Shannon looked at him closely. The cuts on his face were healing well and there was a remarkable change almost overnight as the swelling had gone down. The edges of his bruises had altered from black and blue to a muddy yellow.

She passed her hand over his cheek. No response, not even the flutter of an eyelash. "Looks like you could use a shave, my friend."

Shannon smoothed a clump of hair from his forehead and gazed at him. She was seeing an almost normal-looking man. She looked at him, but not as a nurse looking for signs of health.

"Like Sleeping Beauty," she whispered.

Impulsively, she leaned toward him, her lips pursed.

"Do you believe in magic, that a kiss will awaken you?"

She stopped herself midmotion, straightened up and blinked.

My God, what was I thinking. I've never done anything like that. Never. Professionalism is my middle name.

"That is the last time I pull three shifts in a row!" she exclaimed, and walked out of the room.

"This fast-paced book is the perfect choice for readers who crave romances liberally laced with adventure."
—*Library Journal* on *The Legend Makers*

CATHERINE LANIGAN

CALIFORNIA MOON

MIRA

ISBN 1-55166-578-6

CALIFORNIA MOON

Copyright © 2000 by Catherine Lanigan.

Visit us at www.mirabooks.com

Printed in U.S.A.

ACKNOWLEDGMENT

The brightest star in the heavens is the MIRA star. I have been blessed with the brightest angels to guide me through so many books. *California Moon* shines through the expertise of my brilliant editor Martha Keenan, whom I call friend as well as co-creator. My deepest thanks to Dianne Moggy, Katherine Orr and Stacy Widdrington of MIRA for believing in me and being there for me. To Jennifer Robinson of PMA Literary and Film Management, who aided in the birth of this book, to Charlotte Breeze, founder and owner of CDB Literary Company, who contributed her intellect and love for this story, and to Peter Miller, my agent, whose hope kept it alive.

1

He couldn't be drowning.

He was in too much pain to be dying. No, he was very much alive. At least for the present.

His ribs felt as if they'd been cracked in half. His right arm was numb and flopped against his side. His shoulder was white-hot as if branded. He heard accents, maybe Hispanic, difficult to understand. He had no idea what they wanted from him. He didn't even know where he was or how he'd gotten there. He was shocked to find himself struggling for his own name.

His head throbbed with pain but he tried to stand anyway. Then they grabbed him roughly under the arms and dragged him from the back seat of the car.

Not my car...a rental from the Shreveport airport.

They frisked him and one of the men took his wallet.

"You want money?" he managed to ask.

"Idiot!" one of the men growled as he clumsily shoved the wallet in a jacket pocket. "No identification. No traces," he explained in thickly accented English.

Anger exploded inside him as the realization hit that he might not come out of this alive—whatever this was. That was the hell of it. He didn't know these men. In his bewilderment he reasoned that his wallet was vital to staying alive. He lunged toward the man. "Gimme that!"

A fist slammed into his jaw, stunning him, and his assailant continued frisking him.

"Where eezit?"

"What? I don't have a gun," he tried to tell them, but his cut, bruised mouth barely moved.

Hands moved down his jeans and back again. He shivered, the fleece lining of his Houston Rockets windbreaker doing nothing to cut the biting wind. He shivered.

One of the men laughed.

What do they want?

Suddenly, his arms were pulled behind his back. A fist sank into his jaw again. Pain screamed through his body as another blow hit his midsection and another. His face was pummeled.

He fell to the ground and struck his head on a rock.

He saw stars, tiny swirling lights, but then they faded.

And he remembered. He wasn't alone. He'd been with Adam, his best friend.

He could hear the sound of Adam's frantic pleadings as the assailants turned their attention to him.

"That's only my wallet. I don't have it, I tell you." Adam groaned.

He heard scuffling of feet on gravel and dirt, the sound of fists pounding on muscles. Then he heard a chilling human wail.

"Please don't kill me. No!"

What are they doing to him? And why? Adam, do what they want.

Adam screamed. The sound was frighteningly high-pitched, as if he couldn't take any more.

This is insane! Adam, what have you gotten us into?

He tried desperately to focus his eyes. A dense gray mist swirled around everything. Glancing sidelong toward the long, dark structure to his left, he realized they'd brought him to a bridge.

But where? And why?

He was barely able to make out a sign—the Sabine River. He'd been brought out to Highway 79, south of the city. Down the embankment the murky river flowed deep and wide this time of year.

His arms felt as if they'd been pulled from their sockets. He could barely move his numb fingers as he reached under his jacket for warmth. Behind the Rockets' heavily embroidered emblem he felt the computer disk. It was safe.

He remembered back to his dinner earlier that night with Adam at the Catfish King. "They'll kill me if they get their hands on this," Adam had said, passing the disk across the wooden table. "Thanks for flying in to meet me and not asking why I arranged for your rented car using a phony name. I don't want anyone tracing you back to me. You're anonymous in this thing. I swear, I'll protect you," Adam had said. "Just do this for me."

He knew Adam was in trouble then, but still hadn't fully understood the ramifications at the time. He should have paid more attention. He thought he was helping Adam, but at what price?

His head felt as if it was about to explode. His fingers wrapped around the disk.

Hide it.

His hand moved as if by its own will.

He knew now they were both going to die.

Palming the disk, he slipped it under the bloody rock where he'd hit his head.

No! No good. Think man, think. Your life is at stake!

He moved his hand away from the rock. Pain washed over him. He could barely see them, fuzzy figures looming over him. A booted foot kicked his ribs and shoved hard. He heard the man grunt, then walk away, leaves, twigs and pinecones crunching under his feet.

Adam's screams rent the still night one last time, shocking him alert. He heard the sound of a muffled gunshot.

A silencer! God...Adam....

Suddenly, he was hauled to an upright position.

"Where de fuck eezit?"

"I don't..."

Suddenly his vision was keen and clear. A man with pockmarked olive skin and brittle eyes gritted his teeth and pulled back his fist. The blow to his midsection knocked the wind out of him. He couldn't speak.

They pounded his jaw, neck, shoulders. He folded and sank to the icy mud.

"Give it to me or I'll keel you."

Bastards! I'm dead either way.

The blow to his kidneys sent a searing pain throughout his body. His lungs burned as he gasped for air. The pain was unbearable.

He wanted to feel angry, feel the need for revenge, but that took more energy than he had. Still, if he could survive, he would find them and return the favor.

If I could stall them...get to the car...

Hope was a virtue he'd seldom utilized but right now it was all he had.

"Adam...where's Adam?" he managed to groan.

"Dead. Jes like you will be."

The other man laughed. "No, let's have some fun. We think maybe you keel your friend. Ha!"

They laughed menacingly together.

Even though he knew it was true, the words shocked him. He felt terrible guilt, crucifying guilt. He should have saved Adam. He should have fought back.

His eyes were swelling shut. He flailed his fists at the air halfheartedly.

They just laughed at him. One of them had a quirky, high-resonating titter. Hatred sprouted mighty and fast inside him.

He would never forget that laugh. Never.

They dragged him to the car and shoved him inside, propping him behind the steering wheel. He heard the car door slam, then another door open and close. Scuffling sounds attenuated.

Unconsciousness descended quick and heavy like a steel door. As the world faded to black, he thought, *It'll be good to die.*

2

Shreveport, Louisiana

Shannon Riley had pulled the worst float assignment of her career at St. Christopher's Charity Hospital— the ER during a full moon, half the staff down with the flu and a green intern on duty.

"But I'm just a ward nurse," she said to Helen Mayer, the senior administrator who was standing in the doorway to the staff lounge. "Besides, I just finished my shift. I want to go home." She rubbed her bleary eyes.

"You? Home?"

"I miss my cat."

"She'll survive."

"Aw, c'mon, Helen. I'm tired. I really do have a life."

"Yeah? What's his name?"

"I didn't mean a guy." Shannon dropped her face to her hand, cupping her mouth. "Does it always have to be a guy?"

"It couldn't be anyone else. You don't have any family."

"I know this," Shannon looked away and stared at the wall.

"Sorry."

Shannon was silent for a long beat. "It's okay."

"No, it's not. You're more than just an employee here. You're a friend. And that was unkind of me," Helen said. "Please help me, Shannon. I've always counted on you, my ace."

A slow smile warmed Shannon's face. "You'll note this sacrifice on my record?"

"Sure," Helen agreed. "Come with me. You may be young but you've got more experience than I do." She wagged her finger at Shannon. "You never heard me say that."

Shannon liked Helen. She'd been the one who'd hired her when Shannon came to St. Christopher's six years ago.

"This place has been pandemonium," Helen continued. "Thirteen babies were born before midnight and both the labor and delivery rooms are full. I don't know where we're going to put them all. Maternity is on double shift as it is. On Four an elderly cardiac ICU patient died with no apparent seizure even though his latest prognosis was that he'd be going home in forty-eight hours. On Two, a stroke case, paralyzed on his left side, reacted to his meds and ripped out his IV, got out of bed and tried to walk out the door. It took five staff to get him into restraints and in the process they broke his arm.

"ER has been plagued with that three car pileup on I-20 that was just on the news. God! I can't tell you how I despise minicams! We actually ran out of cast plaster. But the worst part is this flu epidemic. Staff is dropping like flies. The doctors—"

"I've heard all your good news. Now give me the bad news."

"Dr. Scanlon."

"No way."

"Sorry," Helen said.

Rising from her chair, Shannon said, "I like it when you need me."

"Take that grin off your face and promise me you'll do me another favor."

"I haven't actually agreed to the first one yet."

"We've got a coma and a gunshot to the head coming in from Sabine Pass. The ambulance just left Highway 79. They'll be here in ten. I don't have anyone but you. For the record, I'll state that Chelsea Sikeston is taking this shift. That way, if anything goes wrong…"

"Or right, then she gets the credit." Shannon didn't mind the shell game all the administrators played when the situation called for it, but it galled her to no end that twenty-five-year-old Chelsea, fresh out of college with only a year on staff under her belt, outranked her because Shannon was only a practical nurse and not an RN. If it was the last thing she did, she would get her degree someday.

The fact that Chelsea used her affair with the wealthy and very married head of administration, Dr. Thornton, to gain special privileges for herself, incensed Shannon, though she pretended indifference.

Helen's voice brought Shannon back from her musings. "Do I have to say please?"

"Yeah. It would help." Shannon walked past Helen to the hall and headed toward the ER.

Dr. Bradley Scanlon was not only a new resident to St. Christopher's, he was new period. After two weeks on staff he'd lost two patients, both in the past six hours. He was exhausted and wanted only to climb onto a cot in the lounge and sleep for two days straight.

"How could I be so unlucky as to pull another shift?" he complained to Shannon as they changed into fresh greens.

"Triple shift is nothing," she said flatly, cramming her auburn hair into a paper surgical cap. Double wrapping the ties of the smock around her, she heard the ambulance siren at the emergency doors. Two paramedics rushed alongside a gurney bearing the male auto-accident victim the state troopers had dug out from the bottom of the river.

"Is this our John Doe?" Dr. Scanlon asked the paramedic as he quickly checked the chart he was handed. Shoving the clipboard into Shannon's hands, he began inspecting the patient for internal injuries.

"One and the same, Doc," the younger paramedic replied. "Collapsed lung. BP is 190 over 130 and coming down. Possible concussion. He's been out since we found him."

"Chest tube and intubate him. Seven point zero ET 2. Give him Manatol IV and hyperventilate him," Dr. Scanlon ordered Shannon who instantly began assembling the proper dosages for the IV. "CAT scan and X rays," Dr. Scanlon said as he passed his hands along the man's rib cage. "Feels as if they're all broken."

After injecting the proper meds into the IV, Shannon prepared to intubate.

"What's over here?" Dr. Scanlon asked as he turned toward the second gurney coming into the room.

"Again, unidentified. Richard Doe has been shot, Doc. BP is 80 over 60."

"I want an EKG and echocardiogram," he said as he swabbed the blood from the gunshot wound to the man's stomach. Without glancing at the paramedic, he asked, "Any idea what all these burn marks are?"

The young man shrugged his shoulders. "The police were there nearly at the same time as we were. They think he was tortured. I heard one of 'em say it coulda been a cigar."

Dr. Scanlon continued groping into Richard Doe's gunshot wound without further comment. "I can't see dick. It's buried pretty deep. Nurse, suction."

"Yes, Doctor."

"What else did the police tell you?" Dr. Scanlon asked the paramedic.

"That the front end of the car hit the riverbed, squishing it like an accordian. The steering wheel rammed into that one's chest," he said, nodding toward the other patient. "It shoulda killed him. He must be tough. We had to cut the steering wheel away in order to lift him out of the car. Only thing is, I couldn't figure where he got the blow to his head."

"From the same person who shot this man would be my guess," Shannon said.

"Retractor." Dr. Scanlon glared back at Shannon as he held out his hand to her. She properly placed the instrument handle side toward his thumb and forefinger. Using a clamp to clear his view into the interior, Dr. Scanlon dug for the bullet. "He's lost a lot of blood. I'll need a cross-match."

"Yes, Doctor," Shannon replied. But as she cast a sidelong glance at his patient's chalky color and at the readout on the monitors, she mumbled to herself, "Richard Doe won't last that long."

"He needs Methahexol, morphine and valium intravenously, if he doesn't defib," she said.

Just then the heart monitor went off.

"Flat line!" the paramedic shouted anxiously.

"Damn!" Dr. Scanlon blanched.

Shannon grabbed the epinephrine, filled the syringe and handed the hypodermic to the doctor while she automatically spun around and jelled the paddles.

Quickly injecting the epinephrine into the patient's heart, the doctor took the paddles from Shannon and placed them on either side of Richard Doe's chest.

"Clear!"

Shannon held her breath as she watched the patient's lifeless body jerk on the gurney. "Nothing!"

"Clear!" Dr. Scanlon zapped him again.

Shannon didn't wait for results. There was still a chance to save the other patient. "John Doe is still alive and needs to be intubated."

With the chilling sound of the monotone heart monitor behind her, Shannon turned to the bloody, dark-haired man on the first gurney. She looked at his face. Glass from the windshield had shattered throughout his dark hair, cutting his scalp and forehead. Though his clothes were spattered with blood from hundreds of cuts, she noticed numerous hematomas.

"He's been beaten."

She lifted his arm, moving it forward and back while resting her hand on the man's clavicle. Depressing her fingers into his rib cage, she rolled the pads of her fingers back and forth, pressing them into the flesh until they nearly disappeared. She counted seven broken ribs. Then she lifted his side and looked at his back.

"Kick marks. Especially around the kidneys."

Gently pressing her fingers to his kidney area, she felt for lumps or signs of detachment. There were none.

"I've lost him!" Dr. Scanlon said, handing the paddles to the paramedic.

Shannon glanced at the young doctor's ashen face, and realized there was no way he could handle another death tonight.

He stepped next to Shannon. Eyes vacant, he looked at her patient. "Good job, Riley."

"I'll take him up to X ray myself," she said, glancing at the paramedic behind her as he pulled a sheet over the dead man's face.

Police and state troopers scurried in the hallway as Shannon and the paramedics wheeled their patient out of ER.

Brushing past a holstered gun, she shivered. *How ironic. Guns and lifesaving equipment in the same room.*

Police officers jammed the doorway, forming a blockade against the approaching local news-station reporters who couldn't wait to film gruesome live shots of bloody bodies for their early-morning newscasts.

Minicam lights blasted Shannon in the face. She froze. "What the—" Shielding her eyes with her hand, half covering her face, she turned away and quickly pushed the gurney toward the elevator. Accidentally, she bumped into one of the reporters.

"Hey, watch it," he growled.

Her mouth went dry. "Sorry," she said tensely. She

avoided eye contact with the man by keeping her head down.

"Hey, is that one of them?" He turned on his camera.

Shannon felt the blood drain from her face. Though her hands were shaking and her knees quivered, she pulled the sheet over her patient's head. "Please don't," she said meekly.

"I was only doing my job," the heavyset young man said defensively.

"Me, too," she mumbled, hurrying past him.

Grumbling, the cameraman turned away.

Shannon made it to the elevator in a flash and impatiently depressed the button twice. She could hear the barrage of questions and the distinct voice of the chief of police, Jimmy Joe Bremen, talking to Dr. Scanlon as they emerged from the ER.

"Did he say anything before he died?" Jimmy Joe asked, pushing aside his underlings.

"No."

"Did you remove the bullet?"

"Yes," Dr. Scanlon said wearily.

"Forensics will want it. The body as well."

"I understand."

Jimmy Joe's large belly heaved up and down when he spoke and his lungs rattled, reminding Shannon of the pneumonia he'd had last winter when he'd been admitted to the ER with a high fever. He was the most demanding and stubborn patient she'd ever attended.

She hit the elevator button again.

She realized now that Chief Bremen had lied to Dr. Timmons when he said he hadn't touched a cigar for over a year. What bothered her most at the time was that he lied so effortlessly and convincingly. She didn't trust him and it gave her the jitters to be anywhere near him.

Jimmy Joe pressed past the reporters into the hall and Dr. Scanlon followed.

The reporters swarmed.

"What about the other John Doe? Did he say anything? Did you find anything on him we might have overlooked?"

"No, nothing. Should I have?"

Jimmy Joe scratched his head. "Hell, I don't know. These two fellas were in a bunch o' trouble, but without any identification and no witnesses, we're at a loss."

A brash young female reporter stuck a small microphone in Dr. Scanlon's face. "What have you got, Doctor?"

"Other than the fact that I place the gunshot wound at around midnight since he hadn't yet bled to death, the only other medical specifics I can give you at this time is that one man is dead and the other barely alive."

Jimmy Joe pressed his index finger in Dr. Scanlon's bony chest. "When the other one comes around, I want to know about it."

Dr. Scanlon frowned, rubbing the sore spot. "Of course, but it won't be any time soon. He's comatose."

Jimmy Joe slapped his gray hat against his trousers as he walked toward the elevators. "I'll check on him in the morning."

"It *is* morning, Chief," Dr. Scanlon said wearily.

Jimmy Joe smiled wanly. "Then I'll call you later," he said and ordered his men back to the station.

The elevator doors opened. Shannon secured the gurney, IV and respirator on the elevator.

"Appears it's going to be a nice day," Jimmy Joe said, watching her as she pushed the gurney into the elevator.

She held her breath, feeling his eyes free-falling across her backside.

Shannon rammed her thumb against the fourth-floor button and glanced down at her patient. When the doors slammed shut, Shannon exhaled with relief. "Safe once again."

3

Ben Richards was the newest addition to the Shreveport Police Department, and therefore drew the unlucky assignment of standing guard over the comatose John Doe at St. Christopher's Charity Hospital.

"I suppose you want to get reassigned," Jimmy Joe said, exhaling heavily as he spoke.

"No, sir. I'm quite satisfied."

"Satisfied?" Jimmy Joe eyed him suspiciously.

"Absolutely. If this is where you need me, then this is where I'll be," Ben said firmly.

"Good. You let me know the minute that guy comes around. I've got some questions that need answering," Jimmy Joe continued. "You've only been here a few days…"

"And everyone else is needed for more important work?" Ben offered.

"That's right." Jimmy Joe smiled. "Glad to see you understand."

"Of course. No problem." Ben clasped his hands behind his back.

Jimmy Joe grinned widely. "You catch on quick, son." He assessed the tall, thirty-six-year-old man. "You're kinda old for a rookie. Why'd it take you so long to get through the academy?"

"I didn't know what I wanted out of life until two

years ago. I just kinda bummed around, I guess you'd say."

"I see. Just so you know, every case is top priority to this office."

Ben held his palm in the air. "Don't apologize, sir. I'm happy to take this responsibility. If there's any information forthcoming from John Doe, rest assured I'll be on top of it."

"Fine."

"Did we ID the body in the morgue?" Ben slipped the question in easily.

Jimmy Joe nodded. "Even though there was no ID on either one of them when we brought them in, we found his initials inscribed inside his watchband. Then we ran his fingerprints. He had a misdemeanor arrest when he was sixteen. Probably got busted on prom night. His name is Adam Rivers, of New Orleans. I just got the call his wife's coming in. She's probably downstairs right now. Let's go."

Ben followed Jimmy Joe.

Shannon wrapped a pilled black cardigan around her shoulders as she waited outside the hospital, where she was to meet Alice Rivers, then take her to the morgue.

The automatic glass doors opened. Chief Bremen, Ben Richards and Helen Mayer walked toward her.

"Mrs. Rivers isn't here yet?" Helen asked.

"No," Shannon answered, glancing quickly at Chief Bremen. She felt chills surge across her back. She wished she was anywhere but here. She looked away from the older man to Ben. "Who's he?" she asked quietly.

"John Doe's bodyguard," Helen whispered.

Ben overheard Shannon's question. "My name is Ben Richards," he said, putting out his hand.

She looked at his hand and nodded while hugging herself against the cold. "A bodyguard? He's unconscious. He can't hurt anyone."

Shannon looked away from Ben's probing eyes. The wind whipped around the corner, stinging her eyes. It gave her an excuse to close them and pretend she was nowhere near these men. Cocking her head toward Helen, she whispered, "This case gets more bizarre by the minute. And why should Alice Rivers need me…a nurse?"

Helen gave her a sidelong glance, pointing to the squad car as it pulled up. "Wait and see."

Gallantly, Ben opened the car door and extended his hand to the woman inside.

"My God. She's pregnant." Astonishment cut through Shannon's voice.

"Overdue, actually," Helen replied.

"What are these bastards trying to do? Send her into shock?" Shannon glared at Ben.

He ignored her and smiled at Alice.

Helen shrugged her shoulders. "I thought the same thing. They say it's for security. I've alerted Maternity. Watch her closely, Shannon. She's in your hands now."

Shannon moved toward the squad car, intent on taking over from Ben.

Alice Rivers was child-size despite the pregnancy. Her face was pale as she shifted her weight grimly.

"I'm Shannon Riley. I'm here to help you." Shannon said, casting Ben an icy glare and he backed away. Shannon shook Alice's hand. "You're trembling."

"Wouldn't you be?" Alice asked.

"Of course."

"I'm Ben Richards, Mrs. Rivers. If there's anything I can do, please let me know," he said in a comforting tone of voice that surprised Shannon with its depth.

Alice nodded curtly to Ben and Jimmy Joe rather than touch their extended hands.

"You'll be fine," Shannon assured her.

Alice gave her a grateful look.

"Thank you for coming, Mrs. Rivers," Jimmy Joe said. "I must warn you, Mrs. Rivers, this may not be your husband, but from the description you gave the New Orleans police—"

"You think it is," she finished for him.

"Yes."

Alice's eyes went pleadingly to Shannon. "He didn't tell me he was coming here. Adam doesn't know anyone in Shreveport."

"We think he knew the man in the hospital," Ben said.

"What man?" she said, looking at the police officer once more.

"The man we found with your husband."

"Who is he?"

"We were hoping you could tell us that," Ben said.

Alice shook her head vehemently. "We don't know anyone here."

"I understand," Ben replied calmly. "Perhaps we should get this over with."

"Yes," she answered, her eyes going back to Shannon.

Shannon put her arm protectively around Alice's back.

"Everything's going to be okay, Mrs. Rivers." Shannon said.

"How can you say that? My husband is missing, for God's sake. And the best I can do at this moment is pray it's not him in there on a slab."

Shannon saw the tears in the woman's eyes and her heart went out to her. "Believe me, I *do* know what you're going through," she whispered. "It's hell, but we'll do it together. Just you and me. Okay?"

Their eyes met in that knowing glance women share when their hearts are open. Alice clutched Shannon's sleeve. "Okay. Let's do it."

"Good girl."

They went inside to ICU, where three men and one elderly woman were attached to high-tech monitoring equipment. Black screens with waving lines and tiny blinking lights indicated that the still bodies were alive.

Alice braced herself.

Shannon felt her own skin turn cold. "C'mon."

Alice's frantic eyes flitted from gurney to gurney. "This isn't happening."

Shannon's arm tightened around Alice as if she were the one needing strength.

Alice lumbered awkwardly, her arms strapped over her abdomen clearly trying to hold herself together. Fear crept back into her eyes. "Adam isn't here?"

"No," Jimmy Joe said flatly. "We were hoping you could identify John Doe for us."

Ben stood next to the last gurney in the area. "Do you know this man?"

Shannon watched Alice intently.

Alice stared at the mangled swollen face of the man who appeared more dead than alive. She gasped and turned ashen. "My God! Did they crush his face?"

She put her hand over her mouth, holding back her nausea.

"They thought they killed him."

"You mean, like they killed Adam?"

"Yes," Jimmy Joe answered. "Unless this man killed your husband first. We simply don't know."

She gasped and clamped her hand over her mouth. "Did they torture them?"

"Alice..." Shannon's voice was filled with concern.

"I'm okay." She breathed in heavily, obviously anticipating the worst of all possible answers.

Jimmy Joe started to answer truthfully, but Ben interrupted. "No."

The stark terror in Alice's eyes faded. Shannon cast Ben a grateful look. He caught it and smiled back, then gave her a slight nod, letting her know he was there to help her make Alice feel at ease.

How chivalrous. He read the reports. He knows the truth, but he wants to protect her.

Shannon was surprised at the flood of relief that overcame her. She wasn't used to relying on others for assistance of any kind. And certainly not a cop. She wondered why his aid suddenly meant something to her.

Shannon smiled back and Ben's smile widened. She felt her heart flutter. It was a feeling she hadn't experienced in so long, she instantly discounted it.

Jimmy Joe asked Alice, "Are you sure you've never seen him before?"

"I told you, we don't know anyone in Shreveport. My husband and I have a fine circle of friends in New Orleans. My family has lived in New Orleans for two hundred years. We would never, ever associate with anyone so unseemly as this man. For any of this to have happened to Adam is beyond my comprehension. Frankly, it's my belief Adam was kidnapped."

"Kidnapped?" Shannon asked, surprised.

"Yes. That kind of thing is happening more and more these days. People of our class and wealth are more vulnerable than ever to danger. Always have been," she said resolutely.

"I wasn't aware of that," Jimmy Joe said.

"I'm not surprised. You don't honestly believe we involve the police every time one of us is threatened. We have the money to deal with these things."

"Have you ever been kidnapped, Mrs. Rivers?" Ben asked curiously.

"No. But my sister was when I was ten. She was returned unharmed. My father has always believed in a great deal of security."

"I see," Ben said. "Did you receive a call demanding ransom for your husband, Mrs. Rivers?"

"No," she replied sadly.

"Then why would you think he was kidnapped?" Shannon blurted out the question before she realized she'd spoken. After all, this wasn't her investigation. She kept telling herself she could care less. She was assigned. She hadn't volunteered. She wanted to be as far away from here as possible. Yet, something kept her rooted to the spot.

"There's no other acceptable explanation," Alice said. "My husband was a well-educated, honorable man. He wasn't a criminal. Nor would he consort with such people. He was kidnapped and the kidnappers killed him before making the call to either myself or my parents."

Jimmy Joe stuffed his fists in his pockets and

rocked back on his heels as he considered her explanation.

Shannon dismissed her views. She suspected that Alice Rivers not only led a sheltered life, but that her husband had clearly lied to her. No telling what the police would dredge up.

Ben gestured toward the door. "I think it's time we get the worst over with."

The lights in the morgue were blinding as the coroner rolled the slab out of its file in the wall.

Shannon kept her arm clamped around Alice's shoulder while the coroner unceremoniously flipped back the white sheet.

Alice's eyes gaped at her husband's bloodless body.

Shannon felt shock waves rivet through Alice's body. She wished she could absorb the impact, lessen Alice's pain, but she was powerless.

"Oh, God!" Alice screamed. "Oh my God! Adam!" She clamped her hands over her face. Bursting into tears, she turned into Shannon's shoulder, looking more ghostly than the corpse.

"Your husband?" Jimmy Joe asked emotionlessly.

Shannon couldn't help wondering what made him so impassive.

"Yes," Alice groaned and clutched her abdomen. She folded in half.

"She's gone into shock!" Shannon said, casting an imploring look at Ben. "Hit the call button! I need help!"

Ben rushed to the wall and slammed his palm on the red button. He barked orders into the intercom.

"Oh, God," Alice cried. "This can't be happening!" Terror struck her eyes.

"What's going on?" Jimmy Joe asked, flustered.

Ben put his arms around the rotund, but frail woman. "She's going into labor, Chief."

"Shit!" Jimmy Joe said, standing aside as Shannon and Ben lowered Alice to the floor.

Alice's water broke. "Don't let this happen here! I want to go home!"

"You'll be fine," Shannon assured her.

"I don't think..." Pain shot through her again. Her eyes darted to her dead husband. "I'm alone..."

Shannon squeezed her hand very hard. "No, Alice, you have this baby."

"Yes, the baby..."

Shannon tried to lift her.

"Here." Ben put his hands on Shannon's shoulders, easing her aside. "I'll do this." He scooped Alice up into his strong arms. "Where to?"

Shannon gaped at him. She wasn't used to heroes. "Fifth floor."

Ben rushed toward the door with Alice in his arms and Shannon fast on his heels.

"Damn it!" Jimmy Joe grumbled. "Now there's no chance she'll ID our John Doe."

4

Alice Rivers's baby was born healthy. Within fourteen hours her sister from Gretna had driven to Shreveport to take her and the baby back to New Orleans.

Throughout her ordeal, Ben kept telling Shannon he was convinced Alice might have been able to identify John Doe had his features been more normal.

Jimmy Joe blew him off, saying, "Drop it, Ben. Alice Rivers doesn't know him." But Shannon couldn't help thinking Ben was right.

Shannon doubled her shift time to watch over John Doe. Because of the police investigation and the myriad questions swirling around John like a whirlpool, she became fascinated with him. Every time she looked at him, she was amazed the man had survived the torture, much less the car crash. There was little about him that looked human.

But you are human, aren't you, John?

More than that, she sensed he had an incredible inner strength. In the first thirty-eight hours of his confinement, she'd watched his condition improve from critical to stable status. His heartbeat regulated. His breathing became stronger. Even the swelling in his face had begun to subside today as she tended him.

"You want to live, don't you, John?" She held his

hand, counting his pulsebeats. His skin was warm—a good sign. His heart was strong, beating a Morse code that coursed through the nerve endings in the pads of her fingers.

"I want you to live, too. I want you to get well and strong. Maybe then you can tell the police who did this to you. I'll help you, John." Shannon was a firm believer in the power of the subconscious.

Today she'd brought in an old cassette tape player she'd bought at a clearance sale and played classical music and New Age meditation and healing tapes. She owned a collection of subliminal-healing tapes she brought to her favorite patients from time to time. The staff never said anything about her tapes, knowing that Helen Mayers had twice requested financial funding for just such equipment, only to be rejected by the hospital board.

Shannon depressed the start button on the player and turned the volume down low. "It's a Chopin nocturne. I love this part, John," she said, listening closely.

She glanced at him, wanting to believe she saw a tiny tic at the edge of his mouth. But it was only the morning-light shadows playing across his face.

"Keep listening. It will help you wake up." She patted his hand and began marking down his vital signs on his chart.

Routine was easy for Shannon. She'd been through this process many times before, with herself as the healer. She realized she played a catalytic role in all her patients' lives. She believed she was part of the reason John was alive and would, in time, become healthy again. He would awaken. He would heal. They would get to know each other without the machines as interpreters. He would tell her about himself and clear up these mysteries around him. The police would be satisfied. He would tell her where he was from and about his family. About his life. His wife and children, possibly. About how much he loved them and missed them. They would come for him and he would tell her he was eternally grateful to her for helping to save his life. They would bond in a special way that patients did with their nurses. Eventually, he would leave the hospital. He would say goodbye to her and go back to where he came from and she would never hear from him again. It was always like that in Shannon's world.

The John Doe case was more than perplexing to Ben Richards. It bugged the hell out of him. After a week of standing guard at the hospital, Ben had learned little about the man. No one had come to visit him. No one asked about him. There were no calls, no flowers.

Even the police were dumbfounded, it seemed.

Ben stood stock-still in Chief Bremen's office. "Sir, I have a feeling that Alice Rivers knows John Doe. Her ability to recognize him was impaired not only because of his physical condition but because she was stressed over her husband."

"Don't you think I know all that?"

"Sir, I was only recounting your thoughts on the matter."

"Well, then, don't you have any new thoughts to add, Richards?"

"Not at this time, sir."

Jimmy Joe took out a cigar, considered it and put it

back in his drawer. "Doc says those things will kill me."

"Yeah, they tell me that about cigarettes." Ben shrugged his shoulders. "But, what can I do? I'm hooked," he said with a sheepish grin. "You ran John Doe's fingerprints?" he asked, sliding the question easily into his conversation.

"Yes, but we found nothing. No criminal record. No military record."

"And the rental car?"

"Issued to a Harvey Ackerman. But we tracked him down. He's alive and well in Bossier." Chief Bremen answered pointedly and with a terse nod for emphasis.

"John Doe stole Harvey's credit card and driver's license?"

"Apparently," Jimmy Joe said dismissively. "Look, Ben, I handled all this myself. I don't want any more screwups. Your job is to bird-dog John Doe. I'll take care of the rest. You got that?"

Ben watched Jimmy Joe's reactions to his questions like a scientist searching for microscopic clues. Something was wrong. Jimmy Joe was lying through his teeth about something. Ben just had to find out what that something was. "Got it."

"I'm glad we got that straight. Helen Mayer called from the hospital and said they're moving our guy out of ICU. Room 505. I told her I wanted as few people to know about his presence as possible."

"Chief, the fact that he has a guard twenty-four hours a day will draw attention," Ben said.

"I told you to look as inconspicuous as possible."

"Yes, sir."

"Hopefully the guy will come around in another

couple days. So far we've been able to keep the press at bay. We've still got a chance to unravel this thing."

"I understand."

"Dr. Scanlon will continue to be the attending physician and I understand Helen has assigned a permanent nurse." He looked down at his pocket spiral notepad. "Shannon Riley. Wasn't she his nurse when they brought him in?"

"Yes. She's been with him every day," Ben said. "She seems dependable, even taking double shifts."

"She's probably being paid double time and a half."

A moment later, Ben told his boss that he was headed for the hospital. What he didn't tell him was that he wasn't going there immediately. He had some investigating of his own to do.

Ben's conversation with Jimmy Joe bothered him. He was smarter than Jimmy Joe and knew how to read people. The man was lying and Ben had to figure out what he was lying about and why.

After speaking with Jimmy Joe at the station, Ben drove to the airport car rental where John Doe had falsely rented a car. He asked the supervisor to show him the records regarding that particular transaction.

"Mabel Yates, one of our clerks, dealt with that customer. The police were already here once about it. She knows she messed up."

"Messed up?" Ben asked.

"Yeah, she didn't check the signature against the customer's credit-card signature on the back."

"I see," Ben said, nodding. "Did she remember the man at all? Give a description?"

The supervisor shook his head. "Most folks look

the same to us, we see so many. But she did remember that he was short."

"Short?" Ben was surprised. John Doe was at least six foot tall. *But Adam Rivers is short.*

"Yeah. Mabel is tall—five-ten. He was shorter than she is. She says she always notices people's height."

Ben reasoned that Adam Rivers had undoubtedly rented the car under an assumed name, then left it somewhere for John Doe to pick up at a later time. But why? Was Adam Rivers protecting John Doe? Was Adam the gofer, doing odd jobs for John Doe the mastermind? Or was Rivers protecting himself? Or both?

After leaving the car rental place, Ben went to a pay phone. Picking up the phone book, he quickly turned to the Bossier City section. There were three Ackermans in Bossier City, but there was no Harvey nor even an initial "H." He called all three numbers and each call confirmed there had never been a Harvey Ackerman in Bossier City.

Why would Jimmy Joe lie about this? Ben wondered. Or is someone in the department lying to Jimmy Joe?

Ben had thought he'd find answers to his questions.

He'd thought wrong.

John Doe had been assigned to private room 505, located at the end of the hall, surrounded by unoccupied semiprivate rooms. Chief Bremen and the hospital administration had agreed that until more was known regarding the criminal status of John Doe, the safety of patients and staff was of primary concern. No one was allowed admittance to that end of the hall except Ben Richards, Dr. Scanlon, Shannon Riley and Chief Bremen.

"I can understand having Ben around when John was in ICU. But now that we know it may be weeks, months, before John comes out of the coma, is it necessary to have cops on duty all the time?" Shannon asked Helen.

"Chief Bremen thinks so," Helen said. "He doesn't want a gang slaying up here any more than I do."

"Slaying? They think John is in that much danger?"

"Yes."

"My God." Shannon swallowed hard, looking around the nurses' lounge for escape. "I had no idea…"

"Don't cop out on me, Shannon. I need you on this case. You're damn good."

"Besides, no one else will take it?" Shannon offered.

"Something like that."

"Well, I've never worked with an armed guard at the door. All this past week, it's given me the willies."

"He's supposed to make you feel safe."

"Well, he doesn't," Shannon replied tersely. "Maybe I just don't like cops."

Helen nodded. "I've noticed that about you."

"What?" Shannon asked, clearly shocked.

"You shake like a leaf when Ben is around. Chief Bremen, too."

"I do not," she answered with more confidence than she felt. "It's the case that has me rattled. You have to admit, this entire case is out of the ordinary."

"It is."

Shannon rolled her eyes. "How did I get myself into this?"

"You didn't. I did," Helen smiled.

"Remind me to thank you later," Shannon replied. Making no further comment, she walked down the hall toward John's room, closing the door behind her.

"Good day, John," she said cheerily, opening the miniblinds. "Sunny. That's good."

She smiled at her patient. "You look better already without your ICU attachments."

She looked at him closely. The cuts on his face were healing well after only a week in the hospital. There was a remarkable change almost overnight as the swelling had gone down due to Shannon's trick of placing frozen peas inside the fingers of plastic gloves and laying them across his eyes and cheeks. The edges of his bruises had altered from black and blue to a muddy yellow. She passed her hand over his cheek. "I think Mozart has had a hand in this." Shannon had continued to play him classical music each day. She leaned over him, putting her face close to his.

No response, not even the flutter of an eyelash.

"Looks like you could use a shave, my friend."

She prepared water, towels, soap and a plastic disposable razor. After thoroughly washing his face, she smeared a small amount of shaving cream on his left cheek. "Nasty cut on the other side. Better not risk it."

She carefully shaved his cheek, sliding the razor over abrasions with skilled ease. She applied more shaving cream. "I've never shaved a man with such a deep cleft in his chin. How many times did you cut yourself when you first started shaving? Did your father teach you? Did he have a cleft, too?"

She smoothed a clump of hair from his forehead

and gazed at him. She was seeing an almost normal-looking man.

"Or was it your mother you inherited it from?"

She looked at him, but not as a nurse looking for signs of health. In some part of her mind, she knew she was projecting herself onto her patient. Patients projected their emotions onto their healers all the time. It was so common it was a cliché in the medical world. In this case, though, Shannon believed that John was a mirror of herself—a person alone, wounded and waiting.

"Like Sleeping Beauty," she whispered.

Impulsively, she leaned toward him, her lips pursed.

"Do you believe in magic, that a kiss will awaken you?"

She stopped herself midmotion. She straightened up and blinked.

"Stupid. What was I thinking?"

I've never done anything like that. Never. Professionalism is my middle name.

Quickly, she gathered up the shaving utensils. "That is the last time I pull three shifts in a row!" she exclaimed and walked out of the room.

5

Shannon couldn't get used to Ben or his gun. It hung in his holster like a living menace. There were days when it took every ounce of her self-control to keep from lecturing Ben about his gun, though she knew that he had no choice but to carry the weapon.

Only four days after John Doe was moved to Room 505, Shannon discovered that Ben's presence was more than critical. It was crucial.

Dr. Scanlon took John off the respirator. The heart monitor was removed as well. "The monitor is desperately needed in ICU," he explained to Shannon.

"I understand."

"He's doing fine."

Shannon glanced at John. "Except that he's still comatose."

"There is that," the doctor replied, walking out of the room. "I'll be back later. You'll see to the monitor?"

"Yes, Doctor. After I change the IV bag."

Ben questioned the short, Hispanic orderly who came to take the heart monitor upstairs. "What's going on?"

"I've come to get the equipment. That's all I know," the man said.

"Okay," Ben said reluctantly, rubbing the back of

his neck. This was the first break in the regular routine. Something bothered him, but he couldn't put his finger on it.

Moments later a tall, blond orderly appeared.

"I'm here to take the respirator to the ER."

At that moment, the registered nurse, Chelsea Sikeston, rolled a stainless-steel cart down the hall toward John's room. "Hi, Ernie," she nodded to the blond orderly.

"Hi, Chels," he said, then turned to Ben who was keeping everyone outside the room. "Look, man. Let me in. I gotta lot to do."

"Hi, Ben." Chelsea smiled seductively. "You're looking mighty fine today."

Ben ignored her.

Hearing the commotion outside the room, Shannon opened the door. "What's going on?"

The Hispanic orderly pushed past her and efficiently unhooked the respirator. He tapped his foot, waiting for her to remove the chest tube from the patient.

Ernie, the blond orderly, walked into the room.

"Mr. Richards, what are these people doing?" Shannon asked.

"Ben," he corrected her with a smile.

Chelsea's smile vanished as she looked at Shannon and then at Ben.

Shannon didn't miss the glint of jealousy in Chelsea's eyes. "I'm following Dr. Scanlon's orders, Shannon," Chelsea said. "I can see you have other things that are more important."

"I'm John's nurse. I can handle this. You needn't have brought all these people. After all, Dr. Scanlon just left here," Shannon retorted with a distinct territorial edge to her voice.

"The doctor said he needed the monitor, stat," Chelsea said. "As in, now. Here's the new IV bag, linens and sterile gauze." Chelsea's eyes were chastising as she moved toward Shannon. "I'm not about to get written up on your account."

Shannon returned Chelsea's glare. "I wouldn't dream of it." She stood back as Chelsea wheeled the cart into the room, then removed the chest tube. The orderlies left the room with equipment.

Chelsea sailed icily past Shannon.

Ben chuckled, watching what had nearly become a fight. He found it interesting to be involved in part of its instigation. Cockily, he rocked back on his heels.

Shannon's fury burned crimson on her face.

"Your temper is showing," Ben baited her.

"I'm Irish. It's allowed," she said through clenched teeth.

She could feel Ben's eyes on her back but she didn't care if they were sympathetic or scathing. He'd witnessed her powerlessness. And *that* really made her mad.

"Oooo, what I wouldn't like to do..."

"Easy now," he said.

She shot him a damning look, slammed her palm against the door and went inside John's room.

"Ben!" she screamed as she noticed the cloudy nature of John's IV. "Come quick!"

Ben was at the door in a single stride. "What's wrong?"

"His IV!" she shouted, already yanking the tube out of John's wrist. "Someone's tried to poison him!"

She hit the emergency alarm, then depressed the call button to the nurse's station.

"I need a pervasive antidote, stat! Get Scanlon, stat."

John's chest heaved as he struggled to breathe.

"Damn!" Ben raced down the hall. "Hey, you! Come back here!" He pulled his gun. "Stop!"

The Hispanic orderly turned, saw the gun and shot down the hall. Abandoning the respirator, he dashed down the stairwell.

The blond orderly depressed the elevator button. "What the...?"

Chelsea stopped dead in her tracks on hearing Ben's shouts and backed up against the wall to give him room. "What happened?"

"Help Shannon! Poison!"

"What?"

Two nurses raced behind Dr. Scanlon. The tails of his lab coat were flying and he shouted orders as he ran. "Grab that respirator," he said to one of the nurses, who instantly did as she was ordered.

While the medical crew raced to save John Doe's life one more time, Ben pounded down the stairwell to the parking garage where the orderly ran toward the opening onto the street.

His lungs burned, but he kept running.

The orderly wasn't even twenty years old yet. And he was in better shape than Ben, who smoked too many cigarettes and hadn't seen his early twenties for a decade.

The city streets were crammed with morning delivery trucks, semis unloading office furniture and clusters of pedestrians. The orderly rushed down the alley, darted between cars and disappeared in the bright southern sun.

Ben searched the street to the right and left. He inspected the shop fronts in the area and looked into office-building lobbies, but found no trace of the suspect.

Giving up, he turned back toward the hospital entrance, cursing himself for not having seen this coming.

"Damn! I know better!"

Ben was plagued with questions about this extraordinary case. None of the facts gelled, and he was sure Jimmy Joe was lying about something. And Ben didn't believe for a moment there was no trace anywhere of John Doe's fingerprints. Yet, when he'd telephoned his own sources, the answers were the same—no trace of this man.

Ben wondered if John was with the mob. But which one?

He wouldn't know until he got back to the hospital if the attempt today, though bungled, was successful. One thing Ben did know. He wouldn't give up until he knew the answers. All of them.

6

———➤◄———

Arriving home, Shannon shook the icy rain from the army-green raincoat she'd bought at the Barksdale PX. It, and most of the little Christmas gifts she'd wrapped for the mailman, the apartment super and the high-school boy at the corner newsstand were deals she'd bought with the help of her next-door neighbour.

Elliot's father was a colonel at the air force base, which allowed him privileges at the PX.

Plucking a message from Elliot off her door, she smiled at his attempt at British humor.

I'm home. Knock me up when you get in.

Normally Shannon ignored the messages Elliot left, unless, on very rare occasions he specifically asked her to accompany him to a movie or to go dancing at a honky-tonk in Bossier. Because she knew he had few friends, she would accept, though she preferred spending her time alone.

Nevertheless, Elliot continued putting notes on her door, deriving what she thought was sick pleasure out of seeing the notes disappear every day. Because Shannon left for work before Elliot got home, they seldom saw each other.

The note today was similar to most of Elliot missives, but since he was still at home, when he'd usually already left for the garage in Bossier City, where he worked, she decided his request was genuine.

Rapping on his door, she held the note to his face when he appeared. "It's 'ring me up,' silly," she said to the short, dark-haired younger man who held his grease-blackened finger under his nose as if he was about to sneeze, and did.

"Bless you," she said.

"You're wrong, Shannon," he said, shaking his head. "If you watched *Benny Hill* as much as I do, you'd know..."

"That what you really need is two thousand milligrams of vitamin C, ten glasses of water daily and a hell of a lot of sleep instead of staying up all night watching reruns."

"Too boring," he groaned, shoving his arms through his heavy sheepskin-lined leather jacket.

Crossing her arms over her chest, she gave him a scolding look. "Maybe so, but you wouldn't be sick."

"Oh, hell, there's been no heat in the garage for the past three days. And every car in Shreveport and Bossier City decided to break down. I've got work for the next forty years. I had no idea so many people went out of town around the holidays."

"Imagine that," she teased.

"Holidays are gimmicks to..."

"...boost the retail industry," she added in unison with him. "Yeah, you've said that before."

"Well, I'm right."

She smiled, knowing he made such claims because he didn't have any family except for his father who was perpetually overseas. At least Elliot had a father. She didn't have anybody. Trouble was, Shannon did believe in holidays, which made them even lonelier.

There were times she wished she could turn off her heart, like Elliot, and rationalize that her life was neat, orderly and uncomplicated, just as he did. But she couldn't.

Shannon and Elliot had made a pact never to pry into each other's business. They'd never broken the pact.

He was staring at her expectantly.

Shannon shrugged her shoulders. "Yes, Elliot. I have some vitamin C. Open your mouth."

"What?"

"How can I tell if you have an infection if I don't look at your throat?"

"Well, all right," he said and opened wide.

Shannon turned his head toward the hall light. "You might have strep. You should get a culture as soon as possible, Elliot. But until you have time, I have some C Chlor that Dr. Scanlon prescribed for me last month for my sinus infection."

Elliot smiled beneficently and followed her to her door. Because he didn't like having people inside his apartment, he respected Shannon's privacy by remaining outside while she searched for the medicine.

Between sneezes he asked, "Did you have a rough night?"

"Why do you ask?" she shouted from the bathroom.

He leaned against the doorjamb. "'Cuz you worked another double shift."

"Triple."

"Been a lot of those lately, huh? Things must really be busy at St. Chris. Sorta like at the garage."

She returned with a thermometer. "A lot of staff are still battling the flu. And strep is going around," she said, not wanting to admit to anyone her fascination with John Doe. "Here, you might need this," she said, giving him the thermometer. "If you get a fever, take two aspirin every four hours."

"Thanks, Doc." He grinned, showing his large white teeth. "I'll be seein' ya," he said and hustled quickly down the stairs.

Poor Elliot. He's the closest friend I have and I didn't even ask what he was doing for Christmas.

Closing the door, she mumbled, "Maybe he's planning to spend the day catching up on his work, like me."

Just then she heard a jingle bell chime.

"Valentine!"

Her caramel-colored Manx cat jumped onto the back of the garage-sale Chippendale sofa Shannon had reglued and slipcovered last summer. The cat shook her head, making the brass bell she wore on a black velvet ribbon tinkle merrily.

"Did you miss me today?"

The cat scurried over to Shannon and rubbed against her white-stockinged legs, purring loudly to show her affection. Shannon picked up the animal and nuzzled her nose in the cat's neck.

Valentine purred as Shannon carried her to the kitchen where she opened a can of cat food. She watched with a smile as Valentine gobbled her dinner.

Hearing Christmas carols being played on a stereo from a nearby apartment, Shannon said, "I don't know about you, Valentine, but carols make me sad."

The cat looked up at her owner.

Forcing a smile, Shannon said, "Hey, I can't be really lonely if I have you, right? I mean, you could take me out for a holiday drink. And I know you've knocked yourself out shopping for the right gift to give me, just like I've got yours wrapped under the tree."

The cat stared blankly at her.

"Yeah, right," she replied glumly as Valentine went back to her meal.

Flinging a single tear from her cheek, she said, "Let's forget about the Christmas season. This is Tuesday morning. Just another morning..."

The vision of John Doe's face flitted across her mind as she sank into a wicker chair. Valentine jumped into her lap and Shannon stroked the feline's back.

"The weirdest thing happened to me today, Val. It's John again. I have the strangest feelings when I'm around him. I don't know what it is. I feel things so intensely when I'm in that room. It's as if I know things about him that I shouldn't. Today I sensed that he was in danger before it was really evident."

She shut her eyes, envisioning John's face.

"What if John weren't like all the rest and didn't go away? What if he...liked me. What if he was put in my life to make a change?"

Valentine cocked her head to the side.

"Nuts. You think I'm nuts? Well—" she lifted the cat to eye level "—you'd be right. There are no Prince Charmings, and besides, what the heck would I do with one of those anyway?"

Valentine stared at her.

"You're right, Val. Fairy tales are for kids. You and I are women of the world. We know the score."

Suddenly, her face turned glum. Her eyes traveled beyond Valentine, to the window and the rain outside. She put the cat down and Valentine scurried away.

Shannon rose and walked to the bathroom, "A hot shower is all I need. Maybe a foot soak. I could kill for a massage." She rubbed the small of her back.

Valentine followed her into the bathroom as she often did, hopped up on the closed toilet seat and watched. Shannon turned on the shower and steam formed instantly in the cold room.

"I know, Val. It's warmer in here with the shower on, but you have to remember that keeping the thermostat set low not only saves the environment, but costs less. And it's important to save all that we can. Vital," she reminded herself.

The cat stood, stretched, and shook her head negatively.

"Speaking of costs, we'll pay bills today. That'll be fun, won't it?"

Valentine gave Shannon a bored look.

"Forget the bills. We could go to a garage sale this weekend and look for treasures. Maybe I'll splurge and spend fifteen bucks." Shannon never admitted to herself that possessions, material objects she'd purposefully sought out, examined and cherished, were an extension of her own psyche. She was far more fascinated with the mental exploration of attaching imaginary histories to her belongings, of having them provide her with a personal connection to humanity that she lacked.

Each time she looked at a rocker or lamp, she would wonder, *Where did it come from? Was the owner happy? Did they get rid of it for financial or emotional reasons? Did they want it back? Would they come searching for it?*

"Besides, it's dangerous for me to become too attached to possessions. I'm just going to have to leave them someday, anyway."

Valentine curled in a ball and closed her eyes.

"I'm serious. All my overtime this month will really swell my savings. I'm getting close to making our dream come true. Another twenty thousand and we can retire to Greece. We'll have a blast there, Valentine." She rubbed the cat's head affectionately.

"Finally, we'll be able to run so far away no one will ever find us." She sighed deeply as she rose and stared at her reflection in the mirror. "Freedom."

Shannon shook her head as if to brush away the cobwebs. "Don't think about the past, Shannon."

She traced the beginnings of fine lines across her forehead. "God, thirty seems ancient. At least these dark circles match my mood," she said, touching the shadows beneath her eyes.

After her shower, Shannon wrapped herself in a plaid flannel robe and pulled on a pair of warm red socks to match. Of all her traits, she was glad she had regained her ability to fall asleep when necessary. It was the greatest cure for melancholy she'd ever found.

It was raining harder when she closed her blinds and crawled into bed. She didn't think about the fact that she'd saved John's life. She didn't think about running away, or about Ben's increasing affection for her.

All she thought about was escape. Dark bliss. Nothingness.

But in her dreams, she found another life, another world. As she had every night since John was admitted to the hospital, Shannon dreamed of him.

In this dream, when she kissed John, he awakened and kissed her back. She was stunned by the kiss. She had never been kissed in real life the way he kissed her in this dream. It was so unnerving that she told everyone on the staff that John had come around, but no one would take the time to listen to her. They thought that she was crazy or they ignored her as if she didn't exist. She felt herself fading out of their reality. When she went back to John, he feigned being comatose until she came close. Then he pulled her into his arms and kissed her again. The press of his lips was sensual and entreating, urging her to bond with him. She wanted to surrender to him, but she always broke away, her fears flapping around her like predator birds. John fell back into the pillows, unconscious again, leaving her feeling more lonely than before as she struggled to save him.

Shannon tossed fitfully as the dream exhausted her.

The alarm went off at two o'clock that afternoon. Staring at the clock she blinked once, then twice, her mind undecided which reality was best.

What does it matter? John is a part of both.

She flipped the covers across the bed and slammed her palm over the alarm button.

"You'd think after five years I'd be used to starting my workday in the middle of the afternoon," she grumbled and began her day.

7

Shannon Riley had saved John Doe's life—twice. But no one in the hospital thought anything of it. Such heroics were commonplace. That was their job—saving lives.

Only Ben thought she was exceptional. However, when he'd tried to make a point of it, standing with her in the hall outside John's room, Shannon blew him off like winter wind.

"I was just doing my job," she said meekly, hoping to avoid conversation with him. "Just like you."

"Is it that you don't like me in particular, or is it all cops?" he asked, holding out a cup of coffee.

Shannon avoided catching his eye and quickly tried to change the subject. "What's this?" She looked at the coffee askance.

"It's safe. Not the hospital rotgut stuff. I got it from the café across the street."

"What for?"

"It's a gift. You've heard of those?" he quipped with a smile.

"But why?"

"I'm trying to get to know you better."

"That part I understand. You shouldn't spend your money on me."

"Why not?"

She looked down. "Ben, I'm sure you're a nice man, but..."

Frowning, he said, "You don't like me. You can say it."

Sheepishly she looked up at him. A faint smile broke across her face. "I...like you."

"Ah, hope," he replied with mock theatrics. "This is getting cold, Shannon," he said, holding the coffee out again.

Taking it from him, she said, "I really do hate hospital coffee." She sipped it. "And this is so good." She smiled broadly.

He beamed. "More hope."

"To answer your question, it's not you in particular I'm avoiding. It's just that I'm private, that's all."

He took a step closer. "Why is that? You have something to hide?" he joked.

"No," she replied nonchalantly.

"I know there isn't a husband in the picture," he said with a shrug.

"How?" she asked, surprised.

"I asked."

"Oh," she said with obvious tension. "What else did you ask?"

"If there was a boyfriend." He paused, waiting for a reaction. When he didn't get one, he continued. "Maybe my sources aren't so good."

She looked into the coffee and not at him. "There's no one."

"You say that so sadly," he said, touching her shoulder.

Shannon jerked away as if he'd burned her.

"He hurt you that much?"

She felt tears threaten but she fought them. He

would never see them. No one would. It was one of her rules. "I never said there was anyone. Why do you persist with these questions? Why can't you just leave me alone?"

"I can," he said, his eyes caressing her face. "But I don't want to. I told you, I want to get to know you."

Ben hovered over the crown of her head, wanting to kiss her at the top of her being. "I want to be your friend."

"No, you don't."

"Yes, I do." He closed his eyes and inhaled a faint lavender scent from the soap she used.

Still looking into her coffee, Shannon fought her emotions. She hated how they crept up on her without warning and threatened to give her away. She didn't want anyone, least of all a man, to know about her. For so long she'd pretended she was a woman without a past. Without history. She was Shannon Riley—nurse. That was all. "I have enough friends," she said finally.

"But I don't." His voice dropped to a hush.

Empathy nearly bowled her over. Half of her wanted to bolt from this intimacy while the other half wanted the friendship he offered. "Ben, please..."

"So answer my question, Shannon. Is there someone? Was there someone? If so, I'll go away."

"A monster. A long time ago." A tear dropped from her eye.

"I'm sorry," he said, touching her arm. "But I'm not him."

"I don't want that to ever happen to me again," she said. She handed the coffee back and turned away.

"But that's not living," Ben protested softly.

"Sure it is," she said, braving a smile. "People do it all the time. If they're smart."

Ben stepped back to give her full berth. "And you're smart?"

"As a whip," she replied and retreated into John's room.

Standing at John's bedside, Shannon took his pulse, holding his hand a moment longer than necessary.

Just looking at John, she was able to block Ben out of her mind. "It's true what Ben said. I did save your life. There's a saying that if you save a person's life, then you own them. Maybe that's why doctors have such egos. They think they're building up credits like bank balances, that the lives they save make them immortal. That's my theory anyway.

"But I don't want to own you, John. I want to get to know you," she said, borrowing Ben's line.

Shining a penlight into his pupils, she saw no response. Sadly, she closed his eyelids. "It's safe in there. Feels good, doesn't it? But it can't last. That's the sad part. Sooner or later, you have to come out of that cave. But don't worry. When you do, I'll be here. Waiting."

The aftermath of the attempt on John's life was unnervingly tranquil. It gave Ben a chance to chip away at Shannon's wall, brick by brick.

"What's this?" Shannon asked the next day in the hallway.

"No-fat latte. I heard you liked this better than the coffee and you only order it on payday. Extravagances like that will break you," he joked.

"Ben, you're pushing," she said, but couldn't stop the smile parting her lips.

He beamed broadly. "Think it's working?"

She took the latte, pushed against John's door with her hip and said, "Yes."

"All right!" Ben said, pressing his arms down against his sides.

Ben waited a few minutes while Shannon went about her morning routine with John, marking things down. Because she was the only nurse assigned to the case, she was required to administer all medications and even perform orderly's duties.

Ben opened the door and leaned against the jamb. "Need some help with the bedding? He's kinda heavy."

"I can manage," she replied, tugging on the sheets.

Ben entered the room. "Ever heard the old saying that two people lighten the load."

"Yes," she replied as Ben lifted John's leaden legs like feathers. She rolled the sheeting upward.

"Do you like movies, Shannon?"

"Yes."

"What's your favorite kind?"

"Oh, I don't know. Musicals, I guess. Love stories."

Ben slammed his hand over his heart. "Hope abounds! I figured you'd tell me you like those awful Gothic-horror flicks or blow-up stuff."

Shannon chuckled in spite of herself. "Why? Is that what you like?"

"Never. I like westerns. Old ones. Even the silent ones. Tom Mix. I especially like the part where the cowboy kisses the cowgirl at the end."

She looked away. "And then he rides off into the sunset...alone."

"Is that what *he* did to you? He left you?"

Her eyes clouded over and the walls shot up around her. She stiffened visibly but said, "No, I left."

"Oh," he sighed.

Shannon finished changing the linens in silence. "Thanks for helping me, Ben," she said finally.

He went to the tape player and exchanged the tape with one he'd hidden in his jacket pocket. He depressed the button. "I like La Bohème. It moves my soul." He walked out the door.

Shannon looked from the door to the tape player and gasped. "How could he know? It's my favorite, too."

When evening came, the dinner trays were brought by an orderly. Ben took a tray for Shannon and left one for himself outside John's door.

He pushed the door open, announcing, "Break time."

Shannon looked at the tray, not realizing she was frowning.

"If you eat that stuff on a consistent basis, Ben, you'll die."

"This is a hospital. The food is supposed to be healthy."

"I meant die of boredom." She laughed.

Ben laughed with her as he put the tray on the window ledge. "How about we bust this joint and get some seafood. What do you say?"

"We can't leave the patient, Ben. One of us has to be here at all times."

Ben looked at John. "Nothing like having a vegetable for competition."

Shannon's frown was fierce. "Take it back."

"What?"

"You heard me. You could have hurt his feelings. He can hear you, you know."

"He's unconscious," Ben argued.

"The mind absorbs everything in its surroundings awake or asleep." She looked at John empathetically. "He's a human being. Just like you and me," she said softly.

Ben backed away. There was something solemn about that moment and he had the incredible feeling he was not part of it. He realized he was an intruder.

The next day Ben brought in a tiny artificial Christmas tree, complete with lights, and set it up inside John's room.

"What's this?" Shannon asked. "Who sent this to John?"

"I bought it for you."

She looked at the tree. "I told you to save your money."

"Scrooge," he replied, picking up his bantering tone again. "It was only six bucks. On sale."

She examined it. "It's kinda scrawny."

He inspected the tree. "Do you think?"

She crossed to John's bed and lifted his arm to take his pulse.

Ben smiled. "And here I was thinking I'd spared no expense when it came to you."

She took John's blood pressure and recorded her findings on his chart. "Ben, we've known each other for over three weeks now. I've been judicious about letting you know my feelings and concerns. But you keep pressing…"

Before she could finish, Ben crossed over to her. "I'm trying to wear you down."

"Ben, please. I don't want to be worn down. I'm doing fine on my own. Really."

"Have lunch with me."

"I can't leave John," she said.

"I've ordered takeout from the café," he said brightly. "We'll sit with John. He can join us if he likes."

She cast him a semidamning look.

"He'll be safe," Ben assured her.

"You think of everything," she sighed.

"Is it a date?"

She faced him with her hand on her hip. "If I do this, then will you stop bugging me?"

"Probably not." He smiled charmingly at her.

"I didn't think so." She smiled back, dropping her defenses. "Why do you do this to yourself?"

"Do what?"

"Take on impossible challenges."

"Just stubborn, I guess." He chuckled. "So, you want turkey on wheat, Swiss cheese and fat-free Italian dressing. No mayo. No mustard. Right?"

"I'm impressed."

"All I had to do was ask." He shrugged his shoulders.

"Ben, how can you be interested in someone so predictable?"

"Predictable? Oh no, you're quite the opposite. I find you as mysterious as the riddle of Giza."

"How's that?" she asked tensely.

"The owner of the deli says she never knows if you want your brownie with pecans or walnuts. That you are forever changing your mind."

Shaking her head, she said, "I want the one with the caramel filling."

"See? You're fascinating. I'll be back in ten."

* * *

He was back in nine. He spread paper towels atop the hospital tray intended for the patient and handed Shannon a packet of sweetener.

"Just one for the tea, right?"

She looked at him. "You know, it makes me nervous you knowing so much about me. Have you followed me home yet?"

"I'm not a stalker, Shannon."

"Have you?" she asked again.

"No," he replied quietly. "But I've wanted to."

"This isn't healthy, Ben."

He looked at the sandwich. "It's fat-free."

"I didn't mean the turkey."

"I know what you meant," he said.

"You and me. It's not going to go anywhere," she said softly.

"Why not?" Putting his flat palms in the air, he said, "Don't answer that."

She peered at him. "Are you lonely?"

"Yes," he said too quickly. "No. I mean, it's not that, it's you. You remind me of a girl I once knew."

"A girl you loved?"

"Yes."

"But I'm not her," Shannon said, dropping her eyes. She stared at her tea thoughtfully. "What does friendship mean to you?"

Wiping his hands on the napkin, Ben said, "Always being there for each other. Supporting each other. Sharing good times, and bad ones."

"Sounds like marriage. Or what marriage should be."

"I said nothing about sex," he said, purposefully revealing his passion for her.

She glanced at John.

Ben noticed that.

"I...don't think I can do this, Ben. I'm not the chatty type. All this will lead to more questions I don't want to answer. You'll be frustrated...."

"I already am," he said in a low voice, then looked out the window.

"I'm not good at relationships. That's all you have to know about me. I handle them badly."

He stood, gathering his coffee and sandwich. "How would you know? You haven't tried." He left the room without another word.

Shannon stared thoughtfully after him.

For the rest of the day, Ben remained outside John's room, making calls on his cellular phone. She didn't ask who he was calling, not wanting to spark another conversation that would only hurt him in the long run.

Shannon watched Ben as he exited the hospital and stood on the small grassy area five floors below John's window, smoking cigarettes, pacing anxiously, looking confusedly at the sky, then up at John's window. Their eyes would meet and she would turn away.

She told herself she wanted nothing to do with a man who wore a gun. Guns were bad news. Cops were bad news. And Ben was off-limits for more reasons than one.

8

Holidays were special for most people, but not for Shannon. Though the other nurses made a fuss over the gifts they exchanged, Shannon wrapped small boxes of chocolates in simple brown paper, tied them with string and wrote each staff member's name in crayon on the top, the donor's name anonymous. When no one was around, she slipped her gifts under the tree the others had decorated.

She knew they would know the gifts were from her, but this way she didn't have to suffer their thanks, which tended to lead to invitations to their homes. Then to questions and more questions. She could take a lot of things, but not grilling.

Approaching John's room, Shannon realized she'd been effective in her effort to ignore Ben's gun and think of him as a person.

Somehow on Ben the gun had taken on a new aspect and she wasn't quite as frightened. Nevertheless, a gun was a gun. It could turn against her. Ben could turn against her. Especially if he knew the truth.

"Hello, Ben," Shannon said, trying to clip off her words to keep him disinterested.

His eyes lit up instantly. Her ploy wasn't working in the least.

"Hi, Shannon." He smiled. "Merry Christmas." He

got up from his uncomfortable metal chair. "How are you today? Pretty as ever, I see."

"Ben," she said warningly, going into John's room.

Ben followed her inside. He said nothing, only watched her.

She felt the silence, awkward and heavy, slowing her movements. She cuffed John's arm, took his blood pressure, then his temperature and marked them on the chart.

"Any change?" Ben asked, crossing the room and looming over John's face.

"None."

Ben smiled charmingly. "Would you tell me if there was?"

"Yes," she said, as she took out sheets to change the linens. She put her hand on her hip and glared at him. "What do you want, Ben?"

Glancing at his feet sheepishly, he replied, "I wanted us to have a meaningful conversation about our relationship."

"We don't have a relationship."

"Okay. We work together, then. Does that make you more comfortable?"

"Nothing about this makes me comfortable," she replied hastily, putting new cases on pillows and exchanging the old pillows behind John's head for clean ones.

Ben rubbed the back of his neck, and tried another tack. "Would you agree we're more than that?"

She sighed. "Ben, be honest. You said it before. You're lonely. You just don't want to be alone at Christmas. Whether it's with me or not isn't really the point."

"That's not true at all. Damn it, you know that. Why are you being so tough?"

She shrugged. "I'm not tough."

He rubbed his jaw as if she'd hit him. "It doesn't look like that to me."

"Please don't do this to yourself, Ben. I've tried to be nice about this. I'm just not interested in you...like *that*."

"I just don't get you, Shannon. I feel there's a connection between us. There *is* something going on, but you won't let it happen. You said there was no one else, but you act like there is. I went so far as to ask Chelsea and she said you had absolutely no man in your life. So that can't be it."

Grinding her jaw angrily, she answered, "Chelsea doesn't know flip about me or my life. I do have someone." She glanced at John.

"Aw, hell. Why did you lie then?"

"It's very new. Just came up, I guess you could say. And Ben, it's really none of your business."

Holding both palms in the air, he backed toward the door. "I get the picture."

"Ben..." She started toward him.

"No, really," he said, shaking his head. "It's my fault. Just hardheaded."

She could see the pain in his eyes and felt wretched. She hadn't wanted it to be like this. She wanted to consider Ben a friend, and if her life had been different, maybe she might have taken a chance on him.

As the door shut behind him, Shannon couldn't help thinking it seemed so final. And suddenly she realized she'd lost something valuable.

She went back to removing John's open-backed hospital gown—a tedious task given his size and dead weight. She dipped a washcloth in warm, sudsy water and washed his back, then his chest, his arms.

She remembered the dream she'd had and how John had kissed her. Stretching her arm across his chest to dip the cloth in the water again, her breast brushed against him. She felt an immediate heat rise inside her.

"Sorry," she said to the comatose man.

She washed his legs, moving from the thighs to the feet and then back up again. She rinsed him with a cloth dipped in clean water.

"I feel sorry for Ben, wanting to see me. But I just can't." She smiled to herself, wringing out the cloth for a last swipe of rinse water across his abdomen. "You'll always be my special guy." Her voice grew wistful. "More than special. I suppose I can tell you the truth now. I claimed you for myself that first night. I don't know how to explain it. It was as if..." She remembered Ben's words. "I felt a connection between us. As if I knew you somehow. Of course, that's impossible. We've never met. But you're special. That I know."

Just like I know this is crazy. I'm crazy.

She looked out the window at the Christmas lights glittering through the haze.

"I promised you we'd be together tonight and I'm not a welsher." She smoothed John's hair away from his face, fighting a profound sentimentality she thought she'd lost long ago.

Don't do this to yourself, Shannon. It's too dangerous.

She leaned over and kissed him on the forehead, but stopped herself from going farther. Instead, she resoaped the cloth and began on his hands.

She stopped abruptly. "Why hasn't anyone come for you, John?"

Discarding the cloth, she wove her fingers between his, soaping them, massaging them. "Can you hear me? I like your hands. Manicured. It's been a long time since I've known a man who had manicures. Let's face it, it's been a long time since I've known a man, period."

His fingers closed around hers and she smiled. "You're warm..." Suddenly, his fingers tightened.

"God!" She jumped back. "You moved!"

He bolted upright, his eyes clearly focused, his movements swift. He dug his fingers into her wrist, twisting her arm behind her back. A metallic object flashed in his hand.

"What are you doing?" she gasped.

He choked off her words with a twist of her arm. "Shut up!"

Pain shot through her arm and up her neck. "Ahhhh!"

His face was so close she could feel his breath. His eyes were compelling in their frightening glint. "Don't say a word!"

"What..." Her tongue was tied, her eyes wild.

"One sound and I shoot this hypo into your jugular. You know what an air bubble to the brain can do?"

Her eyes shot to the hypodermic needle already piercing her throat. Terror made her numb, she couldn't speak. Time stood still. She couldn't talk.

"Did you hear me?" he demanded.

She couldn't swallow, her tongue was like lead. Only by sheer determination did she manage to say, "Just don't hurt me." She held her breath.

He pricked her skin with the needle. "That's up to you. Do as I say and it's a bargain."

Her lips were so dry from fear they stuck together. She closed her eyes and concentrated on her response. "Okay."

"Unhook this catheter and get this IV out of my hand."

Shannon nodded as he eased his hold on her, but only slightly.

John kept the hypodermic imbedded just beneath the skin, dangerously close to her jugular.

"Easy! Easy! Can't you be more careful?" he groaned as she urgently removed the catheter. "That hurts."

"S-sorry." Her hands were shaking so much that she didn't doubt she'd hurt him.

He kept the needle to her throat while he painfully eased himself out of bed. He was shaky, his muscles weak from atrophy. Shannon noticed he leaned on her a great deal.

"Now, shut the door so we don't wake Sleeping Beauty."

Shannon's eyes darted to the hall. For the first time while on duty Ben had nodded off. Shannon tried to will him awake. She wondered how it was that Ben, who was sensitive to so many things about her, couldn't smell her fear.

John pushed her toward the door. As she closed it, the needle sank deeper.

"Please," she pleaded, tears filling her eyes.

Clamping a huge hand over her mouth, John said, "One more word and it'll be your last. You got me?"

Terrified, Shannon nodded carefully.

"Where are my clothes?"

"In the closet. I had them cleaned."

"Get them."

Shannon handed him the dry-cleaned pants and nylon windbreaker. The glass-matted shirt was torn and completely unwearable so he tossed it in the plastic waste can.

He dressed awkwardly with one arm, still weak from the coma, still keeping the hypodermic plunged in her neck.

"Careful!" she said when he lost his balance and depressed the plunger slightly. The air bubble had moved to the bottom of the syringe.

She had to get away from him as fast as possible. The longer she let this nightmare go on, the more power he gained. Time was crucial. "I'm not going to cause any trouble. I swear. I won't tell anyone where you go when you leave. You'll have plenty of time to get away...."

"I'm not leaving you here. You're going to keep me alive, lady. You got that?"

Ice-cold fear surfaced in a thin veil of perspiration across her forehead and upper lip. If he saw it, he would know she was totally in his power. It was too soon to tip her hand. She didn't want him to think he had all the advantages. "What do you mean?"

He carefully turned her around and held her in a hammerlock while pushing her toward the door. The look in his eyes was so coldly brittle she almost didn't want to hear his answer. "I'm going to need painkillers, antibiotics and whatever else you've been giving me. A two-week supply ought to do it."

"But they're locked up in the pharmaceuticals room."

"Where's the key?"

She considered lying, a habit she'd turned into an art form over the past few years, but then she thought better of it. Her terror was showing too much. To lie effectively, she needed to be more in control. She would have to find another way to talk him out of his impossible scheme.

"At the nurses' station," she replied flatly.

"Then that's where we're going."

He opened the door quietly. Shannon didn't believe for a second his plan would work. He was insane. He had to be. Didn't he realize the coma had zapped his strength? All she had to do was wake Ben and he would rescue her. Even a man in top condition would have a difficult time fending off Ben's obviously well-conditioned body. John was in no condition to fight anyone—not even herself. If she could just get the damn hypodermic out of her neck...

If. What if? What if Ben doesn't save me? John's energy is depleted. He won't last the hour. Or will he? If only I hadn't let my emotions and imagination run wild. I wanted John to be Prince Charming.

They slipped out the door and in two strides John had crossed to the sleeping Ben and delivered a solid punch to his jaw.

She gasped. "Ben."

"I can't take any chances." He looked at Ben. "He won't be coming around for a while, maybe hours," John said.

The needle stung as he jerked it out of her neck. Shannon winced, but didn't take her eyes off the gun he pointed at her.

John took the gun out of Ben's shoulder holster, then searched Ben's pockets for extra clips and put them in his jacket. Cocking back the trigger, he stuck the gun barrel into Shannon's spine. "Do your job. Save his life."

"How?"

"Drag him into my room and tie him up with that adhesive tape in there."

Taking Ben's legs, she managed to drag him into the room. Following John's explicit instructions, she tied Ben to the bed legs using gauze and adhesive tape from her metal supply trolley. As she taped his mouth shut, tears filled her eyes.

If only...I'd gone with you tonight, Ben, none of this would be happening. I'm sorry, Ben. Honest to God. Really sorry.

When she was finished, John cocked the gun again. "You so much as breathe wrong and I'll shoot."

Shannon swallowed hard. "Okay."

"Let's get the meds."

They went to the door and his hold on her weakened.

"That the nurses' station up ahead?" he whispered in her ear.

"Yes."

"How did you get to work today?" He jabbed her with the gun barrel. "Did you take the bus or what?"

"Yeah, the bus."

"Liar." He spat the word like a curse and pressed the gun into her back so hard it hurt.

"Okay! I drove my car."

"That's more like it. Where are the keys?"

"In my purse," she answered. Before he even bothered to ask the next question, she said, "It's in the drawer to the right of the computer."

"Get it. Then how far down this hall to the medicine?"

"The door next to the stairway exit," she replied, pointing to the lighted red Exit sign.

"Just keep your cool."

Nodding, Shannon noticed that no one was at the nurses' station. They'd been severely shorthanded that afternoon and tonight was worse. As the only other RN still in good health, Chelsea had been forced to take on another shift. John was safer than he knew.

"Make it quick," he demanded as they reached the station.

Shannon grabbed her purse, then withdrew the pharmaceuticals-room key from Nancy's personal drawer.

He snatched the purse from her.

"What?" She stared at him.

He rifled quickly through the bag. "Just checking."

"For what?"

"Mace. Pepper spray."

She shook her head. "I don't have any."

"Let's go."

They hurried down the hall, but just as they reached the pharmaceuticals-room door, Shannon heard Chelsea's voice coming from next door. "I'll get you some cranberry juice, Mrs. Raymond."

Shannon fumbled with the key.

Hissing, John warned, "Don't try to be a hero." He pressed the gun solidly into her back for emphasis.

Shannon's mouth had never been so dry. She didn't realize she was crying until a tear fell onto her shaking hand as she finally inserted the key in the lock and pushed the door open.

Just as Chelsea turned into the hall, Shannon and John slipped quietly into the pharmaceuticals room. Hearing Chelsea's rubber-soled shoes slap against the linoleum as she walked past, Shannon finally expelled a sigh of relief.

"Get plenty of painkillers."

"Okay," she said, stuffing the bottles into her purse. When she finished, she nodded at him.

There's still hope we'll be seen. If I can just get away from that gun so that if he did fire, the bullet would miss me, I could make a run for it.

Suddenly, the doorknob jiggled. Then there was a knock. "Shannon? Are you in there?" Chelsea asked.

"Yeah, I am."

"I thought I saw you disappear in there. What are you doing? You're not authorized to dispense medication."

Stepping quickly behind the door, John kept the gun pointed at Shannon. Whispering, he said, "Get rid of her. Now."

Nodding, Shannon choked back her fear, put on a plastic smile and opened the door.

Chelsea was clearly upset with the breach in protocol, and she liked throwing her weight around whenever possible. With Nancy gone, Chelsea was totally responsible for the floor. "What are you doing, Shannon?"

"We've only got a skeleton crew tonight so I thought I'd help you out by preparing the cart."

Chelsea took two steps forward, obviously hoping to push her way past Shannon, but Shannon kept her hand on the open door and barred Chelsea from going any farther.

John glared at Shannon and cocked the gun. She saw the hard glint in his eyes. Though she'd never cared for Chelsea, she realized she could never live with herself if anything happened to her.

"You don't even have a cart." Chelsea tried to glance around her and into the room.

"Yes, I do." Shannon turned her body, indicating the two-tiered metal cart behind her.

John's hiss was a deadly whisper. "Get rid of her."

"You better take care of Mrs. Raymond, Chelsea."

"Yeah, I guess so. Thanks for your help, Shannon. But don't you dare ever let it slip I allowed this. My ass would be in a sling for sure."

"And I'd be in that sling with you."

Chelsea's eyebrow arched suspiciously over Shannon's uncharacteristic camaraderie. "Yeah, I guess so. Thanks."

Shannon sensed John's finger squeezing the trigger. She shivered, thinking how close Chelsea had come to death.

When she closed the door, her knees were trembling so hard, she thought they'd give out.

John darted behind Shannon and took up his armhold on her. He pushed her toward the door. "Is the hallway clear?"

Cautiously, Shannon eased the door open. "Yes."

"Let's go."

They raced around the corner and through the door to the stairwell. Shannon prayed no one was on the stairs while they made their escape down the five flights to the basement tunnel that led to the parking garage. Assuming the other floors were as quiet as the fifth, Shannon believed they'd be safe.

But just as they reached the first floor, they heard voices, both male and female, coming from the underground-tunnel stairway directly below them. John froze. Shannon listened to the conversation and realized the couple was having an argument.

John pulled Shannon back against the wall so the couple could not look up through the metal stairs to the landing where they were standing. His impatience over the couple's loitering was clearly growing as his finger squeezed back on the trigger.

Suddenly Shannon slammed her foot down on the metal step. The thudding sound echoed down the stairwell. The noise startled the couple and they quickly left the stairwell through the tunnel door to the parking garage where the elevator was located.

Shannon and John quickly put the last flight behind them. Checking to make certain the couple was out of sight, John pushed Shannon ahead of him as they emerged into the parking garage.

"Where's your car?"

"Up a half level. A15."

"Let's go."

John followed Shannon as she walked up the incline, taking her keys out of her purse without missing a step. She walked up to the LeBaron and unlocked the door.

John slowly eased himself into the passenger's seat. Wincing in pain, he ordered Shannon to start the car and head out.

"Which way?"

"West. Just head out 79," John groaned, holding his sore ribs.

"To where they found you?" she asked too quickly and suddenly felt the cold gun barrel against her temple.

"You ask too many questions."

"Sorry," she breathed anxiously.

John slumped back in the seat and allowed his eyes to close.

Shannon drove up St. Vincent Street past Schumper Medical Center near the LSU campus, and turned west on I-20 doing just as John told her. As they passed the 220 beltway, John kept his eyes glued to the side rearview mirror. Shannon knew he was checking to see if they were being followed. She drove the speed limit but didn't push the car any faster. She just kept her eyes on the road and drove.

"Slow down," John ordered as they neared the Sabine River Bridge. "It's so dark and I was so..." He looked around. "Drive to the other side, then park the car on this side of the road. Edge off a bit toward the embankment so no one can see us."

Terror had exhausted her and the silence between them was more frightening than anything she'd known.

She drove the car just as he ordered. "Is this good?"

"Yeah."

"No one will see us," she pointed out as she turned off the engine.

"Give me the keys," he said abruptly.

Does he have to think of everything? She shoved the keys into his hand.

"Now, get out and come with me."

"I can wait here."

He stuck the gun to her head. "I'd rather you didn't." He got out of the car, wincing in pain as he did. He kept the gun aimed at Shannon as his eyes scoured the area.

She couldn't fathom what he was looking for. "They took the car away a long time ago, Ben said," she offered.

"I'm not looking for the car." He paused. "It was so foggy that night. I was out of it. And there wasn't any snow," he said, which told her he was looking for something on the ground.

He pushed her toward the bridge sign. Scraping the ground with his foot, John cleared away the snow from around the base of the creosote-coated signpost. "Damn. They found it."

"Found what?"

Growling, he grabbed her arm, pinching the fleshy underside. She noticed that he used her for balance while at the same time keeping her within striking distance. She didn't have to imagine what that gun butt across the back of her head would feel like.

He kept scouring the ground.

Shannon looked for a way out.

He kicked small rocks aside, cursing with each failure. "Where the hell are you?" he asked.

"If you told me what you're looking for, I could help," she said, trying to break free and go in the opposite direction.

He drew up short, dropped her arm and held the gun to her face with both hands. "I don't think so. Just keep pace with me where I can see you. Okay?"

She nodded, pressing her lips together. Turning, he stubbed his toe and nearly fell. The moon glinted off the rock.

"Goddamn bloody rock," he muttered.

Shannon held her breath. Then she saw a shiny object poking out from the rock and tall grasses.

He leaned down. "Is this my lucky day or what?"

John was so intent on his discovery that he didn't see Shannon take a step backward. Then two. Just one more step and she'd make a run for the car.

She didn't know what he was slipping into his pocket, but his face was lit up like a carnival clown's.

Whatever it was, she supposed he had a right to be happy about it—he'd nearly died for the damn thing.

Without even turning his head around, he raised his arm, slowly pointing the gun at her.

"What the *hell* do you think you're doing?"

"What?"

"Cut the crap! Okay? I can feel you moving behind me. You've taken two steps and are ready for the third." He turned. His eyes were blazing.

"I...I..." Her knees were shaking.

He shrugged his shoulders and rolled his head to ease his tension. "Forget it. Let's get the hell out of here." He walked toward her. "I hate this place!"

They walked in silence as he pushed her toward the car.

When they reached the car, Shannon's curiosity had gotten the better of her. "What did you find?"

"Nothing," he said morosely.

"Okay," Shannon replied unsteadily, afraid to get him riled.

"I thought it was here, but it's not. Just some damn smashed beer can," he explained.

Shannon was terrified of provoking him, but her curiosity and quick mind flew ahead of her. "What were you looking for?"

"Frankly, I don't remember."

"You were badly beaten. It's understandable."

A flash of gratitude crossed his eyes. Shannon saw it.

"There's a lot I don't remember. Not who, or why or what they wanted. There were two of them. That's about all I know."

"And whatever it was you left here..." she ventured with a great deal of trepidation.

"Maybe they came back and found it." He rubbed the bridge of his nose. "God! I hate losing part of my life like this. C'mon. Get in."

Shannon closed the car door. Her hands were shaking as she tried to insert the key in the ignition. "Damn. Get in there!"

It wasn't her words that jogged his memory so much as the exasperation in her voice. It reminded him of his own feelings of powerlessness just before blacking out that night.

He'd thought they would kill him and his only revenge was to keep the disk from them at all costs. Now he remembered he'd been sharp enough to slip the disk into the torn lining of his windbreaker, behind the Bulls' basketball-embroidered emblem.

He slapped his chest, feeling for it. "Hell!"

"What?" she asked, her shoulders jumping away from his anger.

"I put it in my jacket. I know I did." He paused, then looked at her. "It was you!"

"Me?"

"You said you had my jacket dry-cleaned."

"I did."

"Where? What cleaners?"

"My usual one in Shreveport."

"Where in Shreveport?

"A block from my house."

He motioned at the ignition with the gun. "Let's go."

"Back to town?" She couldn't believe her good luck.

He nodded. "That idiot stole my disk."

"Okay," she said, smiling inwardly.

How lucky could she get? John was going back where she knew she'd find a way to break away. At the very least, every police officer in the city would be looking for her car. Her nightmare was nearly over.

9

—➤◀—

Ben licked the bloody spot where Chelsea had removed his skin along with the surgical tape. "How long have I been out?" He rubbed his sore jaw.

"I don't know," she replied, untying his hands. "What happened?"

"Obviously, John Doe has been released," he said derisively, yanking at the gauze and tape around his ankles.

"That's impossible!"

"I mean, he escaped!"

"I don't understand. I would have seen him, heard something. Shannon would have told me..."

Their eyes met.

"Damn!" Ben jumped to his feet. "When was the last time you saw her?"

"Hours ago. Oh my God! Do you think he took her?"

"Where did you see her?"

"In the meds room. She didn't act like anything was wrong."

"How did she act, exactly?"

"Like Shannon. Distant, obliging, too helpful."

He glared at her and checked his empty holster. "Damn it! The clips, too."

Chelsea's eyes were wild. "He's going to kill her!"

"Not if I can help it."

Ben raced out of the room and headed to the nurses' station, where he snatched the phone out of a nurse's hand.

"Hey! Wait a minute! You can't do that!"

"The hell I can't," he said, hanging up the girl's call. He dialed the police station. "Gimme Chief Bremen. This is Richards. Make it fast."

"Sorry, sir. The chief's been home for hours."

"He what? What friggin' time is it?"

"Past midnight, sir."

"They could be halfway to the moon by now."

"Sir?"

"Put out an APB on the John Doe we've had on ice here at St. Christopher's. Get me a make on a staff nurse here, Shannon Riley. I think he took her as a hostage. I'll call the chief at home."

"But, sir, it's Christmas!"

"I don't give a damn what day it is!" Ben slammed his hand over the receiver button. He punched out Jimmy Joe Bremen's home number.

A groggy man's voice answered. "This better be important."

"It is," Ben said. "John Doe escaped. I think he's taken a nurse as hostage."

"Don't tell me what you think, just what you know." Jimmy Joe sat upright in bed.

"At some point the prisoner came to. I was asleep, I admit. He knocked me out, took my gun and escaped. I'm on my way over to Shannon Riley's apartment to investigate. Her shift isn't over and she's missing."

"Richards, I don't want to hear that he's armed."

"I'm afraid he is."

"Seal off that room. I want forensics to go over everything. Maybe we'll find a clue to where he would have taken her."

"Sure thing."

"Check out her neighbors. See what they know. Then meet me in my office when you're finished. I want to know every detail of how you screwed up."

"Right."

"And Richards..." Jimmy Joe's breath rattled.

"Yeah?"

"Keep everything on the Q.T."

"Sir?"

"I don't want word of this getting out just yet. I want to know what we're dealing with first."

"Yes, sir."

Ben hung up the phone, went back to Room 505 and locked the door. He instructed Chelsea not to allow anyone but Chief Bremen and the forensics team entrance.

Ben left the hospital and went straight to his car. As he pulled out of the parking lot and headed toward Shannon's address, he reached under his seat for his cellular phone. He dialed a long-distance number.

"We've got trouble. He's skipped."

"I found this, Chief," Mel Anderson, the bookish, thirty-five-year-old forensic assistant said, holding up a hypodermic needle. "It was on the floor."

"So? This is a hospital. I think they might have a few here."

"I hope to hell not."

"Excuse me?"

Mel pointed to the syringe. "This one has a large air bubble. Inject this and there's an empty bed available."

Jimmy Joe examined the hypodermic. "What's in here? Poison?"

"Water. And that air bubble."

"And Shannon Riley being a nurse..."

"...would be scared out of her wits."

"I get the drift. Let me know what else you find. I'll be downtown."

"Yes, sir."

Jimmy Joe walked out of room 505 and found Chelsea giving a statement to his detective. He motioned to the detective. "I'll take over."

"Yes, sir," the man said.

Chelsea waited patiently while the detective walked away, then she turned to Jimmy Joe. "I suppose this means I won't be seeing you later this morning."

"Cut the crap." He glanced surreptitiously over the top of her head at Mel, who quickly looked away.

"You said you had a special Christmas present for me. I've been on pins and needles, sugar."

"We'll have to put it off for now. It's too dangerous for us to be seen right now."

"But you promised." She pouted.

"Later," he snapped and walked away.

Ben got the master key to Shannon's apartment from the superintendent. Taking the stairs two at a time, he was winded by the time he reached her door.

"Damn cigarettes," he muttered, looking at the collage of notes on Shannon's door.

When you get in, knock me up. I'm too sick to sleep. Ben read the note. It was signed, *Elliot.*

"The boyfriend?"

Stepping back, Ben looked down the hall at the

doors. He noticed a blue note on the door next to Shannon's apartment. It was from Shannon to Elliot, with instructions on how to care for his cold.

Elliot's interrogation could wait, Ben thought as he unlocked Shannon's door.

No matter how many times he'd investigated an empty house, office or apartment, Ben never ceased being wary of the unknown. He reached for his revolver and remembered it was gone.

"Damn."

He knew better than to step into a trap. John Doe could be hiding out here in her apartment. A dumb move, but a logical one for a man just out of a coma, perhaps in delirium.

Ben glanced at the crack between the door and the wall. No one hiding there. Then he heard a tinkling sound.

A bell. He braced himself for the worst but then a soft mewing came from the area across the room near the windows. The bell sounded again. A faint glow from a streetlamp illuminated the dark apartment just enough for him to see a caramel-colored Manx cat spring onto the back of the cheap Herculon plaid sofa.

Ben smiled. "What's a nice kitty like you doing in such an...ugly place?" he asked as he turned on the light switch.

Ben's fantasies about Shannon and her after-work-hours life was based on the subdued, confident, efficient and lonely woman he knew from the hospital. He had imagined so many things about her, about being with her. Somehow, he'd pictured a more expressive life-style. What he saw revealed little or nothing about her.

"Except that she lives like someone who is in transition. Between lives," he said to himself after inspecting the entire apartment for would-be kidnappers.

Assured he was alone, he shut the door and took inventory. He picked up a ratty afghan off the floor and placed it on the arm of the slipcovered Chippendale sofa—the only decent piece of furniture in the room.

"Shannon, darlin', you need a subscription to *House Beautiful*," he sighed. "Or a life. Like I do."

The chairs were old, cracked, and had been sanded down to bare wood. Cans of stain, varnish and glue were stacked in a corner ready to heal them.

It hurt Ben's eyes to look from the drab olive hutch with the broken door to the psychedelic wallpapered kitchen with its intensely obvious refusal to indulge in even the smallest appliances. No microwave. No dishwasher. The absence of a dishwasher he could accept, but no electric can opener, no toaster? It was as if she'd deliberately set out to make her life miserable.

The thermostat was set at a bitingly cold sixty degrees. The bedroom was furnished with only a bed and a lamp on a cardboard box that stood in for a dresser. It contained the white utilitarian panty hose worn, no doubt, at the hospital.

There were no frilly things women kept in their lair to make them feel special. Even the clothes in her closet were uniforms or faded jeans and T-shirts. Cotton underwear and bras—no lace, no satin.

"No sex." Ben stopped cold. "*That's* what is missing."

The Shannon he knew exuded sensuality with every step she took. Oh, she kept her eyes averted, her walk brisk, but when she breathed in and out, he sensed that she experienced the swell and contraction of her diaphragm, the press of her breasts against her uniform, the rush of air through her nostrils while tasting the hospital ethers on her tongue.

That kind of acute sensitivity was rare, but Ben knew it when he saw it, because he was like that.

Though he'd never been married, his apartment was furnished comfortably and adequately. His home was a haven for him. He'd expected Shannon to have the same philosophy. It saddened him that she didn't.

His eyes scanned the meager shelves. No stereo. No radio. No music. "No songs to sing," he whispered absentmindedly to himself.

Even the bathroom gave no clues to Shannon's personality. The shampoo was cheap and unscented. A bar of generic soap. A plastic razor. A wide-toothed comb. A brush with most of the bristles broken off. No perfumes. No cosmetics anywhere.

"Doesn't she ever go out? Or is the boyfriend next door a natural-look freak?"

He stopped abruptly, thinking back on his encounters with her. How she'd dodged the personal questions he posed. She never gave clues about her family, her past. He'd been so entranced with her that he'd assumed she was spurning him. Perhaps the answer was not that it was him in particular she avoided, but all people. All relationships. He already knew she was nursing a broken heart. But living like this?

"She's hiding something. And it's big."

Entering the bathroom, he opened the medicine cabinet. Vitamins. Lots of them. Antihistamines. Ibuprofen. Cold remedies galore and several antibiotics.

"She must be prone to head colds," he mused. "But

sleeping pills?" Every over-the-counter brand could be accounted for as well as prescriptions for Seconal, Halcion and Valium. Interestingly enough, all of the prescriptions were long-outdated, as though she'd needed them most in the past.

"My God, Shannon, just what is your secret? Are you in hiding? Or hiding something? Someone?"

He scratched his head. "I must have lost my gift for reading people. That, or Shannon is a split personality."

Going back to the bedroom, he spied a black leather Bible hidden half under the bed and half in sight. He lifted the dog-eared book. There were a half-dozen Catholic holy cards used to mark passages.

"Why do you feel guilty, Shannon? Who or what is riding your back?"

He couldn't recall seeing Shannon in the hospital chapel. She'd never impressed him as being overly religious. In fact, now that he thought about it, she lacked many expected emotional responses.

Was that why he was attracted to her? Ben had always been fascinated with puzzles. The more difficult and tedious, the better. That's why he'd decided to become a cop. Life had taught him, a bit later than most perhaps, that he was a born sleuth. An investigator.

He questioned his interest in Shannon. Was it that he found her fascinating or that she posed a mystery to unravel?

Maybe he wasn't falling in love with her. Maybe he already was. Only time would tell.

He leaned down to put the Bible back and heard the distinct sound of a gun being cocked.

"Who the hell are you?" an angry man's voice growled.

10

— ▶ ◀ —

"I said, who the hell are you?" A short, stocky young man dressed in a worn bathrobe stood in front of Ben holding a Glock.

"The police." Ben held up his badge. "You got a permit for that gun?"

"Damn straight I do." Elliot's hand trembled.

The cat purred in the corner.

Elliot took a deep breath and lowered the gun, uncocked it and stuck it, and his hands, in the robe's pockets.

"You must be her boyfriend," Ben said.

"I wish," he said, still not stepping over the threshold. "I'm Elliot Wilson, Shannon's neighbor. Shannon doesn't have, er, relationships. On that, she and I agree."

"Really?"

"Yeah." Elliot's eyes scoured Ben yet gave no hint to his conclusions. "What did she do?" he chuckled. "Forget to pay a parking ticket? 'Cuz if it's anything more than that, you're off base. Way off."

"You're pretty protective for being just a friend."

Elliot took his hands out of his pockets and balled them at his sides. "Yeah, and you're more than just a cop."

"Not really. I was working at the hospital with Shannon."

"She never said anything about the police."

"It wasn't for public knowledge."

"She's good at keeping secrets."

"Is that so?"

Elliot nodded. "She never talks about personal stuff. Better still, she keeps her yap shut about anything I tell her. I like that in a woman. In anybody."

Ben watched Elliot as he spoke, thinking the guileless man more honest than most people.

Elliot looked down at his frayed slippers. "She isn't hurt, is she?"

"No, nothing like that."

"But you're not sure."

"I just wanted to talk to her," Ben said. "The important question is if you've seen her tonight."

"No, I haven't."

"When was the last time you saw her?"

"A couple of days ago."

"She hasn't come home in the meantime?"

"She came home," Elliot began, "but I didn't see her. I don't always see her. We have this thing."

"Thing?"

"We leave notes for each other. She's coming in when I'm going out. I go to work when she's just finishing. Ships passing in the morning." He laughed at his own joke.

Ben frowned. "She have any other friends in the building?"

"No. She has no other friends, period."

"Why's that?"

Elliot shrugged his shoulders. The hands went back into his pockets where they were less lethal and more comfortable. "She's like me, I told ya. She doesn't like people. She's got her work. It's enough."

"Enough?"

"Yeah. To kill the time."

"I see," Ben said, taking out one of his cards. "Here's my number. If you hear from her, would you call me immediately? Use my cellular number on the bottom of the card. It's easier than reaching me at the station. Sometimes I don't get my messages."

"I know whatcha mean," Elliot said, removing his hands from his pockets to receive the card. "The guys at work never tell me crap. Not that anyone's calling me, you understand."

"Except Shannon, you mean."

"Not even Shannon," Elliot replied and walked away down the hall.

Jimmy Joe Bremen's expression was filled with concern as he spoke to Helen Mayer. "You understand our position, don't you?"

"I'm trying to."

"We don't want anything to happen to Miss Riley. There's no telling what this man could to her if provoked. It's imperative that we keep this incident under wraps. If the media, or God forbid the wires, got ahold of this story, it would greatly jeopardize our efforts."

Helen's cynical eyes fastened on him. "Sounds to me like you're more interested in protecting your department than my employee."

"That's not it at all, Helen. Damn it! I'm doin' my best here!"

"Doesn't look like it to me. Otherwise that bastard

wouldn't have gotten away in the first place. I thought that was why we had a guard on duty."

Jimmy Joe nodded. "He's new and I take full responsibility for putting a greenie on such an important assignment."

Helen's anger deflated with a slow sigh. "I'm sorry, Chief. I'm well aware of what it's like to work with inexperienced personnel. We're the training ground for half the state's medical students. I shouldn't throw stones. It's just that I'm worried about Shannon. She's my best girl. She acts tough, but she's got a heart of gold. I took a shine to her the first day I hired her."

He put his hand on her shoulder. "Tell your staff, those who know about what happened, to keep their mouths shut. We're not even putting out an APB. It's too risky. I've got my best men on this. They work quietly, but effectively. So no gossip about this. No leaks. I'll arrest them for obstructing justice if they do. They've got to understand that one word could kill Shannon."

"I'll do it, Chief."

"Trust me, Helen. We'll have her back here by nightfall."

"I hope so, Chief. I hope so."

Shannon parked the car in front of the motel entrance.

"Give me the keys," John groaned, holding out a hand he struggled to make steady.

She could tell he was in great pain. All she had to do was wear him down. It would be simple enough. Then she could get away. "I thought we had to go back to Shreveport."

"We do."

She was numb, confused. A motel could mean only one thing. She didn't think, just blurted out, "What are you going to do to me?"

"Don't worry, I'm not going to rape you." He winced as he rolled his eyes. "I haven't been charged with anything yet and don't intend to be. Don't flatter yourself. I'm tired."

"How long do you think you can keep up this pace?"

"For as long as I need to." He sat slowly upright, each muscle bending against its will, she was sure.

As a nurse, Shannon had learned the specific ways in which patients tried to hide pain, endure it, overcome it. They held their breath. They focused on objects or people at a distance. They used their minds to convince themselves they were outside their bodies. They willed it away.

But it didn't matter to her what they did. She was what was known as an empath. She felt every torturous breath they breathed. She ached for them. She used her own mind to will their pain away. John was no different. She pretended not to notice his grimaces and moans, but inside she burned with agony. The only thing that negated her reaction to his pain was fear for her own life.

"You don't look so good," she said.

"Thanks."

She needed to make things difficult for him. To run away. Escape. All he had to do was pull the trigger, but his exhaustion was making her feel empowered again. Her hopes for rescue rose.

He looked to the back seat. "You got any other clothes in that mess back there?"

"Just my running clothes and my Nikes."

"That a sweatshirt?"

"Yes. I was taking this stuff to the Laundromat."

"Bring it. You need to change out of that uniform."

"So I won't be recognized as a nurse?"

"That and because I hate uniforms. Any uniforms."

"Okay…" She grabbed the clothes, wadded them into a roll and stuffed them under her arm.

"That's better," he said. "Now, give me your purse. I need some money."

"I'll go sign us in."

"Fat chance." He shoved the gun into her ribs just beneath her breast. "We go together. We're newly-weds returning from our holiday honeymoon. I'll tell the manager you wore me out."

She would have liked to sneer at him, hit him, shove that cold gun up his nose the way he kept doing to her. But she knew this wasn't the time to fight him. She could only pray for the right moment to come and the courage to use it wisely.

They went into the dingy office and greeted an elderly woman whose fatigue appeared to be twice John's. She barely looked at them as she adjusted her bifocals to fill in the blanks on the carboned credit-card slip.

"I'm supposed to have one of them fancy new machines," the old woman said, pressing the credit card into its slot and running the bar over the impression. She shoved the slip at John.

Shannon grabbed the pen attached to the counter with a long metal chain. "It's my card," she said, signing her name.

"You should make him pay," the woman said as she handed Shannon the key. "Merry Christmas."

"Thanks," John said and guided Shannon toward the glass door.

The second they were outside, the old woman locked the office door and shuffled through the doorway to her attached apartment.

Room 6 was small and drab but clean. The bed rested against a white-painted, concrete-block wall, and was flanked on either side by metal faux wood–grained nightstands and cheap chrome lamps. A matching long counter with two drawers was bolted to the opposite wall. A mirror with no ornamentation hung above the counter. The bathroom was minuscule. There was no tub, only a fiberglass shower stall with a clear plastic curtain, a toilet, sink and frosted-glass window.

Still in the bathroom, Shannon paid no attention to John as he nearly collapsed on the bed. All she saw was the window.

"Keep the door open," he said. "Where I can see you."

Normally, Shannon would have had a clever rejoinder for that line. Not this time. She glanced at her reflection in the mirror and saw that she looked as terrified as she felt. She reached around and cracked open the door just enough so he could see her image in the mirror, but that was all.

Running the water, she let the room steam. She wet a washcloth and soaped it just as she'd done a thousand times for patients in the hospital.

Just as I did for you when I thought you were…

Her eyes teared, her back muscles screamed with tension. She exhaled heavily. "A savior."

She scrubbed her face vigorously, almost brutally,

as though she could erase herself from this terrifying situation.

Taking off her top, she washed her arms and back at the sink, afraid to venture into the shower. She couldn't risk being any more vulnerable to him than she already was.

She dried herself with a thin, cheap towel and put on her crop top and the hooded sweatshirt over it, then stepped into her jogging pants. She hung her uniform on a stainless-steel hook on the back of the door.

She walked out and saw John lying on the bed. Her eyes went instantly to the ever-present cocked gun he pointed at her. She jumped, clutching her hands to her breasts.

"You should be used to this by now," he said.

"I'm not."

His eyes met hers. She held her breath, unable to read his expression. This time he gazed at her as if seeing her for the first time. For an instant she thought she saw his eyes sparkle, his lips curve upward at the corner.

"Don't look at me like that," he said tersely.

"How was I looking at you?" she asked curiously.

"Like I'm something I'm not," he said.

"Sorry."

He cleared his throat and pointed to the floor with the gun. "You'll be sleeping on the floor. After I tie you to the bed, that is."

"What?"

"I don't trust you," he said.

She wrung her hands, thinking quickly of how she could retrieve even the slightest hope of escape. "I could have been screaming all the way in here. I c-could be doing it now. I could wake up everyone in this place."

"Not a chance." He shook his head. "You're not that stupid."

She wasn't that stupid. Even if he didn't kill her, one blow of the gun butt against her jaw and she wouldn't be able to speak for days, maybe months.

One of the joys of her training and experience was that she knew precisely the physical repercussions of folly. Unattended wounds, broken bones without proper setting and casting and internal injuries without surgery could all end in death.

He could do that to her, she knew. Beat her, then leave her alive somewhere alone. His conscience would be free from actual murder—if he had a conscience.

Shannon watched as John tore strips of material from the bed sheet. Knowing she had no other options, she allowed him to bind her wrists to the corner of the bed. Tossing her a pillow, he settled himself on the bed above her, keeping the gun clearly in her line of vision. Exhausted, Shannon found her eyes closing despite her terror. She slept fitfully, until John's voice broke through her dreams.

"I need you," he said, his voice a low painful rumble.

"For what?"

"I need one of those painkillers we took from the hospital."

"How am I supposed to inject you if I'm tied up?"

He was in no mood for sarcasm. "First I'll untie you, then the injection." He reached down and loosened the tie on her wrists.

"Can I ask a favor first?"

"No."

"I need to use the bathroom." She lowered her eyes to the floor.

"Oh, all right. Leave the door open."

"Now?" she countered. "I mean, I understand the other...but, couldn't I have some privacy?"

"No."

Taking her purse with her, she went back to the bathroom.

The toilet was positioned behind the door, so if she leaned back enough, she could keep it open and still keep her propriety.

"Hurry it up, will ya? I need that stuff."

Shannon placed her purse on the sink in full view of him. "Demerol."

She withdrew a hypodermic, pulled off the end cap and stuck the needle into the rubber-topped bottle of medicine. She held the syringe to the light next to the small medicine-cabinet mirror. Her eyes were tired and dry. She blinked twice to focus properly.

Three cc's would put him out for hours. Even if I were tied up, I still might have a chance to get out of here. After all, besides the sheets, what's he going to...

Looking in the medicine-cabinet mirror, she saw the reflection of a shadow passing outside the window behind her. She blinked and stared more intensely. There was a man outside the window.

She could tell his hair was short, his head large, and the hand he lifted to the window held a gun. Her skin crawled. She opened her mouth to scream, but no sound erupted. He pulled back his arm.

He's going to shoot the window out! He's going to kill me!

The man's arm moved back away from the window, as if he was retreating. Then it moved forward at lightning speed. The glass shattered and a black-gloved hand snaked through the jagged hole. Frantically, the hand broke more glass, making a frightening frame for the olive-skinned man's horridly placid face. There was no life in his eyes, no soul to his maniacal grin. His attitude was more lethal than his weapon. To Shannon he looked like a...*death mask.*

A gun blasted. Shannon was sure he'd shot her, but she couldn't feel where the bullet had entered her. There was no pain, no heat. Only an iciness that both enveloped and filled her.

He was sneering at her, taunting her to defy him as he pulled the trigger back.

"Bastard!" She felt no fear as she lunged toward the man, sinking the hypodermic directly into his jugular vein. She plunged the triple dose of Demerol into her assailant while grabbing her purse with the opposite hand and flinging it down over his wrist.

He groaned and dropped the gun. His eyes rolled in his head and his head flopped on his shoulders as he fell halfway into the room.

"Shit! You killed him!" John said, suddenly behind her, breathing hard. "I killed mine, too."

"Killed?" Shannon was too stunned, too disoriented to understand him.

"One of them kicked in the front door. I rolled off the bed just as he put a shot through the headboard. Then I shot him."

She remembered the gunshot she'd heard. "I only heard one shot."

John held up an automatic with a scope and silencer. "These guys weren't kidding this time."

He stepped past her and inspected the man in the

window. He took out the hypodermic and felt for a pulse. "Damn, but that was fast thinking."

Shannon couldn't speak. His words made no sense to her. Of course the man was dead. She'd killed him. Hadn't she? And how had she done that? She, who fought so valiantly to save lives. She, who believed she could bring her patients back from the brink of death through the force of her own will. She, Shannon, had killed and the proof was in front of her.

Her mouth was dry, her body immobile and heavy as if she'd been drinking lead.

"I…I killed him," she said, finally admitting to the gravest of all sins.

"No, you didn't." He took her hand, placing her fingers on the man's neck. Her arm retracted as if she'd burned it. "He's alive."

She looked at John. A new horror took the place of the old. "He'll kill us."

"Yes, he will." He grabbed her purse and her hand and pulled her from the bathroom. "Unless we get outta here."

They had to step over the bloody body of the well-dressed man John had shot and killed. Shannon was used to seeing blood and she was shocked that the sight froze her.

"What's wrong?"

John had taken a life. No matter what she did for the fallen man, she couldn't bring him back to life. And if she did, he would simply rise up with only one purpose—to kill her and end John's life.

They raced from the motel. Shannon's world warbled with an unsychronized harmony as her logic struggled to put events in order, to put meaning to the senseless. She was reacting on instinct. Suddenly, she remembered what to do.

Shannon lunged past John toward the car, her toned legs used to brutally hard runs through city streets at daybreak when her night shift ended. She ran now to escape the vision of the dead man.

They jumped in the car. Shannon turned the engine over on the first try.

"The cops will be here soon," she said, backing away.

"Yeah. But not as fast as their buddies," he replied. "Hit it. There's no time to lose."

As they left the motel parking lot, the light in the manager's office was illuminated. Shannon saw the elderly woman pick up the black telephone receiver. Her expression was one of shock. Shannon realized one of the guests was reporting the gunshot and that the police would be arriving soon. Her rescue.

But Shannon would be gone.

11

After leaving Shannon's apartment, Ben reached his car just in time to hear the dispatcher conversing with Jimmy Joe about a shooting at a motel near Bethany.

"The manager at the Lazy Inn says a man and a woman in a nurse's uniform signed in around 2 a.m. It sounds like our missing John Doe and Miss Riley."

"Get Sheriff Dix's number over there and call me back on my cellular."

"Sure, Chief," the dispatcher replied.

Ben's neck hairs stood out like antennae. He didn't take another moment to think, just headed out of town toward the motel.

Ben had already surveyed the scene with the aid of Sheriff Thomas Dix and his men before Jimmy Joe arrived.

"Goddamn place looks more like the Fourth of July than Christmas night," Jimmy Joe grumbled to Ben, who was standing next to Sheriff Dix. "You think you could round up a few *more* squad cars?"

"What's the problem, Chief?"

"Damn it, Tommy, is this your idea of keeping things quiet?"

"Sorry, Chief, but my boys haven't seen any action since Doc Harner got caught screwin' that honky-tonk gal and his wife shot 'em both to kingdom come fifteen years ago."

"Yeah, well, I hope they haven't screwed up my evidence."

"Nah," Tommy said, leading the way toward the motel room where the county coroner's van had just pulled up. "Like I told you, one's deader 'n a doornail."

"Is the other one talking?"

"He's out of it. We got him cuffed in the squad car over here."

Ben followed Jimmy Joe and Sheriff Dix into the motel room. There was no question in his mind that Shannon had been in the bathroom when one of the men had come through the window. Standing amid the shards of broken glass he felt her fear, sensed her terror. What thoughts went through her head as she faced the man whose intent was to kill her? Whom did she fear more, the man in the window or John?

Guilt riddled him. It was his fault Shannon had been taken hostage. There was only one way to make things right. He had to save her.

Looking around the room, Ben found it interesting that Shannon had been in the bathroom at all, much less alone and unbound. Obviously, John had believed himself to be in control of her. And how had he done that? Intimidation? Or had he already hurt her enough to make his threats real?

"I'll kill the bastard if he hurts her," Ben vowed, coming out of the bathroom.

"What's that?" The coroner's assistant lifted his head to Ben.

"Nothing," he grumbled. "It's getting a little crowded in here, isn't it?" He looked around the tiny room filling up with forensic technicians and investigators.

"You think John Doe knew these guys?" Tommy asked Jimmy Joe.

"Who knows?"

Ben looked at the bullet hole in the headboard and the crushed pillows. "I doubt it," he said.

"Why?" Jimmy Joe asked.

"The assailant would never have gotten off the first shot if John had been lying in wait for him. From the way these pillows are stacked, I suspect John was dozing off. The door was kicked in and still John wasn't off the bed yet." He pointed to the corpse. "Guys like that are too well trained to miss. John was quick enough."

"Maybe so," Jimmy Joe replied.

"So was Shannon," Ben said.

Jimmy Joe looked over the well-dressed corpse, his eyes flat as if seeing death was an everyday occurrence, which Ben knew it was not.

"Damn Mexicans." Jimmy Joe didn't so much as glance at the bathroom, but walked away instead.

Ben started to comment on Jimmy Joe's mistake, but thought better of it. There was no question these men were Latin, most probably Colombians.

"Tommy." Jimmy Joe motioned to the man as they huddled outside the motel room. "Do me a favor? Politically, this thing could be my ass if too much gets out about it. Let me handle this investigation. I'll take the body back to Shreveport. I'll question the other guy. I've been working on this case for nearly a month. I need to bag this one. You know what I'm sayin'?"

"Sure, Jimmy Joe." Tommy slapped him on the

back. "We go a long way back. I'll make out my report and say you took over."

"Thanks, friend."

Tommy signaled to his men, who gathered around him while he informed them of the change in procedure.

Ben went up to the sheriff. Lighting a cigarette, he asked, "You've known Jimmy Joe a long time?"

"Yessiree," Tommy said proudly.

Casually, Ben blew out smoke. "He doesn't ask many questions in his investigations, does he?"

The sheriff gave a deep belly laugh. "Yep. He's a bit slapdash. But he gets the job done."

"Does he?" Ben asked.

Tommy's smile faded. "Look, he's got his ways. I don't ask questions. You got that?"

Ben dropped the cigarette and crushed it out with his heel. "Yeah, I got that."

12

→ ←

Terror had stripped Shannon's nerves raw. She was still in shock over being taken hostage by the man she'd fantasized about for weeks.

Until he awoke from his coma, in essence John was a nonentity. He had no personality, no motivations, no actions upon which she could have based her emotional reactions to him.

Shannon realized she'd conjured up an illusion of a man to love and what she'd fallen for was a reflection of her need. John had been in a coma, incapable of responding to her slightest comments. She had invented their relationship.

It was completely false. And now, Shannon's fantasy was a dangerous reality.

Shannon had despised guns on Ben, who did nothing more than try to keep her safe. Now she was staring down the barrel of that same gun.

"What are you going to do?" she asked John as she pulled the car to a stop at the light in Marshall, Texas, the next morning.

"We're going over to that used-car lot. Pull up in the back where no one will notice."

"Then what?" She swallowed hard. Her throat was dry. She was petrified. Each time he changed plans or his course of action, there was the chance he might decide that she was expendable.

"We wait."

"I don't understand—"

He cut her off with a jab to the ribs with the gun. "You don't need to. Just do what I tell you."

She nodded, but remained silent. When the light turned green, she drove to the used-car lot and did as he instructed.

"It's early," he said quietly, as if talking to himself. "The salespeople won't be in for another hour. That gives us time."

Shannon felt hot tears seep from the corners of her eyes. She didn't want him to know she was scared. She wanted him to think she was tough. Really tough. Maybe then he wouldn't hurt her.

"Turn off the engine."

"Okay," she said.

"Give me the keys."

She handed them to him.

Switching the gun in the air rather than poking her again for effect, he said, "Now slouch down. Don't let anyone see us."

She moved lower in the seat. She watched his eyes as he scanned the buildings across the street. His eyes peered at the activity.

Slowly, so as not to be noticed, Shannon glanced across the street. *A bus station.*

"Yeah, we're going to leave your car here," he said without looking at her.

"I wasn't thinking that," she said, her tongue sticking to the roof of her dry mouth. It was amazing her mouth could be so dry when she was sweating all over. She clutched her trembling hands in her lap.

Maybe she could fool him a bit longer. Maybe she could stay alive a little longer. Until...

"No, you were probably wondering if I'm going to kill you."

"I wasn't."

"Don't lie," he growled.

She paused, letting his anger subside. "So why are we leaving my car here?"

"It fits in with the rest of the junk in this lot. The cops won't find it for days."

Anger spiked in her. "Junk? Well, it got us this far, didn't it?" Then she bit her tongue, castigating herself for speaking out. She'd gotten into too much trouble in her former life by speaking her mind. She'd promised never to do it again and now was certainly not the time to start.

But John only frowned.

"I thought we were going to Shreveport," she ventured sheepishly.

"You'd be a lot better off if you didn't make assumptions," he hissed through clenched teeth as he clamped his hand around her arm. "Now, come on. Let's go," he said, opening the door.

Shannon got out and looked at him.

"Don't even think it," he warned.

"I wasn't..."

He shot her a damning look and came up beside her. "I said, don't."

Shannon had come to recognize his intransigent look—when his eyes turned steel-gray. His adrenaline was flowing, masking his pain, pushing them both relentlessly.

He'd taken all her cash from her purse along with her credit cards. He carried not only Ben's gun, but the automatic with the silencer intended to kill them both. In the back of his waistband, he'd stuck the gun from the man who'd come through the window. A face she'd never forget.

Thinking back on that moment, she realized that John had killed one of the assailants. When he'd rushed into the bathroom, he'd thought of saving himself, yes. But he'd also thought of saving her.

He could easily have left her there for another assassin to find. Neither of them had known if there was a third or fourth gunman hiding in the trees or in a getaway car.

He saved me because he needs me as a hostage. I can't forget that.

They entered the jammed bus station. Wooden benches and metal chairs were filled with travelers loaded down with Christmas loot. Children played with new toys while parents snoozed on each other's shoulders. It was the aftermath of the holidays, a vision Shannon hadn't witnessed for a long time.

"I'll get the tickets," John said, easing into the long ticket line, keeping his arm fastened tightly around Shannon's waist.

"Do you have to do that?" She tried to wriggle away from him, but he pulled her closer.

"We're supposed to be newlyweds, remember?"

"That was last night," she whispered, watching the obese woman in front of her give them a sidelong glance.

John flashed the woman a charming smile, then made a show of kissing Shannon on the cheek.

Shannon's blood ran cold. She froze with terror and stiffened in his arms. *Was this the Judas' kiss?*

A loud voice broke them apart.

"Next!" The African-American male cashier called.

John looked up and realized that they were at the front of the line.

"Two for Shreveport. One way," he said, as he took out a small wad of bills from his windbreaker pocket.

"Twelve dollars," the cashier said, handing him two tickets.

"Bus on time?" John glanced at a second ticket window that was opening to handle the influx of passengers.

"That's it pullin' in now. Loads in ten minutes."

"Thanks," John said and ushered Shannon out of the bus station to the curb where the other passengers had gathered.

The incoming passengers disembarked and gathered their luggage from the driver who yanked bags from the underbelly of the bus.

Just as the last passenger left the bus, Shannon glanced at the used-car lot across the wide state highway and froze. John followed her gaze.

"Oh, no!" he gasped.

Two local police squad cars had pulled up to the used-car lot, and the manager was showing the officers the car.

They watched as one of the officers took notes while the other shrugged his bewildered shoulders.

"All aboard! Tickets please," the bus driver announced.

Just as the first passenger walked onto the bus, a second bus pulled up to the station, obscuring their view of the used-car lot.

"Let's go." John shoved Shannon closer to the front of the line. His hands were shaking anxiously as they touched her. They were fourth in line now.

John was preoccupied watching the police. It was the perfect opportunity for her to make a dash for it—the cops were just across the street, the traffic was still sparse, dawn just a moment away, and another bus, this one empty, pulled up to the loading zone.

Confusion frayed the precision of the bus terminal as yet another bus pulled to the loading zone out of turn. The station manager argued with the driver, telling him to back up his vehicle and take his proper turn.

The driver of the Shreveport bus stepped into the middle of the argument, frustrating his passengers who all simply wanted to take their seats.

With John's strong hand on her waist, Shannon moved a step closer to the bus's open door.

She glanced over her shoulder through a narrow break between two of the buses to the car lot. One of the police officers had gone back to his squad car and was speaking rapidly on the car radio. He kept glancing across the street at the bus station. One time, she thought he'd looked right at her.

This is as good as it gets. I should make a break for it now.

The bus drivers' argument was branded with words that would have gotten them fired had one of the passengers chosen to report them. Instead, the catcalls were only getting under way.

"Let's get rollin', buddy!" the burly man in the front seat yelled.

"Yeah, this is my buck and my time yer spendin'!"

The fat woman they'd seen in the ticket line made certain she got her digs in. "I'll sue your ass personally if I'm late to work, Howard!"

The driver stopped midsentence and turned back

to his line of passengers. "Okay! Everybody on. I'll take tickets on board."

The empty bus pulled away, leaving a clear view of the used-car parking lot and the approaching two officers.

Shannon saw their faces, but they didn't see her. She edged away from John as he grabbed the handrail, preparing to step onto the bus.

The teenager behind Shannon wearing earphones and listening to rap music accidentally pushed against John.

"What the..."

Dawn broke over a cluster of billboards, the light hitting John squarely in the eyes. Shannon took a step, then another and another. The policemen were almost across the street. She could tell from their expressions they were looking for someone, looking for her. Her hand began rising involuntarily.

Here I am! I'm the one you've come to rescue!

The younger, shorter policeman's eyes scanned the horde of passengers as they boarded the various buses. His eyes met hers. She thought, wanted to believe, hoped he could read her mind.

Suddenly there were hands on her shoulders, gripping fingers turning her around.

"Don't worry, darling. I didn't forget our tickets," John said loudly enough for the rest of the passengers to hear. "Hurry, or we'll miss the bus." He'd laminated his voice with conviviality, but she sensed his warning in the crushing hold she thought would crack her ribs.

"Don't ever try that again," he whispered menacingly in her ear once they were seated on the bus. "I told you before, I need you. As long as you're with me, they won't try to shoot me."

She glanced out the window as they pulled away from the station. The officers were looking over the passengers, not finding their quarry. The station manager kept shaking his head as if indicating he thought the officers were crazy. They'd probably been given a description of a nurse in uniform and a semi-invalid man. John's dramatics as a newlywed had been effective...for the moment.

Shannon looked back at John. "But are they the ones who will do the shooting?"

"Possibly."

"You know they'll figure this out. They'll be at the terminal in Shreveport when we arrive."

"Yeah, I've thought of that."

"So you'll be riding into a trap."

"Yeah."

"What are you going to do?"

"Do?" He looked at her dispassionately. "Guess I'll have to stay one step ahead of them, won't I?"

13

Ben Richards placed an eight-hundred call on his cellular phone. It was the number he'd dialed many times over the past month, ever since he'd become a part of John Doe's life.

"You got anything for me?"

The cocky, high-pitched male voice on the other end replied, "Your grocery order has been filled, though we're fresh out of tomatoes."

"What do you have?"

"A Doe. But just the one."

Ben smiled to himself. "I'm only interested in one."

"This one's an angel. Gabriel, to be exact. Turner. Shipped out of Dallas. Sells insurance."

"I'll just bet he does."

A derisive sniff, then a self-possessed chuckle preceded the reply, "Four exhaustive weeks of work and all I get is condescension. You want my job?"

"I coulda done it in half the time."

"Methinks not, Maestro. Insurance. Been selling it since he left Special Forces Training in the air force."

"The hell you say."

"He's a weapons expert. Pilot. Did some testing on top-secret aircraft during the star wars years. Stuff said to have broken the time barrier, all of which resulted in screwing up his head and his marriage. Divorced 1988. Bummed around, played around. Now sells insurance to Texas farmers, insuring their equipment against breakdowns. Wish I'd thought of that idea. He makes a hell of a lot more money than I do working for your sorry ass."

"You can quit anytime."

"Nah, I like the hours," he quipped sarcastically. "Anything else, Maestro?"

"Why was this guy so hard to track?"

"Seems the government thought he was a wunderkind. They kept his records off the normal rosters. There's not a trace of him through the usual channels."

"So, the locals here weren't giving me the raspberries about not finding stats on him?"

"They could be giving you black, red and purple raspberries, Maestro, but not on this one."

"And the girl?"

"That's weird, too."

"Why so?"

"There's no Shannon Riley listed as a graduate from any nursing school, college nursing program or university in Louisiana. Nor any other college in the States. We ran the fingerprints you got from her place. No criminal record, no military record, not even a birth certificate. My guess is, her name is a fake."

"Fake name. Fake life. But why?"

"Beats me, Maestro. That's your job. Anyway, I ran a list of sound-alikes. Similar initials. Nothing. She's damn good at keeping underground. Maybe she's had some kind of formal training."

"Or is just well practiced," Ben mused.

"Possible. Anything else, Maestro?"

"Not for now. I'll be in touch."

"You do that—" He paused. "Do me a favor, wouldya?"

"What's that?"

"Don't get involved with this one."

"What the hell are you talking about?" Ben asked.

"I can hear it in your voice. The way you ask about her. Stay above it, okay?"

"Sure, pal. Sure."

Ben pressed the end key, pocketed his palm-size cellular and wiped the sweat from his upper lip.

"Stay above it." He frowned. "No problem." He turned the car too quickly around the bend. His reflexes were slightly off center. The tires spewed gravel, but he righted the car. A bead of sweat trickled down his temple. Though he took a deep breath, the last thing he felt was relaxed.

"No problem at all."

Two miles from the Shreveport bus terminal, John persuaded the bus driver to let them off.

"I've never seen a bus driver let passengers off before the scheduled destination," she said.

"Ridden a lot of buses, have you?"

She glared at him. "It's none of your business."

"Everything about you is my business," he said, huskily.

She glanced away. "What did you say to get him to do that?" she said, looking back at him.

He pressed his hand against his chest, she was sure not for theatrics but to hold the pain at bay. There was no merriment in his eyes when he spoke. "I told him that if he didn't let us off I'd make love to you in front of everyone. He believed me."

She cranked her head around and saw a mischievous glint flit across his eyes. She couldn't believe it. Despite his pain, his criminal act of taking her hostage, he was enjoying his game. Under ordinary circumstances she might have laughed with him, but to her nothing about what transpired between them was a game.

Perhaps that was where she'd made a tactical error. Perhaps she needed to step back and reexamine her course of action.

John took her arm gently. He didn't shove or try to hurt her. It was strange, the way she felt about his touch. Her intuition told her that, in a bizarre fashion, John was protecting her, while her rational mind explained that he was her enemy. He'd put her in harm's way.

A cab pulled up just then. John held the door for her and placed his hand on the small of her back while he glanced around looking for cops, killers, assassins. Unconsciously, he blocked her body from view with his own body.

He's shielding me...like a gentleman would. He'd done it without thinking, instinctively. She looked up at him. His eyes held hers for a fraction of a second too long. Then she saw it—vulnerability, honesty. Time stood still. It was as if her heart and brain had stopped. Shannon realized in that single moment that John was not a monster.

"John." She reached to touch his hand.

"What?" he whispered.

She retracted her hand. "Nothing." Her eyes held his long enough to let him see that she was not afraid of him anymore.

Then she turned at the sound of the cabbie's voice.

"Where to?" the driver asked.

John looked at Shannon without malice. "Sweetheart?"

He slipped his arm around Shannon's shoulder. She knew the movement was painful, but he didn't flinch. If anything, his smile was broad and his eyes flashed with delight.

She had to hand it to him. John was a consummate actor.

He nudged her shoulder. "Where, darling?"

"Regent Cleaners on Dixie Highway."

"You got it," the cabbie said and they drove off.

They remained silent during the ride.

He never took his arm away from her shoulder. His fingers went limp each time she felt his rib cage tighten and she knew he was experiencing a spasm. When the pain eased, he breathed out. His fingers closed around her upper arm. They massaged her shoulder, ever so slightly, as if the movement again was unconscious. He watched out the windows with eyes as alert as those of a hawk searching for prey. His eyes darted from the main street to the alleyways and intersections. He combed the pedestrian crossings. He watched cars departing the fast-food drive-thrus, parking lots and movie theaters. He didn't appear to miss a trick.

She was impressed.

"Here we are," the cabbie said. "Five-fifty."

John paid the man with Shannon's money.

Shannon glanced at her watch. Eight-thirty. She looked up to see a young man departing the cleaners with an armful of clean shirts.

Shannon and John asked the cabbie to wait, then went into the building.

Shannon greeted the girl whose name she didn't

know, but who always waited on her, then said, "A few weeks ago I brought in the windbreaker my boyfriend here is wearing."

"I remember."

"There's something missing from his pocket and I thought maybe you might have put it aside for me and then forgotten about it."

"What was it?"

Shannon looked at John. "A computer disk."

The girl shook her head. "I don't remember anything like that."

"It was the holidays," Shannon offered. "I know there was a lot going on. Maybe you could look around for us."

John smiled charmingly. "It's important."

"Okay," the girl sighed and went to the back.

To Shannon it seemed an eternity as the girl shuffled on slow-moving feet through racks with folded shirts, bins with dirty laundry and finally back to the front to the shelves under the counter.

"I don't see anything like a disk," the clerk said.

"It *has* to be here," John said anxiously. "Let me take a look."

"I can't let you do that, sir," she snapped.

"Look again, please," Shannon asked sweetly.

"Okay, Miss Riley."

While the girl retraced her steps, Shannon used the moment to steal a look at the metal newspaper dispensers just outside the building. From her vantage point she could see the headline banners, but that was all. She supposed her abduction would not eclipse a national disaster like the flooding rainfall on the East Coast, but she was surprised the girl hadn't heard something about her kidnapping on the television news that morning. Then she remembered from her previous trips here that the clerk always had the small TV that was mounted on the wall above the counter tuned to old reruns of sitcoms and soap operas. She had never impressed Shannon as a person who kept up on world or local events. Shannon was just as guilty of noninterference, believing her personal privacy more precious than relationships of any kind. She realized her isolation was costing her her freedom.

It was ironic that her acquaintance with the dry cleaner's attendant could have been the most fortuitous relationship of her life. If only this girl *had* watched the news, perhaps she might have called the police and rescued Shannon. She might even have found herself a heroine, claimed her fifteen minutes of fame.

The girl withdrew a small brown lunch sack. "I can't believe this!" She held it up. "It says Shannon Riley. We had several part-timers during the holidays. One of them wrote your name on this, but didn't attach it to your garments. Sorry about that."

"That's okay. At least we've found it," Shannon replied, taking the sack. "Thanks."

"Yeah, thanks a million," John said. "You saved my job."

"Glad I could help," the girl replied.

They rushed out to the waiting cab.

"Shreveport Airport," John ordered the driver.

As they sped away, Shannon saw a city-police car pull up to the red light. The two officers in the front seat were busily engaged in conversation. The one in the passenger's seat glanced at the shop fronts, looked longingly at the pastry shop, then at the group of children playing with their new in-line skates.

Look this way. See me. Feel my thoughts.

The light changed and the taxi passed through the intersection. The police officers continued their conversation, but they didn't peer into the back seat of the taxi. They hadn't seen her.

Shannon didn't realize until they were blocks away that she'd held her breath. Hoping.

"That was close," John whispered. "But which were you hoping for, Shannon? That we'd escape or be captured?"

She looked at John. His eyes were granite gray. Gone was the tenderness she'd seen only moments ago. Now they were hard, implacable and dangerous.

It was his dual personality that frightened her the most. One minute he was evil incarnate, the next his soulful eyes beckoned to her. The mixed signals he sent would drive her insane—if they didn't lead to her death first.

He waited patiently for her answer.

"I was hoping for a miracle," she said with resignation.

14

—▶ ◀—

New Orleans, Louisiana

Congressman Blane Blair sat in his French Quarter office, across from an expensively dressed Colombian wearing a fedora.

"You needn't have flown all the way from Cartagena just to see me."

The Colombian shook his head and crossed his black-gloved hands rigidly in his lap. He remained silent.

Blane felt his armpits getting damp. He wiped a slick sheen of perspiration off his forehead with a linen handkerchief, then stuffed it in his pants pocket. He didn't need this kind of intrusive bullshit. Everything had been fine until last month when Adam Rivers had fallen prey to the deadliest of all sins—greed.

Now Blane was being forced by circumstances to pay for Adam's sins and he didn't like it one stinking bit.

Adam Rivers had been a fool. He'd pressed Blane to join forces with him in his scheme to embezzle money from the Cassalia Cartel. Blane had flatly refused but Adam had gone forward with his plan.

Even with Adam's death, the drug lord Alejandro

Cassalia still didn't know to what extent Adam had been successful. Nor did the Colombian know how Adam had done it or where he'd stashed the money.

To make matters worse, Blane had the distinct impression that Alejandro had sent Sardia to New Orleans to extract exactly that information from him. Blane knew the time had come to tell Sardia everything he knew and pray to God he made it out of this mess alive.

Blane's box of tricks was empty. He was left with the one finely honed talent he could claim—lying effectively.

He could bullshit, kiss ass, cheat and steal, but he wasn't a murderer. There were limits.

Blane's heart was in his throat when he spoke. He'd been on the hot seat once before, when he'd undergone a congressional inquiry three years ago. It had been Adam Rivers's Washington connections, all of whom had needed Adam's "legal advice" dealing with certain New Orleans hookers at one time or another, who had restored his reputation to lily-white and completely covered his decade-old, lucrative scam of selling Caucasian babies to emotionally distraught, wealthy couples.

However, the heat he was experiencing at this moment was far more intense.

Knowing that the bulge under the Colombian's left shoulder was a holstered pistol, probably of the automatic kind with an expensive silencer, Blane forced a placid expression onto his face. "Alejandro need not worry about anything. That was Jimmy Joe Bremen up in Shreveport I just spoke with. Word about this incident has already been shut down. No one, and I do mean no one, up there is talking. Not to the press.

Nobody. The state troopers have not been informed of the escape. There is no APB. Nothing about this went to the wires. I've kept the path clear for you."

The Colombian uncrossed his legs and crossed them again. He moved his right hand up, as if he was about to unbutton his jacket and go for his gun.

Blane braced himself and continued, hoping to defuse this time bomb. "I have assured Alejandro that I will tell you what I do know, which isn't much."

Still, the Colombian said nothing. Reaching for a glass of water, then sipping it, he said, "Adam Rivers has been embezzling from Alejandro for more than two years. A year ago he came to me and asked if I'd like to get in on his scheme. I flatly refused and told him he was going to find himself dead if he continued. Obviously, that's just what he did. I believe Adam had to have an accomplice. Adam was an attorney, not a money man. He didn't know about investments, or banking, or how to move this stuff around. And to this day, I have no idea how much money Adam stole."

Blane clasped his shaking hands under the desk to hide them from Sardia. "I wish I knew more but I don't. Just tell Alejandro that I'll do all I can to keep a lid on things here in the States. I fully understand the time constraints Alejandro feels with this Cali trial coming up in Miami. Fortunately for all of us, Alejandro has had a tighter rein on his people."

A trickle of perspiration slid from Blane's temple to the edge of his jaw. He chuckled tensely. "Your visit here today confirms that. Right?"

The Colombian's unwavering black eyes stayed locked on him.

Blane couldn't help wondering if the guy ever

blinked. Maybe he wasn't human. Maybe he was a machine like he'd been told—a killing machine.

"Alejandro and I have had a very successful business relationship," Blane said. "And I don't want this mess to disrupt our plans for the future. Tell him that our manufacturing plants are working on double shifts this month. I hope to increase our profits substantially over the first quarter of this year."

Blane didn't know what to expect as the Colombian nodded curtly and rose from the chair.

Just as Sardia reached toward his breast, Blane sucked in his breath.

Now he's going to shoot me. I'm dead.

Sardia's glacial expression did not change as he went to the door. He paused, motioning with his head toward the mock-up campaign posters of Blane leaning against a wall.

Blane Blair for Governor. A Name You Can Trust.

Shooting a sidelong glance at the congressman, Sardia said, "Nice slogan."

He left the room, closing the door quietly behind him.

15

━━━➤ ━━━

Chelsea Sikeston couldn't run fast enough.

For the first time in her life, she was desperate for something besides sex. She needed assurance, needed to know the world, her world, was not falling apart.

Things were happening too quickly. People were asking too many questions. Ones she couldn't answer.

A raw, burning sensation ate at the pit of her stomach as she left the hospital, crossed the street and rounded the corner.

She didn't dare take her car, for she might be seen, recognized. Chelsea knew how to handle clandestine meetings. She'd been doing it ever since she'd first gotten laid by her cousin when she was twelve. She was an expert at slipping through second-story windows, landing on cat's paws and slipping into the night shadows. Chelsea loved the danger and excitement more than the sex.

Her passion for risk was to blame for the peril she was in. They'd always agreed to keep their meeting place far enough from the hospital so that no one would suspect their assignations. Too many times they'd only been able to snatch a few minutes together. Time enough to feed Chelsea's addiction to recklessness.

In the distance she heard the sound of an ambulance.

"Oh, God. What if he's not there? What if he's stood me up?"

She ran faster. Dawn was hours away and this part of the city's streets was not lit. Abandoned offices and empty storefronts yawned openmouthed at her as she raced by. No one saw her, not even the homeless woman armored in black plastic trash bags against the biting cold.

Then she saw the gold Caddy and breathed with relief.

"He never brings the Caddy. It's a good sign. Everything is going to be okay, Chels," she assured herself.

She slowed down. He turned on the parking lights. The engine purred.

She smiled as she leaned provocatively toward the window as it automatically lowered, her image in the tinted glass disappearing.

"Hi, Jimmy Joe."

"Darlin' girl." He grabbed her by the nape, pulled her head into the car and kissed her deeply.

"You're hot," she groaned.

"For you...always," he moaned.

She reached into the car toward his crotch.

His enormous hand clamped over her delicate wrist. "First things first. I'm a busy man and I told you never to call me on my cellular. I call the shots. Remember, baby?"

"Why did you sic Ben Richards on me?"

"What are you talking about?"

"A short while after you left Helen Mayer's office, he showed up asking funny questions."

"What kind of questions?"

"Things he shoulda asked back when we tried to slip poison into John Doe's IV. He found out I wasn't scheduled to be on duty that night. He suspects something."

"He's better at putting two and two together than I thought. What did you tell him?" Jimmy Joe's eyes glittered with accusation.

"Nothin'. Honest."

"Did he ask about you and me? Hint at anything?"

"It wasn't like that at all. But he was askin', Jimmy Joe. Ben never did anything like that before. He just sat there in that hallway cleaning his nails, smoking outside. Making calls on his cell."

"Ben Richards doesn't have a cellular phone."

"Sure he does."

"Why didn't you tell me this before?"

"It wasn't important. Besides, I thought you knew. I thought he was calling you, or the station anyway."

Jimmy Joe knew that Ben rarely called into headquarters while he was on duty. In fact, Richards was surprisingly independent for a novice cop with limited experience. And now he was asking Chelsea questions, without keeping Jimmy Joe informed. It didn't add up.

During that thoughtful moment, Jimmy Joe made his decision. Things hadn't just gone haywire, they'd been manipulated by an outside force—one he believed to be in opposition to his plans.

It was only six months till his retirement, when he could enjoy life. He'd spent years building his network into the smooth operation it had become. He'd amassed over two million dollars in an offshore account in Switzerland. But now there were too many people screwing with his plans. With his life.

Jimmy Joe had always been a man to control his own destiny. He was sick of Blane Blair and his problems. He wasn't about to let some Colombian mobster screw up his life. They could wrestle with each other for all he cared, but they weren't going to be including Jimmy Joe in their plans any longer.

Most of all he didn't need a federal agent, which was what he now believed Ben Richards was, pretending to be his right arm.

Jimmy Joe turned his attention back to Chelsea.

"You look nervous, baby. Did you look this nervous when Ben was drilling you?"

"I'm not nervous, just horny."

His grin was malevolent, but Chelsea only saw desire.

"Then let's not waste any more time," he said. "Get in."

"Okay."

Chelsea rushed to her side of the car. The door unlocked automatically and she slid onto the champagne-beige leather seat, loving the sensual feel of the expensive smooth grain.

"Baby, I'm hard already," Jimmy Joe said, hitting the automatic seat button and leaning back.

She reached for him, unzipped his pants and, as always, marveled over his size. "My God, you're a work of art, Jimmy Joe."

She fondled, kissed, licked, bit, teased and sucked until Jimmy Joe came in her mouth.

"You're the best, baby," he said, kissing her hard and leaning her head back on the headrest. "But you talk too much to the wrong people. I worry about that."

"No worries, Jimmy Joe."

"Yeah, no worries. Never again…" He put his huge hand lovingly on her throat. Just as she relaxed into the kiss, he snapped her neck.

She died instantly.

Jimmy Joe lowered her body onto the seat so that no one would see her as they drove down the street.

Taking a convoluted route out of town, he circled around Cross Lake and headed over the bridge and out the highway to a densely forested area.

Gently, he laid her body on top of a thick pile of leaves. Carefully, he swabbed her mouth, removing all traces of semen. He used a long pine branch to erase his tire tracks and shoe prints. Then he drove back to town.

Chief Bremen went home and gave his wife instructions to have the Cadillac detailed.

"I want it looking clean and shiny for the mayor's New Year's party," he said. "Get that package deal for fifteen bucks where they Armor All the tires."

After she was gone, he took his city-owned car with the painted white emblem on the car door and drove across the bridge to Bossier City to a doughnut shop he used to haunt in the old days. He ordered a cup of coffee, went to the pay phone in back and dialed a number he hadn't needed in years. The call was picked up on the fifth ring.

"That you, Satch?"

Silence.

"Has it been so long you don't recognize my voice?"

The raspy voice on the other end was young and quick. "Bremen, if you're calling me, it can only mean trouble. Or money. Which is it?"

"Both. Trouble if you don't take this job, money if you do."

"Guess that settles that. How much?"

"Ten thousand."

"Twenty. You forget, I know you. If it was easy, you'd have done it yourself."

Jimmy Joe rubbed his jaw.

Ten years ago, Satch Jessel had been a rookie fresh out of the police academy. Six weeks into the job, Satch came to Jimmy Joe and told him he'd gone to the academy to please his father. Now that he was out, he felt he'd paid his dues. He wanted more out of life. He wanted big money.

Jimmy Joe had liked Satch from their first meeting. The gleam in the young man's eye was one Jimmy Joe recognized—greed. But he had to be sure.

Jimmy Joe got Satch to stay for the duration of his internship. It would look good on his résumé that he'd completed his training, he told Satch.

To test the young man, Jimmy Joe deliberately allowed Satch to fire at a retreating robber. Satch killed the criminal without blinking an eye. From that day on, Jimmy Joe knew Satch's button. He liked killing. Almost as much as Jimmy Joe did.

"Okay, twenty it is."

"Ten up front before I start."

Chief Bremen wanted to argue, but the time clock was ticking and his targets were miles away. "Done."

"I've made some changes since our last contract. I've added a partner."

"No partners. I want a clean hit."

"It will be. But Grady is the best driver I've ever had. I need him."

"I suppose now you want more money."

"It's on me. Grady will do it for grins. He's like us, Chief." Satch chortled. "So tell me, Chief. You gonna just watch this time or participate?"

"You do know me. This one's mine. I've spent nearly a month trying to ID this guy. Never send a boy to do a man's job, right? I traced him myself, using my own contacts. Gabe Turner is his name. There's a woman with him. Shannon Riley. He's smart. Military trained. A challenge. I just need you for backup." Jimmy Joe gave Satch a description of the pair. "My bet is they'll come in by car. Planes are too visible. I have the airports covered already."

"Where's this Turner from?"

"Your backyard. Dallas-Fort Worth." Jimmy Joe gave him Gabe's address.

"I can be on his doorstep waiting for him."

"Great. Just follow him if he shows. I'll be there as soon as I can. Keep in touch on my cell, but don't identify yourself."

"Copy."

"And remember, they're mine."

"This a personal thing then, huh?"

"Very. I want to see their faces when they recognize me," Jimmy Joe replied and hung up.

16

Pilots fly.

Ben was banking on that credo to help him find Shannon, or whatever her real name was, and Gabriel Turner, the man who was just as much a mystery to him as the woman he'd become obsessed with.

Ben didn't like knowing he was a candidate for a shrink's lounge, but the point was, he was hooked. He couldn't sleep. He dreamed about Shannon being with this man he'd only known as a comatose victim. What if he'd really hurt her? Killed her? What if Ben never had a chance with her again? Twice he'd bolted awake in a cold sweat. Both times he'd dreamed of Gabe Turner making love to Shannon. The very idea made his teeth rattle.

Coke would have been easier to kick than this obsession.

It had been a long time since Ben had been in love. He'd been obsessed then, too. He'd told Shannon the truth that she reminded him of a girl he used to know. How could a man ever forget Nancy? He would never forget Nancy.

She was so much like Shannon, caring, intelligent, with eyes that ripped his heart in two. Nancy had loved him back, however, and that was the difference.

It was one of those chance meetings that happened once in a million years. In the campus parking lot, she was getting out of her girlfriend's car when her passenger door smashed into Ben's door just as he was opening it.

Ben had stopped dead in his tracks as the most beautiful girl he'd ever seen exited the red compact. He was so breathless he couldn't speak. And that's how it began.

Ben proposed the first time he made love to her.

He knew he'd found his soul mate and so did Nancy.

He would have been with Nancy today if it hadn't been for Blane Blair.

Nancy's traditional Catholic Louisiana parents were as obsessed with keeping her a little girl as they were with expounding their religious righteousness. They never would have forgiven her for getting pregnant with Ben's baby out of wedlock. Ben had wanted to marry her the minute she told him, but she'd made the mistake of not telling him about the baby until she was so far along, her pregnancy was showing. Her parents would have known instantly if she'd gone home at the semester break.

Instead, Nancy left Ben without a word. No note. No forwarding address. She just disappeared off campus.

Ben went insane trying to find her. He skipped finals, even skipped graduation. He combed Louisiana. Four months later, he tracked her down in New Orleans. She'd been living in a flat over a topless bar in the French Quarter with two female roommates who claimed to be dancers and whom he knew were hookers.

He would never forget their names. Brandy and Ice. "It's a sister act. Guys like that. Two-fers, we call it," the sultry brunette, Brandy, said.

"Yeah," said bleached-blond Ice. "We're a hit."

"I'll bet you are," Ben said. "Where's Nancy? And my baby?"

Brandy's face fell. "Didn't you know?"

"I thought you'd tell me," he answered, feeling his blood run cold.

"She sold the baby."

"She what?"

"Yeah, there's a dude who comes around here, buying babies. He sells them on the black market. He bought Nancy's baby."

Ben swallowed hard. "I can't believe this. Not of Nancy. She loved that baby. She used to caress her belly all the time and talk to him...." His eyes welled. "I just can't believe this."

Brandy poured a straight scotch and handed it to him. "That's not the worst news."

He stared at the drink but didn't take it. He knew she was preparing him. He looked up. "And Nancy?"

"Dead."

Ben felt his soul die at that moment. He went cold all over and felt his heart turn into a frozen rock. He knew from that day forward he'd never use it again. His nerves and muscles went haywire. He didn't think he could control his thoughts, emotions or deeds. All he wanted was Nancy and she was dead.

Looking at Brandy, his head bobbed involuntarily from side to side. "No. I won't accept it," he said, scrambling for his sanity.

"Three weeks ago. Killed herself. In there." Ice pointed to the bedroom.

Brandy continued. "We found her. She got some pills...."

"No!" Ben felt rage, sorrow, guilt and hopelessness descend on him like an anvil. His life was over. At that moment the only place he wanted to be was buried beside his precious Nancy. "It's not true."

He stumbled toward the bedroom and stared at the chenille-covered bed. "Nancy..."

He envisioned her there. Without him. Without hope. Lifeless.

Tears sluiced down his cheeks in wide paths. His lungs burned with angry cries he forced himself to hold inside. Finally, he released his pain. He stumbled to the bed and fell on it, heaving with sobs. He pulled the bedspread to his face, wiping his tears, inhaling, scrounging for a scent of her. He needed something, anything, to give him hope.

But there was nothing.

"That's okay, baby," Ice said. "You just stay in there as long as you want. We understand." She quietly shut the door.

Ben blocked out what happened after that. He was in shock for days, weeks. Somehow, he'd gone back to school, took his finals over the summer and received his diploma in the mail. He told his parents he had to go on with his life.

But until the day he'd met Shannon, he realized he'd gotten his wish. He'd been dead, right alongside Nancy, all these years.

Shannon had breathed life into him and she hadn't a clue she'd done it.

Whether she had rejected him or not didn't matter to Ben. He would find her. He would save her. Shannon was not going to die on his beat. Not if there was a breath left in his body. He wouldn't be left alone again.

Unfortunately for them both, he was a walking disaster as he used his off-duty time casing the Shreveport Airport. He was exhausted and driven—a bad combination that produced mistakes.

Ben rubbed his eyes and scanned the parking lot one more time. Watching the doors, he examined every woman entering and leaving.

Too many hours here had produced no results.

It was obvious there was no chance in hell he'd find them here. They were probably halfway to Mexico by now. Or Canada. Or one of a hundred countries.

But Ben wasn't about to give up. He had that feeling, the one that settled in the back of his neck, causing him more aggravation than pain, more insight than logic. And it had never failed him. Yet.

Shannon's eyes were glued to the front doors of the airport as the taxi drove up the departing-passengers lane.

"Which airline?" the cabdriver asked.

"Keep going. I'll tell you," John replied, his eyes hawklike, scanning faces, darting from car to security guard, to patrol car, back to suspicious-looking loiterers just waiting to cuff him.

He saw faces of returning travelers, businessmen, children. All the time he wondered which ones were looking for him.

They were nearing the end of the terminal. Shannon had no reason to believe she'd be rid of John now. He seemed as intent as ever on keeping her with him. But the sight of airplanes had always filled her with wonder. She was childlike in that aspect, she supposed. And just as childishly, she still hoped she would reenter her own dimension. She wanted somehow to find herself in her bed in her apartment, Valentine licking her face, then dashing out the door praying her old car would start and she wouldn't be late to work.

The roar of a jet overhead distracted her. *Valentine...* A cat wasn't much of a family, but she was all Shannon had. Suddenly, Shannon realized she'd be leaving Shreveport. Really leaving. Maybe she'd never come back. *Who's going to care for Valentine? Who'll feed her? Hold her?* Then she remembered her only friend, Elliot. *He'll watch after her. Oh, thank God for you, Elliot.*

"You taking Southwest?"

"I'm...not sure." John avoided the driver's quizzical gaze in the rearview mirror. He reached in his pocket and took out a twenty-dollar bill. "Just drop us off over there, near the parking lot."

"Anything you say, buddy."

John paid the driver and took Shannon's hand, helping her out of the back seat.

"Don't even think it," he said to her as the taxi drove off.

"What?" she asked as he pulled her toward the parking lot and down the middle row.

"About...leaving me."

She was sure of the emotion she heard in the catch of his voice. She would bet her life that John didn't relish the role of kidnapper any more than she found being his victim glamorous. This wasn't a movie. This was real and it was terrifying. But, if her hunch was right and John was softening toward her, he just might let her go. It was about as long as a long shot could be, but she had to try it.

"John, this is Shreveport. I'm home…" She slowed her pace.

He cursed himself under his breath. "You think I don't know that?" Holding her arm, he kept marching toward the parking lot.

"But what I'm saying is…"

"No way." He spun around to face her.

Shannon practically plowed into him. Their eyes locked. She started to plead her case, but he cut her off.

"You don't get it, do you?"

Tears welled in her eyes, but she fought them. He was tough but she could be tougher. "I want to go home."

"So do I. But I can't. Not now, not ever. Somebody else put me in this position. I don't want to be here any more than you do, but I need a hostage and that's you."

Terror filled her eyes as she looked at him. She'd been kidding herself thinking he had softened toward her. In fact, the opposite was true. He was more resolute than ever to reach his goal and she was the means to that goal.

He looked away, then started walking fast, pulling her along with a burst of strength she'd come to recognize would only be short-lived. It made her wonder how strong he must have been before…*they* did this to him. Before…when he had a life.

Getting her bearings, she realized they'd gone past the entrance to the terminal. She pointed back at the main doors. "I thought we were leaving."

"We are," he said. "Just not on a plane."

"I don't get it."

They hustled quickly through the rows, John leading the way as if he knew where he was going. At the far end of the lot he stopped at an old Buick Regal.

"Nice paint job, don't you think?"

She looked at the faded dark blue car. The tan vinyl top had been sun-bleached to beige. The tires were bald and the driver's-side door was dented inward. "Is it yours?"

"It is now." He grimaced and pulled on the damaged door. It swung open. "Get in. You drive."

"I haven't got a key."

He crouched on the ground, reaching under the seat and then the floor mat, searching for a key.

"You're crazy! Nobody leaves the keys in their car."

His search was in vain, except for the screwdriver he found.

There was a split second when Shannon looked back at the doors and realized he was occupied enough for her to make a dash to freedom.

When she glanced back he'd cocked the gun and stuck it in her forehead. "Run for it and I'll shoot you down. Oh, I won't kill you, but you won't be able to run far. You're going with me. Got it?"

Her mouth went dry and her lips trembled when she answered, "Got it."

"Slide in. You won't be so apt to break for it from inside this rusty can."

Shannon did as she was instructed.

John unscrewed the plate on the steering column, pulled out the wires, stripped off the plastic coating with his teeth and tapped the wires together. The engine started instantly.

"On second thought, I'll drive," he said.

Shannon looked out the window. She thought about Valentine, about Helen, about the safe harbor she'd created for herself in Shreveport. She'd even chosen the safe relationship of a comatose man over getting involved with Ben.

There was something about the sound of the running engine that caused her to throw all caution aside. She ignored his warning and bolted for the door handle on her side of the car. Frantically, her hand swiped at the door panel. "Damn!"

John's mutter was laced with dry humor. "No door latch. I checked that out before I hot-wired this thing. I was just testing you."

"Bastard!" She raked her hair with frustration. "You're not going to kill me, you said so yourself."

"That's right. But stupid moves like that *could* get you killed. Until we both know what and who we're up against, I'd appreciate a little cooperation around here!" His voice rose simultaneously in decibels and octaves.

Her eyes were wide. She held her hands to keep them from shaking. "Okay."

He exhaled heavily. "Thank you."

Glancing in the rearview mirror before backing out of the parking slot, he spied a baseball cap on the back seat. He handed it to her. "Here. Put this on. And shove all that hair under there, will ya? It's conspicuous. Cover it up," he replied softly.

Shannon expertly covered her hair as they exited the airport. She stared out the window, refusing to look at John, and watched as they entered the feeder to Interstate 20 West.

"So, are you gonna tell me your real name or what?"

He smiled. "You never asked me."

"Oh."

"It's Gabriel Turner. But you can call me Gabe."

"I like 'bastard' better."

Ben felt his intuition attenuate like a ghost passing through dimensions. One minute he was positive Shannon had been near. He couldn't see her, but he could feel her, almost hear the sound of her voice. But a moment later, she was gone.

He questioned every ticket agent, checked every departure. He called ahead to each arriving flight and its respective city. He checked the charter flights, the cargo flights. His inquisition of the FedEx pilot and ground crew was his last hope.

Five hours later, Ben knew the truth. Shannon and Gabe Turner had not taken a flight out of Shreveport. But they were gone. Whether first thing last night, when they'd escaped the hospital, or early this morning, he'd never know.

The worst part was, he hadn't a clue where to start looking again.

Elliot Wilson blew his nose into a printed bandanna handkerchief as he walked out of his apartment, late for work. He'd telephoned his boss that morning hoping to take a sick day but the promise of double pay had been too tempting. Knowing that the head cold he'd contracted by working overtime in the unheated garage would plague him for weeks if he didn't get some rest, Elliot nevertheless let financial pressure overrule good sense.

As he was about to leave, Elliot glanced at his neighbor's door to see if Shannon had left him a note in response to the two he'd left her yesterday and last night when he'd come home.

The notes were still stuck to the door.

"What's up with this?" he mumbled to himself taking the notes down. "It's not like Shannon to ignore me."

More hurt than angry, Elliot rapped his thick knuckles against the door. Silence. He knocked again. Pressing his ear against the door, he heard no sounds of shuffling feet walking to the door.

Then he heard the sound of Shannon's cat's jingle bell as it hopped from the sofa to the floor and scurried to the door. He could see the shadow of the cat's legs under the door sill as it paced across the floor.

"Valentine? You all right in there?"

Just then Valentine meowed loudly and repeatedly. Elliot realized this was the first time he'd ever heard the sound of Valentine's voice. Valentine was such a contented cat, she never made any noise.

"Valentine. It's me, Elliot."

The cat continued mewing, making even more noise than before. Elliot got the sensation that something was not right. He wasn't sure if anything was wrong particularly, but he intended to find out.

He went back to his apartment and dialed Shannon's number. He let the phone ring four times and it was picked up by a recorder that malfunctioned.

Slamming the receiver down, Elliot grumbled, "I told her to buy herself some decent equipment! Now the damn recorder is on the blink."

Pushing the redial button, Elliot tried again. The results were the same. There was no question Shannon wasn't home.

Curious as to why Shannon's cat would suddenly alter her behavior and start making a racket, Elliot dialed the hospital number and asked for the fifth-floor nurses' station.

"If she's pulled a third shift, she'll be making enough money to buy the whole hospital," he said to himself, checking his watch. "Come on, Shannon. I've got bucks to make, too."

"Fifth floor, Mrs. Burns speaking," she drawled.

"Hello, Mrs. Burns. I was wonderin' if I could speak to Shannon Riley, please."

"Shannon? Who's calling?"

"Elliot, her neighbor."

"Well, she's not here," Mrs. Burns replied tersely.

"She leave already?"

"Leave?" Mrs. Burns's voice had taken on a nervous edge Elliot sensed instantly.

"Where did she go?"

"Home, I think. I'm sure, yes. She said she wasn't feeling well."

Elliot scratched his two-day-old stubble. "Well, I'm at home and she ain't here."

Mrs. Burns scoffed at him. "It's not my job to keep track of my employees once they leave the hospital. Maybe she went out for something to eat."

"Shannon? Eat out? Not in a million years. She thinks it's a waste of money."

"I'm afraid I'm not that familiar with Shannon's personal habits."

"I thought you were friends with Shannon. She's mentioned you from time to time. You have five grandchildren, right?"

"Why, yes. How did you know?"

"I told you, Shannon talks about you and Chelsea and the other nurses. I think she sorta lives vicariously through you all up there."

"I see," Mrs. Burns replied impatiently.

Elliot realized this call was getting him nowhere and he needed to get to work. "Thanks, anyway, ma'am," he said and hung up.

Elliot frowned. "She sure was acting funny, like she knew something about Shannon but didn't want me to know. Now what could she be hiding?"

Leaving his apartment, Elliot was surprised that Valentine was still kicking up a storm, as if she was running in circles.

"Damn cat," he mumbled and did the only thing he knew would help. He went to get the super.

Mrs. Burns called the private cellular number Chief Bremen had given her and the other nurses on the floor. The phone was answered on the second ring.

"How're you doing, Mrs. Burns?" Jimmy Joe asked politely.

"Fine—" she paused, then "—you told me to call if anything came up in regard to Shannon."

Jimmy Joe was instantly all ears. "Yes, Mrs. Burns. What's happened?"

"I got a call from Shannon's next-door neighbor, Elliot, who said Shannon hasn't been home in a while and he was worried about her. Very worried. You told us not to let anyone know about Shannon. I don't know if he can cause any trouble for you. I just thought you should know."

"It's probably nothing but we'll check into it. Thanks for calling. You know, Mrs. Burns, there just aren't enough conscientious citizens like you around."

"That's real sweet of you to say. Thanks."

"Not at all, Mrs. Burns." Jimmy Joe punched End and anxiously grabbed his jacket from the antique-wood hat stand. "Tarnation! How did I get myself into this mess?"

After visiting Shannon Riley's apartment building and finding Elliot not at home, Jimmy Joe spoke with the superintendent who explained that there had been no disturbance at all but that Elliot said he would feed Shannon's cat daily.

The superintendent then gave Jimmy Joe the address of the garage in Bossier City where Elliot worked.

Jimmy Joe arrived at the garage and found Elliot down in a subterranean bay changing the oil on an old Cadillac.

"I'm Jimmy Joe Bremen, the chief of police, and I'd like to have a moment in private with you, Elliot."

"No way," Elliot snapped. "You see this car? I got ten more just like it to do before noon. You come to see me on my time, talk. Otherwise, go away."

Jimmy Joe didn't like this smart-ass one bit, but he was willing to eat crow to keep Elliot quiet. "I understand you're concerned about your neighbor, Shannon Riley."

"I wanted to feed her cat, is all. Since when is that a police matter?" Elliot kept working without so much as glancing at Jimmy Joe.

"Since she works for us."

"Excuse me?" Elliot stopped and put his hands on his hips.

"Glad to finally have your attention." Jimmy Joe

smiled. Elliot did not. "Did you read about that murder that took place last month out on Sabine Bridge?"

"Shannon told me about it and the guy who was still alive she was caring for. She felt like that guy was her own personal assignment."

Jimmy Joe's surprise streaked across his face. He erased it quickly. "That's true."

Elliot stared at him disbelievingly. Something about the man wasn't quite right. His presence in Elliot's garage didn't fit. This was more than a bit suspicious.

Jimmy Joe continued his explanation. "However, that man finally came to and has been transferred to a top-secret facility for questioning. Miss Riley was good enough to volunteer to tend him medically while our investigation is being conducted. The hospital felt that she'd taken a personal interest in his treatment. Coma patients are quite sensitive about such things, so I'm told."

"So why are you tellin' me all this?" Elliot asked.

"Because we don't want to make any trouble for Miss Riley, about her being gone and all. She's helping us out, but until we get to the truth about who the real murderer is, she is in some danger."

"Danger?"

"Nothing serious, mind you, but we don't want to take any chances. You understand what I mean, don'tcha, son?" Jimmy Joe winked.

Elliot stared at him.

Jimmy Joe knew Elliot wasn't buying it.

Elliot wiped his hands on a rag. "You were there the night they brought that guy in, right?"

"Did she tell you that?"

"Nope. Just a wild guess."

"You're good at that."

Elliot sniffed. "You think I'm dumb 'cuz I work on cars?"

"I never said that," Jimmy Joe said with a well-oiled smile. "Did Shannon tell you anything about that night?"

"Nope. She's a private person, like me. It's none of my business."

"Maybe there are things you might not think are important, but to us they could be."

Elliot's eyes narrowed. He felt the hairs on the back of his neck stand on end. Something was going on that he didn't like one bit. "Well, if Shannon's okay, you don't need me."

"Maybe you should come downtown for a bit," Jimmy Joe said with a threatening voice.

"You got a warrant or a writ or something that says I gotta go with you right now?" Elliot spat cockily.

"No, but I can get one."

"Do that. Like I said, I got ten cars to tend to. Time's awastin'." Elliot turned away from the chief.

Clenching his fists, Jimmy Joe marched back to his car. His interrogation had gone sour and it was not sitting well with him in the least. Ramming his fist against the steering wheel, Jimmy Joe said, "There's more than one way to plug a hole."

17

The contorted route Gabe gave Shannon kept them off I-20 more than on. Diverting off the interstate at Jonesville onto old Highway 80 and veering around the north side of Longview, about all Shannon could tell was that they were traveling west.

"Are we stopping in Dallas?" she asked.

Gabe lifted his eyes dully. His adrenaline had finally run its course. Pain of every magnitude raked his body. The mere act of inhaling sapped his energy and talking was pure torture.

"No," he groaned and then coughed. The pain was searing. He coughed again, which led to a spasm of hacking. His chest felt as if it were imploding, his head pounded and he thought he was about to collapse. But he wouldn't allow himself the luxury of succumbing. His driver was much too independent to trust, so he kept his hand wrapped around the automatic pistol in his windbreaker pocket.

"Are you all right?" she asked.

"Control," he mumbled so quietly she couldn't hear what he was saying.

"What?"

"I gotta stay in control. Did it before. Do it again," he groaned.

"You're not making any sense."

"Just drive," he whispered painfully.

"Can't we stop so I can give you an injection?"

"No." He slammed his eyes shut. Fissures crept across his forehead.

She hated being this empathetic. It made her feel impotent. She felt a serious wave of nurturing coming on. "This isn't good, you know, trying to be some kind of martyr. What's the matter, don't you trust me?"

"Not in the least." He coughed repeatedly, pressing his hands against his rib cage. "I never thought I could be so cold." He glared at the chilly heat vents.

Frowning, Shannon replied, "It's an old car like mine was," she said. "I guess the owner didn't have six hundred bucks to get it fixed."

Despite his pain, he was intrigued. "But you made enough money to fix your car, even to buy a new one."

Shannon sensed he measured every intonation of her voice, every facial expression. Gabe was an intense man. She guessed that to him there was no such thing as idle conversation. "I never needed the heater much. I always figured that two months, maybe three tops, of Louisiana's mild winter wasn't enough to justify the cost."

"What exactly do you do with your money, Shannon?"

"Save it," she replied tensely. "For a rainy day."

He opened his eyes enough to cast her an acidic glare. He didn't believe her in the least. "I have a hard time commending your thriftiness," he grumbled as another searing pain shot through his chest. He felt as if his lungs were being ripped from the inside out using his ribs as tongs to do the pulling. The rattling in his chest increased as he was hit with another bout of coughing.

"Tell me about the rainy day. It will get my mind off my pain."

"Oh, the usual."

"You're lying again, Shannon." He kept his eyes closed. "I can always tell when you're lying."

She swallowed. "I don't like telling people about my private life, my thoughts. It makes me—"

"Vulnerable," he injected.

"Well, yes. So, I've made it a rule to keep to myself."

"You thought you'd just sit back and grow old and no one would ever know you were around. Funny, isn't it? I come into your life and I put you in more danger than the next hundred people. Know what I think? I think you were planning to run away."

"I wasn't," she retorted too quickly and with too much shock in her voice.

He opened his eyes and peered at her. "You're saving your money for a long trip. To the farthest place on earth, where no one will find you."

"Greece..."

"Greece..." he said at the same exact moment. "How did I know that?"

"I told you when you were unconscious. Greek heroes and all that."

"I'm no hero," he began when another round of coughing overtook him. "God, I hurt."

"The cold has caused your muscles to contract and spasm, which in turn is causing you just as much pain as the healing that's going on inside you."

He rolled his head slowly on the neck rest, feeling

the knots in his shoulders. "Just how messed up was I? Shouldn't I have healed in a month?"

"Your lungs were punctured by your ribs and collapsed as a result. The worst of the pneumonia, fever, inflammation, passed just last week. You still have a lot of phlegm to get rid of."

"Please tell me you brought something for this."

"An expectorant with codeine. In the brown bottle in my purse."

"Codeine? Isn't that habit-forming?"

Caught off guard, Shannon burst into a cryptic laugh. "You're running for your life from the police and unknown assassins and you're worried you'll get addicted to cough medicine?"

"Sorry. I've always believed in taking care of my body."

"Here," she said, lifting her arm. "I'll get it."

"No," he said. "You have enough to do. I can get it."

Gabe reached in the back seat for Shannon's purse and found the medicine. Slugging back what he thought was the appropriate dosage, he swallowed the bitter liquid. "God, that's disgusting. I hope it works."

"If it doesn't, we'll have to stop in the woods," she said.

"For what?"

"So I can make a poultice of spiders that you will wear around your neck to fight off the ague and fever." She chuckled. Her attempt at levity was meant as much for herself as for him.

"Not very likely," he said groggily, the codeine taking effect. "What nursing school did you attend?" he asked.

Shannon drew in a breath, but was saved having to answer when Gabe cut in. "Never mind. I might not want to know."

He leaned back and closed his eyes. Shannon had driven only fifteen miles when Gabe fell asleep. His head bobbed against his chest and his neck cracked like popping corn. The sound jerked him awake.

"You were snoring," she said.

"Is that unusual?"

"For you it is. You don't snore."

"And, of course, you would know this," he said, watching as her eyelids closed quickly, dispelling her embarrassment.

He was surprised at the pleasure he felt witnessing her reaction to this hint of an intimate bond between them.

"I was your nurse," she replied coolly.

"And as my nurse, just exactly what were your duties?"

"The usual. Check blood pressure, IV, temp—"

His mind raced ahead. "Did an orderly change my bedding or did you?"

"I did."

"And my gown?" His questions came in rapid-fire succession.

"I did."

"Shave me?"

"Yes." Shannon felt her blush start at her toes.

"Wash me?"

"Yes." She cleared her throat.

Resting on the worn headrest, he rolled his head to the left so as not to miss her wriggle, the nervous grip of her fingers around the steering wheel. He was loving this. He'd had no idea. He didn't realize he was smiling.

"And what else did you do with me?" he asked huskily.

Shannon's cheeks were burning, which was ridiculous. She was a nurse. "The human body is like a machine to me."

"Obviously mine wasn't. Or was it?"

"I...I..."

Gabe was grinning. "Tell me the truth, Shannon. I fascinated you."

"It was nothing like that."

He ignored her denial. "What exactly was there about me that intrigued you?"

Too mortified to continue protesting, Shannon answered, "You had bad hair."

"Bad hair? As in, 'He had a bad hair day'?"

"No, as in bad hair. It shows a severe deficiency of the B-complex vitamins A and E. Probably as a result of too much stress, or a thyroid condition, or an unbalanced diet. You probably drink too much, don't get enough sleep and are stressed over work-related problems."

"Well, hell! Isn't everybody?"

"I'm not," she replied confidently.

He lifted the ball cap that she wore and a shiny curl fell out. "Great hair. I see what you mean." He shoved the hat down on her head and stared glumly out the window, mumbling, "Bad hair. Bad hair..."

Entering Dallas, they took none of the freeways, using instead the old highways to the south through Arlington, and on to Fort Worth. Because his directions were precise despite the convoluted city layout, Shannon guessed Gabe had spent a great deal of time here.

"Do you live near here?" she asked as they entered Fort Worth.

He ignored her question. "Take the next right. Go two more blocks and hang a left into the three-story concrete parking garage. Yeah, there. You see it?"

"I see it," she said and turned the car into the garage drive.

"Take the contract parking entrance, not the visitors', and go up to the second level."

Shannon turned on the headlights as she drove up the dark ramp to the blue-coded second level. Spying the elevator, she noted a stairway next to it. There seemed to be no one around. Most of the angled spaces were empty, which told her that this was more of a residential parking garage than commercial. Everyone had obviously left for work.

"Go to the top of this level," Gabe instructed. "The third level is the roof. I'd never park there. Too much sun damage to the car paint."

She did as she was instructed.

"Now drive to the end of this row. The second to the last on the right. Pull in next to that blue Mustang."

Shannon parked the car and Gabe's face lit up as if he'd been reborn. His energy reserves kicked into gear. "Now, get out of the car," he ordered dispassionately, putting the gun to her right temple.

"I thought, after the thing at the motel, that we were in this together," she protested in hopes of diverting his attention from her true motives.

"So did I, but that was before you bolted for the

door. In the pass-fail system, I've found you respond best to stimuli."

She hadn't fooled him a bit.

Keeping the gun pointed at her, Gabe crossed to the Mustang's rear right tire, bent down and retrieved a set of keys.

"Gabe, stop this. I'm not the enemy."

"You have no idea how much I want to believe that. But I know human nature and you'd be crazy not to want to run for it."

"But that was before…"

"Before what?" He put his face next to hers. "Before you realized this really is it, you and me? That you have no life to go back to? That all this private-person, noninvolvement of yours has come to end? Face it, Shannon…this is your life. I am your life."

No gleaming gun barrel, no shots in the night, no man's shadows outside a bathroom window had riddled her with more terror than Gabe's words at that second. He couldn't be right. She wouldn't let him be right. She would find a way to Ben. She could find a way back to the past. Or could she?

He hit an automatic button and the Mustang's lock flipped up. "Now get in."

She made a last-ditch effort. "You could leave me here."

"Not a chance. I told you, I need you until I don't need you anymore."

"When is that?"

"Don't worry. I'll let you know."

"And then what?" she demanded.

He moved her away from the trunk, toward the driver's side. "Never mind."

"Gabe, I have to know!"

"Keep your voice down or I'll tape it shut," he warned.

Shannon clamped her lips closed. He'd do that much, she was sure. Desperate people did desperate things and Gabe was desperate.

He depressed the trunk-release button on his key ring and withdrew what looked to Shannon like last week's dry cleaning. He handed her the clothes. "Here, put everything except my jeans and the blue sport shirt in the back seat."

While Shannon did as he instructed, Gabe took out a leather briefcase, opened it and inspected the contents. He smiled at the cellular phone.

Craning her neck, Shannon was able to see a stack of color brochures and dark blue folders printed with the words Globel Insurance on the cover.

Her eyes flew wide open as she gasped, "You don't really sell that stuff."

"Yes, I really do," he replied, checking the battery on his phone.

"You don't look like an insurance salesman," she said.

"Yeah? What do I look like?"

Shannon didn't answer his question, but asked instead, "What kind of insurance do you sell?"

"Not whole life. Bad investment."

She got his meaning instantly.

Gabe pulled out two credit cards and a checkbook from an inside pocket and put them on top of the trunk. He closed the briefcase, placing it on the floorboard of the passenger's seat. "Get in while I change clothes."

Shannon did as she was told, though she watched his every move through the rearview mirror. Anxiously watching for other cars coming in or going out of the garage, she realized quite a few cars were draped with cloth covers, a sign their owners were infrequent visitors to Fort Worth.

"Now you drive this car to the roof," he instructed. "I'll follow you."

"Aren't you afraid I'll take off?"

"I'll be right behind you. One false move and I'll shoot those bald tires." His eyes were stone cold. He was doing his Jekyll-Hyde thing again. "You're going with me, Shannon. All the way."

"And where is that?"

He glared at her.

"Never mind," she replied, knowing it wasn't the right time to press him. The codeine was giving him momentary false strength. When his pain returned, so would his irritability.

Shannon got in the car, started it and drove up to the roof with Gabe following closely. She parked the car where he indicated and walked back to the Mustang where they exchanged places.

"Let's get the hell out of here. I've got the feeling we're being watched," he said.

Shannon's eyes shot around the garage and carefully inspected the side street as they pulled out. *Watched. But by whom? The men who wanted Gabe dead…*

Then it hit her. Those same men wanted her dead, too. In reality, she'd had no choices since the motel. She'd only thought she had. The assassins would kill her. They thought she was Gabe's girl, at the most, and at the least that she was expendable.

Her world, the one she'd created in Shreveport, was about to come to an end. From this day forward everything about it that she'd created would cease to be hers.

Glancing around, Shannon didn't see anything out of the ordinary, just a man walking to the corner, carrying a briefcase and newspaper. A young boy with a schoolbook bag on his back hurried to the bus stop. There were no signs of police cars, marked or unmarked, not even a crossing guard.

"I don't see anyone," she said.

Suddenly panic froze her thoughts. She'd lived her own lie so long it had become her truth. Police computers were nationwide, connected to each other like a giant honeycomb to entrap the enemies of society.

She swallowed hard. She had been an enemy of society long before she'd come to Shreveport, long before there was a Gabe Turner in her life.

If she wasn't careful, she'd never have to keep another secret again. Everything she'd worked so hard to keep hidden would be revealed.

For the first time since Gabe had taken her prisoner, she didn't want the police to find her. She couldn't let Ben find her. In fact, it might be because of her and her past that Gabe could die.

The irony of her situation would ordinarily have brought her to hysteria, but she didn't have the luxury of tears. It was up to her to keep them running.

Because of her, Gabe would find out what running was really like.

18

Ben started from scratch. He went back to Shannon's apartment and combed it with a vengeance. It still surprised him how little life she had outside the hospital. There was no address book, no Christmas list of names, no hidden family photographs, no coupons for favorite foods. There were no shopping lists, or even notes to herself stuffed in the bottom of either of the two purses he found in her closet. The only routine excursion he found was a stack of dry cleaning stubs. He'd hit a dead end.

"Shannon the phantom. How is it I still know nothing about you?" He scratched his head. "Nobody is this nonexistent."

Ben glanced around the small apartment one last time and realized that since he'd walked in, Shannon's cat had done nothing except sit facing the wall.

"Shouldn't you be hungry, kitty? Don't you want to be petted? Your mommy has been away for over a day and a half now."

The cat refused to acknowlege him.

Ben went to the kitchen and found that, indeed, the food bowl and water bowl were empty. But the cat hadn't budged. Something wasn't right.

Ben went over to the cat, crouched next to it and stroked her back. "What's the matter, kitty? Miss

Shannon?" He noticed the cat was sitting on a floor vent. He thought that maybe she was warming herself, but when he put his hand on the metal vent it was cold. Just like the rest of the apartment.

Then he heard the sound of a stereo being played. The music was faint but he could hear that the record was skipping, repeating itself over and over.

"You can hear that, can't you?" The cat blinked and looked away.

"My guess is the owner isn't home. Maybe they left the music playing before going away for the holiday." He looked at the cat. "What do you think?"

The cat stared at him, cocked her head and blinked again.

Ben picked her up and stroked her neck. "You don't want to listen to that, do you?"

With a lightning-quick movement, the cat scratched Ben's hand angrily, drawing blood, then jumped out of his arms and immediately sat on the vent again, facing the wall.

"This is too weird." Ben looked at the wall. There was nothing but old faded wallpaper there.

Suddenly, he remembered Shannon's neighbor, Elliot, whom he'd questioned. This wall was shared by Elliot and Shannon.

Ben leaned against the wall. The skipping record came from Elliot's apartment. Ben looked at the cat again.

Her chest barely moved as she breathed, looking like a sphinx. Rigid as stone.

"You aren't being weird at all, are you? Animals do this, sit watch over the dead."

Ben bolted to the door, threw it open and darted to Elliot's apartment.

"Elliot!" He banged on the door with his fist.

No answer.

"It's Ben Richards, Elliot. Open up!"

Still no answer.

"I'm coming in. I have the master from the superintendent."

Ben opened the door and the sight that greeted him made his heart sink.

"Shit." He closed his eyes, then opened them again. Ben didn't like being right all the time.

"Damn it!"

He raced into the room and grabbed Elliot's legs. The young man swung by the neck from a rope wrapped securely around a bicycle hook in the ceiling.

"Shit!"

Ben looked around for a chair so he could get high enough to reach the rope. The computer chair, which had rolled to the opposite side of the room, threatened to slide out from under him several times as he mounted it. His hands shaking, he untied the rope around Elliot's throat. The body fell against him with a heavy thud.

"No!" Ben felt for a pulse and found none. Ben couldn't help the tears in his eyes. He tried not to react when things like this happened, but most times he did. He hid his feelings as best he could when others were around, but this time, the only one to see him crying was Shannon's cat who had come to sit in the doorway.

The Shreveport police arrived in record time. Ben was impressed with their efficiency.

"What was Chief Bremen's reaction to this?" Ben

asked Investigative Lieutenant Sanders as they wandered around the kitchen and bedroom looking for clues in closets, under beds and in drawers.

"He didn't have one."

"What?"

"His wife said he wasn't to be disturbed."

Ben slapped his hand on the back of his neck, a gesture to contain his anger. "Suicides are that common around here?"

Sanders smirked, took out a piece of chewing gum and folded it into his mouth. "Not at all. It's been a hell of a Christmas for the chief. He needed the rest."

Ben's eyes filled with disdain. "Life's a bitch."

"Yeah," Sanders said, looking at Elliot's body. "Guess he thought so, too."

Ben turned the incident over in his head a hundred times. Something wasn't right about Elliot's suicide. A brief note typed into the computer complained of loneliness, yet Elliot had told Ben that what he'd liked about Shannon was that she kept her distance. Elliot hadn't even stepped foot in Shannon's apartment, not wanting to invade. He was as judicious about protecting her privacy as he was about his own.

Ben didn't believe for a second that Elliot had killed himself due to despondency or "the holiday blues." Loners were never lonely. They were alone. There was a difference.

Ben also found it odd that, given that Elliot was nearly a foot shorter than himself, the computer chair, the only one in the room, couldn't have been the one Elliot had used to stand on to hang himself. For a man Ben's height, the chair was the right size. Elliot could have put the noose around his throat, looped it around the hook and then kicked the chair away. But he was still hanging too high for that to have happened.

Ben wished now he'd taken measurements himself, but the photographs the Ident team had taken would give him a better approximation. When they came back from processing, he'd put in a request for them.

Ben called Chief Bremen's cellular and it answered on the second ring.

"The cellular number you are trying to reach is unavailable. Please leave a message at the tone."

Ben hung up. He needed time to think.

Driving to the Sonic hot-dog stand, Ben ordered a large root beer, two hot dogs and fries from the carhop.

It had been a hell of a day and the only thing he'd turned up of any value was Shannon's dry-cleaning stub. Just as he turned it over, noting the address, his cellular phone rang.

"Make it good. Make it snappy," he said dully to the only person who knew his very private number.

"Aren't we in a good mood," the familiar cocky voice replied.

"Tell me why I should be."

"In one word or two?"

"I'll take whatever you've got as long as it's good."

"Fort Worth."

Ben straightened up. "No kidding?"

"Turner lives in a neat-as-a-pin, anal-retentive apartment on the northwest side. Our man scanned the interior with his infrared zoom lens an hour ago. No signs of life. But something interesting."

"What's that?"

"Turner's car is missing from his slot."

"I'm fresh out of Kewpie dolls, but I owe you." Ben smiled. "Tell me we made the car."

"Blue Mustang. Hasn't gotten regular plates yet. Paid cash. I like this guy more every minute."

"Any make on the two Hispanics from the motel?"

"Out-of-towners. Way out. Try Cartagena, the Cassalia Cartel."

"Turner's making a bundle all right, but it's not from insurance."

"Possible. We dug up last year's W-2's. I dunno. He coughs up a chunk to Uncle Sam. The point is, he's in deep shit if he's tangling with them. They take no prisoners."

"And I thought we were after the Cali Cartel. What the hell are Alejandro's men doing this far north?"

"You're the Maestro. You tell me."

The carhop interrupted Ben's conversation. He handed her a ten-dollar bill as she hung his food tray on the half-opened car window. "What else did you find?"

"Our gal Sal you mean?"

Ben's ears pricked to attention. He sat up straight as anticipation shot through his spine. "Yeah."

"She ain't."

"Huh?"

"We've run every initial combination of the initials SR we can think of through records, files and databases. None of the Shannon Rileys are nurses. Three are deceased and none are in or from Louisiana. Nor can we find records of anyone changing their name to Shannon Riley, legally or not."

"Which tells me she's hiding something," Ben said.

"Or from someone. Sound familiar, Maestro?"

"I'm not listening," Ben said, frowning, then

crammed half a hot dog in his mouth and guzzled his root beer.

"You won't have to for much longer. Word from the brass is you'll be coming home soon."

"How so?"

"Certain Cajun comrades are about to show their hand. The fires are red-hot."

"Good," Ben said. "I'll check in later." He pressed the end button.

Ben drove back to the police station, his hot dogs not sitting well in his stomach.

"Where's the chief?" he asked the desk sergeant as he came through the door.

"Gone." The sergeant shrugged his shoulders and went back to the conversation he was having with a middle-aged man wearing a grossly obvious toupee.

Ben took the stairs two at a time. His instincts had kicked in the minute he'd walked in the station. When things went wrong, they were always hot. He could feel the heat.

"The chief in, Thelma?" he asked, breezing past the auburn-haired administrative assistant.

"No!" she replied, bolting from her chair and trying to stop Ben as he walked straight to the chief's desk and rifled through the papers on top. "What are you, nuts? Get the hell out of here, Richards."

"No way. The St. Christopher's fiasco is my fault. I intend to rectify my mistakes." There was nothing out of the ordinary on the chief's desk, except a notepad where he'd scribbled #304 at 1:05. An address? Time of a meeting? Or a plane flight and time? He flipped the notepad and saw the impression of other words he would try to make out later when Thelma wasn't around. He palmed the notes quickly, to keep her from seeing them.

"Thelma, did the chief get a make on John Doe yet?"

"Not that I know about."

"But Thelma, darling, you know everything that comes across his desk. This place can't survive without you."

"Don't patronize me, Richards," she barked.

"Nothing about the guy we brought in this morning from the motel incident?"

"Nada. Chief said they were just drunked up, looking to make a quick heist is all. And the dead one was real unlucky."

Those two men were assassins and Chief Bremen knew it. Clearly, the chief was either keeping a lid on the case or he was covering something up. He was in deep. Up to his eyelids was Ben's guess.

Ben wondered for a moment if the Colombians had accomplices who might have killed Elliot, but discounted the idea. He realized the connection just wasn't there. Shannon was Elliot's friend. She might have told Elliot something about Gabe Turner, but if they'd been savvy enough to track down Elliot, they wouldn't have needed to be so meticulous about the execution. The existence of the phony note told Ben that someone else had wanted Elliot dead and had wanted it to look like a suicide.

Whether that someone was associated with Shannon or Gabe Turner was yet to be seen. It was possible Elliot had an enemy. Lots of people did. But not probable from what Ben could discern about him from the man's surroundings.

The truth about Elliot's death was only one of a litany of questions plaguing him. Why wasn't there more information on his desk? By now, Ben should have received the report from Marshall, Texas, about Shannon's car being found in the used-car lot. What was the holdup? Why didn't he or the chief have a pile of faxes on his desk about that alone? Ben also didn't see a report from the bus driver who'd identified Turner and Shannon; the same bus driver who said they'd gotten off the bus miles away from the Shreveport station.

Ben thought it more than curious that Turner had decided to come back to Shreveport. Why would Turner take such a risk? And what about the cab-driver who took the couple to the airport, but then didn't see them enter the terminal? What about the Colombian down in holding? And the dead one in the morgue? Why hadn't either of them been identified yet? No police department was this slow.

Most important, to Ben's thinking, why wasn't Chief Bremen asking the same questions as Ben?

Ben realized he was the only one on the case who smelled a rat—or two.

Ben hid his concern under a placid expression as he looked at Thelma. He shrugged his shoulders. "Doesn't give me much to work with, does it, Thelma?"

"And I thought you were a wizard."

He grinned. "Nah."

She grinned back affectionately.

"Anything else I should know?" he asked.

"Not that I can think of. Oh, say, there was a call from the hospital. Helen Mayer I think she said her name was. Administrator there."

"That's right. What did she want?"

"I told her it was nothing to worry about, but she said one of her nurses was missing. Since this girl worked on the same floor as Shannon Riley, she thought maybe you should know about it. She hasn't reported to work since…your fiasco, is that what you called it?" Thelma smirked.

"What's her name?"

"Chelsea Sikeston."

"Thanks. I'll look into it."

"Then it's time you scram." She jabbed her thumb over her shoulder.

He promptly went to his desk and went through his paperwork. He punched in a call to Helen Mayer at the hospital.

"This is Ben Richards. I was wondering if you'd heard from Chelsea yet."

"No, Ben. The nurses tell me she has a habit of doing this kind of thing. They also tell me she had a date this morning with one of her…friends."

"So, it's likely she could be shacked up in a motel and still show up for work."

"I'm sorry I called. Personal heebie-jeebies since this thing with Shannon. Any word about her yet?"

"No, but I expect to hear something any minute."

"Good. Let me know, will you?"

"Sure, Helen." Ben hung up.

Ben found Chelsea's number in the hospital roster of names and numbers he'd been given his first day on duty. He dialed it, let it ring, left a message on the answering machine and hung up. There was no doubt in his mind, Chelsea was simply having too much fun to go to work.

He leaned back in his chair compiling the hard evidence he'd found that day. He almost smiled to himself.

Ben's suspicion of Jimmy Joe Bremen's involvement with a drug ring had landed him this assignment when he'd first linked Blane Blair to Shreveport over eighteen months ago.

Blane Blair—Ben's own personal sworn enemy.

He knew the stats on Blair by heart. Rich kid gone bad. Princeton preppie with nothing to do with his life. Hangs out in Malibu for years after graduation living off Daddy's sugar-refinery millions. Daddy gets miffed and cuts him off. Blane moves to San Francisco and makes his own fortune selling black-market babies to other misguided rich kids like himself who did too many drugs to risk a pregnancy or who simply can't have a baby. Daddy dies, leaves Blane the business and the mansion on Lake Pontchartrain. Blane brings his California big bucks back to Louisiana, but it's not enough to buy Blane big-daddy status. So Blane decides to try politics. To fund his new toy, he needs lots of cash. He revives his black-market babies and dips into a new business venture—drugs.

All this Ben knew. What he didn't know until today and hadn't even suspected was the magnitude of Blane's connection.

"Blane Blair and Alejandro Cassalia. Now there's a pair."

He remembered the notes he'd palmed off Chief Bremen's desk. Taking a pencil, he scratched the lead over the impressions he'd seen. The lettering spelled out "Fort Worth." Turner's apartment was in Fort Worth. Obviously, Bremen was on his way there.

And so was Ben.

Walking out of the station, Ben couldn't help thinking that the truth never seemed to strike him full force, but came in tiny seeds of intuition that grew into hunches.

Ben had lots of hunches. They formed the melody of his life and he strung them together, pearls of evidence, facts and prosecution witnesses that blended harmoniously in courts of law, resulting in convictions against a sea of drug traffickers. Pearls weren't worth much individually, but tied together they were priceless...like good music. Like Ben's favorite song, "String of Pearls" by Glenn Miller.

Ben loved good music. Hearing drug traffickers inform against each other was opera to Ben's ears. There was nothing he liked more than conducting an interrogation and making scum sing. That's why his fellow DEA agents called him the Maestro. He'd created magic before. He could do it again. He needed this encore.

The only flight leaving Shreveport at 1:05 was #304, bound for Fort Worth. Ben's genius was alive and kicking.

It was possible that Jimmy Joe kept his whereabouts secret in order to bag Gabriel Turner for himself. Landing a headliner case like this would insure his reelection the following year. But something told Ben that Chief Bremen wasn't interested in his political status—not this time.

Ben had personally tapped Jimmy Joe's phone lines. Only once had the chief made a phone call to New Orleans. When they'd run a check, the call was to a phone booth. Nothing criminal in that.

But this hunch was personal to Ben. It would be played out until the end. It had to be.

Ben's knowledge about Blane Blair's black-market babies was personal. Unsubstantiated and inadmissible in court, but it was all true. Ben knew the story well, for he'd been part of it when Nancy was alive.

Ben's painful past had remained buried until Blane Blair's name turned up on a file-folder label of the top-secret case he was investigating for the Department of Justice. Ben dreamed more about nailing Blane Blair than he did about sex.

Before coming to Shreveport, Ben had put a man on Blane Blair. They had photographs of Blane making phone calls from a phone booth. Ben would know later if the phone numbers matched. If they did, he'd count it as a pearl.

Ben booked the next flight to Fort Worth at five o'clock that afternoon.

He cracked his knuckles anxiously. He didn't like the feeling he was getting.

Jimmy Joe was in Fort Worth right now and Ben had three hours to kill before his flight took off. It was too much time. These days the world could blow up in a millisecond, much less three hours.

The hot dogs churned in his stomach. There was just enough time for him to go back to Shannon's, get her cat and take her to his place. Then he'd call the cat-sitter service he'd heard one of the detectives talking about.

He knew it wasn't much, but just having Shannon's cat around would make him feel closer to her.

19

—→ ◄—

"You know anything about computers?" Gabe asked Shannon.

"Why?"

"I want to rent a computer and find out what's on this disk."

Getting a bearing on their location, he said, "Drive about three more miles. You'll see a strip mall with white brick and green awnings. A doughnut shop. Best in Fort Worth. There's a twenty-four-hour Kinko's next door. Pull in at the doughnut shop. We'll walk the rest of the way."

While Shannon drove, Gabe banged out a series of numbers on his cellular phone. Counting the number of digits he punched, Shannon realized he was calling long distance. The first call was answered with a busy signal. Noticing that he glanced at the digital clock above the tape player, she deduced that whomever he was dialing was most probably in a different time zone. Gabe called the same long-distance number again, getting no answer.

"Doesn't he believe in answering machines?" he said.

"Who?" Shannon couldn't help asking questions; there was always a chance she'd get lucky and Gabe would answer her.

"No one."

The third call he placed was a local call. She guessed he was accessing his answering machine or contacting his call notes. After listening to his messages, Gabe put the phone in the glove box.

Pointing up ahead, he said, "There's the doughnut shop." He put the gun in the back of his jeans waistband, then concealed it with the windbreaker.

Shannon parked the car at the far end of the doughnut shop away from Kinko's. They went inside the copy center.

"I'd like a half hour on one of your computers," Gabe said to the clerk.

"We rent by the hour. Fifteen dollars. Diskettes are three dollars each."

"I'll take two," he said and followed the assistant to the computer.

When they were alone, Shannon inserted the disk into the drive and pulled up the information on the screen.

Gabe stared at a column of names next to which were the names of worldwide banks, corporate-account names and numbers and lists of stocks and commodities.

"What is all this?"

"I haven't got a clue."

Shannon scanned the accounts. "It's bookkeeping. But of what? I'm not a numbers person."

"My first thought was that this had something to do with the IRS, but these transactions are worldwide. And look, here's an Irish corporation. Cayman Islands." Gabe sucked in his breath. His eyes went wild. "My God, they're offshore accounts."

"Who would need something like that?" she asked.

He swallowed. "People who move money from one country to another. Look at these transfers. This took a lot of work on someone's part. I think we're in a lot of trouble," he said, concentrating on the data on the screen.

"*We're* in trouble?" Her eyes shot from Gabe back to the screen. "This isn't our stuff."

"The information is ours."

"What information?" She looked from the screen to Gabe's fear-filled eyes and back again. "Gabe, what is all this?"

"Millions, if my addition is right."

Stunned, Shannon's voice quaked. "Dollars? Millions of dollars? Whose money is it?"

"I don't know, but I can guess."

Her eyes shot to the columns. Maybe there was something here that would save their lives. Quickly, she tried to memorize everything she saw on the screen, but knew it would be impossible to remember this nonsense.

He scrolled down the seemingly endless list of names, some of whom he'd never heard of, finally seeing a pattern. "This isn't good."

"I figured that. Is there something specific you're referring to?"

She followed his eyes to a name on the screen. *Blane Blair*. She knew Congressman Blane Blair was running for governor of Louisiana. But what was his name doing on this list? None of the other names were politicos she recognized.

"No. Nothing specific," Gabe said, studying the columns.

All Shannon's adult life she'd shied away from investments, stocks and corporate portfolios because she didn't understand them. As she surveyed the computer screen, she wished she'd learned more about accounting. When Elliot had taught her how to use his computer, he'd suggested she use home-accounting software to make the job easier. She'd refused even to learn, thinking it would be too complicated. Now she wished she'd at least taken a stab at it. Perhaps then she might understand the reasons behind her inevitable murder.

All she knew as she skimmed down the columns was that Jimmy Joe Bremen was listed and, therefore, was somehow involved with Adam Rivers's death.

"Is there anything more on here?" Gabe asked.

Shannon scrolled down the page and brought up the second page.

"I know these people," Gabe whispered to himself, tapping the screen as he recognized one name after another. Nearly half were his insurance clients. But he didn't understand what they were doing on this list.

Suddenly, it hit him. They were all referrals Adam had given him. According to the entries, Adam paid them regular but fairly small sums of cash over a long period of time. The entries went back nearly eight years. What could Adam have had in common with Blane Blair eight years ago? Blane was a state senator at that time. "You're from Louisiana," he said to Shannon. "You know anything about their politics that goes back eight or more years?"

"Politics? I don't have time."

Looking more closely, Gabe realized there were numerous small-town Texas politicians on the list as well as several law enforcement officials. One of them was a state trooper, a client he knew didn't make more than thirty thousand dollars a year. Yet, he was listed as having deposited a hundred and twelve thousand dollars in a numbered Swiss account.

Everyone on the list received the same amount of money on the fifteenth of every month. "Just like clockwork," he said. "How do I make a copy?" he asked, handing her one of the floppies he'd bought.

"I'll do it," she said, starting the process in motion.

Gabe kept scrolling. The next set of entries showed that Adam had invested large amounts of money for the same clients. Oddly, they all had variations of the same initials—A and C.

Gabe read the list. "Andrew Cassidy. Charles Atwater. Abe Castleman. Amelia Carrington. Cindy Ames."

He pointed to the screen. "This is a set of client names I've never seen. And the numbers are staggering." His insurance clients' accounts were paltry compared to the hundreds of millions these half-dozen names had deposited in the same Swiss bank. Gabe didn't believe for a minute they were real people.

He looked at the last column. Each of the six accounts from the A and R list had regularly transferred a half-million dollars to a single account under the name of Angelo Rodriguez. The total was over fifty million dollars. Curiously, this was the only account in Grand Cayman not Credit Suisse.

A and R were Adam's initials. He realized that the accounts using the A, C initials were dummy accounts belonging to one man but what kind of man had nearly a billion dollars. What did this guy do, and did he even want to know?

Gabe had visions of being implicated in an espionage scheme if this disk got to the FBI. He wasn't sure what all this information meant, but he knew enough to memorize the number of the Grand Cayman National Bank in Georgetown.

Suddenly, Shannon pointed to the screen. "Cartagena? Isn't that in Colombia?"

"Yes...." Gabe swallowed hard as reality sharpened his senses.

"What's this?" She pointed to the call letters—DIF.

"Man!" Gabe recognized them as the call letters for Dominic Investment Firm in San Francisco. The corporation was owned by his best friend, Peter Dominic, whom he'd been trying to call for help.

"Peter..."

He didn't realize he'd said Peter's name aloud. All he knew was that he'd believed his friend was his salvation, his way out of this mess.

Reality seemed too much for him. It was one thing to have misjudged Adam, who'd always tended to look for the quick buck, the easy deal. Even in college Adam had had a habit of falling in with the wrong crowd. He'd desperately wanted to be rich. But Pete had been the solid one and was certainly more stable than Adam and Gabe combined.

What if Gabe's idol had feet of clay? It would kill him if it was true.

There was no question in Gabe's mind that Adam and possibly Pete had been involved with a Colombian cartel. If his speculation was accurate and Adam had tried to bribe the cartel with the list of names on the disk in exchange for the money he'd siphoned from their bank accounts, then word about his disappearance from the hospital had to have gotten back to Colombia. By now, everyone who'd been on the take from Adam was probably gunning for him as well.

Gabe wondered what Adam had been thinking when he'd called him and suggested they connect in Shreveport. Adam couldn't have possibly thought Gabe would want to be part of his scheme to steal from a cartel. Adam wasn't that stupid, was he?

Then again, perhaps he'd never intended to tell Gabe at all. Perhaps he'd meant for Gabe to be the patsy. Maybe Adam had been just that desperate, just that disloyal.

Shannon didn't like the flush of anger she saw in Gabe's face. The betrayal hurt him deeply. She knew how that felt for she'd felt it herself once.

Whoever this Peter was, he was causing a severe reaction in Gabe. It would have to be someone very close to upset him this way.

Cautiously, she surveyed the area around her. It was busy for the day after Christmas. Mostly she saw young office types, clerks, a young mother with two children.

From the other side of the store she heard a raspy, rattling cough. Then the man coughed again. It was deep and lingering.

Suddenly, her skin crawled. She'd heard that particular cough before—in Shreveport. She glanced over her shoulder and sucked in her breath in shock.

Her alarm brought Gabe out of his thoughts. He followed her gaze to the overweight man in the khaki pants and white shirt. "Who is it?"

Gabe looked at Shannon. There was no fear in her eyes. She'd obviously recognized someone who would save her. Suddenly, Shannon had become the enemy, too.

Lightning-fast, Gabe slipped the gun out of the

back of his jeans and put it in his windbreaker pocket.
He ejected his disks, then stuck the gun in her back.

She gasped. "What?"

Gabe was startled by how alone he felt at that second.

"Time to leave. Any heroics would be an unwise decision."

Fear rattled in her throat. "Okay."

Gabe eased Shannon away from the computer area, past the cashier's desk and toward the sliding-glass front doors. He didn't know who the person was that Shannon had recognized, but the overweight man had suddenly left his copying on the machine against the far wall.

"Keep walking," Gabe ordered.

For a moment Shannon contemplated stepping back into Gabe to throw him off balance. He was fighting fatigue and the drugs she'd given him. She had a chance to break away, get to Chief Bremen and...

Suddenly, she remembered seeing Jimmy Joe Bremen's name on the computer. *And now he's here.*

She combed the place looking for another cop. There were no uniforms, not even anyone watching her protectively. Chief Bremen was alone.

But why? Didn't he need backup to save her from this lunatic with Colombian drug-lord friends?

Shannon had too many questions and things were moving too quickly. She didn't understand why Chief Bremen's name was on that computer disk, but she knew Gabe's gun could go off at any second.

Oddly, it didn't frighten her half as much as seeing Chief Bremen in plainclothes. Intuition told her Chief

Bremen had not come to save her but was here to save himself.

The glass doors seemed an eternity away, but Gabe kept his eyes glued to them. Jimmy Joe's coughing spasm was well under control as he easily walked right up behind Shannon and Gabe. Gabe could feel the man's heated anger flay the air between them.

"He's got a gun," Gabe whispered in Shannon's ear. "He'll use it. Don't panic, just go slow. Don't draw attention to us."

She nodded.

They were almost at the doors.

Suddenly a hand clamped down on Gabe's shoulder and a gun barrel rammed into his spine.

"See that van out there?" Jimmy Joe said to Gabe.

"Yeah."

"That's where we're going."

Gabe nodded as the automatic door opened. The rush of air was cool, but not cold, the sun blinding.

Shannon squinted, then stumbled. Her involuntary action was enough to give Gabe the edge he needed. He folded in half and rammed an elbow into Jimmy Joe's testicles.

"Oooomph!" The older man's knees buckled. His face turned red and he sank slowly to his knees.

"Run!" Gabe ordered Shannon.

Jimmy Joe raised his gun and fired. The bullet zinged past Gabe's head, just missing his skull by inches.

Shannon opened her mouth to scream but made no sound. Instead she bolted forward. Gabe ran faster.

In the distance the van engine started. Its tires screamed as it backed up toward Gabe and Shannon. It was gaining speed.

Shannon darted to the right of it, Gabe lunged to the left.

It raced backward, then stopped, and a man with a blond crew cut and camouflage T-shirt leaned out the window. He aimed an automatic rifle at them and began firing. Bullets flew everywhere.

Shannon covered her head with her arms, but she kept running. Gabe's legs were lead. He felt as if he were running in place, going nowhere, going to die.

"Hit the deck!" Gabe yelled to Shannon, but she didn't hear him. Gabe lunged for the pavement, then rolled onto his back, aimed the gun at the van and fired a round.

Shannon kept her eyes on the Mustang. No matter how fast she ran, it seemed to keep moving away from her, shrinking as it faded away. She ran harder.

The driver's window of the van rolled down and another automatic appeared. The van screamed as it skidded across the parking lot.

Gabe watched it move toward him, gaining speed, practically kissing his cheek. He fired at the van's tires and the front right tire blew. The van whirled, made a doughnut and slammed into a trio of parked cars, the driver falling unconscious against the steering wheel. The horn blared incessantly.

Gabe scrambled to his feet and took off toward Shannon.

Shannon felt as if she were flying. The Mustang was only steps away.

"Oh God, the keys!" Shannon remembered she'd left them inside the copy center.

"Shit!" Gabe couldn't believe what he was hearing.

Just then another round of bullets pinged off the Mustang's trunk as Jimmy Joe fired again, but his aim was misdirected by an ear-splitting woman's scream from behind him.

Gabe ducked the bullets. "Get in the car!"

"I left the keys inside!" she yelled, pointing toward the copy center.

"I'll go back."

Gabe's legs were on fire as he raced directly toward Jimmy Joe. The old man's eyes were bulging with pain and victory as he raised his gun, patiently waiting to get a clean shot off.

Gabe turned on the heat. He ran awkwardly due to his slack muscles, his body like a sail flapping in the breeze as he shifted his weight from right foot to left.

A quartet of people had exited Kinko's, morbid human curiosity putting them in harm's way.

"Get back inside!" Gabe yelled at them, flapping his arms overhead. "He's got a gun! I'm a cop! Call the police!"

Gabe shot across the distance up to Jimmy Joe, and kicked the gun out of his hand before the stunned man could pull the trigger. Then he kicked him in the jaw. Jimmy Joe rolled backward like a humpty-dumpty doll.

Gabe broke through the gathering crowd and yelled out to the cashier, "I'm a cop! Call 911. Get an ambulance and tell them to send me backup!"

The cashier was too rattled to ask questions and did as Gabe instructed.

He was nearly out of breath as he bounded up the single step to the computer area, snatched his keys and retreated.

He sailed past the unconscious Chief Bremen, still not knowing his identity, and one of two assailants stumbled out of the van, dazed.

"He's not Colombian! My God! How many people does Cassalia have working for him?"

Gabe knew the cops would be crawling all over the strip center in minutes. Every second counted. His lungs felt as if they were about to explode, but he managed to get to the Mustang, where Shannon was already seated behind the wheel. He saw her anxious eyes watching him from the rearview mirror. She was rooting for him. The passenger's door was open. She'd opened it—for him.

He tossed her the keys. She started the car and peeled away from the parking lot in record time. Just as she pulled into traffic, a black Mercedes pulled alongside them. Gabe knew before he looked—the Colombians had come.

"Damn!"

Shannon's eyes were wild.

"Gun it!"

"I am!" she yelled.

Traffic was heavy as cars positioned themselves in the turning lane, focused on the band of fast-food restaurants. Gabe shoved his foot against Shannon's, forcing the accelerator to the floor.

"You're crazy!" she screamed as they plunged ahead.

Gabe grabbed the steering wheel, ramming them from one side of the road to the other. The Mercedes began to gain ground. Shannon saw the red light ahead. Traffic was already moving through the intersection.

"Hold on!" Gabe warned as the Mustang's tires careened around a trio of cars, nearly broadsiding them. The Mercedes pursued relentlessly, but just as it lunged ahead, about to overtake them, a city bus drove through the light.

The Mercedes slammed against the connecting rig between the bus and its trailer and the bus dragged the Mercedes a half block before coming to a stop.

The uninjured passengers leaned out the windows, cursing and flipping the bird at the Mercedes driver who had interrupted their scheduled transit.

Gabe watched the chaos behind him increase through the rear window. His heart was pounding and his lungs were raw, but he was alive. They were alive.

"Drive west four miles, then I'll show you a short-cut."

"To where?" she asked, shooting the car down the feeder to the interstate.

"California."

"What did you say?"

"California."

Shannon slammed on the brakes so hard, if Gabe hadn't been wearing his seat belt he would have been kissing the silver hood ornament.

"Are you nuts?" he demanded.

"No, you are. I can't go to California."

"You can and will."

"The hell I will! Don't you understand? I can never go back to California! Never!" Fear crystallized into panic. Shannon started crying hysterically. Her eyes were as big as saucers as she began hitting Gabe with her fist, screaming over and over, "I can never go back! You bastard, why can't you see that?

"I can't take this anymore," she sobbed, reaching for the door and missing the handle. "I've had it with you. I'm outta here!"

"Shannon! Stop!" he shouted back, trying to grab her arm. She swatted back at him, clumsily missing her mark.

Gabe finally grabbed her hands, fending off her attack. "Shannon, what's the matter with you? Snap out of it. I have to go to California. You have to go with me."

"I can't," she cried, her face awash in tears.

"We can't stay here. We'll die."

"I'll die if I go to California."

"That's a long time between then and now. Right now, step on that gas and get us out of here."

"I won't, I tell you! I won't! I won't!"

"Shannon, stop!" Gabe said, slapping her across the face to quiet her hysteria.

Her hand shot to her cheek. She held her breath and glared at him, but she stopped fighting.

"I'll drive," he said. He got out of the car and raced to the driver's side while holding his hand to his painful ribs. Breathing seemed impossible, but he was learning how to forget the pain. Getting back in, he said, "You're going to have to learn to trust me."

"I c-can't, I can't," she said quietly to herself repeatedly.

Gabe floored the engine as sirens screamed behind him.

20

Shannon had outsmarted the dream for years.

She'd worked double shifts, even triple shifts, so that she'd be too exhausted to think. She knew the alternative was worse.

She had not chosen to visit the dream again; the situation had been forced upon her. Gabe had robbed her of her free will. She was a target for murder just like him. But unlike him, she could not escape the horror of her reality in sleep.

The dream was more than a nightmare—it was hell.

Flames leaped around her, consuming her, burning her flesh. She could smell her hair as it melted from the heat. She was being tortured, body and soul. She knew the identity of her persecutors, the ones who lived peacefully now that she was gone. Now that she was not in California anymore. They promised to come after her if she ever returned. She had promised herself she never would.

From the edges of her mind she heard Gabe's voice. He was yet another among the horde of tormentors sent to seek her out, make her pay reparation. But for what?

Even in those few short hours she was forced to sleep, Shannon continually asked that same question.

What had she done that had been so evil, so wicked? Why hadn't she found solitude in obscurity? Why was it life kept pulling her from the shadows? Revealing her?

Fears crept over Shannon as she slept. Then it began again. The screaming. The incredibly heart-ripping screams of her child.

My baby! I must save him! Save him! As always, Shannon ran. Ran away from the flames, then into the flames.

But the screaming continued. It filled her head, then her heart. At last, it scathed her soul.

She stood amid the flames in the dream. She wanted to burn. Incinerate. Be one with her child. But it was too late. Her baby was dead. He was never coming back. Not even in a dream.

"Shannon! Wake up!" Gabe shook her shoulders.

"What..." She opened her eyes, but all she saw was white.

"What the hell's the matter with you?" Gabe asked.

"What?" She tried to focus, but she still saw nothing but white. Then Gabe's face came into view.

Pain, like an ax splitting her head in two, nearly blinded her. She was slumped over in the passenger's seat. Gabe was driving.

"You were screaming," he said. His hand was gentle as it caressed her shoulder, rubbed her neck.

"You hit me."

"You were hysterical."

"Where am I? I thought I was leaving you."

He nodded. "You fool. I had to save you. If I'd let you go, they would have caught you. They would have killed you, damn it."

"That's my choice."

"Obviously you have a death wish. Otherwise you wouldn't have done anything so stupid." He leaned over the steering wheel, squinting through the opaque windshield.

She realized they were in the midst of a snowstorm. "Where are we?"

"North of Wichita Falls," Gabe said. "Heading to Amarillo."

"I can't see a thing."

"Neither can I. Good thing I know these old roads."

"I thought only Interstate 40 went from Amarillo to Wichita Falls."

"Right. Where the cops can make the car. Not to mention a few other fine folk we left back there."

Shannon kept silent.

Gabe let his anger fade. "So when did you last drive this way?"

"I haven't," she lied. She'd crossed Amarillo when she'd come to Louisiana from California.

"I see that being on the edge of death hasn't forced you to tell the truth yet."

"I heard it somewhere," she replied, putting her hand against the window. "Frost? Inside?" She needed to change the subject.

He nodded. "A bullet screwed up the electrical system. Only the wipers and lights work."

"Great." She folded her arms over her chest to keep warm.

"So you gonna tell me about your nightmare?"

Shannon's back muscles constricted. "No."

"Fine."

A strong gust of wind whiplashed the car, but Gabe kept the spinning wheels on the road.

"You're good at this," she remarked, hoping to take his mind off her. "You really do know this road."

"Yeah...." His voice trailed off. "I can see lights ahead. Streetlights and...a truck stop and motel."

They should have been on the other side of Amarillo by now. They were way off the schedule he'd set for them.

He was exhausted, hungry and thirsty, but if they stopped too long it could cost them their lives. "We better keep going."

Strung to the limits of her patience, Shannon smacked him on the arm and grabbed the steering wheel from him. "Like hell we are!"

The car swerved off the road, skidded on gravel and hit a patch of ice, throwing them into a severe tailspin.

"Are you crazy?" He pried her hands off the wheel. He took a deep breath and looked at her huddled angrily against her door.

"I've got a splitting headache, thanks to you, and I have to use the bathroom. *And* I'm hungry. So hungry, in fact, I don't really give a damn if they kill us or not. Okay?"

He glared at her.

Her eyes were rigid, unyielding.

"Okay!" he said.

He drove into the snowy parking lot and parked away from the restaurant in the shadow of a billboard. The snow was nearly five inches deep, erasing parking-slot demarcation lines and covering curbs.

"Do you need an injection before we go in?" she asked him.

"Yeah, but I'd fall asleep. And as tired as I am, I

might not watch you as closely as I did the last time to make sure you don't give me too much."

Shannon cast him a sidelong look.

Gabe smiled. "I've been around a few blocks."

"Just how long were you conscious in the hospital before you tried to kill me?"

"I never tried to kill you. I *threatened* to kill you. There's a difference," he said, pulling out his gun.

"Oh, for God's sake," she groaned and opened the door, involuntarily shivering at the sight of the weapon.

Gabe was equally as tired of it all. He put the gun in his waistband. "Let's get some coffee, then I'll decide if we stay here tonight or press on."

Locking the car with the remote, Gabe followed closely behind Shannon as they walked into the brightly lit diner.

Plastic poinsettia garlands festooned the windows and an artificial tree sat in a far corner, reminding Shannon that this was the season of peace and goodwill toward men. She couldn't help thinking that maybe the saying had been misinterpreted and was meant to be: "Peace to men of goodwill."

She wanted to laugh aloud at the irony. The last thing she felt was peaceful. Fearful, yes. Peaceful, no.

From Gabe's gun to the perilous weather it seemed fate wanted her destroyed. Whether she ate or slept was immaterial. She was as good as dead.

In the far corner was a red-painted sign indicating the rest rooms. Quickly, she noted there was no exit other than the front door. Outside, huge diesel trucks pulled up underneath a fluorescent-lighted canopy to the pumps. The snow was falling so thickly she almost missed seeing a row of four phone booths beyond. If she could get to one of those phone booths, she could try to call Ben.

He would take her back to Shreveport and she wouldn't have to return to California. She'd be home-free.

"Where do you want to sit?" she heard Gabe ask.

"By the window," she replied, glancing away from the counter where every stool was occupied with overweight truck drivers conversing about the storm. Realizing Gabe saw through her lies, he'd know she was already praying for a bathroom window. She slid onto the sticky plastic seat at the booth, making certain she faced away from the rest room. If she could just get to those pay phones...

"Coffee, burgers and fries for a start," Gabe ordered for both of them.

Shannon blinked at the peroxided waitress with the Dolly Parton body. She'd been so preoccupied she hadn't heard the young woman approach them.

"Y'all want those burgers all the way?" she cooed directly at Gabe.

"All the way," he said, handing the menus back and looking directly at the woman's enormous breasts. "Dixie."

Dixie sucked in a huge breath as she shoved her order pad into her apron pocket. "All the way is best," she purred.

"No onions for me," Shannon said.

"I understand, honey," Dixie said familiarly. "If I had a hunk like him, I'd wanna be real close, too."

Shannon sipped her ice water. "They give me gas."

Dixie's eyes bounced away from Shannon and back to Gabe. Her face was lit with lust. "Y'all staying the night?"

Gabe bit his tongue to keep from laughing. "I was thinking about it. Do you happen to know if there are any vacancies next door?"

"Sure do. My mama runs the motel and this place. She's the cashier. You can pay for your meal and the room at the same time. We take Visa and American Express."

"How about cash?"

"That, too." She winked and left to place their order with the cook.

Gabe smiled to himself as he watched Dixie's backside. "Nice place."

"You're disgusting."

"Yeah? Well, welcome to my world. This is the kind of place I'm used to—country highways, diners, truckers and truck stops. People who are just trying to make ends meet. They're my clients."

"Yet you have wealthy friends as well. People like Adam. And what about that man—Peter? I bet he's rich, huh?"

"I suppose."

Shannon wasn't giving any quarter. "Suppose or know?"

"Okay, so I went skiing with him in Aspen a couple times. He's got a suite at the Little Nell Hotel, the only five-star in Aspen. Even the new Ritz-Carlton isn't that expensive."

"Is it pretty there at Christmas?" she asked, still thinking about the pay phones.

"Incredibly," he answered.

Dixie returned with two cups of coffee. Winking at Gabe and then sashaying away before he had a chance to accept or reject her flirtations, Dixie effectively garnered the attention of every man in the room.

Shannon couldn't have asked for a better diversion. "When she comes back, ask her for some cream," she said, rising, picking up her purse that held Ben's card.

"Wait a minute. You're not going anywhere by yourself."

"Fine. Come with me to the ladies' room for all I care."

"Go," he replied sheepishly.

Shannon didn't miss Dixie's broad smile as she passed, nor the fact that she made a beeline back to their booth.

I couldn't have planned this any better. If Dixie keeps Gabe busy...

Entering the ladies' room, Shannon's hopes died. "Damn! No window!"

But Shannon had noticed that the entrance to the kitchen was next to the men's room. If there was a door out the back, she could make her way through the kitchen, then out to the phone booths, make her call and be back before Gabe knew what had happened.

Flinging back the door, Shannon took three giant strides to the kitchen entrance. Suddenly her body slammed up against Gabe. He wasn't smiling.

"Hey, honey. Dixie here was just introducing me to her mama. I was telling her to make my burger rare. How did you want yours?"

Shannon's glare was lethal. Gabe's was serious.

Shannon plastered a simple smile on her face as she glanced over Gabe's shoulder to see an older version of Dixie standing over a griddle waving a spatula at her.

"I'll make yours well done, honey, just like your husband says you like 'em."

Shannon's eyes flung back to Gabe. "Husband?" she whispered.

"It was the only way I could get the room. Seems they're Baptists."

Shannon began to lose it. "Since when did you get religion?"

He grabbed her by the elbow, escorting her to their booth. "Ever since you thought you'd make a run for it out the back door."

"But I didn't—"

"Bullshit. I'm hungry, tired and I really don't want to get into a domestic squabble here in front of all these people."

"Don't even try to be cute with me, Gabe," Shannon muttered, angry at herself for not making good her plan.

They slid into the booth.

"Damn it, Shannon. Why do you make this harder on both of us than it needs to be?"

"Oh, now I'm the one to blame for all this crap you've gotten us into. I was just going to the bathroom."

"Do you think I didn't see you casing this place when we walked in? Where did you think you were going to go? Hop on one of those rigs? Stow away in a van? Or maybe you just wanted to phone home."

The instant his words struck their target, Shannon's head jerked back.

"Bingo."

She hated him, really hated him. "If you're so smart, why didn't you do something with your life instead of selling insurance? You could've been an attorney."

"Nah. The drop in income would have killed me."

"Huh?"

He leaned closer, his eyes boring menacingly into hers. "How long is it going to take for you to realize I'm not the kind of stupid jerk you seem to have obviously known too well in your past. I make a damn good living. I've been places and seen things you couldn't imagine. Just because I wound up at your charity hospital does not make me indigent. I know exactly what I'm doing, Shannon. I'm not about to give in or give up. We're going to make it through this. You got me?"

"And what if we don't?" She swallowed hard.

His eyes were earnest. "We will."

21

Ben answered his cellular. "Make it good," he said, lighting his twenty-fifth cigarette of the day.

"Bremen's disappeared into thin air."

"I'm not hearing this."

"And those two buddies of his? Lunatic-fringe material all the way. Satch Jessel and Grady would barbecue their mothers for laughs. They look country, but they're both well trained by Uncle Sam. Now they're on a Colombian payroll."

Ben rammed his palm against the steering wheel of the car he'd rented at DFW Airport. "Damn! Is there anybody in this part of the country *not* working for Alejandro?"

"Only you, Maestro."

"I don't believe this!"

Ben flipped his cigarette out the window, the bright orange cinders looking like a comet's tail as he sped down Interstate 40 at ninety-two miles an hour.

"Give me some good news."

"I haven't got any, except a make on our gal Sal."

"Where is she?" Ben heard the anxiety in his own voice.

"She's at a truck stop east of Amarillo."

"That's more like it," Ben replied, smiling.

"You want me to have the local authorities go in and pick her up for you?"

"No way. I don't need someone botching this up. I don't want her to be afraid or do something stupid and get hurt. If she sees me, she'll stay calm."

"Always the Boy Scout, eh, Maestro?"

"Have you gotten a make on her yet? Her real name?"

"No. She's a phantom…which makes me wonder what she's hiding. I bet it's a doozy."

"Keep looking. I want to know."

"Read you loud and clear."

Ben knew now that Shannon was either in hiding or hiding something and his hunches had never been wrong. He'd observed her for nearly a month at the hospital. He thought she was aloof, withdrawn and incapable of hurting anyone's feelings, much less murdering someone. He'd found himself responding to a deep sadness in her. He sensed it was a strain on her to remain distant from her co-workers, from him.

Each time she pushed him away, she'd pulled him in closer. She was like a magnet and he was nothing more than steel. He couldn't have stayed away from her if he'd tried. And Ben hadn't wanted to try.

He liked to imagine her laughing freely with friends, going to parties. He believed he saw a brilliant inner light in her eyes, though she often kept her eyes lowered. He believed she chose nursing due to a profound altruistic drive, unlike others he'd met at the hospital.

No, he was convinced Shannon was more than special.

He remembered her apartment and the fact that he'd not seen the first clue to her past. The place was strange, possibly fanatical in its detachment, its lack of personality. He'd sensed she was hiding from life amid possessions once owned by others.

He lit another cigarette, then paused, noticing his hand was shaking. Shannon had gotten under his skin but good.

Ben rubbed the back of his neck. It was best he keep his mind on finding her rather than on what he wanted from her once he saved her.

"How could one woman slip through the cracks like that?" Ben asked, chewing his bottom lip.

"Hundreds do it every day, Ben. You know that."

"Yeah, but they have reasons. Motivations," Ben said gruffly. "Is this a nightmare, or what?"

"You okay? You sound like you're losin' it."

"I'll be fine."

"Good. When you get closer to the motel, I'll give you an update. Okay? And Maestro, stay off the cell as much as possible."

"Why?"

"Remember our South American buddies from the motel?"

"Yeah."

"We finally impounded their Mercedes away from the local police. These boys are good to themselves. They buy the real expensive toys. Trust me, they can hear a bird fart from miles away."

"I'm off then," Ben replied, ending his call and shoving his foot against the accelerator.

An hour before dawn, Chief Bremen dialed New Orleans from a pay phone near Amarillo. He used coins to pay for the call. He was paranoid of traces and any tracks that could indict him. He was too close to winning not to be careful.

"You can tell our Spanish friend to ease up."

"You've got the disk?" Blane Blair asked anxiously.

"Just as good as. We spotted them at a motel. In the morning when they head out of Amarillo where we won't have witnesses, we'll nail them."

"Call me the minute you have that disk." Blane started to sign off. "Oh, and Bremen."

"Yeah?"

"Just remember your Swiss trust fund was one of the accounts these bastards cleaned out."

"Why do you think I'm out here in the middle of nowhere looking for them myself? I coulda had Satch and Grady take care of this alone. What's on that disk is my life. I don't trust anybody that much. And when I find this bastard, I'm gonna skin him alive. The girl, too, now that she can make me." Chief Bremen's blood pressure skyrocketed.

"I don't care what you do with them. Just get the disk."

"Am I going to have any more interference from Alejandro's men?"

Blane laughed. "Idiot. His ace patrol is across the street watching you."

"What the hell for?"

"Follow you, he finds the disk. Besides, Alejandro doesn't trust you, or haven't you figured that out?"

"Damn it!" Chief Bremen slammed down the phone.

22

Sardia stood squarely in Chief Bremen's path.

"I will take care of this," Sardia said flatly, pulling his Magnum .357 with silencer out of his shoulder holster for Bremen to see.

Jimmy Joe snorted. "You candy ass." He pushed past the Colombian, walking toward the Amarillo Motel where Gabe and Shannon had booked a room three hours earlier.

Sardia's expression was implacable. As always when serving Alejandro, Sardia experienced no emotion. He didn't ask about his targets. He didn't want to know anything more than their identity. Names meant nothing to him. People meant nothing to him. Money, power, possessions meant nothing to him.

Loyalty. That was the virtue he esteemed. Sardia was loyal to Alejandro because Alejandro had saved him from his sexually abusive father when he was nine years old.

Sardia didn't remember the first time his father raped him, but he remembered the last. That was the day he turned on his father with a knife, trying to cut off the man's dick. Instead, his father had grabbed the knife and sliced Sardia's face, leaving a wide gash.

Sardia had run into the street, bleeding profusely, carrying his pain inside him as he had all his life.

Alejandro's white limousine had been stopped at a tobacco shop where more dope was sold than cigars. Sardia's tears had obscured his vision and the young boy had bumped into the impeccably dressed man.

Alejandro's bodyguard had been incensed that Sardia had bled onto his employer's fine white wool suit, wanting to strike Sardia. But Alejandro stopped the guard and took Sardia into the limousine, ordering the driver to take them to the hospital, where Sardia's cheek was cleaned and stitched.

Alejandro coerced the truth from Sardia. In return for his honesty, he promised to take care of Sardia as long as he did everything he was told to do. Sardia promised.

He was a natural assassin. His skills came easily, as if he'd been born to the job. He simply pretended that each target was his father. Having buried his emotions with his childhood, Sardia killed with clarity, precision and dispassion.

Therefore, it wasn't anger that caused Sardia to ask, "What did you call me?" It was a well-calculated tactic.

"Candy ass."

Jimmy Joe glanced back over his shoulder just enough for Sardia to put a bullet through his forehead.

Jimmy Joe dropped to the ground with a heavy thud.

Sardia stepped over the body and crossed the highway to where his driver was parked in the Mercedes.

Satch and Grady walked out of the Pancake House just in time to see the man in the expensive dark suit shoot Chief Bremen.

"Holy hell! Did you see that?" Grady asked.

"Get back," Satch ordered as they both slid into the shadows behind their pickup truck.

"Is that him? The Colombian Bremen told us about?"

"Has to be."

"I say we get outta here!" Grady said.

Satch smiled a half grin, his eyes steely. "Just when things are gettin' interesting? Not on your life."

Grady rubbed his stubble as he watched the Mercedes pull into the motel parking lot, then circle around to the back.

Though the lighting around the motel was poor, there was no mistaking the two slim figures carrying assault weapons with silencers as they positioned themselves on either side of the door to room 105.

Sardia signaled his partner, who picked the door lock, then cut the door chain with wire cutters. They burst into the room and fired a round of bullets into the two sleeping figures in the bed. Down and feathers flew as the bullets hit pillows bunched under the blanket and bedspread Gabe had formed to look like bodies.

Before the assassins realized their mistake, Gabe sprang from the closet, fired the pistol he'd stolen from their colleague and killed the driver.

Sardia's eyes were cool as they met Gabe's, assessing his ability to react, seeing the flash of fear, anxiety and triumph in his gaze.

Sardia calculated his own victory. "Give me the disk and you live!"

"It's on the nightstand, asshole." Gabe's eyes shot to the black and silver disk on the night table.

Sardia followed his gaze. It was only a brief flick of

the eyes, but it was the break Gabe had planned on, prayed he'd get.

Gabe fired.

Sardia's eyes filled with surprise and he fell to the floor.

Gabe sprinted across the room, frisked both bodies for ID, money, car keys, ammunition and guns. He crammed as much as he could into his pockets and fled the room.

He raced to the far end of the building and across the back parking lot to the Dumpsters. There, he opened the Dumpster lid.

"Come on!" He reached his hand inside, half expecting Shannon to be gone.

"Is it over?"

"Yes." He hoped she wouldn't ask for details. Gabe didn't want to think about what had just happened. "Lucky thing you saw that Mercedes when you did."

"But that was hours ago. And you said it wasn't them," she replied, climbing out of the bin, brushing filth off her clothes.

"Yeah, but it got me thinking. The last two they sent after us were well equipped. We'd gone too long without seeing anyone. I could almost feel them closing in. I've always had good instincts."

"Well, you called this one right."

They dashed across the lot to the parked car. Gabe took out the keys and hit the remote. The door locks popped open.

Gabe drove the Mercedes through a back alley to a service road that led to the south, away from the interstate.

Shannon looked over her shoulder through the

back window at the motel as it disappeared from view.

She didn't see Sardia stumble from the room, holding his side where the bullet had narrowly missed his lung. And she didn't see him flag down a trucker and hitch a ride. Nor did she see the pair of men across the street jump into their pickup truck, drive past the dead body of their former friend and take up pursuit.

Shannon was too busy thinking that Gabe was right. She looked at him. "How many were there?"

"Two."

"Just like the last time? Or were they different?"

"The same. Colombian."

"Did you kill them?"

"No."

"But they'll come after us."

"Shannon, even if I killed these two, there would be two more to take their place, then two more."

"Until they kill us."

"Yes," Gabe replied quietly. "Their boss probably has an army of hit men. We know where his fifty million bucks are and he doesn't."

"You left the disk in the motel like you planned?"

"The copy I made, yes."

"What's the difference?"

"At the copy center, just as we were leaving, I made an adjustment to the Swiss-account number where all the money is stashed."

"I thought you didn't know anything about computers."

"I'm a fast learner," he said. "Anyway, that's the information they'll get on the disk."

"And the original?"

"I still have it. There's only one flaw to my plan."

"Flaw? What kind of flaw?"

"These guys are smart. I'm afraid they'll figure out what I know...that my friend, Peter Dominic, is involved in this thing somehow. I was hoping to get to Peter before they did."

"How can Peter help us?"

"Hopefully by telling me what the hell is going on, for one." Gabe didn't tell her that he needed to hear Peter admit he'd plotted against Gabe, let him rot in that hospital without coming to his aid, betrayed him. Gabe's sense of justice needed closure.

Gabe didn't mind a lot of the crap he'd been dealt in life. He'd chalked it up to fate. But when his best friend screwed with his life, that was something different. Gabe had trusted his friends blindly, and it had nearly gotten him killed. If he was going to die, he wanted to know why.

He couldn't help thinking how good it would feel to sink his fist into Peter's traitorous face.

"So what do you plan to gain from this?" she asked.

"At the very least some time."

"Time..." she said, thinking the word meant so many more things to her now than it did before. Only days ago, she'd meant nothing to anyone. Now she knew everything on the computer disk, just like Gabe. She'd read the screen at the copy center even though she hadn't understood much at the time. Now she did. She understood too much.

Gabe was no longer the enemy, but she almost wished he were. Gabe had a conscience. These assassins who seemed to come in waves, overtaking them, nearly annihilating them, had none. It was their job to kill.

As ludicrous as it was that she should be their target, she realized that Gabe was right—no matter where she and Gabe went, these men or others would track them down. They were relentless. Their numbers alone tipped the odds in their favor.

As the Mercedes sped through the snowstorm, Shannon couldn't help thinking their flight superfluous, a waste of time.

"What makes you push so hard?" she asked as hopelessness flooded her. "There's too many of them. They'll keep after us until we're dead."

"I don't give a damn what the odds are! We're not dead yet."

"But we will be." She looked out the window, the cover of night obscuring the scenery. She felt tears stinging her eyes, but she refused to let him know how scared she was.

"I'm not going to let them hurt you, Shannon."

She looked at him then. His eyes were focused on the road, the lights from the dash casting an eerie glow over his features. She noticed the determined set of his jaw, as if he could, and would, take on the world. She could almost see the barrage of thoughts careen through his head, and with each he chewed his bottom lip while he analyzed their merit.

He mastered the slippery road better than she could. The snowstorm posed no more threat to him than did the near-death scene behind them. What made him so indomitable? So fearless? Shannon had never known a man like him. Her father had died in a car accident with her mother over ten years ago, long before she'd looked at men as possible mates. Long before she'd gotten married and become a mother.

She had little adult criteria for what a man should

or shouldn't be for her. But she had known she wanted to feel safe. Safe from the abandonment she felt when her father died. Safe from the pain she'd known with her husband, David.

She closed her eyes.

"What's wrong?"

"Nothing," she replied, putting the past away. "I was just thinking."

"About what?"

When he turned to look at her, the moment became surreal. Even in the dim light his eyes probed hers. This time there was nothing guarded in them. She'd never looked so deeply into another person before. She almost felt her breath taken away. He was no longer a fantasy imbued with qualities born from her imagination. He was flesh, bone and spirit, and more real to her than anyone she'd ever met.

"Us," she finally said.

"What about us?"

Suddenly, it mattered very much to her that they survive. Her smile was slow to blossom. "Maybe we'll make it after all."

With survival on his mind, Gabe hadn't realized the shift that had taken place until he saw Shannon's smile.

Its effect on him was shattering. Up till now she'd just been his conduit to freedom. He'd needed her. He'd needed someone to get him through those first hours.

Callously, he told himself that she'd simply been in the wrong place at the wrong time. He'd intended to get the hell out of the hospital and find out what was on the disk. Naively he'd thought he'd go back to his old life in Fort Worth.

But none of that had happened. Instead, he found himself giving more than a damn about Shannon. He'd managed to rationalize that his sexual desire for her was simply a reaction to the intensity of their flight, danger and anxiety mutating into a passion of sorts.

Now he realized he'd been shortsighted. He desperately wanted her to be safe.

Unfortunately, he couldn't whisk her off to a mountain cave or lock her in a secret room. Safety was nowhere to be found at the moment, except in transit. As long as they kept moving he could keep them alive. And he wished to hell he was smart enough to know what to do after that.

23

San Francisco, California

Peter Dominic lived in a three-story condo on the side of a high hill in Tiburon overlooking Richardson Bay and the Golden Gate beyond.

The security system in the house was unsophisticated and out-of-date, an indication to the Colombian assassin approaching the house that Peter Dominic probably did not own valuables.

At the front door, he broke the security laser beam with a circuit interrupter. The alarm was silent. He entered the house. The door to the right of the vestibule led to the garage, which he found empty.

Stealthily, he climbed the Persian-carpeted stairs to the second-floor main living area. Just beyond the closed French doors he saw a gold and cobalt blue velvet–draped room, elegant French antiques and a person's shadow lying across the highly polished wooden floor.

The shadow moved back and forth as if pacing in the room beyond, which he guessed to be a kitchen since he could see the dining room from his vantage point. Inspecting the door, he found it electronically free. He opened it noiselessly.

"I was like, wow, when he asked me!" the young

girl's voice said into the telephone. "No joke. Tif, you gotta see this place! Frisco guys are rich. Forget that crap in Oakland. The money's over here, I tell ya."

The assassin scanned the living room, then crossed it on cat's paws. Opening the door to a huge armoire, he found expensive stereo equipment, but no television, VCR or cable box. He eased the door shut. Keeping his back against the wall, he inspected the dining room. An incredibly expensive chandelier hung in the middle of the room. The wall coverings, drapes and hardware would cost a fortune, but the room was devoid of any furniture and there were faded rectangles on the walls where artwork used to hang.

"Divorce," he mumbled. He shrugged his shoulders and lunged soundlessly back to the French doors and the staircase that led to the third floor.

The girl in the kitchen was squealing now. "Tif, this guy is paying me five hundred bucks to hang for a week and water plants, for God's sake. I dunno, he's skiing someplace. You know I only like the beach, so I didn't pay much attention. Yeah, yeah. I got a number."

The assassin found exactly what he was looking for in the sitting area off the bedroom. The personal computer was ancient, nearly twelve years old, but it didn't matter.

He smiled. "A hard drive is a hard drive is a..."

Booting up the PC, he scanned the screen. "C'mon baby, show me the money. Swiss money."

He frowned as he searched directory after directory. Nothing. He opened the desk drawers, then he inspected the collection of colored plastic computer-disk boxes that sat in a neat row on the desktop. Still nothing.

"Who are you?" the young girl asked, clearly startled to find a stranger in the house.

"Joseph," he replied as naturally as if his mother had walked into the room. He continued his search for the disk.

"How did you get in?" Her surprise was infused with indignation.

"I have a key."

"I don't think so," she replied smartly, putting a hand on her narrow hip. "Peter said I had the only key."

"Peter forgot that I have one, too." Joseph went to the closet, hoping to find a shelf filled with more plastic disk containers. "What's your name?"

"Melanie."

"And you are...?"

"The house sitter. Now, are you gonna tell me who the hell you are and what you're doing here?"

"I'm from the office. Peter gave me a report to get done before the end of the year. The only problem was, he failed to give me the disk in order to do the work. So, if I don't find it, it's my ass."

"Oh," she said casually, tossing her overpermed blond curls over her shoulder. She chewed on a black-painted fingernail as she watched him march into the bathroom. A wall of white cabinets faced sliding mirrored closet doors, making the place look like a honeycomb.

Joseph inspected one cabinet after another, his frustration mounting with each unsuccessful attempt. He should have been out of here long ago and it didn't help that the valley girl gold digger had discovered him.

"Must be important, huh?"

"Yeah, real important."

"Does it tell you how to make money in the market? What stocks to buy? Insider-trading secrets, maybe?" She grinned greedily.

"What kind of classes are they teaching in high school?"

Haughtily sticking her chin in the air, she replied, "I'm a sophomore at USF."

"Majoring in?" Joseph rifled through another half-dozen cubbyholes.

"M-o-n-e-y," she said, eyeing Joseph suspiciously.

"Accounting? Finance?" He banged another door.

Melanie jumped, then she started backing away toward the bedroom door. "Are...are you sure Peter said this thing was here?"

"Yeah."

"Then how come he didn't tell you *exactly* where it was?"

Joseph was getting exasperated. "He said it was on the computer."

"And it's not?"

"No." Losing his temper, he furiously slammed the last door shut. "Damn!" he muttered to himself.

His anger startled and frightened Melanie. "I...I think I'll get a Coke while you finish." She raced down the stairs.

Joseph rolled his eyes. "Bitch!"

Melanie couldn't get to the portable phone fast enough. She double-checked the number for Peter's office that he'd left her under the refrigerator magnet. Her hand was shaking as she punched out the numbers.

"Hello?"

Joseph ran down the stairs in leaps. He shot to the

kitchen and snatched the phone from Melanie by cracking her wrist with the side of his hand aikido fashion. He struck her again just above the elbow, which made her arm go limp.

Her terrified eyes locked on his. Her jaw dropped as she attempted to scream.

His third blow cracked the thinnest area of the skull at the side of the right eye next to the temple, which killed her instantly.

She dropped to the floor at his feet.

Putting the earpiece to his ear, he heard a recording. "Thank you for calling Dominic Investment Firm. Our offices are closed for the holidays. We will resume our regular office hours on January second at nine o'clock. In case of an emergency, please dial 555–9456. At the tone please leave a message."

Joseph smiled and dialed the emergency number. He heard a second message.

"This is Peter Dominic. I'm unavailable right now, but I check my messages every hour. Please leave your name and number and I'll get back to you."

"Damn technology," Joseph said and hung up the phone.

24

Shannon drove the Mercedes deep into New Mexico. The road was virtually empty since most farmers in the area were already home. Small houses and a trailer here and there sat long distances from each other, plastic wreaths and garlands sparkling in the late-afternoon sun.

Though drained physically, Gabe was still unable to doze off for more than fifteen minutes at a time. Allowing Shannon control of the car was still a risky proposition.

"I'll take over for a while."

"That's okay. I'm fine," she said.

She *was* fine. From the looks of her she seemed well rested and at ease. He couldn't figure it out. If anything, she was under more pressure than he. Just her continual search for a way to break from him was bound to sap her energy.

"How do you do it?" he asked.

"Do what?"

"Manage so well with virtually no sleep."

Her smile died quickly. "Sleep is the last thing I need."

"You mean, because of your nightmares."

"You know about them?" She glanced at him, hoping he was only stabbing in the dark searching for the truth. But his sharp gaze told her she wasn't that lucky.

"You talk in your sleep."

She swallowed hard. "What did I say?"

"Mumbles mostly, stuff I couldn't make out. Except for the terror." He sat up, facing her. "Who was dying, Shannon?"

She didn't know how it happened. She'd been able to control her emotions for a long time. A lifetime. Two lifetimes, it seemed. Her stomach knotted as old memories brought back the agony she'd struggled to forget but never could. Tears sprang to her eyes. She choked when she tried to speak. "My...son."

"God, I'm sorry. I didn't know."

She jabbed her fist to her lips to hold back her sobs. Her breath came in spasms. She'd been wrong to try to forget. She'd been shoving back her pain for so long, it now shoved back with relentless force.

She shook her head. "It's okay."

"No, it's not," he said as he reached out and carried her tear away on the pad of his finger. "How old was he?"

"Six months."

"What happened?"

Tears spilled when she shook her head. "He's dead, okay? What does it matter now?" Her tone was blasting.

He recoiled. "It doesn't matter to me." But Gabe could tell it mattered to her. She wore her guilt like a lead suit. He wished to hell he could help her, but he believed she wouldn't let anyone help her, least of all himself.

He put his hand on her shoulder, caressed her back and lingered on her arm. He could tell she was back there, in that horrid moment, reliving her terror, feeling every pain again.

She was unaware of his touch, as if she was numb.

She blinked away a rash of tears, but all she could see was the past. All she heard was the past—David's voice screaming at her one more time.

Damn you, Shannon! You've always been nothing but a bitch! Why can't you leave me alone? Or just go away? You know I don't want you. I don't love you.

Do it my way, Shannon, or hit the door!

Always so high and mighty! Miss Goody Two-Shoes. Too good to take a hit with me. If you love me, you'll do it. Show me you love me…me, not just my kid!

David's voice was always a hideous concoction of ego, drugs and self-pity. He hated his parents. He hated her. He hated the life she was trying to make for them.

Shannon knew the truth was that David Randall hated himself.

But all that belonged to the girl she used to be. She was Shannon Riley now. And she was still on the run, still caught in a life she didn't make.

Gabe watched as she wrestled with her demons, then came back to the present. Her face was furrowed and drawn, the exercise draining her more than their flight.

Gabe was astonished at his own reaction, hating the specters that threatened her. A latent chivalry emerged within him, spawning an intense frustration and impotence he'd never experienced before.

How could he help her if she wouldn't let him? And yet, how idiotic of him to want to become her champion when his role was that of kidnapper.

Again, he reached out to her, but the glare she gave

his hand was searing in its intensity. He retracted his hand. "Shannon, isn't there anything I can—"

"No. Nothing. Forget it." She took a deep breath. "I have."

"You have not! Let me help take your pain away."

"You?" Her laugh was high, trilling and raked with hysteria. "Now you want to be my savior? I don't think so. You've screwed with my brain enough already. One minute you look at me with eyes that make me want to run for my life, and the next I feel like my insides are melting. Suffice it to say, I liked you best when you were comatose."

What was there about her that made him think he'd lost his mind? She didn't just jerk his chain, she rattled it, yanked it and cast him out to lure. Somehow she'd managed to make him want her to want him. That was bad enough. But now he wanted to win her respect.

He had it bad, all right.

Gabe's voice was tender when he said, "I think I understand now why you refuse to deal with people. You have enough going on just dealing with your grief. But if you'd let me in...I could try—"

"It's my problem, okay?"

Her rejection hit him like a shot. He almost recoiled from the brunt of it. He wanted her pain to be his pain. He wanted to be her savior.

He looked away from the trouble he found in her face. "Okay," he said. "But would you step on it? There's no one around for miles. We need to make some good time."

"Sure," she replied, wiping her tears with her palm. She was glad to focus on her driving once again.

She glanced in her side-view mirror.

The last of the sun's rays glinted off a shiny red metallic short-bed pickup truck, complete with an expensive row of lights on the roll bar. The truck was coming up on them very fast.

"Who are they?" Shannon pointed behind her with her thumb.

"They?" Looking in the side mirror, Gabe's instincts shot into warp speed. "Gun it!"

"What?"

"Just do it!"

Gabe pulled out his gun and checked to make sure it was fully loaded.

"Oh God!" Shannon slammed her foot down on the accelerator.

Gabe saw the automatic rifle appear out of the passenger's window. Before he could roll his window down, the man on the passenger's side of the red truck fired off a volley of shots. The back windshield of the Mercedes shattered, spewing glass inside the car like hail.

Shannon screamed and tried to cover her head.

Gabe steadied his aim with both hands. He fired at the truck. "Faster!"

"We have to get help!"

"Where? We're in the middle of nowhere!" He emptied the gun into the truck, but inflicted no damage.

"They're eating our bumper!" Gabe shouted. "Move it!"

"Okay!" Shannon whipped the Mercedes to and fro on the road, making it tough for the shooter to make a direct hit. Bullets pinged off the back and side of the car.

"Duck!" Putting his hand on Shannon's head, he shoved her down so low in the driver's seat she couldn't see the road.

A round of bullets zinged just over her head and shattered the front windshield. Gabe shouted a string of curses as glass blew over their faces.

"Are you trying to kill me, too?" Hysteria had taken Shannon over. Tears filled her eyes. Her head pounded.

"I just saved your life!"

"The hell you did!" She rammed her foot down on the accelerator. "I'm saving my own ass!"

The road straightened for what looked like a half mile to Shannon before rounding a particularly bad right curve.

A bullet whizzed just past Shannon's ear and kept sailing through the missing windshield. Cold air blurred Shannon's vision, but not her brain.

The Mercedes's wide wheel base would help her hug the road. If she could stay to the outside, then slip back to the inside lane and slam on the brakes as she'd done before, she just might send the truck off the road.

"Hold on!" she shouted to Gabe.

Gabe's thoughts were solely centered on making his next shot count.

The red truck was gaining on them again, which was just what Gabe wanted. "Come on," he whispered to himself as he peered carefully around the seat. "Just a little closer. That's it. That's the way..."

The shooter had just finished reloading when Gabe fired.

He clipped the man in the shoulder. Without a second lost, he fired his second shot into the driver's side of the windshield, hitting the driver.

The truck swerved.

Gabe shot the front right tire.

Shannon raced around the bend just as she'd planned.

The red truck went screaming over the side of the road and flipped over, rolling down the embankment, slamming into a group of mesquite trees and bursting into flames.

In the rearview mirror Shannon watched the flames leap into the darkening night sky.

"Don't look back," Gabe warned.

Shannon obeyed and kept her eyes on the indigo horizon.

25

——►◄——

Sheriff Douglas Creighton stepped over a twisted piece of metal. Holding his handkerchief over his nostrils to filter the stench of burning flesh, he stared at the charred remains of what looked like a five-foot-eight-inch-tall man. Age was indeterminable. The corpse's hair was gone and his scalp looked as if it had melted into his face. Otherwise, there was little left to describe.

Glancing over his shoulder to his deputy, Burt Kincaid, he asked, "Anything over there?"

"Another man. Taller, heavier. This one was the driver. Part of the steering wheel melted into his hands. What a stinking mess," he said, looking up at the road. "Here they come, Sheriff."

"Right on time," Sheriff Creighton said.

A string of headlights snaked down the country road toward them. Three county patrol cars, four tow trucks, an ambulance, the coroner's van and a half-dozen curiosity seekers drove toward the accident scene.

Burt removed his hat and scratched his head. "Does it always have to be a party?"

"Comes with the territory, Burt," Sheriff Creighton said. "Besides, who could miss this much smoke?"

"Yeah, I guess they figure this is the most excitement we've seen since that rapist escaped from Huntsville Prison."

"Don't remind me," he replied, casting a sidelong glance at the farmer standing on the edge of the road, bandanna tied over his face and signaling to the arriving cars. "It's bad enough Harvey Silber nearly lost our prisoner for us back then—trying to be a hero. Damn idiot nearly got himself and us killed. Now these two fools blow themselves up in Harvey's front yard."

"Sir, Mr. Silber did call us immediately."

Sheriff Creighton pointed to the blue Ford sedan. "Yeah, us and the local press."

Harvey Silber flagged down the lead patrol car, which directed its headlights onto the scene. The tow trucks followed suit while Harvey rushed over to the blue sedan. The area reporter jumped out of his car and started taking notes as Harvey gestured theatrically with his hands and arms, describing the crash. The reporter pulled out a camera and flashed three shots of Harvey before rushing toward the scene with Harvey running alongside him.

Frowning, Burt said, "I guess Harvey's never gotten over you going off to Desert Storm and he didn't."

"Who the hell knows," Sheriff Creighton said as he picked his way over the wreckage to meet up with the aging, cranky county coroner, Ted Meadows.

"I don't mind telling you I was about to sit down to one of Mrs. Meadows's fine chicken dinners, Sheriff. Being called out like this isn't good for my system. This is what I get for playing Santa Claus—letting my staff take vacation," he grumbled.

"I understand, Ted," Sheriff Creighton said.

"The hell you do. I'm too old for this crap."

Sheriff Creighton nodded while Burt rolled his eyes.

"You'll need dental records to identify the bodies," Sheriff Creighton said.

"No chance of getting prints?" Ted asked.

"None."

"Dad blast it!" Ted grumbled. "I'll do the best I can, Sheriff," he said, fastening a sterile white cotton mask over his face and adjusting his glasses as he surveyed the area. "Holy cow! What kind of joyride were they on?"

"I don't know but the truck was riddled with bullet holes. I found an automatic rifle the likes of which I haven't seen since my Navy SEAL days."

"This used to be a God-fearing county and in the past four years it seems we've been thrust into hell," he criticized.

"Ever since I took office?" Sheriff Creighton, the first African-American elected official in the county, wanted Ted to know he wasn't as stupid as the coroner believed.

The older man pretended not to hear him and shuffled off toward the nearest human-shaped cinder.

A series of flashes went off in Sheriff Creighton's face. "Burt!" he shouted. "Get Harvey Silber and that idiot reporter out of here until I find out what the hell's going on."

"Yes, sir!"

"And Burt, tell him 'no comment' from my office. I'll deal with the press later."

"You got it!" Burt rushed over to Harvey and the reporter.

Sheriff Creighton pulled out his cellular phone and punched in the number of the New Mexico State

Highway Patrol. "Hello, Doris. This is Sheriff Creighton again. Did you find anything I can use?"

"No, sir," she replied. "There have been no new APBs of any kind since you called in a half hour ago. No mental-patient escapees, no prison breakouts. No robberies. Not even a speeding ticket. No unusual activity of any kind. It's as quiet as a graveyard."

"It's the Fourth of July over here, but thanks." He hung up.

"Damn." He made a second call to the FBI office in Austin, Texas. Chances were strong he'd inherited a problem from the neighboring state. "This is Sheriff Douglas Creighton calling Randall Sinclair. Is Randy back yet?"

"One moment," the male voice replied and put him on hold.

The call was picked up in a second. "Doug. What's up?"

"You tell me."

"I got your message, but our guys are quiet. We've been laying low ever since the drug bust over in Mineral Wells."

Sheriff Creighton rubbed the back of his neck to ease his tension. "I've got a truck that's been shot to hell, two toasted bodies and what looks like one of your automatic rifles."

"No way it's one of ours." Randy paused. "It could be stolen."

"That's what I figure, but my point is, these yokels were after somebody. And that somebody is out there racing around my county making me look bad. I figured the least you can do is be up-front with me."

"Damn it, Doug. You know I can't share privileged

information with you. Friendship is one thing, but my butt's on the line."

"So, you *are* active over here."

Expelling a heavy sigh, Randy continued. "Until these methamphetamine labs are shut down for good, we're prowling. You got that? But what I can tell you is that in the past two hours your district is silent as a lamb. Okay?"

"Then what the hell is going on here?"

"You tell me, Doug. What exactly *is* going on?"

"I haven't got a clue, but I'm sure as hell going to find out."

"I always get nervous when someone else is dealing the cards. Keep in touch. And Doug, watch your ass."

Chuckling to himself, he said, "I will." Sheriff Creighton signed off with his friend.

Sliding into his patrol car, he used the radio to contact one of his men who was combing the western part of the county. "Matt. What's it look like over there?"

"Nothing."

"This guy can't just vanish into thin air. He couldn't have gotten too far, either. From the looks of this truck, the other guy ought to be in a whole lot worse shape. I found three empty clips. Somebody's car is a mess. Personally, I can't believe it's still running. They have to be on foot."

"It would take an army to comb this county tonight. But I'll do it. Just give the word."

"Keep checking for hitchhikers. I've put out a CB alert. If we're lucky some trucker might spot them. I doubt a roadblock would do us any good."

Creighton's ringing cellular phone caused him to

cut his conversation short. Taking the call from the Texas Department of Motor Vehicles caused his eyebrow to cock. "You wanna tell me that again?"

"There's no registration for the '96 metallic red Ford pickup with Texas license plate WHX356. The VIN number you gave me is nowhere in the system. Are you sure you got it right?"

"It's a bit obscured due to the damage," the sheriff said, "but try variations of the last three numbers. The rest of the number is legible."

"I'll do my best. Personally, I think it's a waste of time."

"I know. Just do it anyway," he said and signed off.

Burt waited for Sheriff Creighton while he finished his calls. "The coroner's finished. He said to tell you he'll have a report for you by morning. He wants to—"

Sheriff Creighton held his palm in the air. "I know. He wants to finish his supper. But he'd better have it first thing in the morning. At this point these two guys are phantoms."

"Pardon me, sir?"

"DMV says this truck doesn't exist. I'm getting a real bad feeling about all this." His dark eyes searched the black night. "He had to take one of the farm roads off here. He couldn't have gotten far."

"I've called some of the local farmers and ranchers. Vince Harper, Suellen Prather and the Mileses. Told them to be on the lookout. They said they haven't seen or heard a thing."

"The trouble is, this all took place about suppertime. Families are busy clanging around the kitchen, watching the news on television, closing down their barns and such for the night. Hell, Chuck Simpson told me he was still plowing, getting ready to plant his winter crops."

"What are you saying, sir?"

Sheriff Creighton's eyebrows knit. "They could be anywhere. Even backtracked for all I know. But I've got to find them." Massaging the back of his stiff neck, he said, "This thing has the earmarks of something bigger than a local shooting."

"Like how big?" Burt's eyes rounded. He'd never been involved in anything more than routine police work.

Sheriff Creighton's seasoned background had taught him to consider the most sinister of options. He made a practice of looking deeper than surface evidence. He'd know a lot more once he had that coroner's report. The acrid smell of burned corpses was nothing to the stench of organized lynch law.

"The fact that this truck was not registered tells me that these two guys are no ordinary accident victims, if they're the victims at all. They had something to hide. They thought they were above the law, but they were wrong. Nobody gets away with dick in my county."

"I hear you, sir."

"Let's get back to headquarters. I have a long night ahead of me. Our men will comb this area but good. We'll find the guy who did this."

"And then we nail his ass, right?"

"Maybe. Maybe not."

Burt looked at his boss with surprise.

Sheriff Creighton was still at his desk at ten o'clock that night. The place was empty and the light in his office was the only one burning. He was perturbed when the front door opened and a tall man with dark hair walked in.

The man's eyes slipped imperceptibly around the room. His movements were catlike, his every pore breathing in details.

Sheriff Creighton would bet his last buck this man was a fed.

"I wasn't expecting vistors. How can I help you?" Sheriff Creighton asked.

"I'm here to help you. My name is Ben Richards."

"And which department are you with?"

Ben grinned. "You're good."

"I know." He folded his arms over his chest, his mind on alert. He motioned for Ben to sit.

"Thanks. It's been a long day."

"For a lot of us." Sheriff Creighton waited patiently.

"I'm here about the two unidentified men you called the bureau about today."

"You made them?"

"Yes. Satch Jessup and Grady Conners were both members of a drug ring that runs from Louisiana across Texas into New Mexico and, we believe, has ties to California."

"Are you telling me I've got a drug war in my backyard?"

"Yes and no." Ben rubbed his forehead then spied a half-filled coffeepot. "May I?"

"Yeah, sure."

Ben rose and poured coffee into a foam cup. He patted his breast pocket for his cigarettes.

"No smoking in here," Sheriff Creighton said.

"I'm out anyway."

Sheriff Creighton leaned forward in his chair. "Just

what the hell's going on and who am I dealing with here?"

"The Cassalia drug cartel out of Colombia."

Sheriff Creighton whistled. "And I thought I was dealing with big potatoes with the meth labs around here."

"The labs belong to Alejandro himself."

"No way."

Ben nodded. "I've been working on this case for nearly two years. I've tracked Alejandro's network to New Orleans and was just about to close in when everything blew up in my face the first of December."

"I didn't hear about anything."

"I know. We kept things quiet once I went undercover again. The chief of police over there was the superintendent, so to speak, for all the labs. He reported directly to New Orleans and they reported to Alejandro. The fly in the ointment was an attorney, Adam Rivers, who embezzled over fifty grand from Alejandro. We have an investigative team in Colombia who tapped into Alejandro's cellular phones and overheard him telling one of his people here in the States that Rivers somehow pawned off the information to an unsuspecting friend of his, Gabriel Turner, of Fort Worth. After Rivers's death, our men went over Rivers's house with a vengeance. The computer in the office was blank. I mean, there was nothing on the hard drive. That's when I deduced that Rivers downloaded his information to a disk and that was why he set up the meeting in Shreveport with Turner. Both men had to travel to a place they seldom visited.

"Alejandro's men were already in New Orleans and probably followed Rivers to Shreveport. My guess is that they thought Turner was his accomplice.

Alejandro's men executed Rivers and thought they'd killed Turner, but he not only survived, he's got the information Alejandro needs to recover his money. It's all there on that computer disk."

"Ain't technology a kick in the ass?" Sheriff Creighton smiled.

"It's scary stuff if you ask me." He drained his coffee. "Alejandro lives in seclusion a continent away, yet his network is global. He's got assassins and collection men in every country. He never has to dirty his hands, seldom travels to check on his operations or control his men. He orders extortion and murders by e-mail. Painless, bloodless and efficient as hell. It's worse than Big Brother. It's electronic apocalypse. And the bitch of it is, we can't nab him. No one can. He's untouchable."

"Yet you're here. Something's got your attention."

"This Turner I told you about? He was in a coma for weeks. He wakes up and splits from the hospital, taking a nurse hostage. I believe he's got the disk because Alejandro's men, both the locals from Louisiana and imported Colombians, have been all over him."

Sheriff Creighton was contemplative. "You think Turner was responsible for the incident here this evening?"

"I'd bet my last buck on it."

"You're sure?"

"We last had a bead on them at a motel near Amarillo. By the time I got there, the place was shot to pieces, I had one dead Colombian and Chief Bremen's body to contend with. Turner set up the Colombians like a pro. He remembers his military training well, thank God. However, we believe one of the assassins got away and is tracking Turner."

"And the toasted fellows I found…"

"Were on Bremen's payroll. Either they killed Bremen or the Colombians did. They both had the same assault weapons."

"And so what do you want from me?"

"You're a former Navy SEAL. An expert in tracking both with high-tech equipment and by gut instinct. I need to find Shannon."

"Shannon?"

"She's the nurse with Turner."

"The hostage?" Sheriff Creighton watched as the nerve in Ben's jaw jumped.

"Yes. I want to find them before the Colombians do—for obvious reasons."

"Yes, they're quite obvious indeed." He paused. "From what you tell me, I think the smart thing for you to do is let Turner go. Seems to me he's shutting down the methamphetamine operations here all by himself. Bremen's dead. Two of his lieutenants are dead. He's got Alejandro's money or knows where it is. Hell, man, we ought to put him on the payroll." Sheriff Creighton smiled broadly.

"The government needs that disk to shut Alejandro down completely," Ben said. "And…there's the woman. She needs to be rescued."

"I understand."

26

"We have to ditch this car," Gabe said as he and Shannon watched a farmhouse from behind a group of trees and wild evergreen bushes.

"I agree," she replied.

The kitchen and dining-room lights were still on and music played loudly when the front door opened. A man standing next to a late-model truck called out to the woman inside. She emerged in the doorway, putting her arms through the sleeves of a winter coat, then hurried over to him. They got in the truck and drove away.

"Let's go," Gabe urged.

"But the lights are still on and so's the music. What if there's someone home?"

"People like these don't worry about things like that. My mother used to do it all the time when we lived on a farm."

"You? On a farm?"

"Is that so hard to imagine?" His look was indicting.

Acutely aware of how little they knew about each other's pasts, Shannon envisioned Gabe possessively surveying his land, feet planted shoulder-width apart on frozen, furrowed ground like this. At that moment she realized he was that blend of determination, intractability and loyalty that defined "salt of the earth." He was from good stock.

So was she.

She broke their gaze. "Not hard at all," she said, wishing they had time to spend exploring each other.

Shannon eased the car up the dirt driveway and over to the left of the barn where an old Cutlass Supreme was parked.

"I don't know about this, Gabe," Shannon said.

"Look, we can't keep the Mercedes. Once it's daylight, these shot-out windows are a red flag to anyone who passes us."

"God, we're always stealing something. I hate it!"

"Trust me, these folks could use a new car. So they replace the windshields and the Mercedes is all theirs. They'll make a great profit. Let's pray this Cutlass runs."

"You're right, but I still don't like it."

"Your morality is commendable. Now, let's go."

Looking back at the house, Shannon said, "This is so risky. If someone's still inside, they'll call the police."

"All right. I'll go check it out."

Gabe eased his door open. "Stay here and keep low."

Shannon grabbed his sleeve. "Be careful."

Though surprised at her concern, Gabe nodded. "I will."

Crouching low, Gabe hurried across the weed-filled yard to the steps. Quietly, he approached the front door and peered through the wavy old glass. From what he could determine no one was home. He knocked on the door and waited. Leaning closely, he couldn't hear a sound.

"It's okay," he said, walking back toward Shannon who was already getting out of the Mercedes.

Shannon used the remote to pop the trunk. Gabe removed their belongings, including the arsenal he'd accumulated in the past two days.

"I just thought of something. If there's a car key, I won't have to hot-wire it. Maybe the back door is open."

"What makes you think it's unlocked?"

"I told you before, I know these parts and these people. They're trusting."

He went around the back of the white-painted house to the concrete steps leading up to the back door. Judging the house was built during the Depression, he rightly guessed the door's lock would be worn. Opening the screen door first, he turned the scratched metal knob and found the door was indeed unlocked, just as he thought it would be.

Turning to his right, on the landing wall, on a corkboard next to a red-and-white-checked apron were various sets of keys. The GM keys were hard to miss.

"I've got them," he told Shannon as he got into the passenger's seat.

While Shannon nearly flooded the Cutlass trying to get it to start, Gabe drove the Mercedes around to the back side of the barn where it couldn't be seen from the road.

Driving away, neither of them looked back.

They'd only gone a quarter of a mile when Shannon glanced at the fuel gauge. "We're going to have to stop soon. We've only got a quarter of a tank."

"I was afraid of that. It'll be close, but I know of a place about thirty miles from here where we can fill up. If it's still there. We'll get something to eat and then lose ourselves on the country roads north of here."

"If it's still there? Do you know this area?"

"I grew up here. I buried my father here..." His voice trailed off as old memories filled his mind.

Shannon felt his grief more acutely than his physical suffering. "How old were you when he died?"

"Fourteen," he said softly. "Could I have ever been that young?"

"Was it awful? Burying him, I mean."

Shrugging his shoulders, he pretended her question had no impact, though it sliced his insides. "At the time, it seemed like just another day."

Gabe's thoughts catapulted him back to a place in his life when he'd needed Adam and Pete. A time when they'd been there for him.

"My parents didn't know many people, really. It was 1970 and half my dad's friends had come home like he did. In a box."

Shannon held her breath as she asked, "Vietnam?"

Gabe nodded gravely. "My mother lived on a ranch not far from here all her life. Funny, that house back there reminded me of it. They all look the same, I guess. She hated it, though.

"Growing up, my dad and gramps taught me and my friends, Adam and Pete, how to ride, rope and brand cows. When my dad died, I thought the world had ended."

Shannon's eyes were filled with compassion when she asked, "Adam and Pete helped you through that time?"

"They made sure I was included whenever their fathers took them to football and baseball games. They kept going with me out to the ranch all through high school. They shared their families with me. I never felt alone.

"Even when I went to the Air Force Academy in Colorado Springs, we still made a point to see each other on Christmas break. They went to UT in Austin, made new friends. We graduated. Adam, the attorney, Pete, the investment banker, and me... I intended to be a career officer."

"Follow in your dad's footsteps?" she asked.

"Precisely. I even married a farm girl just like Dad did. I thought I had the world by the nuts. On our second anniversary, I decided to surprise Mary by coming home two days early. I showed up at our apartment in Fort Worth and found her in bed with another guy." Gabe stopped for a long moment, the angry heat of that moment rushing over him.

"What did you do?" Shannon asked, looking at his balled fists.

"I wanted to beat him to a pulp, but I didn't. I took off. I filed for divorce, quit the air force and began my second career."

"Which was?"

"Bumming. I bummed around. Bummed off Adam, and when he got disgusted with me, I bummed off Pete. I took advantage of my friends, and you know what they did?"

"No."

"They worked twice as hard to redeem me. Adam used his influence to get me one job after another, begging his friends in New Orleans to give me a chance. I did everything but get my act together."

"Then one day I saw an ad on television for an in-

surance school. I enrolled and got my license. I started
selling right off the bat, thanks to Adam and Pete who
both gave me referrals. When I started my own
agency and branched out by implementing my brain-
storms, I became the all-American version of suc-
cess."

She watched his face contort each time he mentioned his friends' names.

"Just a regular guy," she offered on a cheery note.

"Yeah, sleazy friends and all." His voice clutched.
He glanced away, then down at his hands.

"It's not your fault," she said. "What they did, I
mean."

His eyes were damning, intense and unrelenting.
He blamed himself unmercifully and she doubted she
could dissuade him. She knew that kind of intractability because she was like that. *We're the same, you and
I, Gabe. More than you realize. More than I realized.*

"I should have seen it coming," he said softly. "If I
had, neither of us would be in this mess."

"So you're not telepathic. So, big deal."

Pinching the bridge of his nose with his thumb and
forefinger, he said, "When I was younger I didn't give
a damn. Then I learned to manipulate my destiny. I
never in a million years thought anything like this
could happen to me."

"Neither did I."

"Shannon, I feel so guilty about dragging you
along. I guess what I'm trying to say is that I'm sorry.
The hell of it is, if I let you go, I know you wouldn't be
safe. They'd hunt you down and I wouldn't be there
to defend you."

"Defend me."

"Ironic, isn't it? Gabe Turner, kidnapper or champion. Take your pick. Both are true."

Her eyes held his for a long moment. "I've always wanted a champion, Gabe."

"Well, you have one now."

27

They made fast time in the Cutlass. Still crisscrossing the countryside using back roads and county highways only when they needed to find fuel or food, they avoided detection. Only once did they pass a state trooper who was too busy issuing a ticket to a teenager in a black BMW to notice them.

"By morning the cops will know we've stolen this car. We need to get as far as possible," Gabe said.

"I know, but I'm exhausted," Shannon said. "If you want me to stay awake and keep driving, you'll have to at least feed me," she said.

He reached over and began rubbing her neck and shoulders. "Maybe I should drive."

"In your condition? You conk out in midsentence half the time."

"But look at you. I was better off the night I came into the ER."

"Thanks a lot."

He chuckled good-naturedly. "It's eighteen miles to the next town. We'll gas up there."

The village was little more than a crossroads with no post office or bank. A small dilapidated Baptist church sat next to a graveyard. Shannon saw only three houses none of whose lights were on this late at night. A blinking yellow caution light suspended over the pavement at the intersection of the highway and a gravel road slowed whatever traffic there might be.

The sole business was a gas station with one pump attached to an old clapboard house with a hand-painted sign saying Thelma's. On the side of the house fading and chipped paint formed a forty-year-old image of a pack of Lucky Strike cigarettes. Every light in the house was on, a mixture of smoke and steam spewed out a side exhaust and the smell of cooking onions and hot grease filled the air.

Shannon pulled the Cutlass to the gasoline pump.

"This place is jumping," Gabe said, pointing to the five parked cars in front.

"Can you blame them? We're in the middle of no-where."

Gabe read the collage of stickers on the glass door. "Looks like you can have anything you want. Beer, hard stuff, burgers, play the lotto."

The gasoline pump is as antiquated as the house, Shannon thought as she looked at the side-mounted lever. Pushing it, she found the numbers rolled on a drum to zero. *I haven't seen one of these since I was a kid.* She filled the gas tank with the old-style nozzle that allowed her to top it off. "Coffee. Lots of it. A burger is fine. And fries, too."

"Deal," Gabe said, going into the house to pay for the gas.

Stepping through the doorway into a smoke-filled room, he found he was the center of attention. A dozen men and women looked up as he entered. He gave them a short wave. They stared blankly at him then went back to their conversations.

"Can I help ya?" an obese woman with raven-dyed hair asked from behind the counter.

"I owe you for the gas," Gabe said.

"How much did you get?"

"You use the honor system?"

The woman continued to stare at him as if he were an idiot. Gabe went to the door, strained his eyes and read the numbers on the pump. "Fifteen-forty."

"Anything else?" the woman asked.

"A couple burgers with everything. Two fries, two coffees and...these Ding Dongs. And two Hershey bars."

She wrote everything down on a green-colored pad. Turning around, she slapped two precooked hamburger patties into two buns, added the condiments and wrapped them in paper. Under a warming lamp there were just enough fries for Gabe's two orders. The coffee was blessedly fresh. She put plastic tops on the foam cups, neatly stacked the food in a brown paper bag, then added a half-dozen paper napkins.

"Anything else?"

Grabbing a Lubbock newspaper from a small stack, Gabe said, "Just the paper."

Without wiping her hands, she pulled out her pencil and pad, added the total of the food cost to the gasoline, and said proudly, "Twenty-one ninety."

Gabe handed her twenty-two dollars. "Keep it."

"Gee, thanks, mister," the woman grumped.

Carrying the food and newspaper in one hand, Gabe balanced the coffee in the other, placing his chin on the top cup to keep it from spilling. When he reached the café door, he was about to back out when two men opened it for him.

"Thanks," he said, keeping his head down to avoid spilling the coffee.

"No problem," one of the men replied.

Gabe walked out gingerly, careful of his purchases. He raised his eyes to the car. It was gone and so was Shannon.

His shock froze him. His eyes scanned the parking lot a second time.

"Aw, man! Just when I was starting to trust her!"

Disappointment was sliding quickly into bitter betrayal as he stomped the ground.

"Shannon, how could you leave me?"

Walking past the pumps toward the highway, Gabe moved out of the puddle of light from the house and into darkness. He paused for a long moment, still scanning the area.

He peered carefully into the darkness, listening for any sound of a retreating car, but there was only silence.

He listened just as intensely to his own intuition. Shannon wouldn't leave him. Not now, not after what they'd been through.

He looked around the parking lot again for a sign of her. Nothing. However, he had the eerie feeling that he was being watched. He looked back over his shoulder. The coffee teetered in his hands.

"Shannon?" He whispered her name. He felt as if she was close, as if she was with him.

He felt a warning chill race up his spine. "Something isn't right. None of this is right." Then it hit him.

There was something about the two men he'd seen at the door to Thelma's, but he couldn't put his finger on it. Because he'd bent his head and placed his chin on the stack of coffee cups, Gabe hadn't been able to see their faces. They had been wearing jeans and light jackets, he remembered that. Because his eyes were lowered, his focus had been at their waist level where their waistbands had bulged peculiarly, as if they'd been carrying guns.

Quickly he glanced back at the roadhouse and noticed the newest vehicle to join the five was a white Dodge truck. That was the truck the two men must have been driving. Then the door to Thelma's banged and the same two men crossed to their truck and got in.

Gabe's eyes flew to the passenger's side. He'd seen the sharp-featured man before.

"Amarillo! He's alive!"

"Gabe!" Shannon shouted from a short distance.

The Cutlass seemed to appear out of nowhere.

"Get in!" She motioned excitedly, leaning over to open the door for him.

Rushing toward the car, he managed to keep the coffee in check as he hopped in. Shannon sped away from the roadhouse before Gabe completely shut his door.

"I thought you'd left me back there."

"I thought about it."

Alarm filled his face.

"I'm kidding."

"I'm glad you didn't," he said gratefully. "How is it they didn't see you?"

"I got back in the car just after I finished pumping the gas. I guess I've become addicted to watching this rearview mirror more than I realized."

She rammed her foot against the accelerator and they sped away.

Gabe grabbed his guns from the back seat.

"The minute I saw headlights coming toward the roadhouse," she said, "my instincts kicked in. I pulled away from the pump and hid the car behind that Quaker State sign and the clump of bushes."

"That's smart," Gabe said.

"Yeah? Well, you got any idea how I can lose them now?" she asked, her eyes glued to the rearview mirror.

"Yeah, drive like hell!"

Shannon already had the Cutlass up to ninety-five.

"Kill your headlights and don't hit the brake," he said anxiously.

"Are you crazy? I won't be able to see the road!"

"I know this road. It's flat as a board...so is the shoulder. Several miles up here is a small road that leads down to a couple of farmhouses. What a lot of people don't know is that the road goes northwest and connects with a highway...I forget the number."

"They're gaining on us!" Her voice cracked. Gripping the steering wheel, she willed the Cutlass to go faster.

"Here's the turn! Now, Shannon!" Gabe yelled while still keeping his eye on the headlights behind them. "Don't slow down, and for God's sake forget you have a brake!"

"I know! I know!"

The car hit the gravel at breakneck speed, but fortunately, the land was flat for miles. Years of nursing, lifting patients to bathe them and change their linens had helped to develop her upper-body strength. To keep the car steady and on the road, Shannon used every bit of muscle power she had. She let up on the gas, but kept her foot off the brake. She wanted to see what was happening behind her, but she was too busy keeping the car from rolling over.

As if reading her thoughts, Gabe said, "Great cars, these old buzzards. All that steel and weight keeps 'em grounded."

The recent snows in the area had wetted down the otherwise normally powder-dry land. As they sped down the back road, there was no rooster tail of dust to reveal their position.

"What are they doing? Are they following us?" Shannon asked, still keeping her eyes glued to the barely visible path in front of her.

Gabe watched anxiously as the headlights approached the turn. His heart hammered against his chest, causing his ribs to ache. His mouth was dry with fear. If that truck followed them, they were dead meat for certain. The old Cutlass was no match for any new engine.

All this time he'd thought about dying. Not about being caught. The alternative flashed through his mind. The thought of these butchers torturing Shannon, or worse, turned his blood to ice.

Dying quickly sounded inviting to him.

He'd gotten Shannon into more than just trouble. The reality was, they were about as safe as a couple of people sitting on a discharged napalm bomb.

Reaching under the seat, Gabe realized he had a little over half a box of shells left. He could hold them off for a while, but not forever. He couldn't help thinking, as the Dodge truck headlights hit the turn-off, that this whole situation was anything but real.

Gabe knew he was just an ordinary guy. But how in the world was it possible that he was fighting for his life, killing people he didn't know, guilty of dragging a perfectly innocent woman along with him. He should get a medal. A stupidity medal.

Shannon didn't want to watch the rearview. But she couldn't resist. "I don't believe it!"

"Oh, no!" Gabe's voice was a rush of relief. "They didn't turn off. They didn't turn!"

"Wait! They could still double back."

Gabe's exhuberance vanished. "You're right. They could." He held his breath. "Keep driving. Don't let up on that gas!"

Shannon passed a lone farmhouse and a rusting tin barn that was surrounded by flat grazing land. She could make out a dozen cattle slumbering near a windbreak of mesquite and cypress trees.

How was it possible everything around her could look so tranquil when she felt as if she'd explode any moment? It seemed impossible a human's nerves could endure being rubbed this raw hour after hour, day after day.

Even when they thought they were safe, they weren't. Maybe they never would be. Maybe this chase would go on forever, for eternity, for as long as she lived.

And how long would that be if these men caught them? They would kill her. She knew it. She could feel its certainty in her bones.

And what if they weren't caught tonight? There would be another pair or three or four after them tomorrow or the next day.

She envisioned her future a stream of mercenaries stalking her, making her life hell. Maybe she'd be better off dead.

Continually watching the rearview mirror, expecting to see the truck turn onto their road and follow,

Shannon was stupefied at what happened. "I don't believe it."

"They're still going straight," he said as the headlights disappeared altogether into the night. "We're not licked yet."

He faced forward. "There's another road to the south about five miles from here. Hopefully, they'll think we took it. Maybe they'll get lost. But one thing is for sure, by morning they'll figure out what we did."

"But they're going in the wrong direction. They won't find us."

Reaching across the dash, Gabe turned on the headlights and said, "Don't ever presume anything. I had enough special forces training in the air force to know that once you let your guard down, you lose."

"Ever?"

He purposely gave her a hard look. "The only thing that stops the enemy is winning. For them to win, we have to lose."

"Or concede," she offered. "What if we anonymously sent them the disk."

"Oh, sure. And to whom should I mail it? Maybe I should arbitrarily pick a name from the list. Close my eyes and point? Shannon, I'm trying to plan our lives here! Gimme a break!"

"I just wanted—"

"To get rid of the damn thing. Then everything would be the way it used to be. Right?"

"Yes," she answered quietly.

Gingerly, he laid his hand over hers. She glanced at his hand, looking as if he were helping her steer. Gabe removed his hand. "You can't go back to your old life, Shannon. Neither can I." He looked thoughtfully ahead. "Nobody can. Not really. For you and I there's only the future. It's as if the past never happened. It'll be tough, but that's the way it's got to be." He paused and then looked at her to see her reaction.

She dropped her eyes. She didn't want him to see her cry. She couldn't take the truth. *How many times have I said those precise words to myself? It's got to be like this, kid. This was the hand you were dealt, Shannon. Play your cards. Make a bet, but keep playing.*

"I wish we could be like normal people and do regular stuff. You know, rent a movie or go on a picnic," she said.

"Not our style…anymore," he replied regretfully.

"Still…"

He expelled a deep sigh. "There's this little Mexican restaurant on the banks of the Guadalupe River near New Braunfels that serves the best enchiladas you've ever tasted. And fresh *pica de gallo*…it crunches in your mouth. At night they turn on these cheap Japanese lanterns they've got strung between the mesquite trees. But when the moon is full and the breeze is blowing, those colored lights dance along the river like water sprites. There's a trio on weekends that plays sad Spanish ballads. I'd give anything to take you there…"

"And we'd dance under the moonlight?"

Gabe touched her hand. "All night if you'd like." He knew he'd never let her go.

"Yeah," she replied, driving into the darkness, imagining how it would feel to be normal. To dance in the moonlight with Gabe and pretend neither the past nor the future threatened their idyll.

28

One of the dozen people sitting in Thelma's road-house when Gabe had walked in was Lester Bell, brother-in-law of Sheriff Douglas Creighton. Lester didn't know much about police or detective work, but he knew trouble when he smelled it. And he smelled it.

When the Latin men came into the roadhouse and began asking Kitt about a man and woman traveling together, the first thing Lester noticed was their accent. In and of itself, a Spanish accent was commonplace in the Southwest. But the second thing he noticed was their guns.

Though Lester was an out-of-work oil-field driller formerly from Odessa, he'd been blessed by the good Lord to call Douglas Creighton his brother-in-law. When Lester lost his job, Douglas had generously taken his family into his home. During that time Lester hung around his brother-in-law and his deputies enough to pick up their lingo, tactics and the particular way their brains worked. He'd learned that in crisis situations, a calm person could mean the difference between life and death.

From the disquieted look on Kitt's face, Lester realized something was wrong.

He knew a thief when he saw one and it was his guess these fellas were going to rob Kitt.

Leaving his Coors beer on the table, Lester walked up behind the two men. "Kitt, mind if I get another order of fries?" He winked at her.

She shrugged her shoulders. "I just turned the fryer off."

"Well, turn it back on, Kitt. I'm hungry." He elbowed his way between the two men. He nodded cordially to them both, memorizing their faces. The man to his right had a face like a hawk. Razor-sharp and lethal. The other man was thinner, with a goatee and even darker eyes than his friend.

"Evenin', gentlemen."

They only nodded.

Lester stepped back, keeping his eyes on their concealed guns.

"They're asking questions," Kitt said to Lester.

"Questions?"

The man to Lester's right whirled around. "Yeah. We're looking for a white man and woman. We got a report they stole a Cutlass Supreme."

"Oh, you're cops then. Where you from?"

"Dallas. Have you seen the car?"

"What year is it?"

"Eighty-three."

Lester was dumbfounded. "You're working overtime tracking down a car that's not worth more than three grand tops?" Lester laughed.

"Yeah," Sardia answered sternly.

Lester couldn't help having a bit of fun. "What? Is it lined with gold? Got a body in the trunk?"

"What of it?" Sardia grumbled.

"Don't you get up in my face," Lester roared. "I

know some things about the law...and law enforcers."

"Like what?"

"Like this stinks to high heaven. I don't know what you're after, but your dog don't hunt here." Lester's thick neck muscles pulsed as his temper shot through his voice.

The man to Lester's left went for his gun, but his partner stopped him. "No."

Lester stepped a pace back. "I suggest you look elsewhere. Nobody here has what you want."

The men left.

Lester went to the pay phone in the back of the diner and placed a call to his brother-in-law.

"I know I must be waking you, Douglas, but I thought I should tell you about what happened to me tonight."

"It's quite all right, Lester. I wasn't sleeping. I'm in my car. I've had all my calls forwarded to my cellular. It's strange you should call, I was just thinking about you. Now, tell me what happened."

Sheriff Douglas Creighton believed in destiny, ESP, fortuitous circumstances, serendipity and the ability of the mind to create them all.

He needed a miracle to find the man and woman from Shreveport.

Thanks to Lester, he'd gotten one.

Thanks to the area-wide APB he'd placed on the Cutlass Supreme, he'd gotten a second miracle.

"Sheriff Creighton, this is Kent Marsalis at the state park over at Sumner Lake. I found your Cutlass Supreme."

Sheriff Creighton jotted down the particulars and

immediately punched in Ben Richards's cellular-phone number.

"I found them," Sheriff Creighton said.

Ben exhaled relief. "I'll meet you there."

Ben drove as if Satan himself were on his tail.

His cellular phone rang.

"Make it fast. Make it good."

"Her name is Kathleen Shannon Randall."

Ben held his breath. After so many calls with no information, now that he was about to receive this holiest-of-holy news, he almost didn't want to hear it. In a few hours he would be with her. She would be thrilled to see him. Overjoyed that he was her savior. She would come to him the way he'd imagined in his dreams.

His nerves were raw. An ominous shadow drifted over him. Something told him he wasn't going to like what he was about to hear. He started to ask if it was good or bad news. Instead, he said, "Shoot."

Listening to the rain of information about the woman he'd fallen in love with, the woman who so reminded him of his beloved Nancy, at first shocked him. Then he felt betrayed. And then came the pain.

He felt gutted as his informant continued spewing facts and data with one shocking tale after another.

He couldn't believe it. Didn't want to believe a shred of it.

But what cut him the deepest was the same thing that had hurt him about Nancy.

Shannon, or Kathleen, had not turned to him. She had not confided in him. She'd never needed him and he wanted so desperately for someone in this world to need him.

Easing his foot off the accelerator, Ben wiped the tear from his cheek that had trickled down to his jaw.

His lungs burned with a sadness he hadn't felt since the day he'd discovered Nancy was dead.

At this moment, he nearly succumbed to believing that Shannon was dead to him, too.

"No," he mumbled to himself.

"What's that, Maestro?"

"I mean, no, I won't be contacting you until after I find the girl and Turner."

"Sounds good. Catch you then."

"Right." He hung up and stared into the dark distance ahead of him.

Only his headlights lit the country road.

Multibranched trees arched over the road, and at night they could almost be mistaken for carrying the leaves of summer it was so dark. But their bare branches reminded him of the death of winter. The kind of cold he felt in the depths of his soul.

"Why couldn't you trust me, Shannon?" *Why couldn't you love me?*

Shannon wrapped her arms around herself and leaned closer to the fire Gabe had built at the edge of the lake. "Are you sure we won't be reported for having a bonfire?"

"Do you want to freeze to death? Besides, who's going to see us? Nobody comes to these parks during the holidays. It's not a Christmas thing to do."

"I guess you're right. The fire does feel good." She smiled, warming her hands.

Gabe threw a dried cypress branch on the fire, then sat near Shannon, their shoulders touching. "Sleepy?"

"Hmm."

He fought an incredible urge to put his arm around her and pull her into him. Maybe she'd lay her head on his shoulder.

The fantasy was compelling.

She hummed a tune as she took a stick and poked at the fire.

"I've heard this song before," he said, remembering a faint echo in his mind. "It was you." He gasped. "You sang that to me in the hospital."

"I did!" She smiled. "But not when you were coming around. It was long before that. When you...first arrived."

"But I remember it so well. Is that possible, for me to remember something like that?"

"Of course. The unconscious records every word, every nuance of things our conscious minds don't recall."

A cold blast of wind cut through the trees.

Shannon hugged herself and moved her face closer to the fire. She began humming again.

Gabe manipulated the moment to put his arm around her. She did not shirk him, but accepted his touch instead. He thought he could remember other things Shannon had said to him and done for him while he was unconscious, but they were enveloped in thick shrouds of forgetfulness and buried too deep.

"Tell me the words," he said.

"I don't remember them all really. It's about a man wanting to have wings to fly his lady past the night to another world where they could be free to love."

"That's what you'd like me to do, isn't it, Shannon?"

She stared silently at the fire.

Watching the fire's shadows dance across Shannon's face, Gabe lifted his fingers to her chin. Slowly, he turned her face to his. "Wanted me to do that long before I was awake...before I even knew you."

She felt a tear slide down her cheek. "Yes."

His eyes smoldered as they dropped their gaze to her lips.

"Shannon..."

His lips captured her mouth in a kiss so passionate yet tender it shocked her to her core. His hand quivered as he touched her cheek and she knew he was as struck as she. His lips were eager in their apology and desperate in their need. He started to end the kiss, but instead, his lips plundered hers. He seemed unable to satiate himself.

His arms encircled her body and drew her in to him.

She leaned against him, taking the comfort he offered. She slipped her arms around his back, pressing her palms to his shoulders, pulling him closer, closer still.

She hadn't been prepared for the need she felt, nor the sense of wonder that overwhelmed her.

He slanted his mouth over hers as his kiss grew more powerful, then demanding. His fingers clasped her nape, holding her hostage. Only this time she wanted to be his captive.

This time she knew she held him in equal measure.

He ringed her lips with his tongue, then plunged into the interior of her mouth, setting off a series of shock waves she'd never experienced before.

"Gabe..." She exhaled his name as she broke from him.

"Please, don't," he said, eyes smoky with passion.

"I've never…"

"Neither have I," he whispered and cupped her face. "This is insane."

"It is," she said and kissed him with explosive intensity.

Shannon felt as if her heart had opened. A rush of love like she'd never known poured from her.

His arms tightened around her, pressing her so close to his chest, she felt his heart pound.

She wanted it to be like this always, ardor accelerating to delirium, but she knew it wouldn't. It couldn't.

She told herself she was caught in a romantic web.

She'd been needy, love-starved, for a long time. It made sense she would feel this lust.

What she couldn't explain away was everything else between them. The way she'd fallen in love with the fantasy of Gabe from the moment she'd seen him lying half-dead on a gurney in the ER. She'd spent her nights with him for weeks, talked to him about everything in her heart, sang to him, joked with him and miraculously, somehow, he had stored all her secrets deep in the labyrinth of his unconscious.

She had stolen him away into the night without his knowledge. Had she programmed his mind to fall in love with her? Had she manipulated his emotions when he was unconscious, making him respond only to her?

Or was it something more mystical? Magical, perhaps? Were they long-lost soul mates who, through quirks of fate and twists of destiny, had been finally brought together? Was she living the dream? Or was it possible…this was reality?

She didn't dare to hope.

Gabe was lost in the kiss as he leaned back, taking Shannon with him until they were lying on the ground. He slipped his hand underneath her sweat-shirt and unhooked her bra. She was surprised at the heat emanating from his hand as he filled it with her flesh. Even more shocking was the intense pang of craving that shot from her nipple to her loins.

She had wanted him since that first day in the ER.

Now she wanted him inside her.

She reached underneath her clothes and took his hand, pushing it lower…over her belly and down farther still.

Gabe's mouth covered hers in a protracted, rapacious kiss, then he stopped abruptly. He pushed himself away from her on his elbows. His eyes locked with hers.

"Shannon, I want you…more than you could know. But I want you to want me just as much."

"I do, Gabe. So very much."

"Shannon…"

"Gabe." She raised her face to his. "Shut up," she said and took him.

Gabe lowered his body to hers while she unbuttoned his waistband and unzipped his zipper. She wriggled out of her jeans, then grasped his hips. He fitted himself between her legs.

He filled her completely then, making love to her with a sweetness she hadn't dreamed possible. His kisses covered her lips, cheeks, temples, and fell like spring rain against her hairline. He drove himself deeper inside her as if gently marking her soul for eternity.

"You were meant to be mine, Shannon," he whispered tenderly as she arched her hips to him.

Like wedding vows, his words engraved themselves on her heart. Shannon had always felt displaced by life, even as a child. Suddenly, she felt as if heaven were watching over her and over them, blessing them.

She wasn't aware of his climax nor of hers, only of a spiraling sensation gently lifting her out of her body, carrying her through the night to another world. It was exactly like the song she'd hummed to him earlier.

She could feel his arms around her, cradling her as they floated still united, still one body, back to earth.

A profound awareness suffused every nerve in her body. She was in love with Gabe.

"Gabriel," she said and opened her eyes. *"My guardian angel."*

He buried his face in the crook of her neck. He was crying, but he didn't want her to know. He sniffed and rubbed his nose. Then he pulled her head into his shoulder, keeping their bodies close to stay warm. He was speechless. Sex with Shannon was nothing like what he'd expected.

But now that he thought about it, he wasn't sure what he'd expected. They had bonded, sure. They had come to have an affinity for each other. He'd needed her compassion. Her empathy. But somewhere after their initial kiss, everything had changed.

He'd been alone so long. Loved no one for so long, he didn't know he had a heart. He did now because it was open and screaming for nurturing.

He took her hand and placed it over his heart. Instantly, the pain began to ease.

Gabe didn't want to fall in love. Didn't want to so much as care for anyone. Especially not Shannon.

He knew nothing about her.

Yet he knew everything.

He knew he wanted to be inside her again. Not just inside her body, but inside her heart, inside her mind.

He felt like a greedy, hungry child. He wanted to know everything about her instantly. Had she ever loved anyone before? Had he been a better lover? Was she still in love with that man?

Or could he possibly hope she could love him?

"Shannon, you're cold," he said, reaching for her jeans and his. "Here, let me help you," he said and sat up halfway.

"Gabe?"

"Yes?" He pulled on his jeans and zipped them. Then he grabbed a stick and poked the fire. It blazed, warming them.

"Are you all right?"

"Am I—?" He turned back to her.

He sank his fingers into her nape and pulled her to him and kissed her.

When he released her, she said, "You wish you hadn't made love to me."

"Yes," he replied dourly.

"Why? I thought it was…"

"*Pointless* is the word you're looking for, Shannon. I had no business letting myself get carried away like that. We have no future, you and I, even if we get out of this alive, which I hope we do. But I have to remain realistic…you won't stay with me. You'll want to find your way back to your old life somehow."

"My old life…" She looked away from him to the fire.

She shivered from its memory. "My old life, Gabe, is not what you think."

"What is it, then?"

She hugged her knees and placed her chin on them, staring into the fire. "Everything you think you know about me is a lie, Gabe."

"I don't believe you."

"It's true." She glanced up at the full moon. "That moon up there reminds me of a night in California. Of why I can't go back there. Back to my old life."

She could feel that night coming forward like the rumble in the earth before it quakes.

The truth.

Her truth.

Maybe it was the pull of the moon, she wasn't sure, but Gabe was the first person she'd trusted in a long time.

"You don't have to tell me this," he said gently.

"I know."

She looked at him, the firelight crackling against the pain he saw in her eyes.

"It…it hurts. You know?"

"Yeah."

"I've never told anyone. My life in Shreveport is a lie, too. My name isn't Shannon Riley. It's Kathleen Shannon Randall. I'm not even really a nurse. I faked my application. I've only had one year of training. Charity hospitals are so desperate for help, they don't check records all that well, if they check them at all. When I was in college in San Francisco, I wanted to be a nurse. I've always known I had a talent for helping people, for bringing them back to health. But I didn't finish school because I got pregnant."

"Why did that stop you?"

"Money was hard to come by back then, being on my own and all. But the fact was that David's parents were very high-profile Californians. The Randalls still are."

She continued. "David and I met at a political fund-raiser where I'd volunteered to help serve food with some of the other pledges in my sorority. Supposedly, these things were only attended by a much older crowd. I learned later that several of these older men dated college girls. Some of the girls liked the grand-father image, but I didn't. Anyway, David was there with his grandfather—"

"Who made a play for you first," Gabe interrupted.

"How did you know?"

"Because I would have," he said softly. "Go on."

"Anyway, David and I fell in love at first sight. I know it sounds corny but it was true. When I met his parents on our first date, he announced to them that he intended to marry me once he graduated that year."

"And his parents hated you on sight."

"Yes. He was their darling whom they intended to groom for governor one day. He was dashing, charm-ing, handsome as the devil and graduated summa cum laude in political science. He was a shoo-in."

"Did they have another woman picked out for him?"

"Not really. Amelia, that's his mother, told me not long after we met that she 'had wanted better for him.' Since she knew every Californian's pedigree go-ing back to the Spanish dons', I didn't doubt she had a very long list. I was a nobody in David's parents' eyes. Be that as it may, they wanted David to be happy. So, they paraded me around from parties to weekends at luxurious ranches in northern California to charity-sponsored operatic events. My name was in the society column every month."

"When I got pregnant two months before David's graduation and the wedding had to be moved up, Amelia hit the ceiling. She was devastated because now her friends would know me for the real tramp I was, she said."

Gabe watched the furrows in her forehead deepen as Shannon placed herself back in time. He felt as if he were back there with her. "And the baby?"

Shannon's face instantly glowed. "He was exquisite. Healthy. I wanted to call him Thomas after my father. But we named him Laird, after David's father. Laird was only a month old when I discovered David was a cocaine user. Not just a little bit. A lot. It got out of hand fast. I couldn't believe his high energy and sexiness came from drugs. I pleaded with him to stop. But he wouldn't. Couldn't. I threatened to tell his parents. It was a waste of time."

Taking a very deep breath, she continued. "Then, when Laird was six months old the whole family was invited to a family picnic in Carmel. I remember how excited I was. Amelia was actually warming up to me by then. Laird had made the difference for me where she was concerned. She loved being a grandmother and showing him off. The money that woman spent on his nursery and clothes was incredible. She paraded the baby around San Francisco society announcing someday Laird would show them all and be president of the United States. Lord knows, the Randall family fortune could pay for his campaign single-handedly.

"David's using was totally out of control by then. He started at six in the morning and didn't stop. Since he didn't actually work at anything other than politics, making himself visible at one function after another, there was nothing for him to do but be charming. For that, he needed coke.

"For me the picnic was a disaster. David was verbally abusive day and night. After being out till two and three in the morning, he'd wake me up to abuse me. He got his kicks out of seeing me cry, plead with him not to hurt me, then thank him when he didn't. I begged to leave. He refused. This time I did more than threaten to tell his mother, I did. She called me a tramp and said I didn't know what I was talking about. The past six months of our bonding vanished. She wanted the baby and David and wanted me to disappear.

"We left the party. David's abuse turned to screaming, ranting. I realized his rage was directed against his mother, which he'd projected onto me.

"I was driving. He started hitting me while I was driving. The baby was in the back seat in his car seat. Laird started screaming. David hit him to get him to be quiet. Of course Laird screamed louder. I hit David. We struggled over the steering wheel. He called me names. I told him I would take the baby and walk back to San Francisco, but we weren't staying with him anymore. I told him I was filing for divorce. He swore he and his parents would take Laird from me."

Tears tumbled out of Shannon's eyes as she continued. "We were driving along the Pacific Coast Highway. I slowed the car as I remembered a lookout point just around the next bend. David went crazy and rammed his foot down over mine, flooring the accelerator. I screamed. David grabbed the wheel, saying, 'You'll never take my son away from me.' I barely remember what happened next, but somehow I kept the car on the highway for quite a while. Suddenly, we were rolling over and over and over. Then we smashed up against the guardrail. I was upside down. David's head had gone through the windshield. I don't think there was an inch of flesh left. The baby was silent. I remember the flames. I always remember the flames. The way they smelled, not like this campfire, but acrid from my own flesh burning. From Laird's body…"

Her hands were shaking. Her voice quaked, but she knew she had to tell the whole story.

"I…I don't know where the fire started. Somehow, I got out of the car and got Laird out of his seat. Mercifully, he was still alive, though not breathing. I crawled away from the car just as the gas lines exploded. At least that's what I think happened. It was like that truck exploding today. I tried to revive Laird with mouth-to-mouth, but he was too…small. He was just a baby. I was burned myself. My hair was gone. I had a concussion and must have passed out at that point. There are days and days I don't remember at all, when I was taken to the hospital. When I woke up, my burns had begun to heal, but that was when I was told Laird was dead. My mind seemed to explode and my heart shattered. I wanted to die then. So badly…"

Shannon burst into tears and let her face fall into her hands. "My God! Will I ever be able to forget?"

"No," he said softly, putting his arms around her. "But you'll go on. You have no choice."

She pressed her face into his shoulder.

"Cry. Cry all you want for as long as you want," he said.

A long moment later, Shannon composed herself. "I've cried for years, Gabe. I don't know how I've got any tears left."

"I'll always give you time for tears." He caressed her hair. "So, you left California?"

Nodding, she said, "Amelia and her husband didn't believe my story. They were in total denial about David's using. They pressed murder charges against me, claiming I'd trapped him into marriage, making false accusations about me extorting money from them. They said they'd seen me drinking to excess at the picnic. I knew their kind of money and influence could buy a guilty verdict in court. I couldn't afford the kind of attorney it would take to fight them. So I jumped bail, disguised myself and started driving East. I didn't know where I was going, just as long it was the other side of the earth. I got as far as Shreveport when my car broke down. While I was having it repaired, I read an article in the newspaper about the crisis St. Christopher's was having finding nurses and doctors to staff the charity hospital. I sold the car to a young college guy who was planning to relocate to Chicago, used the money to get my apartment and got hired as a nurse. That was six years ago."

"And so you're afraid that if you go back to California, the Randalls will find you and put you in jail."

"I'm sure of it."

"Have you ever thought of really fighting them?"

"With what? How?"

"In court. They couldn't make those charges stick through a formal hearing."

"But that takes money. Lots of it."

Gabe reached in his pocket and pulled out the computer disk. "What do you think this is?"

She wiped her eyes with the flat of her palm. "What are you saying?"

"That we take this drug money and right a wrong with it. You lost your son because of drugs. That money has come back to you. It can give you back the life it took away from you."

"Gabe, please."

"I'm serious."

"How can we make it out of this alive?"

"I'm not sure, Shannon," he said, pulling her close to him again. "But I promise you, I'll do everything I can to keep you safe. I swear I will."

His eyes were filled with tenderness and commitment.

Maybe Gabe was right to conjure his dream of surviving.

After all, there was nothing else to keep them alive.

29

Ben stood over them, watching, feeling his heart sink.

This was not what he thought he'd find. He'd expected Shannon to be tied up. Terrified. Instead, he found Shannon and Gabe spooned against each other like lovers.

Ben felt sick inside.

He unholstered his gun and nodded to Sheriff Creighton, who signaled back.

A cold metal rifle barrel pressed into Gabe's left cheek.

"Wha...?"

Sheriff Creighton increased the pressure.

Vividly remembering the last time he'd been similarly stirred, Gabe half expected to hear Hispanic accents. Instead, he looked up to see an imposing figure dressed in a sheriff's uniform looming over him.

"All I want to know is who the hell are you?" Sheriff Creighton demanded.

Gabe reached protectively for Shannon, pulling her against him.

"What's the matter?" She awoke and focused her eyes, then gasped. "Ben?"

"Kathleen," he replied, surprised at the bitterness he heard in his voice.

"You know?"

"Everything," he said, his eyes riveted on hers.

Gabe tightened his hold on Shannon. "Are we under arrest?"

"You didn't answer my question," Sheriff Creighton boomed, pushing the rifle into Gabe's flesh.

Gabe didn't flinch. He was too busy analyzing the interplay between his former guard and Shannon. Ben stood pantherlike, ready to defend with a kill. His eyes were relentless, his jaw grinding angrily as if he'd already devoured his enemy. Everything about him was territorial.

Gabe realized he had invaded Ben's space.

It hit him that Ben was in love with Shannon.

Gabe didn't dare look at Shannon. He didn't want to see her eyes and see the truth. He knew she'd been trying to escape him from the get-go. All along he hadn't blamed her. She was terrified, of course. But it had never dawned on Gabe that there might be another reason for her wanting to leave.

Sure, she'd told him her story about her past life with David. Sure, they'd made incredible love last night. But what if she was just acting?

Even if she had had a momentary lapse and had fallen for Gabe, would it last?

Gabe couldn't believe how faulty his thinking had been. He'd never factored in the Ben quotient.

Gabe could feel Shannon's reaction to Ben as she straightened her back and moved away from him just enough that their bodies no longer touched.

Gabe felt as if he'd stepped off the earth.

He swallowed and looked down at the black metal rifle.

"Turner. Gabe Turner. I sell insurance."

"Right." He stuck the rifle in Shannon's face.

She sucked in her breath.

Sheriff Creighton said, "Maybe you'll be more co-operative. You're *supposed* to be the hostage."

Shannon didn't miss his inference. "I am the hostage."

"Doesn't look like it to me. Does it look like that to you, Agent Richards?"

"*Agent* Richards?" Shannon parroted.

"Hell! No wonder they found us!" Gabe exclaimed. "Why didn't you come a little sooner? Maybe you could have saved me from doing your job for you back there in Amarillo," Gabe said bitterly. He didn't like the way Ben's gaze didn't waver from Shannon. Gabe didn't like it at all.

"Thanks," Ben said.

"That's it?" Gabe hit the ground with his hand.

Sheriff Creighton stuck the rifle barrel on Gabe's forehead. "I've got papers here that say you're wanted for the federal offense of kidnapping. Agent Richards has done an exemplary job of bringing you to justice. Least that's the way I see it."

"I'm sure you do," Gabe said, his territorial instincts as intense as Ben's.

Shannon dropped her eyes as she realized the emotions underscoring their encounter. Suddenly, she was in the middle of something she wasn't sure she understood.

Ben wasn't a city cop. He was a federal agent. He'd been assigned to Gabe's room to spy. To haul him off to God knew where the moment she and the doctors had made him well.

Betrayal knifed her. She'd been used, by Ben and by the system. She was sick of it. Sick of other people dictating her life, her direction based on their needs. She'd let it happen in California and now it was happening again.

Suddenly, she didn't give a damn.

With her forearm she swiped at the rifle barrel, shoving it away from Gabe's face. "If you're going to shoot us, then shoot!" She was on her feet. "I don't care what you do!"

"I do!" Gabe said, slowly inching upward into a stance.

"They're going to kill us." She turned blazing eyes on Ben. "Aren't you, Ben?"

"Shannon..."

"It's Kathleen to you. Remember?" Hands on hips, she took a bold step toward him. "So before you cart his butt off and then trump up some phony charge that I'm an accomplice to what, I don't know, why don't you tell me what you really want, Ben?"

He stared at her, hair sleep-tossed, her eyes wild as fire. She took his breath away. And he hated it. He had no idea he could feel like this about a woman. Especially about one who was about to nail him. Unless he did it first.

Either way, he was screwed.

"It's about money," Ben said. "Cartel money. Turner knows where it is. The United States government needs that information to put the Cassalia Cartel out of business. Forever."

"And after Gabe does his patriotic duty for the country? What happens to him then?"

Her method was convoluted, he thought, but she was defending Turner.

And she saw Ben as the enemy.

He steeled himself. He knew the situation was only going to get worse for him.

"He'll be protected."

"Like one of those federal witness-protection plans?" Gabe laughed aloud. "Sorry, I'm not buying."

"Fine. Go to prison. I can arrange that," Ben shot back.

Gabe glared at him. "So then I have a new identity, new place to live, new work. Never see my mother again? Never see my friends?"

"You'll be safe," Ben replied.

"Bullshit! There's no such thing as security. You can't promise diddly. You'll have what you want...all the way. I get zilch. Sorry, pal."

"And me?" Shannon asked.

Ben knew he'd had hours to prepare for this moment. This question. But he'd never come up with the answer that would satisfy her. Or make himself happy. It was a piece-of-crap reply and he knew it. But it was the truth.

"The same," he said.

"That's not a life!" she said.

"You call living like you were a life? Always on the run? Hiding out? Come on, Kathleen. You think you know what you're dealing with here, but you don't. The Cassalia Cartel is huge, bigger than the Cali Cartel. It has more Americans on its payroll than Colombians, including Chief Bremen, who is about as ruthless as they come. Do you know that he's responsible for the murders of two of your friends?"

"My friends?" Shannon asked. "He doesn't know anyone..."

"Bremen tried to fake Elliot's suicide, but I can

prove he murdered him. Our men found a witness who saw Chief Bremen entering your apartment building at the time of the murder. He left fingerprints on the front door. Chelsea Sikeston? She was his girlfriend. He broke her neck and left her in the woods."

Shannon's body went rubbery as the shock hit her. "Elliot? But he never hurt anyone. He was the kindest..." She felt faint with disbelief.

"Bremen was afraid you'd told Elliot something about Turner in confidence. He thought Elliot knew something. Chelsea was the one responsible for the Mickey Finn in Turner's IV that day," Ben explained.

Shannon was disbelieving. "Why would Chelsea..."

"Money. She was paid."

"They died because of me?" Her eyes swam in tears.

"No! It's not your fault!" Gabe was angrily defensive. "What the hell are you trying to do, Ben?" Gabe shot him a damning look.

Ben was undeterred and continued his onslaught. "I'm not telling you this to make you feel guilty. I'm telling you so you'll understand that these people are everywhere, Kathleen. As soon as the department puts away one or two links in their chain, another pops up, greedier, more vicious than the last."

"We managed to get away from Bremen in Dallas," Gabe said.

"You were lucky. Besides, Bremen is dead."

"What?" Gabe asked.

"Shot by one of his men. A gang hit. In Amarillo."

"He was there at the motel?"

Ben nodded. "Across the street."

Gabe faltered back a pace. "My God, is it just luck that we're alive?"

"I'd say a miracle," Ben said. He turned back to Shannon. "So is this what you want? Dodging bullets forever? Never going back to California to find out the real truth about what happened that night on Highway 1?"

Ben stopped himself. He'd let his need to win, to always be Maestro, take over. It was a sin he'd never committed until now. But he'd said too much.

Gabe picked up on it first. "*Real* truth?"

Shannon felt as if time stood still. She heard the clacking of the bare tree limbs above. A night owl hooted. A rabbit scurried over dry pine needles. Inside her mind, she heard a baby's scream and the anguish of her own voice.

How could Ben know anything about me? How could anyone? He's bluffing.

"What are you saying, Ben?" she finally asked.

"That you've been running away when maybe you should be going back. That your baby isn't dead."

"What?" Gabe was incredulous.

"*What?*" Shannon felt the earth reeling. "That's impossible."

"Is it?" Ben replied. "After you dragged yourself and the child from the wreckage, what did you do?"

"Mouth-to-mouth. I tried to revive him. But he was dead."

"Not according to the eyewitness who called the paramedics. We tracked the medical records, too. You passed out, Shannon. You were comatose for ten days after the accident."

"I know."

Gabe stared at her. "You? Comatose?"

Suddenly, he understood how Shannon knew to have so much empathy for him. She knew from personal experience that he would hear her voice even when unconscious.

Shannon pressed her fingers to her temples, clearing the muddled scenes of the past. "I remembered hearing a nurse's voice when I was out. Coming to and finding her there with me. Everyone in my life was gone, but that nurse. That's why I took your assignment. I wanted to repay the favor."

Ben continued. "During that time you were out, Amelia placed your son in a private hospital. His burns were treated, he had plastic surgery, and when he was released, the hospital records stated that he was put up for private adoption."

"This is ludicrous! You're saying all this to trick me! To make me think my son is alive!" Her insides were on fire. She wanted to strike Ben for giving her false hopes. False dreams. Especially when she knew the truth.

"Laird is alive, Kathleen." Ben's voice was filled with compassion. He hated seeing her upset. Knowing he was responsible.

He would have given the world if she would have fallen against him, the way she was now doing...but to Gabe.

"Who could be so barbaric as to take a child from his mother?" Gabe asked, his eyes clamped on Shannon.

Shannon thought the world had stopped. She shook her head. "Some people can be just that desperate."

Ben's eyes rested softly on her face, hoping to God she could take the rest of the truth.

As she watched Ben's expression change, Shannon felt her body tremble and her skin crawl. Her adrenaline raced. She saw the pain in his eyes. And she knew he was holding the worst back.

"What else do you want to tell me, Ben?"

He didn't want to tell her the rest. He didn't want to be the messenger of bad news. Messengers were too often hated and blamed as if they'd been the perpetrator rather than simply the deliverer.

"You know who adopted Laird, don't you, Ben?"

"Yes. I got the report just hours ago."

"Who was it?"

"Amelia."

Her hands flew to her mouth as she gasped. "Oh my God! It can't be true!"

Gabe shook his head and put his arms around Shannon, folding her next to him. He looked at Ben. "Her own mother-in-law?"

"Amelia Randall couldn't pry David away from Kathleen or bring him back to life. But she could and did arrange for the baby to be brought to the private hospital herself. She got her doctor to falsify information, make a new birth certificate and thus became Laird's legally adoptive mother. Everyone in San Francisco thinks she's a bit daffy, wanting to replace David with a surrogate. Not even her husband knows the real story."

"And my son? He's healthy? Happy? He doesn't remember the accident?"

"It appears that way though we don't know that for sure. All we know is that he's six years old, in the first grade at a private elementary school in San Francisco and being brought up as any other wealthy kid."

Shannon's legs gave out from under her. She sank to the ground.

Sheriff Creighton made a show of putting his rifle away. He didn't want anyone to know he'd been holding his breath all this time. Turning to Ben he said, "Remind me not to go on another arrest with you."

Ben shot him a sidelong glance. He took a step toward Shannon. "I could take you to him."

"What?"

"I'll take you to see your son. To California."

Her eyes narrowed. "You said I had to go into protective custody. That I'd have to be like Gabe."

Ben's voice was softly earnest. "You want to see him, don't you?"

Ben wanted to be her savior, had to be her savior.

Her eyes held his for a long moment. A space in time where she felt Gabe struggling with himself not to demand she stay with him. She had guessed Gabe would be self-sacrificing. He would care more about her feelings, her needs, than he would his own.

She remembered making love with him and the sweet passion they'd shared. She felt part of his life now. Part of his struggle. Even now she felt the pressure of his hand on her arm, supporting her, comforting her, and yet their tentative pressure was ever so slightly telling her it was okay to leave him if that was what she wanted.

What do I want? For weeks I wanted only Gabe. Wanted him to be conscious. Wanted to get to know him, and now I know him as much as I know myself. I can't leave Gabe. It would be like leaving a part of myself behind.

Glancing up at Ben she felt his heart open to her, a flood of compassion and emotion wafting over her.

She realized he was giving her a chance to go back to the past. A chance to hold her son. An hour ago she hadn't thought such a miracle possible. She would have died herself for the chance to hold her baby one more time.

Ben was giving her the moon, stars and heaven, too. He loved her enough to jeopardize his career for her.

She was suspended between two men. Both loving her. Both with their lives on the line. For her.

For her son.

Fate's crossroads were paved in broken glass. Torture to choose and impossible not to experience.

She couldn't...wouldn't ask him to take the risk.

"And what happens to Gabe?"

"He goes one way. To Washington with Sheriff Creighton. You and I go to California."

"Ben..." She reached for his hand.

Gabe swore the world went black as he watched Shannon make her choice between them.

It seemed an eternity, watching Shannon's hand link with Ben's and fuse with another.

Gabe touched his lower lip with his tongue, still tasting her kiss. He didn't want to imagine his life without Shannon in it.

She dropped her eyes away from Ben and let go of his hand. "I can't let you do this, Ben."

"Why not?" Ben asked disbelievingly.

"It's too much to ask. You have a life. A career. You have a need to make the world a better place. I'm as selfish as humans come. All this time I haven't cared about anyone. Anywhere. I've only wanted a chance to hold my baby again. You gave me that chance and I'm going to take it."

She reached for Gabe's forearm and let him pull her up. As she did, she surreptitiously slipped her hand into his jacket pocket and pulled out the disk.

"Here," she said to Ben. "This is what you want. This is what you really came here for. Not for me. Not to cage us for the rest of our lives. You'll have your drug lord."

Ben laughed in spite of himself. "You think I'm just going to let you go?"

Sheriff Creighton started to pull up his rifle. "Turner is going to D.C. with me."

She noticed that Ben and Sheriff Creighton never took their eyes off the disk she held up. It was confirmation that she was right.

She guided Gabe toward the Cutlass. He took her cue and darted toward the car, got in and started the engine.

"Everything you need is on this disk. Your job depends on this information."

"She's right," Sheriff Creighton said to Ben.

Shannon kept backing away. The Cutlass was only a few feet away.

Ben was undeterred. "The cartel will kill you. You have to know that! They'll never let up! You'll be running forever!"

"I'm going to see my son!"

"And after that?"

"I don't know."

"Shannon! Don't do this!" Ben shouted.

Sheriff Creighton had had about all he was going to take. He cocked the rifle and aimed. "You're under arrest. You have the right to remain silent. You have..."

"Ben..." Shannon said across the distance. "Ben, you've helped me this far. Let me go all the way?"

"God help me, Shannon, I can't let you go. I lo—" Ben's words caught in his throat.

Shannon pitched the disk toward Ben.

He lowered his gun and caught it, then grabbed the rifle out of Sheriff Creighton's hands.

"Are you nuts?" Sheriff Creighton asked him.

Shannon got into the Cutlass and Gabe hit the gas. Ben waited to see if she would look back. She did.

"Yeah. I'm nuts." Ben smiled.

"So now what do we do?"

Ben looked down at the disk. "We make out our report. We retrieved the disk. We have the evidence we need."

"And?"

"I get a flight to San Francisco."

Sheriff Creighton smiled. "Now you're talking."

30

Shannon had gone to the gift shop and bought a New Mexico T-shirt, a pair of black leggings and a few toiletries. Then she'd gone to the ladies' room and given herself a sponge bath using paper towels. She'd washed her hair with the travel-size bottle of shampoo, and after drying it under the hand dryer, had shoved it beneath her ball cap.

While Shannon was changing, Gabe placed a call to Peter Dominic at his San Francisco home. This time the phone was answered.

"H-hello?" Pete's voice cracked.

"Is that you, Pete?"

"My God! Gabe! Can I call you back?"

"No! Pete, you have to listen to me. You're in danger."

Pete stared horrified at Melanie's dead body at his feet. "You're telling me. You wouldn't believe what's happened here."

"Adam is dead, Pete," Gabe blurted.

Pete said, "I know. Did you go to the funeral?"

"Not exactly."

"What the hell does that mean? I was in New York on business. Where were you?"

"Lying in a coma in Shreveport."

"That was you?"

Gabe swallowed hard. "How is it you know so much, Pete?"

"Adam's family called the office to tell me about the funeral arrangements. My secretary asks a lot of questions. She called me in New York and said Adam had been found in Shreveport. Shot. Murdered. There was an unidentified man with him in the car. The murderer they thought. What the hell's going on, Gabe?"

"I was gonna ask you the same question."

Melanie's blue eyes stared up at Pete out of her lifeless face.

His stomach lurched.

He turned away from her.

Pete swallowed hard. "I think we need to talk."

"No joke."

"Where are you?" Pete asked.

"I'm on my way to see you, but it can't be at your place."

"I agree. This isn't…convenient for me, either."

"Can we meet at your cottage in Carmel?"

"Yeah, sure. So tell me where you are."

Gabe didn't like the way Pete asked the question. There was too much edge. Too much desperation. He couldn't be sure. Hell, at this point, he wasn't sure about anything.

"Albuquerque airport. I'm flying out in less than an hour. I need another favor. Do you still keep that Taurus at the airport?"

"Yeah. I mean, I think it's there unless one of my employees used it."

"I'm on my cellular. Find out and call me back. I

need that car to get to Carmel and I don't want to risk renting a car."

"What's your number?" Pete scribbled down the number on a notepad. He tore off the top sheet and put the number in his pocket. "I'll call my secretary and see if she loaned it out to anyone. I just flew in from Aspen and took a cab to the house."

"You still hate driving, don't you, Pete?"

"It's a phobia. People have them."

"Is the Taurus still on level four, section H?"

"Yeah. 4H. Easy to remember. What airline are you flying?"

"American," Gabe answered.

"I'll arrange to have the keys left for you at the American Airlines ticket counter like I've done in the past. I'll tell them you're a client. It's too risky to use your name. Tell them you're Paul Huber."

"Great. I'll give you a call when I land."

"Don't call me here. I'll be in Carmel. Just meet me there," Pete said.

"All right," Gabe said and hung up.

Pete backed away from Melanie's body and surveyed the rest of his house. Sofa cushions had been upended and the throw pillows tossed on the floor. Going upstairs, he found his closet a mess and his toiletries strewn on the floor. He made certain not to touch anything. He went back downstairs, picked up his ski bag, suitcase and portable computer bag and walked out of the house.

At the next block he went to a phone booth and called a cab. He dialed his office.

"Susan, is the company car at the airport?"

"Yes, sir. Are you on your way in from Aspen?"

"Not yet."

"Dina called yesterday and left a message on your voice mail."

"I'll get it later. Do me a favor and have a messenger run the Taurus keys out to the American Airlines ticket counter. Tell the attendant they're for Paul Huber."

"Certainly. Anything else?"

"No. I'll check in tomorrow for my messages. Have a good day," he said and hung up.

A cabbie servicing the area pulled up to the booth. Pete placed his bags in the trunk and pulled out a hundred-dollar bill. "There's another one of these if you go off duty for this trip."

"Consider it done," the cabbie said and took the money. "Where to?"

"Carmel," Pete said.

Shannon walked out of the ladies' bathroom and found a very agitated Gabe.

"What took you so long?" he asked.

She didn't like the constriction she heard in his voice. She could tell he was nervous, but this was something else. Every time she was out of his sight for a moment longer than he expected, he started acting this way.

"Gabe, I'm not going to run off."

"I know," he replied, still feeling tenuous after his recent victory over Ben.

Gabe realized that Shannon didn't give her heart easily. She was in love with him. He'd bank on it. They'd been to hell and back together, but her love for him was new. The love and need she had to see her son again had history and a deep well of emotion he saw every time she thought about Laird.

Gabe's gut turned inside out at the thought of losing her to the one male he could never fight—Laird.

With this call to Pete, they were on their way to San Francisco. Gabe had to face the fact that Shannon might not stick with him all the way to the end.

Shannon glanced at the clock above the ticket counter and then down at her watch. "I'm sorry, Gabe. I didn't mean to worry you. I guess my watch stopped."

He took her hand and started toward the gate. "We have to hurry or we'll miss our flight."

"Did you find Pete?"

"Yes."

"Thank God. And everything is arranged like we talked about?"

"Yes. Everything," he said, his eyes scanning the crowds. He could see no one following them. They walked down the corridor to the gate.

They fast-walked up to the tall male attendant who was motioning to them to hurry onto the plane. Holding their boarding passes out to the attendant, Gabe glanced back over his shoulder.

Still safe.

"Are we the last ones?" Gabe asked the man.

"Yes, sir. This flight is already a minute late."

"Sorry," Shannon said nervously and darted in front of Gabe onto the jetway.

Gabe rushed behind her.

As Gabe entered the plane, the jetway captain closed the airplane door behind him. The airliner immediately taxied away from the terminal.

Sliding into his seat next to Shannon, he cupped her face with his hand and pressed her head into his shoulder. Her pulse was beating at triple time just as his was. "It's okay. We made it."

"Yes, we have," she said with a sigh. Settling back into her seat, she prepared for takeoff.

Once they were airborne, Shannon watched the earth fall away and clouds hold the plane in the sky by its belly. They had been running and hiding every second since the moment Gabe told her they had to go back to California. She'd never let herself think about Laird and who he would be now. She thought he was dead, frozen in her memory as an infant.

She couldn't help wondering about him. Did he look like her still or had he grown into a replica of David? He would be six now, going into school. She wondered what toys he played with. Did he have a computer? Kids all seemed to know how to use one better than she did these days.

What was his favorite food? Did he have friends or pets? Did he like fairy tales? Did he remember the Irish lullabyes she used to sing to him even before his birth? Had Amelia told him anything about her?

Shannon kept her eyes closed to hold back her burning tears. She didn't want to think about the lies Amelia could have told him.

Still, she would brave those walls of lies, just to see him again.

Her arms went around herself, and she wondered what it would have been like to hold him. Suddenly, she realized she'd never known such emptiness. Such a hollow feeling this was…a mother without her son.

At that moment, she cried for all the mothers who had lost their sons to war or illness or accident. For all the mothers whose hearts were broken and left torn by life. She cried for her child and herself. She cried for the world.

Gabe put his arm around her and curled her into his shoulder. "There, now, Shannon," he said.

It was just the way he said it, its inflection and color and tone, that Irish lilting way of speaking that reminded her of the times when her mother had held her, comforted her and given her hope again with just a squeeze.

For that moment, Shannon knew she would love Gabe forever.

31

![arrow decoration]

"We're here already?" Shannon asked, opening her eyes as she felt the plane descend.

"I'm afraid so," Gabe said, pulling her closer and kissing her temple.

"I'm scared, Gabe," she said.

"I know," he replied. "But I'll be with you all the way," he said as he tilted her face to his. "I want you to know that I hate it that I'm the one who brought all this down on you. I swear I'll make it up to you someday."

"Don't..."

He kissed her.

Gone was the passion and in its place was sweet melancholy, as if he were saying goodbye.

"Shannon, I lo—"

She placed her fingers on his lips, quieting them. "Don't say it," she said. "Please."

He peered deeply into her eyes. "You know I love you. I'd take a bullet for you, Shannon. But I don't know if I can watch you walk away from me."

"Gabe. I have to go. He's my child."

His expression recoiled as if he'd been struck by a viper. "I'd be putting you both in danger if I went."

"I know."

There were tears in her eyes and the sight of her

open love for him tore at his insides. Placing his hand on her crown, he gently pressed her head to his shoulder. "It's okay, Shannon. I'll help you find him."

"You love me that much?"

"More. So very much more," he said as the pilot touched the aircraft to the runway.

Walking off the airplane, Shannon was instantly on guard again. Her adrenaline raced as she scanned the sea of passengers. Every life-and-death scene she and Gabe had experienced in the past few days came spiraling back to her.

"Gabe, hold my hand. Don't let me go."

"Never," he assured her as they pressed their way toward the American Airlines ticket counter.

Glancing at Shannon's pale face and frightened eyes, he said, "Please try to smile."

"I wish I could, but I know that at any moment we could be killed."

"I don't want to draw attention to us. Pretend we're on vacation."

"Sure. Right. Fine," she grumbled. Trying to put herself in the role, she glanced at the foreign-travel posters that lined the corridor. "Where are we going?"

"Where do you want to go?" he asked, still searching for the American Airlines counter.

"Greece."

Gabe kept a false smile plastered on his face as he watched people rush by. "I'm not into ruins," he said.

"Okay, then we'll go to one of the small islands. Santorini perhaps. We'll sit in an outdoor café and have coffee, listen to the sound of goats' bells as the goatherders take their flock up the mountainside. I'll sunbathe on a rock and watch the sun set across the Aegean."

"That sounds better."

"Then we can go?"

Gabe halted momentarily and said, "I promise."

They walked up to the ticket counter.

"May I help you, sir?" the fresh-faced young woman asked.

"I'm here to pick up some car keys for Paul Huber."

"I don't know anything about any keys. We don't ordinarily do this kind of thing."

"I'm a client of Peter Dominic's and I..."

"Oh." The girl blushed crimson. "Mr. Dominic. Of course. Let me check."

Gabe looked at Shannon. "Girlfriend," they said in unison.

"Yes, Mr. Huber. I have them. The messenger must have brought them over while I was on break." She handed the keys to Gabe. "Please give Mr. Dominic my regards when you see him."

"I'll do that, Miss..." He looked at her bronze name badge. "Patterson."

Shannon held her breath as she and Gabe walked away.

"I thought it would be tougher than that," she said.

"That's because you don't trust Pete."

She glanced at him. "Neither do you."

"You're right," he said.

They walked quickly to the parking garage and took the elevator to the fourth level. As they passed the sections in the first third of the alphabet, Shannon noticed they seemed to be the only ones in the garage.

The rows were numbered in purple-painted letters

of the alphabet. "Row H." She looked down the row. "There it is!" she said, pointing to a clean white Taurus.

"Great!" Gabe approached the car.

Suddenly, he stopped in his tracks.

He didn't know exactly what it was, the dark cloud that passed over the sun or the way the sun's rays cut through the concrete opening and cast eerie shadows, but something felt menacing.

He grabbed Shannon's arm and pulled her back alongside him.

"What's the matter?" She quickly glanced around her. "Is someone following us?"

"It's not that, but…"

Gabe pulled the keys out of his pocket and stared at them, cocking an eyebrow.

"But what?"

"Pete never had a remote on these keys before. He always said this was a company car. No leather. No sunroof. No tape deck. It was intended to be a plain-Jane car for clients who come into town and don't have time to rent a car or who have a particular aversion to cabs. Sitting here at the airport most of the time, he figured no one would steal it because it isn't worth much."

"So? He changed his mind." She'd no sooner said the words than she instinctively began backing away from the car.

As Gabe did the same, he hit the unlock button.

The Taurus exploded. The sound was deafening and thundered through the concrete caverns of the parking garage. Fire billowed from beneath the Taurus and smoke rose like a dragon spreading its wings.

Pieces of metal and glass hurtled through the air toward Gabe and Shannon.

"Run for it!" Gabe shouted but Shannon was already ahead of him.

Debris hit the concrete roof, then deflected instantly to the concrete floor, sounding like an avalanche crushing everything in its path. Waves of heat surged toward them, threatening to singe their backs.

Shannon thought she could smell her hair burning. Terror struck her.

Visions of the past—flames, her baby—flooded her. "I'm on fire!"

"No, you're not!" He pointed to the car. "It's the cloth seats and carpet."

She glanced back at the sizzling debris.

Escaping serious injury, they raced down the ramp to the second level.

"Look for something old, dusty. A car that looks like it's been forgotten by someone who doesn't show up here very often," Gabe instructed.

Shannon found a black early eighties vintage Cadillac Sedan de Ville. She tried the door. "It's locked," she said, "and we don't have a wire coat hanger or anything else to jimmy it."

"I know," he said, wrapping his windbreaker around his forearm, breaking the passenger's rear window. He unlocked the back door, slid inside and unlocked the other doors.

Going around to the driver's seat, he hot-wired the car and in minutes they drove away.

Shaking her head, Shannon asked, "You do this so well. How many cars have you stolen?"

"I'm not stealing this car, I'm borrowing it."

They pulled up to the payment booth. Because of

the explosion, the attendant had left the booth and was racing up the ramp with a security guard. Siren sounds approached from outside the garage. In the lane next to them sat a silver Mercedes whose driver had gotten out of his car and was yelling at the attendant.

"Hey! You! Come back here and open this gate! I've got a meeting to get to!"

Gabe laid on his horn. "Hey! Buddy! My wife's gonna have a baby!" Placing his hand on the top of Shannon's head, he pushed her down in the seat. "Groan," he instructed.

Grimacing with accompanying painful-sounding moans, Shannon convinced the onlooker she was in dire straits.

"Oh my God!" The man raced over to the black-and-white-striped wooden arm and lifted it manually for Gabe and Shannon. Gabe waved to the man as they drove through the turnstile.

Joseph Valerosa pointed to the fourth floor of the parking garage from his vantage point in the Volvo across the street. "It's up there," he said to Sardia. "The car was parked next to the outer wall." He checked his watch. "They should be almost there…"

A huge explosion sent fingers of flames through the opening in the concrete wall that both ventilated and lighted the interior.

Joseph crossed himself, but smiled at Sardia's implacable face.

Sardia's dark eyes were hidden behind reflective sunglasses. When Joseph reached for the ignition key, Sardia placed a black-gloved hand on Joseph's arm.

"Wait."

Sardia kept watching the garage.

Long moments passed, the sound of falling metal and glass shattering dissipated. Sirens screamed toward the garage. Pandemonium from pedestrians entering the garage blended with cries and shouts of hysteria all around the garage.

Sardia tapped Joseph's shoulder and pointed to the garage exit. A black Cadillac with a single driver left the building. It was followed by a man driving a silver Mercedes.

"What?" Joseph looked at Sardia.

"Follow the Mercedes," he ordered brusquely.

"Why? Our pigeons blew up!"

"Do it!"

Joseph pulled away from the curb as two squad cars sped into the garage followed by a fire truck and ambulance.

Gabe took the 101 out of San Francisco International Airport and headed toward San Jose. Shannon kept her eyes plastered on the traffic behind them.

"What are you looking for?" Gabe asked.

"Cops, of course."

He glanced in the rearview mirror. "It'll take them a while to put two and two together, if they ever do. No one is going to notice this car being gone. The only one who can describe us is the guy in the Mercedes and he won't talk."

"Why not?"

"Are you kidding? He's a businessman. He's got a meeting to go to. Talking to cops will take up too much time. He'd have to file a report. He'll say he didn't see a thing," he said glibly.

"Do you really think so?"

Nodding, he warned, "I'd be looking at passenger cars if I were you."

"For who?"

"For our friend from Amarillo and the airport."

"You think he knows we're here?"

"I'm certain of it." He paused. "That explosion sent a very large signal. Frankly, I didn't think we'd get out of there alive. Even without the car being rigged to blow."

Gabe's eyes were stern, holding pain.

Shannon sensed what he was thinking. "Pete set us up?"

"Yeah," he replied sourly.

"If Pete set the bomb, or his people did, then why are we going to Carmel to see him?"

"I've always believed in keeping my friends close and my enemies even closer."

She touched his arm. "Are you sure about this? I mean, we'll be walking into a trap for certain."

"You won't."

"What?"

"I told you I'd take you to see your son. That's what you're going to do."

"Gabe, I…"

"Look, if Pete's network stretches from San Francisco to Texas and Louisiana, he'll have that cabin surrounded. I can't risk anything happening to you."

He looked at her as he eased through traffic.

He could tell she was thinking about Laird, from the faraway, aching look in her eyes. It hurt him to see that much hope in anyone's eyes. He couldn't help wondering if his own eyes looked like that whenever he looked at her.

He bit his lower lip to keep his emotions in check.

He wished she was thinking about him but this was a place in her life he couldn't go.

What amazed Gabe was the depth of his own emotions. If any of his friends had told him he would fall so inexorably in love with a woman, he would have scoffed. He'd done such a good job distancing himself from relationships, he realized now that he'd missed out on most of his life.

Ironically, it had taken a coma to wake him up.

He knew he'd acted too late.

He knew how much she wanted to go back to the life she had once had with her son, but she was a hunted woman now. All of which was his fault.

A riptide of guilt pummeled him.

There was always a chance she could figure out a way to stay in San Francisco, he thought. She could go undercover again. After all, Shannon's former mother-in-law had obviously once had incredible pull to invent facts and distort reality. She could do it again if Shannon could convince her.

In a way, Shannon was in no more danger hiding out in San Francisco incognito than she was running to the ends of the earth with him.

He saw that hope in her eyes that made her believe maybe, just maybe she could stay here and watch her son grow.

And Gabe would be somewhere else, on the other side of the world, missing her every day for the rest of his life.

A burning ball of emotion stuck in his throat. He had so many things he wanted to say to her, but he couldn't speak.

He was trembling when he took her hand and kissed it.

"So, Shannon, are you going to give me the address or do I look it up in the phone book?"

32

───▶ ◀───

Rain clouds moved over the Santa Cruz Mountains obliterating the afternoon sun. The temperature dropped fifteen degrees, allowing a blanket of familiar thick, gray fog to descend upon the area. Blinking yellow hazard lights from the road-repair crews on Highway 17 out of San Jose were a blessing in the dense fog.

"We're moving so slowly," Shannon said, continually looking behind them. "But I guess it doesn't matter much. I couldn't tell if we were being followed anyway. How could I ever forget this fog...?" Her voice trailed off.

With every inch they covered, she was going back. Suspended inside the cocoon of fog, she felt like a time traveler. She remembered Laird, the sweet baby smell of him, his velvety skin still unmarred by sun or injury. She remembered how his eyes lit up when she walked into the nursery, how it felt for her face to crinkle with a smile so wide it nearly hurt.

Suddenly, it was yesterday and Laird was alive again, resting in her arms. How could she have forgotten the weight of him as he slept soundly in her arms? Or the high pitch to his screams when his ears became infected and his fever rose frighteningly high? As if it were happening now she felt her insides ache with the need to heal his winter colds, to feed his hunger, and warm his body.

Gabe ground his jaw anxiously, gripping the wheel as if it were a life preserver.

She saw the white of his knuckles. She heard the numerous times he parted his lips to speak, then pressed them together, keeping his thoughts to himself.

"What are you going to do?" she asked finally.

"I told you," he replied. "Find Pete and get the truth."

"And then?"

"I haven't thought that far ahead," he said.

"Liar." She smiled softly and reached for his hand. "You always seem to be one move ahead."

"Comes from playing chess."

"I guess I should have learned that game," she said, looking straight ahead.

She felt ripped up inside, as if she was betraying Gabe by wanting to see Laird.

"I keep thinking of all those times I tried to get away from you. And now..."

"Now you are. You have to. I understand."

"But I..."

"Look, Shannon, I love you, but I can't take you with me to Carmel. It's too dangerous. It's—"

"Gabe, stop."

"What? I was only..."

"It's dangerous no matter what we do. Split up or stay together. We don't even know if we're being followed right now." She glanced behind them. "Though I hope not."

Driving through the residential section, Gabe watched her as her eyes scanned the houses. He

wanted to ask her to stay with him, but he couldn't.
He wanted to believe she would actually consider it,
but he knew better.

All the reasons he'd had for coming to San Francisco—getting the truth from Pete and revenge for
Adam's death—suddenly weren't important anymore.

Gabe wanted Shannon. He loved her. It was as simple and as complicated as that.

At the stoplight he grabbed a tooth-marked ball-
point pen from the overhead visor and scribbled on a
piece of paper. "Shannon, here's my cellular number.
If you should need me... I mean, I'll keep the phone
on. In case anything happens."

She took the scrap of paper. "Where will you go,
Gabe?"

He looked at her. "You shouldn't look for me. I
want to know you're safe."

She touched his cheek. "None of us ever really are,
are we?"

He shook his head. "I'll be on that rock in Greece,
waiting for you."

"Don't look at me like that. I can hardly bear it,"
she said, kissing him.

Tracing his fingers down the column of her throat,
he said, "No one's ever loved me enough to do what
you did. To stay with me and fight my fights. You
could have ditched me and been safe with Ben, but
you didn't. I'm so lucky to have had you, even for a
little while."

Shannon's heart pounded and a wave a heat exploded through her body as she unleashed her emotions. She threw her arms around his neck and held

him tight. "Gabe, you have it all wrong. I didn't bring you back to life. You gave me life."

Gently he touched his lips to hers. "Ben gave you your old life back. I didn't do that."

"That's not what I meant. I want so much to live again now, Gabe. I haven't wanted that since I was very, very young."

"I know what you mean." He peered deeply into her eyes. "We were just two lost souls, huh?" He paused thoughtfully and then said, "I thought we were pretty good together, didn't you?"

Tears welled in her eyes. "More than pretty good," she replied, her words tasting of melancholy.

"Good," he said. "Now keep my number with you. Promise?"

She nodded and stuffed the scrap of paper in her jeans pocket. "I promise."

A car honked behind them, signaling that the light had changed.

Unwrapping herself from his embrace, Shannon suddenly felt unsure of her choice. It was killing her to say goodbye to Gabe. She hadn't expected to be this torn. When Ben had told her about Laird being alive, she'd thought her dreams had come true.

Now she realized her dreams had expanded and she wanted so much more for herself. Gabe had taught her to value her own feelings and her own life. She'd been his equal, his confidante, his savior as much as he'd been hers.

He was right. They were two lost souls. The only problem was that leaving him meant she'd be lost again.

Shannon looked out the window, but in the reflection she saw Gabe's face behind her. She saw the anguish in his eyes that he hid so well when she wasn't watching. She remembered how he'd made love to her and how she'd known in her soul it would never be like that for her again with any other man. Gabe had made her his that night.

She felt as if she had one foot in heaven and the other on earth. She needed to see her child, but she might never see Gabe again.

"I really do love you, Gabe," she said.

He reached over, took her hand and held it to his lips. "I needed to hear that."

"Gabe, I was afraid that if you knew how much I loved you, you'd make the wrong decisions, make the wrong move and wind up dead because of me."

"Don't think like that," he said. "I'll make it."

They stopped at a stop sign.

She turned abruptly. "Gabe..."

Suddenly, they were kissing. It was a soul-wrenching kiss born of tears, regrets and futures unearned. She tasted him, devoured him. She promised herself she would remember this kiss every night for the rest of her life. She was Gabe's. And he was hers.

"Shannon..."

"I gotta go, Gabriel."

"I know," he said, feeling the fire of her kiss, the strength of her resolve.

The car across the street moved through the intersection. Gabe eased onto the gas.

"Make sure you watch your back," she said, lowering her head, letting her tears fall freely.

"I will." He swallowed hard.

She was looking out the window again at the houses. He purposefully went exactly the speed limit.

He only had these few minutes left. He didn't want to lose them too quickly.

"Have you thought about what you're going to say when you see him?"

"Yeah."

"That's good. A plan is always good." His mouth was dry. He licked his cracked lips. He felt as if his blood had turned to powder, as if his emotions had dried up with her leaving.

"What did you say the house number was?" he asked.

"Seven fifty-two."

"Oh, yeah. I remember now." His voice sounded hollow, empty. Shannon was practically glued to the window. She looked like a little girl, her nose pressed against the glass.

Gabe's heart ached for her. He wanted her to be happy but he'd never thought he could know such pain. At least he would always know he'd given her life back to her. He owed her that much.

He couldn't help thinking of the irony of it all. He'd started out their relationship as the villain and now he'd done the one deed that turned him into a hero. He'd saved the day, but not himself.

"This must be it," Gabe said, pointing to the mansion on the hill. He retracted his hand. It was trembling.

"Oh my God! It is," she said with a rush of elation that died as quickly as it came.

The yellow stucco and white-trimmed mansion seemed even larger than she remembered. The landscaping was more lush, the flowers more exquisite and costly. New awnings graced the leaded windows. She could see that a side yard had been outfitted with a swing set, a Western-style log fort and a tree house. She saw a boy's blue metallic bicycle lying near the front door, as if he'd ridden too fast, jumped off and let the bike fall.

The mansion had become a house, a home filled with life. Filled with her child.

A Mercedes station wagon passed by them on the street and pulled into the driveway, the black wrought-iron gates opening automatically.

Then she saw him.

"Laird."

Shannon strained to watch through the window.

"Get out, Shannon. You can't see anything from here."

Gabe leaned over and opened the door.

Shannon heard nothing, not the traffic or Gabe's hollow voice. All she heard was the sound of a little boy's laughter. It pulled at her, mesmerizing her.

"Bye, Shannon," Gabe said.

She turned back to look at him.

He was alarmed at the torture he saw in her eyes. There was still a chance for him. He knew she was still thinking about staying with him. His emotions, fueled with hope, skyrocketed.

"You better go," he said, damning his own integrity. If only he were a bit more selfish.

Shannon's tears glistened as she touched his cheek. "Thanks, Gabe."

He knew he'd lost her.

She looked at her little boy again. Her face was glowing. She was happy. He'd never seen anything so beautiful in his life.

"You take care of yourself, Shannon."

"I will, Gabe," she said.

She opened the door, got out and crossed the sidewalk. Her ears filled with Laird's laughter. She felt giddy, incredibly light and hopeful.

God in heaven. She was hopeful again.

She stood at the black iron bars that surrounded the mansion. Peeking through the crimson bougainvillea she saw him. Her heart skipped a beat, then two.

Laird.

He was romping on the grass with a golden retriever puppy that was no more than four months, tops, she guessed.

His hair was flame-colored auburn like hers. She couldn't see his eyes, but she wondered if they were green like hers as well. They'd been blue when he was born.

"Mother!" Laird yelled loudly to the well-dressed woman emerging from the Mercedes.

Shannon's heart jumped.

"Yes, darling!" Amelia replied happily, more genuinely happy than Shannon ever remembered her being.

"Mother, are we going to the Wharf tonight?"

"Yes, dear!"

"Can Bebe come, too!"

"Darling, I hardly think a restaurant is the proper place for a puppy."

"Daddy won't mind, will he?" The puppy licked Laird's face incessantly. He laughed and fell to the ground, rolling over and over with the frisky puppy.

"Please don't ask your father. He's mush in your hands."

"Mother, please. Puhleeeezzze. I'll leave her in the car and bring her mashed potatoes for dinner. Nanny could stay with her while we eat."

"Oh, you are such a salesman. You think of everything."

"I thought you said I was a good attorney."

"That, too." Amelia replied, helping one of the servants with the grocery sacks.

"Maybe I'll be an actor!"

"Fine with me, darling. Only don't get grass stains on your new uniform pants. They take forever to order new ones."

Just then the puppy took off, running directly toward Shannon.

"Bebe! Come back here!" Laird yelled at the dog.

Shannon saw her son racing toward her—from out of the past to her own present.

He was like the north wind rushing toward her. She'd never seen any child so beautiful. His smile was infectious and she felt herself smiling back.

Hope filled her soul. Joy burst through her heart. She was breathless watching him. Her anticipation of what it would be like to fold him into her arms again ignited the cells in her body. Her fingers itched to tousle his hair. Her mind spun years ahead to what it would be like to see him playing at the beach. She could almost hear his laughter and excitement at the amusement park she would take him to. She envisioned him learning to drive, tossing his black cap on graduation day from high school, his wedding day.

Laird's entire future flashed across her mind in an instant. What she couldn't see was what her own life would hold. Stricken with the fear that she'd made the wrong decision, Shannon turned to leave.

Then she heard his laughter again. "Bebe! You silly dog!" he shouted.

She had come too far.

"Bebe! Stop! Don't go there! It's dangerous out there!"

Amelia dropped the groceries. "Don't let her go near the fence! She can get through the iron!"

"Mother! Help me get her!" Laird raced down the hill, across the perfectly clipped thick grass, his feet tumbling over themselves, yet somehow holding steady.

As he came near, Shannon could see his face, see the scars.

Then she knew.

Her son would never look like a normal child.

The burns had been rectified by plastic surgery as well as could be expected, but the shiny flesh, smooth without line that only skin grafts produce, attested to the horror Laird had known with her.

Her unmended heart shattered. She had dreamed of him as whole and as a baby. But this was a child, a real person who had grown healthy and happy despite nearly dying in a fire.

All this time she'd frozen his memory in her mind, but her memories were not even close to the reality.

Chills blanketed her body as a pain gashed her solar plexus. In that instant, she relived every moment of the car crash. She felt the flames, the heat, the torture of trying to breathe life into her baby son and knowing she'd failed.

Shannon's soul had died that day. Now it was dying all over again.

The pain her son must have endured during those surgeries was something she couldn't have withstood had she known he was alive. She knew enough about medicine, what it could and could not do, to know that the torture of watching his agony and pain would have been her undoing. She would have lost her mind, and, in the process, lost him.

She clutched her throat, hoping to hold back the burning ache inside. Her hands were shaking and her legs sagged with the onslaught of emotions slamming through her. To steady herself, she clung to the wrought-iron bars.

"Bebe!" Laird yelled at the puppy. "Stop!"

Laird's eyes sparkled with confidence as he raced to save the puppy. Already she could see an inner dignity not common in children.

He had been through a great deal, yet he'd triumphed in his short life. Possibly even more than she in her own.

"Bebe, you come back here right now! I'm your master and you will do as I say!" he shouted to the puppy.

Just as the puppy was about to tumble into the bougainvillea, she skidded to a stop on all fours, then turned toward Laird, panting. Waiting for him to come to her. Proud she had obeyed him.

Shannon held her breath. She could almost touch the puppy.

Laird stopped and shook his finger at Bebe. "Bad puppy."

Amelia was fast on his heels, racing down the hill. She came toward Shannon, her Hermès scarf blowing around her neck, her Italian shoes catching in the grass.

Shannon was astounded at the change in her. Though six years had passed since they'd last spoken, Amelia had never looked younger. Her skin was fresh, devoid of all but the subtlest makeup, with only the faintest webbing around her eyes marking her years.

Shannon realized that Amelia was happy. More than happy, she was content, satisfied with her life. She believed she had everything. She had her son back...in Laird.

And here was Shannon, about to destroy her nemesis. Ready to rectify past sins and bring justice into balance.

Amelia waved her arm at Laird. "Darling, be careful!"

Laird stopped, bent and picked up the puppy who licked his face furiously.

Shannon felt time pressing in on her. She looked at Amelia running closer, keeping her from her son—again.

Laird was almost within reaching distance. She should say something. She might never have the chance again to tell him.

What? Tell him what, Kat? Tell him I'm his mother? That I've come to take him home? Back to...Shreveport? Back to where my friends are being murdered for my sake. Friends who don't even know my real name. Friends who've done nothing wrong in this world except be kind to me.

And to what life, Shannon? To running from men who make their fortunes selling coke to kids, to weak men like your father, Laird?

"Hello, Kathleen," Amelia's voice broke through Shannon's thoughts.

"Hello," she replied softly, unable to take her eyes from her transformed mother-in-law.

Laird looked up at Amelia, his scars shining in the sun. "Do you know her, Mother?"

"Yes," Amelia replied, blanching.

In the space of a millisecond, Shannon held all their futures. Destiny gave her the power to reclaim her son, punish Amelia and claim a victory for herself.

She should have been ecstatic. Instead she felt profound sorrow. Sad for the little boy Laird had become and whom she didn't know. Sad for the boy who undoubtedly faced cruel taunts from children and seemingly endless stares from rude adults.

She was sad that she didn't know him and even more sad that he did not know her.

"How are you, Amelia?"

"I'm doing well."

"You look well...wonderful in fact."

"Thank you," Amelia replied warily.

Laird set the puppy down. "If she's your friend, shouldn't we invite her in? You always told me that was the polite thing to do."

Shannon's gaze held Amelia's.

"Yes," Amelia finally said. "Would you..."

Shannon interrupted her. "I was just passing by, actually. I really don't have time for tea or a chat. I saw the puppy running toward me and heard your—" Shannon swallowed the tears in her throat "—son shouting for the puppy to stop. I thought to catch him, should he get through the fence."

"She. It's a girl," Laird corrected her.

Shannon dropped to her knees so that she was eye level with Laird. He looked so fragile and her arms ached to hold him. It took every ounce of will and determination not to blurt out the truth to him, not to claim what was rightfully hers.

"I had a puppy once," she said, her voice faltering

dangerously close to the edge. "I loved him very much. He was the world to me."

Laird moved a step closer. "Really? What was his name?"

She held her breath. "Starshine."

"I like that. I like starry nights. I have glow-in-the-dark stars stuck on my ceiling in my bedroom."

There was a star, moon and angel mobile in your crib.

"What happened to your puppy?" Laird asked, coming even closer.

Tears filled Shannon's eyes. She didn't want to cry. She wanted to carry on more conversation, get to know her son better. Instead, she was overwhelmed with emotion and her heart broke all over again.

"He died," she said over the burning lump in her chest. She felt as if she were dying inside.

"I'm sorry," Laird said, coming to her finally, putting his tiny hand on her shoulder and patting her affectionately.

She placed her hand over his. She wanted to kiss it, to touch her lips to his flesh.

Instead, Laird wiped her cheek with his fingers, carrying her tears away. "Please don't cry," he said. "Mother—" he turned toward Amelia "—we should help her."

Shannon couldn't stand the pain. She dropped her face to her hands and sobbed.

"Kathleen..." Amelia stepped toward her, trepidation in her voice and movements.

Shannon looked up. She saw that, by virtue of what she said, she could rip their world apart just as hers was being rent at this moment.

Laird turned back to her. "You are so sad and it's

not good to be so sad. I will let you take Bebe home
with you for a day or two."

Shannon realized suddenly she had to find the
courage to pull herself together. "Oh, I couldn't do
that." She swallowed. "Besides, you would miss her
and I would never want you to be sad, either."

Laird considered this for a long moment. "I know
what you should do."

"What?" She sniffed back her tears.

"Maybe you should get another puppy. If my
puppy died, I would want another one right away."

"You would?"

"Yes. That way I would always have someone to
love."

She gasped and nearly lost her balance. He touched
her heart so deeply. How was it possible for one so
young to be so loving, so wise and complete?

Then it hit her. Laird was the man David should
have been. Laird was the senator-in-the-making
Amelia had wanted her son to be. Laird at six already
had the stature that set him apart from other children.
He bore his scars as medals of honor.

And I gave them to him.

It was odd how, at that moment, she realized that
perhaps her destiny had been served after all. Perhaps she was to be Laird's mother in heart, soul and
body, but not in presence.

The thought was almost too much for her.

She wanted to scream at God, "Why me?" She
wanted to shake her fist at the fates who would be so
cruel as to do this to her.

A pain more excruciating than any she'd experienced rocked through her. She felt as if her heart had

been ripped from her chest. She was bloodless suddenly. She felt nothing but utter hopelessness.

Her future yawned at her as a black gaping hole in the universe, a void she could never fill.

Looking at Laird, feeling the warmth of his smile on her face, she realized that she had inadvertently put his life and Amelia's in danger. She couldn't be a hundred percent certain she was not being followed.

What if the Colombians saw her? What if they discovered her truth?

She would never forgive herself if she was the cause of even the slightest ripple of fear to come to her son.

She knew in that instant that she had no options. She had to leave Laird with Amelia and leave forever.

"That's very good advice. I'll think about it," she said, touching his cheek, gazing into his eyes one last time. She didn't think she'd have the strength to stand, but she did.

She also found she had the strength to stand up to all her fears. She found that loving never dies, that once a person experiences their ability to love, it never goes away.

To love was to be alive. And Shannon wanted to live and she wanted even more to make certain Laird would not be harmed.

"I really have to be going," Shannon said slowly, peeling her fingers off the wrought iron and backing away from the fence.

"Kathleen!" Amelia took a step forward.

"Yes?"

"Thank you." Their eyes locked.

Shannon felt as if she knew every emotion Amelia was feeling. "For stopping by to help, I mean."

"Think nothing of it."

"Oh, but I always will." Amelia's voice was filled with intense gratitude.

"Goodbye, young man," Shannon said.

"My name's Thomas."

Shannon's eyes flew to Amelia's face. _My father's name! Amelia, you named him after my father!_

Amelia only nodded, tears glistening in her eyes.

Shannon turned away then, her eyes awash with new tears. She thrust her arm in the air behind her. "Bye, Thomas. Bye, Amelia."

Her eyes streaming with tears, Shannon could barely see the sidewalk in front of her as she walked away. Every day of her life, she would remember the sound of her son's voice. She would keep this scene locked in her heart, taking it out in private moments when she wanted to visit him again.

Never again would she think of the fire. She had extinguished the flames, the terror. For the first time in her life, she realized that, sometimes, self-sacrifice is the best choice. Sometimes the best thing is to put others and their happiness ahead of one's own.

Self-sacrifice could not be equated with weakness for it could only be accomplished with strength and deep abiding love.

Shannon could still hear Laird's voice behind her, but she didn't dare look back. She wasn't sure she could be that strong—twice.

"Goodbye, Miss Kathleen!" Thomas waved, then picked up the puppy's paw. "Say goodbye to the nice lady, Bebe." Then he looked up at Amelia. "So, Mother, what do you think? Can I take Bebe to the restaurant with us?"

"Yes, darling. Puppies don't last forever. You should spend every second you can with her."

Amelia watched after Kathleen, wiped away her tears and put her hand on Thomas's shoulder. Then they walked back up the hill toward their home.

33

Gabe stopped the car at the light at the bottom of the hill. In a little park he could see young mothers, just like Shannon, walking their babies in strollers, chatting happily with each other. Kids played on the swings, pushing each other, laughing.

It was life. It was all around him. And he hated it. It reminded him of what he didn't have, might not ever have, and worse, didn't want if he couldn't have it with Shannon.

He'd been right to let her go. Maybe she would be safer away from him. She had a right to be with her son.

The light turned green and the car behind him honked its horn impatiently.

His cellular phone rang. He answered it. "Pete?"

"No, it's Shannon," she said. "Could you come get me?"

His breath came in spurts between his words. "What happened? I mean, where are you?"

"At a pay phone two blocks down from Amelia's, at a little coffeehouse."

"I don't remember it," he said, making a U-turn.

The car behind him honked again and gave him the finger.

Gabe hit the gas. "Where?"

"A cappuccino place really," she said, turning around to look at the street. "Gabe!" She waved. "I see you...."

She left the receiver dangling as she raced toward the old Cadillac.

Quickly, he eased the car against the curb and opened the door for her. She slid inside and into his arms.

"Oh, Gabe!"

He kissed her and it was a kiss of desperation, joy, reunion and love.

"Are you sure about this?" he asked between frantic kisses.

"Yes."

"I can't give you anything, Shannon. Not even a future. I told you that."

"I can't go back, Gabe. Not ever. That's not my life back there. I don't know where it really is, but that's not it. I was a part of someone's life before, but I'm not anymore."

He held her face between his hands. "You're a part of mine."

She nodded, holding his eyes with hers. "And you, mine."

He kissed her deeply again, his heart thudding.

"We should go, Gabe. Now. I've put us in danger...taking so much time here."

He smiled, kissed her one more time very quickly and said, "It was worth it."

North of Carmel's central business district and a block off the beach, Peter Dominic's cottage hugged the base of a low hill. Clusters of pines, redwoods and aspens formed a canopy over the small house, holding it in the shadows. Fog crept around the foundation on ghostly feet.

Seeing not a single light burning through the windows, Gabe killed the car's engine as he rolled the Cadillac to a stop a half block away.

"Maybe he's not here yet," Shannon said.

Gabe checked to see that his gun was fully loaded. "Trust me. He's here. Just maybe not in the house."

Shannon opened her car door. Gabe grabbed her arm and pulled her back into the car. "What the hell are you doing?" he asked. "You're staying in this car. Here are the keys. If anything happens to me—"

She cut in abruptly, "Then it'll have to happen to me, too! I'm a sitting duck out here. Our only safety is in numbers."

"I never, ever planned for you to go in there with me."

"It's not your call."

They kept to the shadows as they approached the house, their eyes scanning the shrubbery for any sign of movement. When they reached the front door, Gabe tapped on the door lightly.

Silence.

He tried the knob and the door opened. With his gun in hand, Gabe stealthily entered the house with Shannon close behind. The room was pitch-black with all the shades drawn.

"That you, Gabe?" a man's voice asked from the shadows in the corner of the living room.

Gabe pointed the gun at the darkness. "Pete?"

Shannon's nerves were strung out as she peered into the corner. She swore she saw what looked like a gun pointed right at her. Bracing for the impact of a gunshot, she held her breath.

A light flicked on, its suddenness momentarily blinding Shannon. With her eyes still focused on the man in the corner, she realized he was holding a black plastic cordless phone.

"What's the gun for, Gabe?" Pete asked.

Gabe swallowed back his relief as he holstered the gun in the waistband of his jeans. "Since when do you greet your guests sitting in the dark?"

"I have to be careful...even of my so-called best friend," he said as he rose, "who comes into my house toting a gun." He leaned toward Shannon, extending his right hand. "Hi, I'm Pete."

Shannon only nodded.

Still not trusting Pete, Gabe's hand went to his gun.

Pete glared at Gabe.

Gabe didn't back down. "Can the charm, Pete, and explain to me why the Taurus blew up in the garage!"

"It what?"

"It's toast. Scrap metal now. The little gizmo on the remote control was cute."

"What remote control?" Pete asked.

"The one on the—" Gabe paused as he looked closely at Pete's stunned expression. "You really don't know?"

"No. I don't know what the hell you're talking about. I called my secretary and asked her to have the messenger service take the keys out to the airline counter. I haven't seen those keys in months."

"Damn you, Pete!"

"What?" Pete threw his hands up in the air.

"I almost believe you."

"Well, hell. That's a start." Pete put his hands on his hips angrily. "Now, why don't you explain what you're doing out here and what this has to do with Adam's death."

"Murder, Pete. He was murdered by Colombian-cartel hit men who thought they'd murdered me as well. They executed Adam and beat me within an inch of my life, so my nurse, Shannon, here tells me. Then they put me behind the wheel of a rental car and sent the damn thing into the river. Somehow, I lived through it. When I woke up from a month-long coma, I had a guard at my door who was packin' this rod." He held up the gun.

"So, I kidnapped Shannon, my nurse at the hospital and we hit the road. The cartel leader has sent an army to kill us, but so far we've managed to stay alive. The Shreveport police chief tried to kill us in Dallas, but he bought it in Amarillo when his Colombian colleagues killed him. Seems the chief was busy murdering Shannon's next-door neighbor and a nurse friend of hers just before he tried to pop us off. Then we finally make it as far as New Mexico and find out that the guard at my hospital door is an undercover fed who wakes us up with a gun in our noses, but he lets us go."

Shaking his head disbelievingly, Pete said, "Let me get this straight. The bad guys nearly kill you, but the cops let you go? This doesn't make any sense."

"I don't give a shit what you think." Gabe was losing control, but he didn't care. After all he'd been through, it was allowed. He reached inside his jacket pocket and pulled out the original computer disk.

Shannon gasped. "What's that? I gave the disk to Ben."

"Who's Ben?" Pete asked.

"You reached in my pocket and took out a copy.

Remember, I bought two disks from the guy at Kinko's."

Shannon was incredulous. "Then what does Ben have? The altered version or the real one?"

"Who is Ben?" Pete asked again.

Shannon ignored him, as did Gabe.

Gabe continued. "It was altered somewhat, but it doesn't matter. He's got what he needs."

"Everything but the money. Right?" Shannon asked.

"Precisely," Gabe answered her.

"Who the *hell* is Ben?" Pete yelled.

Shannon and Gabe looked at Pete. "Shut up!" they said in unison.

"Fine!" Pete snorted. "I can tell that is a computer disk, but why is it so important?"

"Don't look so innocent, Pete. You know damn well what this is."

"The hell I do!" Pete protested.

Shannon looked back to Gabe. "What if he's telling the truth?"

"Pete and I are the only ones who know where he parks that car."

"Right," Pete said. "You and a hundred of my clients. Not to mention they could have listened in on our phone call with one of those phone scanners. Hell, two years ago I took a company public that makes a scanner with the longest range out there...over a mile. Besides, haven't you read the papers lately? Just yesterday there was an article in the *L.A. Times* that California, southern California in particular, is the drug-laundering mecca in this country. Cartels have their tentacles everywhere out here—"

Pete stopped abruptly. His eyes widened and his face paled.

"What?" Gabe asked.

"Man, we're in a lot of trouble."

Shannon rolled her eyes. "Catches on quick, doesn't he?"

Pete looked at Gabe. "While I was in Aspen I hired a young college student to house-sit for me. I came home two days early and found her dead."

"Dead?" Shannon's shock rattled through her voice.

"Yeah," Pete continued. "Her neck had been broken. There was no forced entry. She must have let the murderer in. I figured the guy was some stalker kind of boyfriend of hers. I panicked. I just wanted to get out of there. I was planning to call 911 anonymously when you called."

Shannon was incredulous as she leaned into Gabe's side. He slid his arm around her. "Is there no end to this nightmare?"

"Yes. There always is."

"But how?"

"I'll think of something," Gabe assured her.

"No," Pete said. "We have three heads to put together on this thing now."

Gabe addressed Pete. "We need to keep in mind that the cops will be looking for you once they find the girl's body. They'll be looking to question you."

"I thought of that."

Gabe eyed him suspiciously. He still wasn't buying all of Pete's story. "You're smarter than to get caught with your pants down. That's why I think you're up to your ears in this thing."

"What thing?"

Gabe pointed to the laptop computer Pete had sitting on his desk at the opposite end of the room. "Turn that thing on."

Pete did as Gabe asked. Inserting the disk, Pete studied the screen.

"No wonder you think I'm mixed up with these guys. I know these people. I set up these accounts."

Shannon stood behind Pete and peered over his shoulder. "You did this?"

"I know it looks suspicious." Pete cast Gabe an accusatory look. "Did you steal this from my office?"

"Is that where it came from, Pete?" Gabe held his anger in check.

"You tell me," he blurted then scrolled down farther. "Wait a minute. Mackindorff. Johnson. Bremen. I've never seen these names before. But these others, these are the names of two divorcees Adam had referred to me. Nice ladies. They both made a killing in the stock market this year. Software-technology companies were a favorite pick of mine," he said proudly.

Gabe frowned. "Keep going. Show me how your company is not involved in drug laundering, Pete."

"I know it looks that way, but... Hey! Wait a minute. Where did this Angelo Rodriguez account come from? I've never seen this name."

"Really?" Shannon asked. "Why is it you know some of them and not all?"

"This isn't from my files. I swear it."

Shannon couldn't help thinking Pete was telling the truth. Still, she reserved judgment. She was learning fast that things are never what they seem. She thought of Laird. Of Amelia. Truth was twisted like a pretzel too easily. What once gave the appearance of evil could transform to good. And goodness too easily turned bad.

Of everything, she'd learned to be flexible. Expect surprises and be prepared to defend herself.

Pete's eyes were glued to the screen. He whistled. "I set up these accounts for Adam's clients. Andrew Cassidy was four years ago. As was Cindy Ames. Abigail Carrington was two years ago. Charles Atwater, Alexandra Cline and Al Castleman were all about eighteen months ago."

Shannon said, "The initials are the same. Did you create their names, Pete?"

"No way. In fact, I never noticed it before. They didn't come to me in one batch, you know. They were spread out over long periods of time. But now I can see…"

"It's like a code?" Gabe asked.

"Yeah. Easily identifiable."

"By someone who makes a habit of opening so many accounts around the world he needed to create a trigger for his memory?" Shannon asked.

"Precisely."

"But not so smart," Gabe said.

"There are other ways of doing it," Pete said.

"Lucky for us this guy isn't all that astute," Shannon said.

Pete's eyes were sincere when he faced Gabe and Shannon. "I swear to you that I didn't move fifty-three million, one hundred thousand, twenty dollars and twelve cents to this account."

"Yeah, sure," Gabe groaned, still unconvinced. He pointed to the account in Cartagena, Colombia. "You say you don't know about this, either?"

"No. I had no idea any monies came from anywhere but the U.S. Many times Adam wired me money out of his client trust account. Look, I know those are my call letters, but I didn't do this. But it sure looks like Adam could have."

"How's that?"

"I sent him complete documentation on all his clients. I invested their money in the Vancouver exchange, in Hong Kong, wherever the deals were hot. I have his clients' files, deposits, copies of stocks, and especially a list of their brokerage fees."

"Adam died for this disk, Pete. This is his computer file."

"God, he moved a hell of a lot of money," Pete said.

"Yeah. And somebody is really pissed about it."

Suddenly, bullets sprayed the house like hail. The sound reverberated around the cottage like Armageddon.

Shannon screamed and covered her head.

"Shannon, get down!" Gabe yelled.

She dropped to her knees.

Windows shattered and glass flew everywhere, pellets of tinkling crystal embedding themselves in furniture and drapes, skittering across the hardwood floor.

Another round of bullets chewed up the plaster walls and scarred the wooden tables, Pete's desk and the bookshelves. The television screen was hit and exploded like a fireworks display.

"Hit the floor!" Gabe yelled to Pete who sat woodenly at the computer.

Pete's shock kept him riveted to the chair.

Thinking quickly, Shannon scooted across the floor, then over the throw rug, bullets narrowly missing her legs and feet. She found momentary shelter behind the sofa.

Shannon looked to Pete. Her heart pounded. Her ears were filled with the deafening sound of gunfire. She thought there must be an army outside the size of Santa Ana's at the Alamo.

They were going to die.

This was it. She should have resigned herself to it, but she just couldn't. She was a fighter, not a quitter. She had to keep going. Had to keep believing they had a chance, slim as it was.

Pete was still at the computer.

Her mouth was dry, her tongue immobile with fear, but she managed to shout to Pete. "Get your butt down, Pete!"

Finally, Pete's brain slipped into high gear. He slammed down the computer screen, fell to the floor, and from under cover of the desk, began dismantling the printer and unhooking cords. He turned to Gabe and handed him the laptop. "Watch this!"

Pete crawled on his belly into the den. He opened a gun-case door and withdrew two .357 Magnums, a Glock and several boxes of bullets.

Gabe had doused the lights and signaled to Shannon to stay low while the bullets riddled the air around them.

Returning to the living room, Pete held two guns at Gabe and Shannon.

Gabe was right. Pete's the ringleader and he's going to kill us both.

All she could see was the gun barrel pointed at her. Time stood still as she waited for death. The zinging bullets and gunfire from outside the cottage seemed to fade, while Pete's movements looked as if they were in slow motion.

She closed her eyes. She didn't want to see death coming.

"Gabe!" Pete shouted and tossed one of the guns to him. "Keep low, keep shooting and try like hell to hit something."

The .357 spun in the air toward Shannon. "That goes for you, too," Pete said. "I'm in this thing with you whether you like it or not."

Gabe nodded to Pete.

Like the sound of a tornado, one of the assassins hurtled himself at the front door and crashed into the room.

More terrified than courageous, Shannon jumped up from behind the sofa, intending to pull the trigger as fast as she could. But she froze. Just then, Gabe emptied the full round into the man, killing him.

Watching the man's blood ooze from his wounds sent Shannon into a paralyzing state of shock.

"Shannon!" Gabe yelled as another spray of bullets riddled the room.

She dropped to the floor just as a second assassin rushed into the house through the doorway. His automatic M-16 shattered everything in its path.

Aiming smartly, Pete shot the man in the leg. He dropped to the floor screaming. Gabe fired two shots to the man's heart and killed him.

The room was silent.

"Come on!" Pete shouted at Gabe and Shannon. "The cops will be crawling all over this place in seconds."

"Where're we going?"

"My car," he said, quickly gathering his computer,

cords, printer, briefcase and cellular phone. He
handed half the equipment to Gabe and the rest to
Shannon.

"Where's your car?" Gabe asked, following Pete
out the back door.

"Three houses down."

"Why did you park so far away?" Shannon asked
as she ran across the yard.

"Are you for real? I get cockamamy phone calls
from Gabe. I find a dead girl in my house and you
think I'm not gonna plan for a getaway? The way I see
it, my life here is over."

Tossing all the equipment in the back seat with
Shannon, Pete got behind the wheel while Gabe rode
shotgun. Just as they rounded the corner, they heard
the sound of sirens in the distance.

"We have a great Neighborhood Watch here," Pete
said, taking a back road out of the residential area. He
drove for several blocks before turning on the headlights. Not until they were on the highway and speeding northward did any of them take a full breath.

"Where are we going?" Gabe asked cockily.

"Frankly, I believe we have only one option." Pete
glanced sternly at Gabe.

"You're not serious?" Gabe asked.

"What the hell did you think was going to happen,
Gabe? That you were gonna come out here, press me
into a confession that I'd stolen this money, which I
didn't, and then you were gonna turn me in to the
feds?"

Gabe remained silent.

Pete's laugh was hearty. "You never change, do
you? Always gotta be the hero. Well, guess what?

This is real life. Things don't clean up that good. What we have here is a mess."

"Yeah? Well, smart-ass, what do you propose we do?"

Pete glanced back at Shannon's distrustful gaze and then to Gabe's expectant look. "Boys and girls, I say we take the money and run."

"Are you out of your mind?" Gabe raked his fingers through his hair. "The cartel will kill us for sure!"

"Not if we outsmart them," Pete reasoned.

"Oh, right. We just killed two trained hit men. They're going to send an army after us, man!"

"I'm with Gabe on this," Shannon cut in. "This isn't just a few dollars they're missing. It's more than fifty million!" she shrieked. "We'll be running forever. I don't know about you, but living on the edge like this, wondering where the next round of bullets is going to come from...I can't take it."

"Ha! Trained hit men. We killed them, didn't we?" Pete countered.

"We got lucky," Shannon replied angrily.

"So, we'll get lucky again."

Gabe looked at Pete. "Just how long have you been behind a computer, Pete? I think it's warped your brain."

"Will you two hear me out?" he asked, looking at their rigid expressions. "All we need to do is disappear...permanently. Fifty-three million dollars can buy all kinds of anonymity."

"This is insane!" Shannon said.

"Do you have any better ideas? Gabe's plan is a no-go. Neither of you can walk into the sunset at this point, can you? You're dead any way you look at it. So why not be totally dead?"

Shannon looked at Gabe, who cocked an eyebrow at her.

She said to Pete, "Keep talking."

34

Shannon could hear the drone of helicopter blades whirling in the night sky behind them. Police sirens screamed through the quiet tree-lined streets of Carmel toward Pete's cottage. She was driving in the opposite direction and expertly made their escape without detection.

She almost couldn't remember what it was like to live a life so structured it bordered on the boring. Never had she thought she would be caught in a life-and-death struggle. She'd known grief and pain, but never this kind of fear. How odd it was that she didn't so much fear for her own life as for something happening to Gabe. It was a life without him in it that scared her most.

She remembered harboring that kind of fear when Laird was a baby and David's cocaine habit was the enemy. Her role then had been to protect her son. It still was.

Shannon knew she'd do anything to shield Laird, even if she was the one posing the threat.

She'd never realized how much love she had in her heart to give until now. She'd spent so many years blaming herself for her mistakes, she'd forgotten to look for the goodness inside her.

As she headed Pete's car into the foggy blackness

down Highway 1, she guessed their chances of being alive tomorrow morning were slim. If the cops didn't find them, the assassins would.

Gabe saw the hopelessness in Shannon's eyes. He put his hand on her thigh. "I'm here. Don't forget that," he said to assure her.

"I know." She choked back her misgivings. "So am I."

Gabe heard a series of bleeps from the back seat as Pete punched out a number on his cellular phone.

"What are you doing? Any scanner in the area can pick up your call," Gabe said.

Shannon glanced at Pete in the rearview mirror.

Pete frowned at them both. "Quit looking at me like I'm Lucifer," he said. "I know what I'm doing."

"Prove it."

"I am! Give me a chance, will you?" Pete snapped while listening to the ringing telephone on the other end. His call was picked up. "Buzzy! How the hell are you? It's Peter Dominic."

"How's my stock doing?" Buzzy asked.

"Great, and I've got a new company I want to tell you about. You could get in on the ground floor. A real opportunity for someone like you. I usually only offer a deal like this to big players, but you're such a friend that I—"

Pete's eyes cut to Shannon and she glared menacingly back at him.

Buzzy's voice was so loud and harsh on the other end that Shannon and Gabe could hear nearly every word.

"Cut the crap, Pete," Buzzy said. "What's it gonna cost me?"

Gabe stifled a snicker.

"I need a favor," Pete said, huddling his shoulder into the leather seat.

"What is it?"

"I've got a couple friends who want to elope to Santiago...tonight. I need to charter a plane."

"No can do."

"This is an emergency," Pete protested. "You must have something."

"Oh, I got the plane all right. A Citation. But, in case you haven't noticed, we've got pea soup out there. I can't send a pilot up in this stuff."

"I forgot about the weather." Pete looked out the window as Shannon drove them through low-lying mists. "It doesn't look that bad down here."

"Where are you?"

"North of Carmel."

"No kidding? I got a report a half hour ago that said the fog was lifting, but it's so thick here I didn't believe it. Tell you what. You come on in. I'll see if I can get one of my guys to take an extra gig."

"I really appreciate it," Pete said.

"Pete, I want you to know I believe in favors as much as the next guy, but I can't afford a free charter—"

Pete cut in, "I wouldn't dream of it. And no discounts, either. In fact, if you can pull this off, there's a bonus in it for you. Cash."

"You're talking my language, Pete."

"Good. I'll call you back and let you know when we're close. And thanks again, Buzzy." He hung up.

Pete then dialed the home number of his most trusted assistant, Sid Gillis.

"Sid, I'm arranging for a wire transfer to come into

the company account first thing in the morning. Don't be alarmed when you see the size of the transaction."

"How much are we talking?" Sid asked.

"Over fifty million."

"What's it for? A corporate merger?"

"Something like that. I want you to go to the office right now and get some money out of my vault for a client who's leaving the country tonight," Pete instructed.

"But I don't have the combination."

"I'll give it to you. I trust you, Sid," Pete added. "Five hundred thousand ought to do it."

Sid struggled to hide his surprise. "I...had no idea you kept that kind of money around. Will you want me to have the combination changed afterward?"

"In the morning. Have the locksmith send the combination to my personal e-mail address. Susan has it."

"What else?"

"I'll meet you at the American Airline baggage claim in San Jose," Pete said.

"That'll take some time, Pete."

"I understand, Sid."

"What am I supposed to do about the fifty million?"

"I'll be taking care of it," Pete said. "Use my canvas bag for the five hundred thousand. It's in the closet in my office. Take your cellular with you and call me when you're close to the airport. I'll keep mine on if you need me."

"I'll take care of it," Sid said and signed off.

In the black Mercedes less than a mile behind them, Sardia used an ultrahigh-frequency phone scanner to listen to Pete's cellular call. When the communication ended, Sardia turned to Joseph.

"San Jose Airport."

Joseph turned off to Highway 156. "This is the fastest way. The fog is starting to clear. We'll get them this time."

Sardia nodded coldly.

35

Ben's ace attribute was his ability to curse himself out.

He did just that for nearly half an hour after leaving Amelia Randall's house, a round of questioning that got him nowhere except to know that Gabe Turner had done the right thing, the gentlemanly thing, and let Shannon go.

Amelia had said Shannon was alone.

"Damn, it almost makes me like him," he grumbled.

Ben didn't know where Shannon had disappeared to after her visit with Amelia and the boy. He didn't have to wait long.

Ben didn't need a live report from the CNN helicopter over Peter Dominic's cottage to know the story. His cellular link with Washington was better than being there—almost.

"Make it good. Make it fast."

"Don't be so edgy, Maestro. Think about it. You nab these guys, your career is golden. You'll be immortal. That's what you've always wanted, isn't it?"

"I did," he replied, hearing sadness in his own voice. "I mean, I do."

"Hey, man. You've got it bad."

Swiping the back of his hand across his lips, he

couldn't help wondering what it would have been like to kiss her, to hold her the way Turner had. He felt his guts roll over. "Not so bad," he lied.

"Yeah, right, and I'm the pope."

Ben closed his eyes, momentarily shoving his emotions back inside. "I'm coming up to the freeway."

"Head to the San Jose Airport."

"Have they seen her?"

"She's driving Dominic's car."

Suddenly, Ben felt a pang right in the center of his heart. If he'd had any doubts about what was tops on his priority list as of the last several weeks, he knew now it was certainly not his damn career. It was Shannon. First. Last. Always.

He remembered the first day he'd seen her at the hospital. She'd barely glanced at him, but in that millisecond, his eyes had locked with hers. Fire and cool apathy, he'd thought of her green eyes. Every day he'd watched her go into Gabe's room. He'd heard her read poetry to the comatose man and he'd been jealous as hell.

Ben inhaled deeply. He could almost smell her scent. Like fresh clean soap. Not perfume. Never perfume. Never obvious. Like Shannon, who subtly eased herself into his heart and took up space, he'd never forget the scent or the woman.

What kind of fate put a woman like Shannon on the planet and wittingly positioned her between two men?

For weeks Ben had been able to fool himself into thinking that he was the good guy while Gabe was the bad guy. The truth was, they were both good guys—except when it came to Shannon.

Ben would have kidnapped her himself, given half

the chance. And he probably would have forced himself and his affections on her.

Ben was the Maestro. He was used to getting what he wanted. He would have taken Shannon no matter what the consequences—and Ben knew he would have screwed it up.

"Ben? Are you listening to me?"

"Yeah. So tell me, why do I detect a certain evasiveness to your voice?" Ben asked.

"Because…they lost her."

"You've *got* to be kidding me." He raked his hand through his hair, expelling a frustrated sigh. "This isn't happening."

"It's bad fog. We got the info from a local chopper. Then she lost the chopper and we haven't gotten a bead on her since."

"I'm betting she's alive and that's something."

"I wouldn't take that bet. I don't think Shannon's luck can last much longer."

"So what makes you think they're headed for the airport?"

"Maestro, you're slipping. It's a hunch."

"Of yours?"

"I'm entitled." He laughed.

"Not on my mission, you aren't."

"Okay, fine. We overheard portions of a cellular call Peter Dominic made."

"And?"

"He's making plans to leave the country."

"I'll check it out." Ben hung up.

The drive seemed interminably long. When he got to the San Jose Airport, the place was a zoo. Planes downed, canceled and then brought back made for a nightmarish sea of angry, pissed-off travelers. Area motels and hotels were packed with holiday travelers who wanted to be anywhere but in the airport.

Ben combed through the crowds, several times thinking he'd found Shannon.

Discouraged, but unwilling to give up, he questioned the ticket clerks.

"Sorry, Charlie. There're plenty of redheads going through here," the last clerk said. "My wife went red this year. It's the in thing ever since Julia Roberts, she said. I can't help you out."

He found nothing. No one matching Shannon's or Gabe's description was traveling internationally, domestically or bound for cities or airports with international travel connections.

Ben had hit a dead end and he didn't like it one bit.

36

Gabe felt ancient. He'd been running, physically and mentally, from the Colombians for what seemed like forever. Part of him wanted to confront the cartel bastards. The other part wanted to disappear somewhere safe with Shannon.

The truth was, they were far from safe. Every time a car passed them on the highway, he braced, expecting a rain of bullets. When they stopped to get gas, he watched every face. He was beginning to feel as if his hand was glued to his gun.

"I wish to hell you didn't make sense, Pete," Gabe said.

Shannon shot him a glaring look. "We'll never get away with this. The cartel will find us."

Pete's voice was sincere when he said, "I know you don't know me at all, but tell me what you've got to lose? Parents? Kids?"

"No," she replied sadly, her eyes finding Gabe's. "There's no one."

"I'm in the same situation. Now that my divorce is final and my ex is paid off, even she wouldn't miss me."

"Gabe's the only one who could get hurt," Shannon said.

"Me? How?"

"Your mother." Shannon watched as fear flickered in his eyes.

"Gloria..." Pete's voice trailed off pensively.

Looking in the rearview mirror at Pete, Shannon asked, "How do we protect her?"

Pete didn't have an answer. He shook his head, his eyes escaping Shannon's damning look.

Gabe had felt protective about his mother ever since his father died. Gloria was a self-sufficient woman with many friends and her real-estate work. She'd never been a loner. She wouldn't understand if Gabe sent her money to relocate in Europe. Gloria wasn't a vagabond.

Gloria was in jeopardy.

They arrived at a private hangar marked with a blue-and-white sign that read Pacific Air.

Buzzy MacGregor wore a broad smile, tan overalls, duck boots, a crackled brown leather jacket lined in sheepskin and a leather aviator's hat that looked like the World War II relic it was. He walked up to Pete and slapped him on the back. "How the hell are you, Pete?"

"Great. You're looking a bit overfed, Buzzy," he said, swatting the Scot's round belly.

"A bit too much holiday cheer." He laughed as Shannon and Gabe walked up. Seeing their anxious, grim faces he dropped his banter and turned instantly to Pete. "Must be a shotgun weddin'. They don't look happy to me."

Pete's smile disappeared as he glanced around the open area. "Where can we talk?"

"Inside," Buzzy said and quickly ushered them into the hangar.

They went into Buzzy's windowless office and he closed the door. Reaching up to the television that was mounted to the ceiling in the corner of the room, he turned the switch. "I was channel-surfing earlier and turned on the news. First it was just on the local news, but now CNN has picked it up."

"What?" Pete asked, watching Buzzy flip past the Weather Channel to yet another station. "I know one of these stations will have it. Ah! Here we go...." He turned up the volume.

The CNN newscaster switched over to a live on-the-scenes reporter. "We're here in the quiet art colony of Carmel, California, where two men have been found dead, both from apparent gunshot wounds. Neither of the men have been identified, though the police are saying these murders have all the earmarks of a gangland slaying. The time of death has been put at approximately seven o'clock, Pacific time, when neighbors heard repeated gunshots being fired and called police. Two M-16s were found on the bodies. Police believe the owner of the house, Peter Dominic, was not at home at the time. Neighbors stated they did not see Mr. Dominic, nor any lights in the house this evening. Whether Mr. Dominic rented his cottage to unknown parties is not known. Police have not located Mr. Dominic for questioning at this time. Now back to you, Jennifer."

The newscaster came back on the screen. "I have just been handed an update. Police have found the body of a young woman, in her early twenties, at the home of Peter Dominic in Tiburon. The name of the young woman will not be released until her family has been notified of her death. Police believe she was a student at the University of San Francisco. Mr. Dominic is being sought for questioning."

Buzzy turned off the television. "Mind telling me what's going on?"

"I could, but I won't," Pete said. "I don't want the same thing to happen to you, Buzzy."

"You saying it could?"

"Yes. I didn't kill that young girl. I did kill one of those assassins at my cottage."

"I killed the other," Shannon volunteered.

Buzzy took off his cap, revealing a head full of strawberry-blond curly hair. He scratched his scalp and said, "I don't think you have enough cash for this favor, Pete."

Gabe instantly stepped in. "Look, none of this is Pete's fault. He has nothing to do with these drug dealers, but neither do Shannon and I. The truth is, Pete and I got caught up in a scam our high-school buddy, Adam Rivers, was pulling on a Colombian cartel."

"Holy cow!"

"By being a friend to Adam, both Pete and I are in danger. We didn't ask for any of this to happen, but it did and now we're running for our lives. You're our only chance to get out of the country. You can see," he said, pointing to the television set, "these people will stop at nothing. Since Christmas Day I've been running across this country. I've been shot at so many times, by so many different hit men, I should have been stopped three states back.

"The thing is, Buzzy," Gabe continued, "I have information that the DEA has needed desperately. I know where half the methamphetamine labs are located across the South."

"God almighty!" Buzzy whistled. "I'd better get the Citation filled up."

Pete slapped Buzzy on the back. "Thanks. You're a real friend."

Cranking a bushy eyebrow upward, Buzzy asked, "Pete, am I going to see my Citation again?"

Gabe and Pete exchanged a look. "I hadn't gotten that far with my plan."

"That's what I thought," he grumbled. "In that case, you'll need to do me a favor."

"What's that?"

"This plane was supposed to drop some cargo in Cabo San Lucas. If you're headed to Santiago, you'll have to stop in Cabo to refuel anyway. Most of this stuff goes to the *Commandante* there."

"Really?" Gabe asked. "Do you know him?"

"Yeah. My wife and I've been down there on vacation. We met in a restaurant seven, eight years ago. Real nice guy."

"Would you say you were close friends with him?" Gabe asked.

"I know him pretty well...."

"Well enough to know if he's bribable?"

Pete threw Gabe a cautious look. "Gabe, I don't think you should be..."

Gabe cut him off. "I'm doing what you failed to do, Pete."

"What's that?"

"Plugging holes."

Pete borrowed Buzzy's Suburban to drive over to the American Airlines baggage claim to meet Sid. Shannon and Gabe remained in Buzzy's office.

Hugging herself, Shannon sat in a chair near the

space heater. "Do you think we'll be able to take off soon?"

"It depends on the fog. Buzzy said if it didn't lift by the time Pete got back, we'd have to stay here till morning."

"Can we risk that?"

"No," he answered honestly.

"That's what I was afraid of."

Pulling her into his arms, he said, "Mark my words. Someday you'll never use that word again."

"What word?" she asked.

"Afraid."

"I keep thinking this has to be a nightmare. That I've been dreaming this horror."

"I know." He caressed her hair. "I'll do everything I can to keep you safe."

"I know you mean that, Gabe, but I've got to be realistic." Tears filled her eyes. "Our chances of staying alive are used up. I can feel it. All it's gonna take is one bullet. Just one time when we don't watch where we are going, or what we say or who we trust."

He held her tighter, wishing his arms could shield her. He'd never felt his mortality so keenly.

Pete parked the Suburban in a metered parking place at San Jose Airport and rushed up to Sid's car. Pete got into the car and Sid handed him a canvas duffel bag.

"I didn't think you'd come," Pete said, aware of the suspicious look Sid gave him.

"I thought about it."

"So, why did you do it?"

"I've known you for fourteen years, Pete. The Peter Dominic I know wouldn't have killed a young girl

like that. You're ex...now, that's different," he said
with a half smile, then his expression grew serious
again. "What's going on, Pete?"

"You never saw me and you didn't get this money.
You got it?"

"The police have already called my house. They'll
know about the money transfer in the morning. How
do I explain that?"

"I've decided not to transfer it."

"What?"

"At least not through the company. That way, you
and the company won't be under suspicion of any
kind."

"So, you're just going to disappear, is that it?"

"Not exactly. You're going to tell the police that I
was brokenhearted after my breakup with my girlfriend in Aspen."

"You broke up?"

"Yes, but I'm not brokenhearted. Then I flew back
to the city, which they will verify when they check my
plane reservations. I did go by the house and saw
Melanie's body. I panicked, went to the office, took
my personal cash and left the country. In a few
months when things die down and the police figure
out Melanie was killed by one of the hit men they
found at my cottage, which is my personal theory,
then I'll contact you from Africa."

"That's where you're going? Africa?"

"Sure, why not? I've always wanted to go on a sa-
fari."

Sid eyed him carefully. "You've lost your mind."

"Not at all. I'm actually doing something noble. I'm
being a friend."

"Huh?"

"It's all right, Sid. You don't need to know any more than what I've told you. Just stick to this story." Pete shook his hand. "You'll be an asset to the company, Sid. You're more innovative than I ever was. I'm not sure how many more years it would have been until my ways of handling investments would be outmoded. Who knows? I might have lost a great deal of investors' money, and I couldn't live with myself if that happened. It's time I retired."

"I've never heard you talk like this, Pete."

He smiled. "I know. Maybe I'm growing up."

"Peter Pan? Never."

The fog lifted, releasing the Citation for takeoff.

After slipping into their Pacific Air uniforms, Buzzy's pilot and copilot walked out of the hangar toward the Citation.

"The Raiders are getting their asses kicked this season," the pilot said. "Who do you think will be playing in the Super Bowl?"

The copilot never had a chance to answer.

Sardia and Joseph used their gun butts to knock out the two men. They dragged them back behind a row of scratched and dented army-green lockers and undressed them. Then, wearing the pilot uniforms, Sardia and Joseph headed toward the Citation.

37

Pete met with Buzzy in his office while Gabe and Shannon went out to the plane with Pete's computer equipment.

"I've got the Citation fueled and my boys are bringing that cargo around from the back of the hangar. I appreciate your taking this to Cabo," Buzzy said to Pete.

"No problem."

Buzzy handed him a slip of paper. "Here's Commandante Miguel Torres's number. The second number is his home. His wife's name is Rosa. He's expecting this shipment. I told him you were a good friend and to take care of anything you needed."

"I can't thank you enough, Buzzy."

"About that cash bonus..." Buzzy said, rocking back on his heels.

Gabe unzipped the canvas bag. "Here's twenty-five thousand now."

Buzzy whistled. "I've never seen that much money."

"As soon as the banks open in the morning, I'll have a cashier's check sent to you to cover the cost of the plane. I'll fly your pilot and copilot back first-class from Santiago. I'd appreciate it if you wouldn't say anything to them about that. Not that I don't trust them, but they could slip up and say something over the radio. It's too easy for information like that to be picked up."

"I know. I invested in that scanner company you told me about." Buzzy laughed. "You better get going."

"Thanks for everything," Pete said and left.

Gabe and Shannon went to the reception counter in the front of the hangar. The ground crewmen were busy loading the plane and finishing their inspection. The room was empty.

Gabe opened drawers and rifled through the in and out baskets.

"What are you doing?" she asked.

"Don't ask. You'll think too well of me," he said, finding a brown padded mailing envelope. He took out the computer disk and placed it inside. He scribbled a short message and enclosed it as well. After stapling the envelope shut, he scribbled an address in Washington, D.C., used the automatic mailing machine to mark the postage and placed it in the basket marked Out.

Shannon glanced at the addressee. "You're sending it to Ben?"

"Yeah. Seemed the right thing to do considering I got the girl."

She smiled.

Just then they heard a gun cock.

"I wouldn't exactly say that, Turner," Ben said.

"Ben!" Shannon exclaimed.

He looked at her. Was it possible she was smiling because of him? Or was the gleam in her eye because of the man standing next to her? Ben didn't want to know the answer to his own questions. He didn't like losing. More important, Ben believed deep in his soul that he was the only chance Shannon had of living at all. He had to show her that he was her savior.

"How did you find us, Ben?" she asked.

"I told you I would find you." Ben felt a burning lump in his throat. He walked forward carefully.

Gabe held out the envelope. "This is for you."

"Not a chance. This time I'm after the whole enchilada." Ben cast a sidelong glance at Shannon.

Gabe stood Ben down. Neither was prepared to compromise.

Ben didn't like it. Shannon wasn't running toward him, wasn't welcoming him as her savior. She stood riveted to the floor. He felt as if he were sinking in quicksand.

He did the only thing he knew to do. He took action. "I have to take you both in. My backup will be here in seconds."

"I'm sure they will." Gabe's eyes were level with Ben's. "But she's not going. She hasn't done anything wrong."

"Goddamn it! I'm trying like hell to save her ass!" Ben nearly shouted.

"I thought that was my job," Gabe retorted.

"You're not helping her. She's instrumental in our case...she's... Goddamn it, Turner! I need her."

Shannon walked toward him. "For what, Ben?"

"I just told you." He felt his armpits get wet. His hand was trembling.

"Ben," Shannon said, her eyes unsettling him even more. "This disk is all you need. I know it and you know it." She took the envelope from Gabe and handed it to Ben. "This is the original. It has everything. When you report to your superiors—"

"You'll be with me," Ben interrupted.

"I can't, Ben."

"You mean you won't...." He barely got the words out. For days he'd wanted to force the issue with her. Now he wasn't so sure. "Don't you see? I'm the only chance either of you have. I can protect you," he pleaded earnestly.

"I'm going with Gabe," she said, reaching out to touch Ben's arm.

He lowered his gun.

She expelled a deep sigh. "I hate guns, Ben. Thank you for that."

"I shouldn't, you know."

Her gaze was piercingly sincere. "I love him, Ben."

His head snapped back ever so slightly as her words struck him. "I...thought so."

"Please try to understand. I don't have a life here. Not with my son anymore. Not in Shreveport anymore. They were only way stations for me. I'm sorry I got you messed up in my struggles."

"You didn't do anything, Shannon," Ben said. "I just..."

"Don't say any more," she replied. "I know." She looked at him as if in some way he had been her savior after all. "I'll always be grateful for having known you, Ben. You've kept those bastards off our backs. Probably even saved our lives a time or two. That's pretty unselfish, come to think of it."

Ben looked at Shannon. "Goddamn, I need you, Shannon."

She squeezed his hand. "But I need this," she said.

"Him or the freedom?"

"Both."

"I guess I knew that."

Her eyes were imploring. "So will you let us go?"

Ben looked over Shannon's head to Gabe. "You don't deserve her."

"I know that, but I intend to work on it."

"See that you do," Ben said, taking a step back and releasing Shannon's hand.

Ben motioned toward the door with a tilt of his head. "You better get going. The locals are right behind me."

Gabe rushed up to Shannon and took her elbow with one hand while extending his other hand to Ben. "Thanks, old man."

Ben looked down at Gabe's hand, but refused to take it. He half smiled. "Sorry, but I'm not *that* gracious a loser."

"Fair enough," Gabe said.

Shannon started to leave with Gabe and then stopped. "Can I take just a minute alone?" she asked Gabe imploringly.

Gabe saw the tears in her eyes. "Sure. I'll be outside."

"Thanks."

Gabe shut the door on his way out.

Shannon walked back to Ben and she took his hand. "I'll always remember you, Ben. What you did for us."

"For you," he corrected.

She gazed at him, eyes full of grateful tears.

"When all this started, I had this personal vendetta against Blane Blair. It hasn't gone away. I was driven by hate. I wanted revenge for something that happened to me a long time ago."

"Does it have anything to do with the girl you were in love with?"

"Everything."

"I see."

"I thought I was bringing this case in for her. To get Blane. It started that way. But it's not ending that way. That's what I want you to know." He took a deep breath for courage. "I would have combed the earth for you, Shannon. And it's not because I need your testimony. I've realized that you're not the kind of woman I'll get over. I'll never forget you. And I'll never give up on you."

"Ben, please, don't..."

He put his fingers to her lips. "Don't say anything. Just let me say this." He paused. "I'm grateful to you. I didn't know I was capable of loving anyone this much. I would crawl over glass for you. I would have died for you. And I know I'll keep on loving you. I don't want to forget. If you ever need me, no matter where you are, I'll find you again. I guess that's what you've taught me...that loving doesn't just stop."

"No, Ben, it doesn't. And you can't pick it. It chooses you. Love just is."

"It's like this for you with him, isn't it?" he asked, tilting his head in the direction Gabe had left.

"Yes," she said softly.

"You knew it when he was in the coma, didn't you?"

She nodded. "When he came in off the ambulance I touched him and something just happened to me. I can't explain it."

"So, I lost you before I even had a chance?"

She kissed his hand, tears streaming down her cheeks. "Ben."

"Just know you'll never lose me. I'll always be there for you. Always."

"Ben, it's not fair of me to ask. You should have a life. You should have—"

"Hey," he interrupted, "you're not asking. I'm offering. There's a difference. Remember?"

"Yeah, there is." She smiled.

"Can I ask a favor since I may never see you again?"

"Sure," she replied.

"Can I kiss you before you go?"

"I'd like that."

Cupping her face with his hands, Ben brought his lips to hers, barely brushing the surface, not daring to imbibe too much of their splendor. He ached too much already. He was only torturing himself.

His lips were trembling. A tear fell from her eyes and slid onto his hand as she opened her eyes and moved away.

"Goodbye, Ben," she said, turning away.

He lifted the tear to his lips and drank it. "I'll be seeing you," he said, a crack of emotion splitting his words.

Shannon closed the door behind her.

"Thanks for giving me that, Gabe," she said.

"How could I not? You love him, too."

She nodded. "In my way."

Gabe took her hand as they rushed away from the building.

Ben watched them race across the concrete toward the Citation. "Look back, Shannon."

But she kept running—with Gabe.

* * *

Joseph Valerosa checked the instrument panel and donned his earphones.

Looking back at the hangar, Sardia nudged Joseph and pointed to the ground crewman who was hauling eight huge canvas sacks and numerous crates out to the plane's cargo hold.

"You see that? It is Alejandro's money!"

"Did he ever tell you how much?"

"Fifty-three million U.S. And change." Sardia laughed.

Joseph turned back to watch the crewman. "Just how much do you think it weighs?"

As Pete climbed into the plane, the ground crewman wheeled the steps away and signaled to the pilot to begin his taxi.

Gabe told Pete about Ben.

"The feds will be swarming over this place in minutes."

The engine revved, then backed away from the hangar.

"Just in time!" Gabe said, relieved.

Pete pulled out his laptop and inserted a new battery. He turned to Gabe and pointed to the in-flight telephones. "Can you believe it? Buzzy's always got the best!"

Pete turned on his computer and hooked it up to the telephone. "Time to go to work."

Canceling the wire transfer to Dominic Investments was the first order of business. He then placed a transfer of half the drug money into his private Swiss account.

Gabe leaned across the aisle. "What are you doing?" He looked at the screen and saw Pete's name at the top of the screen.

"This will be an interbank transfer from the Rodriguez account into mine. I set this account up during my divorce so my wife wouldn't take my retirement fund."

Gabe looked at the account balance. "Pete, you're an investment banker and you only have seventy thousand dollars in your account?"

"Okay." He shrugged his shoulders. "So, I didn't plan well."

"I told you to buy whole life!"

Pete waved him off. "I screwed up, okay?"

Shannon kept watch out the window. In the distance she could see a platoon of police cars snaking down the street toward the airport. "My God, they've sent in the militia!"

"Damn!" Gabe turned to the window. "Ben wasn't kidding."

Shannon was aghast. "They needed this many just for us?"

"I think they were planning to catch much larger fish."

Shannon nodded. "Ben will be disappointed."

Gabe kissed the back of her neck. "That's not what's eating at his craw, believe me." He slipped his arms around Shannon and kissed her ear. "I know how I'd feel if I'd lost you."

The Citation taxied farther down the runway, but the squad cars were gaining.

Pete glanced up from the laptop. "Where are they now?"

"Close," Shannon said, putting her hand on the window. "Someone's opened the gate!"

Gabe peered over her shoulder. "They're coming onto the runway."

"What's taking the pilot so long to get us airborne?" Shannon asked.

Just then the Citation picked up speed, outracing the police cars.

Shannon watched the office building. She saw a man come rushing outside. "Ben…" she whispered to herself, placing her hand on the window.

She saw him smile at her. Then he lifted his hand and gave her a terse salute to acknowledge the fact that he'd seen her smile back at him.

"Say!" Pete said, "don't you want to know what I'm doing?"

"Not now!" Shannon and Gabe exclaimed in unison.

Pete kept working feverishly. "Well, for your information I'm putting the rest of the money into my other account in Grand Cayman."

Gabe cranked his head around. "Cayman? You have two offshore accounts?"

"Yeah. I told you, I was a little paranoid during the divorce. There's not much in this account either."

Gabe glanced at the screen. "To me it looks like you've got all the money in your name, and Shannon and I don't have a penny."

Pete ignored him and continued working. He dialed the phone number in Geneva and sent the e-mail wire transfer. After the transaction was completed, he typed instructions for a series of small ten-thousand-dollar deposits to be sent to the Cayman National Bank. Then he dialed the Cayman National Bank.

"The bank in Cayman is closed for the night, but the computers are kept on. They pick up the wires and input them in the morning. I have several accounts under different corporate names and I can wire ten thousand dollars to each. I don't want anything too suspicious-looking right now. By law you can only withdraw ten thousand dollars at a time out of Cayman. I'll make flight arrangements for the three of us and once there, I'll introduce you to my attorney and my banker."

"What for?"

"It isn't easy to move this much money around. It's going to take a lot of work and travel, quite frankly. Maybe you'll learn to appreciate me," Pete said.

"Yeah, maybe even trust you," Gabe replied.

Pete gave Gabe a flinty look, then said good-naturedly, "I put all your information on my hard drive back at the cottage." He patted the laptop. "All stored away, safe and sound. I just need a few more minutes...."

"You may not have it!" Shannon jammed her finger anxiously at the window.

"How *is* our company?" Pete asked, to change the subject.

Shannon looked out the window. "Closing in fast," she reported, then her eyes looked past the stream of oncoming squad cars to the hangar.

She watched Ben's shadow against the sea of flashing red and blue lights. He stood immobile, watching her leave. Then he raised his hand as if waving good-bye to her. She splayed her fingers against the windowpane as if their fingers were touching.

"God bless you, Ben."

"Ready for takeoff," the copilot announced their ascent.

"It's about damn time!" Gabe said, leaning his

head against the headrest and closing his eyes. He didn't want Shannon to know that seeing her bid farewell to Ben cut him to the core.

Turning, Shannon saw the pained expression on Gabe's face. "What's wrong?"

"I just discovered I'm jealous. Crazy bad jealous." He opened his eyes.

"I would be, too, if the tables were turned." She kissed his cheek. "But I love you most."

He kissed her back. "Thank God."

"Gabe! They're gaining on us!" Pete said.

The Citation picked up speed.

"Oh God." Shannon was wide-eyed watching the swarm of police cars zoom forward, closing the gap. To Shannon they looked menacing. She couldn't help thinking of the irony of their position in her life since she'd known Gabe. She'd always thought of police as the men who "serve and protect." She knew Ben thought he was protecting her and Gabe thought he was protecting her. All her years in Shreveport she'd thought she was protecting herself. But, she'd just been running away.

If she'd stayed in California, confronted Amelia and stood up for herself, perhaps she wouldn't have ever come to this.

The choreography of the red and blue lights cleared Shannon's brain like healing lasers. There was no time for regrets.

"Come on! Hurry!" Shannon said, urging the pilot on.

A half-dozen cars pulled alongside the Citation. Shannon knew they were going to try to cross in front of the Citation's flight path, forcing the plane to remain grounded. Then they would board the plane and take them into custody. She might never see Gabe again.

Her adrenaline kicked in. She felt as if she could lift the plane herself.

"Come on...come on," she whispered the litany as the plane's engine burned. Still it wasn't enough. The squad cars matched the Citation's speed.

Shannon pounded her fist into her palm while she watched out the window.

A rapacious taste for victory overwhelmed her, but it was in equal measure to the powerful force of the police. She couldn't help thinking, Right over might. No matter how much she willed herself, Gabe and Pete to escape, the police had the law on their side.

She was part of a trio of outlaws now—one of the bad guys.

The Citation was nearly surrounded.

Her hope dying, Shannon pushed her nerves to the limit. "What can we do? Damn! There's nothing we can do!"

"Pray!" Gabe said, taking out his gun, preparing himself for action he'd almost believed he would never be forced to take again.

"What if they board us?" Shannon asked, her eyes clamped on the gun.

Gabe swallowed hard as his eyes cut back to the scene outside. "I'll deal with that when the time comes."

"Gabe...I can't...I won't shoot at cops. It's against my principles."

"Mine, too," he said and kissed her cheek. "It's not gonna happen. But this time, let's try not to think so far ahead."

Gabe looked out the window. The cop cars were

running neck and neck with the Citation. They were so close Gabe swore he could make out the numbers on every one of their badges.

"Why can't we get this crate off the ground before it's too late!" Gabe exclaimed, casting a damning glare toward the closed door to the cockpit.

As if he'd heard Gabe's directive, the pilot nosed the plane into the air.

The squad cars shot underneath the plane's belly, racing farther down the runway. One by one they slammed on their brakes, many skidding to a halt, others spinning like lighted tops.

"Oh my God! We made it!"

"We're up!" Shannon yelled and hugged Gabe.

Pete kept pounding away at his keyboard, seemingly unaware of the tension in the cabin and their narrow escape.

"I sure hope there's no fog farther down the coast," Pete said drolly. "Night flying is dangerous as it is."

Shannon watched the flashing squad-car lights below. They had stopped moving. One by one they were turned off. The feds, the cops and Ben were below her.

She was on her way to another world and realized she'd been holding her breath so long her lungs burned. She wiped beads of anxiety from her upper lip, then clutched her hands in her lap.

"Relax," Gabe said. "We're almost home-free."

"Why do I feel that almost doesn't count?" she quipped.

Gabe gave her a reassuring look. "We'll make it. I'll call up to the pilot and get our estimated flying time. That way, you can see how very close we are to home plate." He unbuckled his seat belt and reached for the

intercom phone located in the bulkhead in front of
them.

Shannon nodded as she looked over at Pete who
was hitting the enter key, then closing the laptop.

"Say, Captain, what's our ETA?" Gabe asked.

There was no answer so Gabe asked the question
again. After a long pause, a thickly accented voice
said, "Sorry."

Gabe's neck hairs prickled. Instantly, he tossed his
gun to Shannon. "Cover me," he said.

No sooner had the words left his mouth than Sardia opened the cockpit door, aimed his gun and
pulled the trigger.

Gabe slammed his back against the bulkhead wall,
just missing the bullet.

Pete froze as the bullet zinged past him and imbedded itself in the seat upholstery only a fraction of an
inch from his right ear.

"No!" Shannon screamed, forgetting all reason,
forgetting her fear of guns. She aimed Gabe's gun at
Sardia before he had a chance to fire again.

She fired and hit Sardia in the heart. Blood spurted
from his chest. He clamped his hand over his heart,
impotently trying to stop the flow.

Wild-eyed, he stared at Shannon as if she were the
angel of death delivering retribution. Then he sank to
his knees and fell facedown, dead.

Hands shaking, Shannon dropped the gun. "Now
Laird will be safe forever."

In the next instant, Joseph appeared in the doorway, leveling his gun at Shannon. Gabe whirled
around from his hiding place against the bulkhead
and pounced on him before he had a chance to react.
He rammed his fist down on the man's outstretched

arm and Joseph dropped his gun. Gabe yanked his arm, pulling him out of the cockpit and into the cabin. He grabbed his collar with his left hand and sank his right fist into Joseph's jaw. Joseph barely reacted to the pain.

Quickly, Joseph delivered a right-handed punch, landing it in Gabe's chin, then a left hook, which Gabe dodged expertly.

Gabe sank another blow to Joseph's jaw, then shoved him enough to stumble against Sardia's body.

Seeing Sardia's dead body on the floor, Joseph's shock caused him to falter a second too long, allowing Gabe to land a punch to his midsection. Joseph doubled over in pain.

Gabe brought both fists down on the back of the man's shoulders and neck, knocking him unconscious.

Gabe looked at Shannon's terror-filled eyes. "You all right?"

She didn't react, only stared at Sardia's body. Slowly, she raised her eyes to Gabe. "I killed him."

Gabe's heart went out to her. "I know, but you had no choice."

Nodding, she said, "It was him or us."

"Yes."

Her eyes burned. She'd never taken a human life. She'd spent her life saving lives. "I saved Laird, too," she said with a raspy voice.

"It's over," Gabe replied tenderly. "You saved your son and us. Even my mother is safe now, thanks to you."

Tears sluiced down her cheeks. Gabe climbed over Sardia and Joseph and went to her. Enfolding her in his arms, he tried to comfort her.

"It's an awful thing I did," she said. "I didn't even think about it. I just did it. Is that how it is in war? When men fight for freedom? Is that what this was? A war? A personal war?"

"Yes," Pete said from across the aisle. "And we won. The righteous vanquished because of you."

She looked up at Pete and gave him a grateful look.

Suddenly, the plane pitched to the side. They yelled in unison.

"We're going down!" Pete said.

"The hell we are!"

Gabe rushed into the cockpit and took the pilot's chair. Pete and Shannon followed behind.

"What are we going to do now?" Shannon asked. "We don't know how to fly a jet!"

"I do!" Gabe said, taking the plane off automatic pilot and banking it out to sea.

Pete watched as they changed course. "Where are you going? Cabo is the other way!"

"Don't worry. I know what I'm doing. We've got to get rid of these bodies. You and Shannon get ready. When I tell you, toss them overboard."

"What good will that do?" Shannon reasoned. "We still can't go back. Like you said, they'll just send more killers after us. We'll never get away from these bastards."

"I guess we're just gonna have to die!" Gabe declared as he shoved the plane into a vertical dive.

The plane felt as if it had dropped out of the sky. They descended at a dizzying speed.

"Gabe? What are you doing?"

The plane kept screaming toward the ocean.

"Gabe! Damn it, man!" Pete yelled, eyes like saucers as he watched the ocean rise up to kiss them.

Shannon screamed. "Gabe, are you crazy? What's the matter with you? Pull up! Pull up!"

"You asshole!" Pete yelled as his voice blended with Shannon's terrified screams.

38

➤ ◄

Shannon wouldn't believe they were going to die.

"Damn it, Gabe, do something!" Her eyes were filled with horror knowing impact with the ocean was only seconds away.

"I am!" he said, grabbing the radio mouthpiece. "Mayday! Mayday! This is flight 756 out of San Jose. I'm fifteen miles south of Monterey, headed out to sea, bearing west southwest. I've lost my right engine. Left engine is smoking. I'm going down! Explosion in number-two jet! I'm down…" He shut off the radio, disconnecting it.

Shannon looked out the window at the second engine. "What explosion? There was no explosion," Shannon said, her eyes cutting back to Gabe.

"I know," he grumbled, fighting with the controls.

"What the hell are you doing, Gabe?" Shannon demanded.

"Saving our asses!"

"I don't see how…"

"Help me depressurize this plane. Those switches there…" He pointed above her head.

"Okay," she said and did as he asked while Gabe used all his strength to pull the plane upward.

Gabe felt as if he were wrestling Atlas. His muscles burned, his ribs felt as if they'd snap, but he wouldn't give in to his pain. Only he could save them and he knew it.

"Man, I hate this hero crap."

Just as it looked as if he was about to crash into the water, Gabe leveled the plane out at five hundred feet.

"Oh my God! You did it!" Shannon said, taking a deep breath as the blue they saw through the windshield was sky now and not ocean.

"You're a genius!" Pete said. "There's no radar detection under five hundred feet. Everyone who heard that broadcast will think we crashed and burned. We're as good as dead."

Shannon nearly snapped her neck looking quickly at Gabe. "Really?"

He winked at her. "I told you to trust me."

She smiled. "Good thing I did."

"Yeah," he said, checking his instruments. "Both of you need to get back to the cabin and throw out everything you can. Food, bottles, blankets, pillows. Rip out a seat cushion or two. Everything that isn't nailed down I want floating around out there. Use the emergency-exit window."

"But we'll get sucked out!" Shannon said.

Gabe shook his head. "That's why I had you depressurize the cabin."

She got out of the copilot's chair and squeezed Gabe's shoulder appreciatively. "That really was genius."

Gabe patted her hand. "Nah, bringing you with me was the smartest thing I've ever done."

She leaned down and kissed him quickly. "I think so, too."

Pete opened the exit window. "Come on, Shannon," he said, lifting Sardia's upper body. "This trash is rotten."

Shannon took Sardia's feet and helped Pete shove the body out the window.

"What about him?" Shannon pointed to the unconscious accomplice.

Pete lifted his shoulder. "He'll wake up when he hits the water."

"What if he can't swim?" Shannon asked.

"Let's pray he can't," Pete answered, hoisting him out the window. Pete dusted off his hands. "Flotsam."

Shannon ripped the cabin interior apart. She yanked out the in-flight phones and tossed them overboard.

"What a waste of good equipment," Pete moaned regretfully as he watched the debris hit the water.

Shannon emptied everything out of the bathroom, galley and storage bins. When they finished, they put the window back and joined Gabe in the cockpit.

"All set, Skipper," Shannon said.

"Good. As far as the world is concerned, Peter Dominic, Shannon Riley and Gabe Turner are dead. Their bodies have been washed out to sea. The disk is in Ben Richards's hands and a drug lord somewhere has lost over fifty million bucks."

"Shame." Shannon smiled.

"Yeah, ain't it though." Gabe chuckled.

Shannon looked at Gabe. "We're a long way from being safe. What happens when we land? Won't the authorities identify this plane and know we didn't crash after all? What if that information gets into the wrong hands?"

"She's got a point, Gabe," Pete said.

"I have a plan."

"Please tell me this plan is not a work-in-progress."

Gabe only smiled.

Cartagena, Colombia

Alejandro had been unable to sleep. Courvoisier and a particularly well-made Habana cigar did not ease his tension.

The ringing telephone interrupted Alejandro's thoughts. Thinking the call was from Sardia, he beamed as he picked up his private-line receiver. *"Sí."*

He heard not Sardia but the frantic babbling of one of his lieutenants, Pedro, based in California, whose only job was to monitor the airwaves.

"Señor, I have just picked up an emergency call from the jet your party was flying."

"What kind of emergency?"

"A Mayday, *señor.* They…crashed into the Pacific."

"Impossible!"

"I've been trying to reach Sardia's cellular phone and the calls haven't gone through. Joseph's pager hasn't worked, either. What do you want me to do?"

"Did you get the location of this so-called crash?"

"Yes. So did the Coast Guard."

"And their report?"

"Debris was found. No bodies. The Coast Guard says the plane sank with all the passengers."

"Gone? Everything?"

"Everything."

"Thank you for the report."

"Yes, sir."

Alejandro leaned back in his chair and looked out

to his garden. His beautiful wife wrapped a shawl around her shoulders and gazed up at him. She smiled seductively, picked up a rose from the table and walked through the French doors to their bedroom.

He rose from his chair.

"Sometimes, I take all of this too seriously."

He walked out the door, across the terrace past the blooming bougainvillea and into the bedroom.

Cabo San Lucas, Mexico

Gabe landed the Citation on the Mexican airstrip and taxied to the private hangar where the ground captain directed him.

After deplaning, Gabe kept his arm around Shannon as a black Lincoln pulled up and a rotund man got out of the car. Dressed as he was in official uniform, they knew instantly he was Commandante Miguel Torres.

"Thank you for meeting us so late, *Commandante*," Gabe said.

"Buzzy called me earlier when we heard over the radio that your plane was down. He told me he had a feeling you would be arriving. He's very smart." The *commandante* smiled knowingly.

"It's very important that no one know of our arrival," Gabe said. "Besides the controller, the ground captain and yourself, are many people aware of our presence?"

"I wouldn't worry about it," he said. "They are my cousins."

"Excuse me?"

The *commandante* shrugged his shoulders. "Buzzy

said you would take good care of me," he said, his eyes gleaming.

"And right he was," Gabe said, taking the canvas bag Pete handed him. "Family is very important, don't you think? Now, how many cousins would you say it took tonight to help us."

The *commandante's* eyes were wide with greed. "Three...I mean, five."

"How about six?" Gabe asked.

"Oh, yes. I forgot Luis. Thank you for reminding me." The *commandante* grinned wider.

Gabe pulled out a stack of bills and handed them to him. Miguel stuffed the money into his pants pockets.

"I know it's probably rude of me to ask, but I need another favor," Gabe said.

"Another, *señor?*"

"Yes. A very big favor. One that will require many more cousins. Some uncles as well."

Shannon stared quizzically at Gabe.

"I need a crew to cut up this plane."

"What?" The *commandante's* shock was evident on his face. "It's a beautiful jet! Worth three million dollars!"

"I know that. Think how valuable all its parts will be to your family when you sell them."

"Ah!" He held up a finger in the air. "This is very smart of you. I will need to have my cousin fly the plane out of here immediately and deposit it in the jungle not far from my home. We do our best work there."

"I'm sure you do," Shannon said, pulling another stack of bills out of the canvas bag.

"*Señors, señora.* You are most generous."

Gabe put his arm around the *commandante's* shoulders. "Buzzy told us we could depend on you to make very certain our arrival went unnoticed."

"No problem," he said, waving generously. "I know lots of people who never came here," Miguel assured them.

"Good," Gabe said, and gestured toward the car. "Shall we go?"

"Of course."

Gabe sat next to Shannon in the back seat and put his arm around her. "There's only one thing I want to know."

"What's that?"

"Just what was there about me that made you fall in love with me?"

She put her arms around his neck. "I think it was the fact that you were comatose. I figured you wouldn't give me any trouble," she joked.

"I was afraid of that. And now?"

Her eyes plumbed the depths of his. "I love you, Gabe."

"Not as much as I love you," he replied and kissed her tenderly. He touched her cheek. "So, do you still want to go to Greece?"

"We can. But I don't need to," she said, smiling. "I've got my hero."

"And I've found mine," he said, kissing her again.

Epilogue

━━▶ ◀━━

Ben Richards and Sheriff Douglas Creighton, both in plainclothes, walked past Blane Blair's startled secretary and into his office just as Blane was stuffing a handful of files into his electric shredder.

Ben darted across the room and unplugged the machine. "Not so fast."

"Who the hell are you?"

Ben pulled out his badge. "FBI. Read him his rights, Sheriff," Ben said as Creighton yanked Blane's hands behind his back and handcuffed the man.

"You have the right to remain silent..." Sheriff Creighton began.

Over the sheriff's voice, Blane sputtered protests, his spittle raining on his newly polished dress shoes. "This is preposterous! You can't arrest me!"

"Yes, I can. And I am," Ben said smugly.

"On what charges?"

Ben held up a packet of papers. "You want me to start with the ones from California for extortion and fraud?" He shuffled the stack like playing cards. "Or Louisiana? Accomplice to murder one. How about the federal charges for drug trafficking? Money laundering. You name it."

"The hell you say." Blane stood upright, the furor

in his eyes dying quickly as reality hit him. "I get a phone call."

"Maybe," Sheriff Creighton said, hustling Blane past his election posters, past the banners, past the American flag.

"I want to talk to my attorney!"

"Yeah?" Ben snarled. "I'll bet he wants to talk with you, too."

They were all out the door in less than two minutes from the time Ben and Sheriff Creighton had entered.

Ben nodded to the secretary as they passed her.

"Is he coming back?" she asked.

Ben turned on his heel, cocked his head to the side and said, "Better book him out."

"For how long?"

Satisfaction warmed Ben's toes as he curled them inside his shoes. He'd waited a long time, worked what seemed a lifetime to bring Blane Blair down. There was nothing he despised more than a rotten politician. Blane was all that and more. Devil seed, his mother used to call people like Blair.

He thought of Nancy. And Shannon, the girl who was the impetus for his chase across the country, the catalyst and the reason he had the evidence to stop Blane before the election. Before he could do more harm to more Americans.

And Ben knew he'd been right to follow his instincts, to follow his heart.

There was no question in Ben's mind that somehow, someway, Gabe and Shannon had escaped death. He would know if she was dead, because he'd be able to feel it deep in that place where it still hurt when he thought about her.

The corner of his lip turned up, unable to deny the

triumph he felt. He looked the secretary straight in the eye.

"For the rest of his life, if I have anything to do with it."

Shannon stood on the balcony of an eight-hundred-year-old villa carved into the side of a cliff overlooking the Aegean Sea in Santorini, Greece. At sunset, the sky was ablaze with orange, pink and lavender ribbons of light wafting across the horizon. A gentle warm breeze fluttered her long white linen skirt and tickled her sandaled feet.

Gabe stepped through the French doors and said, "I have something for you."

She closed her eyes and inhaled the sea air. "I don't need a thing. This is bliss."

"You'll need this," he said, placing a beribboned bouquet of stargazer lilies in her hands.

Turning around to face him, she said, "You look dashing in your wedding suit."

"I should hope so. All heroes look that way, don't they?"

Lowering her eyes to the lilies, she said wistfully, "All my life I've wanted to come here. I wanted to know what it was like to live among the ghosts of ancient heroes. And it's more incredible than I'd imagined. But even more mystifying to me is that I've realized all of us are heroes, aren't we, Gabe? Just surviving this life with our hearts intact requires courage. You, me, Pete and Laird. Amelia, too."

"You forgot Ben," he said.

She raised her eyes to him, shining and full of love for him. They quelled Gabe's last insecurity. "And Ben," she replied softly.

He held her chin between his finger and thumb. "I want you always to love him, Shannon. That's just you. You have enough love in your heart for the whole world. Don't ever let anyone, even me, stem that flow. It's what makes you so special."

"Thanks" was all she could say before a tear crept to the corner of her eye. Wiping it away, she asked quickly, "Is Pete here already?"

"Uh-huh. And the priest."

She gazed at him. He kissed her sweetly. "I'm amazed you were able to arrange all this."

Gabe slipped her arm through the crook of his own. His smile was mischievous. "But darling, haven't you heard? Money may not buy you love, but it can sure help to make it legal."

Playfully, she tapped his temple with her bouquet. "Oh, you!" She laughed.

Gabe laughed with her. "I'm not going to be really happy until I see that ring on your finger."

"Really? And then what?"

He stopped dead in his tracks. "And then we do what all the real heroes in this world do."

"What's that?"

"Why, start a family, of course!"

Her smile erupted from the bottom of her soul. "Yes, that *is* the most heroic adventure we could have."

"Glad you agree," Gabe said, walking Shannon inside.

"Always, Gabe. Always."

Dearest Reader,

I hope you enjoyed *California Moon* as much as I loved bringing it to you. This was an intense story to write because so much of the work was done by me while still living in Quito, Ecuador. During that time the communications systems to the United States were far from stellar, to say the least. I am amazed I ever got it assembled, considering that my copiers, printers and fax machines conked out on me constantly. However, after years in the making, as they say in the movies, it finally comes to you.

For those of you who collect my recipes, I have a follow-up to the "Quick and Easy Tortilla Soup" I offered years ago. This one requires a bit more work, but the result is outstanding.

If you'd like a copy and a *California Moon* bookmark, please send a self-addressed, stamped (legal size is best for the bookmarks) envelope to me at: 5644 Westheimer Road, PMB #110, Houston, Texas 77056.

I would love to hear your comments!

God bless you all,
Catherine

HELEN R. MYERS

Six years ago the town of Split Creek, Texas, was rocked to its core when a young woman was brutally murdered. Her killer was never found. Now another girl has disappeared....

When Faith Ramey's abandoned car is discovered, the town feels an unwelcome sense of déjà vu. Police Chief Jared Morgan doesn't want to believe there's a connection, but Faith's sister Michaele is beginning to suspect otherwise.

LST

As secrets and scandals are exposed, old fears—and new—spawn doubt and suspicion. Is a sinister stranger lurking behind the murder and Faith's disappearance—or does someone in Split Creek have blood on their hands? Only Michaele's fierce determination—and her trust in Jared—will help her see the truth hidden in plain sight.

"Ms. Myers gives readers an incredible depth of storytelling."
—*Romantic Times*

On sale mid-March 2000 wherever paperbacks are sold!

MIRA

MHRM572

If you enjoyed what you just read,
then we've got an offer you can't resist!

Take 2 bestselling love stories FREE!

Plus get a FREE surprise gift!

Clip this page and mail it to The Best of the Best™

IN U.S.A.	IN CANADA
3010 Walden Ave.	P.O. Box 609
P.O. Box 1867	Fort Erie, Ontario
Buffalo, N.Y. 14240-1867	L2A 5X3

YES! Please send me 2 free Best of the Best™ novels and my free surprise gift. Then send me 3 brand-new novels every month, which I will receive months before they're available in stores. In the U.S.A., bill me at the bargain price of $4.24 plus 25¢ delivery per book and applicable sales tax, if any*. In Canada, bill me at the bargain price of $4.74 plus 25¢ delivery per book and applicable taxes**. That's the complete price and a savings of over 10% off the cover prices—what a great deal! I understand that accepting the 2 free books and gift places me under no obligation ever to buy any books. I can always return a shipment and cancel at any time. Even if I never buy another book from The Best of the Best™, the 2 free books and gift are mine to keep forever. So why not take us up on our invitation. You'll be glad you did!

183 MEN CNFK
383 MEN CNFL

Name	(PLEASE PRINT)	
Address	Apt.#	
City	State/Prov.	Zip/Postal Code

* Terms and prices subject to change without notice. Sales tax applicable in N.Y.
** Canadian residents will be charged applicable provincial taxes and GST.
All orders subject to approval. Offer limited to one per household.
® are registered trademarks of Harlequin Enterprises Limited.

BOB99   ©1998 Harlequin Enterprises Limited

INTERNATIONAL BESTSELLING AUTHOR

DIANA PALMER

FIT FOR A *King*

They were friends, neighbors and occasional confidants. But now Kingston Roper needs a favor from Elissa Dean—he needs her to get caught in his bed. Elissa's glad to play the temptress in order to help King out of an awkward situation—just to be neighborly, of course. But she's not supposed to want the make-believe to become a reality. And he's not supposed to find such passion. Could they go from neighbors to lovers without destroying their friendship...or their hearts?

"The dialogue is charming, the characters likeable and the sex is sizzling..."
—*Publishers Weekly* on *Once in Paris*

Available mid-March 2000 wherever paperbacks are sold!

MIRA

CATHERINE LANIGAN

66517	THE LEGEND MAKERS	__ $5.99 U.S.	__ $6.99 CAN.
66435	IN LOVE'S SHADOW	__ $5.99 U.S.	__ $6.99 CAN.
66420	TENDER MALICE	__ $5.99 U.S.	__ $6.99 CAN.
66286	ELUSIVE LOVE	__ $5.99 U.S.	__ $6.99 CAN.
66163	DANGEROUS LOVE	__ $5.99 U.S.	__ $6.99 CAN.

(limited quantities available)

TOTAL AMOUNT	$_____
POSTAGE & HANDLING	$_____
($1.00 for one book; 50¢ for each additional)	
APPLICABLE TAXES*	$_____
TOTAL PAYABLE	$_____

(check or money order—please do not send cash)

To order, complete this form and send it, along with a check or money order for the total above, payable to MIRA Books®, to: **In the U.S.:** 3010 Walden Avenue, P.O. Box 9077, Buffalo, NY 14269-9077; **In Canada:** P.O. Box 636, Fort Erie, Ontario L2A 5X3.

Name:_____
Address:_____ City:_____
State/Prov.:_____ Zip/Postal Code:_____
Account Number (if applicable):_____
075 CSAS

*New York residents remit applicable sales taxes.
 Canadian residents remit applicable GST and provincial taxes.

MIRA

Visit us at www.mirabooks.com   MCLBL0300